F. C. Burnand

My Time, and what I've Done with it

An Autobiography. Compiled from the Diary, Notes, and Personal Recollections of

Cecil Colvin, Son of Sir John Colvin, Bart., of the Late firm of Colvin, Cavander and

Co.

F. C. Burnand

My Time, and what I've Done with it
An Autobiography. Compiled from the Diary, Notes, and Personal Recollections of Cecil
Colvin, Son of Sir John Colvin, Bart., of the Late firm of Colvin, Cavander and Co.

ISBN/EAN: 9783337124120

Printed in Europe, USA, Canada, Australia, Japan

Cover: Foto ©Raphael Reischuk / pixelio.de

More available books at **www.hansebooks.com**

MY TIME,

AND WHAT I'VE DONE WITH IT.

AN AUTOBIOGRAPHY.

COMPILED FROM THE DIARY, NOTES, AND PERSONAL RECOLLECTIONS
OF CECIL COLVIN, SON OF SIR JOHN COLVIN, BART., OF
THE LATE FIRM OF COLVIN, CAVANDER & CO.

BY

F. C. BURNAND.

THIRD EDITION.

London and New York:

MACMILLAN AND CO.

1875.

CONTENTS.

CHAPTER XXII.

CHAPTER XXIII.

CHAPTER XXIV.

CHAPTER XXV.

CHAPTER XXVI.

CHAPTER XXVII.

CONTENTS.

CHAPTER XL.

MY TIME,

AND WHAT I'VE DONE WITH IT.

CHAPTER I.

I COME TO TIME.

I BEGAN life with punctuality.

My nurse Davis—an authority to be trusted implicitly in such a matter—has often said that no infant as she'd ever known, and she'd known a many, had ever been so satisfactory in regard, as it were, to keeping an appointment, as I had been. The other nurse, a temporary official called in for the important occasion, expressed herself as under a personal obligation to me, on account of her having a pressure of business on hand at the time. In fact, I had been as nicely calculated as a comet, and came exactly to the minute. I fancy that this must have exhausted at one effort my powers of accuracy and precision. I can honestly affirm, that, since the first day of my existence, I have never been noted for my punctuality, nor have I ever been able to acquire those habits which the world calls business-like, and which, I am ready to admit, however much it may tell against me, are of the very essence of respectability. Commerce and trade go to make up that business-like body of Respectability, whereof the soul is Punctuality.

S   A

When I entered upon the scene, nobody was put out, everybody was prepared. The traditionary basket was on the neatly appointed table. Grandmamma Pritchard, my mother's mother, was enthroned in state. The special nurse was in waiting. The doctor, representing science, was on the spot to receive me. My father, Sir John Colvin (of the old stockbroking firm of Colvin, Wingle, and Co., with Wingle long since out of it, and Co. nowhere), was in his dressing-room, so bewildered and helpless as to be able to do nothing more than sit and stare at the fire. My extraordinary punctuality had completely taken him by surprise. His energies were paralysed. To be a father at all was startling; but to be a father before he had thoroughly prepared himself for the part, had scared him. Nurse Davis, my informant on a good many matters connected with my early history, has said, that "he sat like one dazed, as though he were complaining to the fire and saying, 'Look here, what next?'" He had been married scarcely three years when my mother died, and I, christened Cecil, after her, was left to my father's care.

We were not, on my appearance, in our own house, owing to my father's want of faith in the calculations above mentioned. It was not yet ready to receive us, and thus my first character chanced to be that of a lodger. Yet it really was a capital place to be born in. If I had my time over again, I couldn't wish for a better.

Our apartments were over a dairy, where everything seemed to be new and fresh every morning. The dairy itself was an old-established affair, but having been years ago started as "The New," it had retained the title, and I believe does so to this day. There was a white marble slab for a counter in the shop, which looked as if it had been just a moment before washed with milk, and dried with polishing leather. The butter, too, in shape like logs which had been chopped off some upright butter-tree, had quite a marvellous colour of its own,—bright but not bilious. Milk was announced on a framed board as fresh from the cow; and there was such a picture of *The* Cow, as spoke volumes for the imaginative faculties of the artist, but was of itself scarcely calculated to inspire nervous customers with confidence. It had queer reddish-brown blotches over it, suggestive of having signally failed in an attempt at self-vaccination. Fortunately no one believed in the painted cow, merely looking upon it as the poetic side of the business, and not to be trusted for milk any more than that legendary animal supposed to have achieved the tremendous feat of jumping over the moon, with which marvellous creature, on becoming acquainted with the nursery rhyme, I at once associated my spotted friend in the dairy window.

The shop undertook also to provide fresh eggs every morning, laid in fulfilment of a previous contract by some responsible hens in the country. Within two doors of us was a baker's, a little way down the street a butcher's, and at the corner was a natty tavern, which had a large private connection in the neighbourhood, but did little as a public house. So that our wants were supplied within a limited radius.

"Man wants but little here below," said Nurse Davis, "but he likes to have that little good and within reach."

Of my mother I have no recollection whatever. She died, as I have said, when I was about two years old. A son passes through the best part of his lifetime before he can estimate all that he has lost by his mother's death. I have often stood before her picture, and wondered what I should have been, had *she* lived. It is a sweet gentle countenance. It has always affected me deeply, as though I were looking on a face lighted by a dying smile.

Perhaps I judge in this case by the event, but I have, since, seen portraits of living people, which have impressed me as strongly with the same mournful presentiment. I fancy I can trace this kind of superstition, in its origin, to Nurse Davis, the kindest soul in the world, and very fond of my mother.

Not long after my poor mother's decease, my father went to India on some business matters, and I was left to the care of Grandmammas Pritchard and Colvin, who, with my aunts Susan and Van Clym, and my uncles Charles Van Clym and Herbert Pritchard, formed a sort of board of directors, "with power to add to their number," for my benefit. This was but a very nominal affair, resulting in a formal visit once a week to Grandmamma Pritchard's; and, on the first Sunday in the month, a dinner, at one o'clock, at my other grandmother's, and, on the second Sunday, an afternoon, including tea, at Aunt Clym's (my father's sister), which was—as it finished up with prayers in the evening, and a sermon—quite a religious solemnity.

Practically, Mrs. Davis, my nurse, was my guardian. With her I was always happy, generally having my own way in every respect, and becoming remarkably obstreperous when thwarted in the slightest degree. Still, there we were alone in our lodgings, now and then undergoing a visit of inspection from one of the above-mentioned directors.

After Nurse Davis I was much attached to my grandmother Mrs. Pritchard, and my aunt Susan, for whom, at an early age, I entertained so strong an affection, that I could not endure the notion of her marrying anybody except myself; and I remember having been very jealous of a gentleman to whom I heard she was engaged. I rather fancy now that I wouldn't shake hands with him (I was between five and six at this time), and ultimately, when he laughed at me, for something or other, in the back drawing-room, attempting a violent attack on his legs, which was the only part of him I could conveniently get at with any chance of success.

Among these relations, my body, so to speak, was distributed. Each chose a portion, and stuck to it. For example, my Pritchard Grandmamma, representing my interests on the maternal side, looked after my head, generally; her strong points being my ears and teeth. Of the latter she had a magnificent set herself, white and regular, which she used to exhibit to me as a shining example for my imitation. It was the only pleasant way that ever occurred to me of "showing one's teeth." My Colvin Grandmamma, on the paternal side, inspected my nails before allowing me to quit her on my monthly visit. My Aunt Susan (maternal interest again) looked after my exterior as to dress, with the exception of my boots, about which my Uncle Herbert Pritchard—who spent his time, it appeared to me, in lying on the sofa with his legs up—was very particular, taking a considerable pride in showing me the size and shape of his own foot. As for my interior, not physically but morally speaking, that, as far as it was looked after at all, fell to the lot of my Aunt Clym, who ruled her own family, and Uncle Van Clym, with a severity that caused her husband to regard her with the greatest possible respect.

Uncle Van Clym was a Dutchman, not a double-Dutchman—being, in fact, only half a one, the other half having been, long ago, naturalized as British. He was a flabby, colourless man, of whom there wasn't much left over, after measuring five feet eight, He had a quick, short laugh and a high-toned voice with a snuffle in it. On the whole he resembled what an unappreciative mind might suppose to be the appearance of a light-haired oyster, and recent theorists would have marked him out as the perfection of a superiorly gifted mollusc.

I usually found him on the doorstep of his own house—I don't know why—but he always seemed to be either going out or coming in. Here he stopped, perched like a sparrow, and economized his power of vision by using only one eye at a time, the other being, for the nonce, screwed up.

"Hallo!" he'd exclaim on seeing me,—he was always being taken by surprise, and when he had recovered himself, he'd laugh (always with the snuffles), as if at the most humorous thing in the world, no matter what it was.

"Hallo! He-he-he! Come to dine wiz my wife—he-he-he—see your aunt an' your couzans, hey?"—and then off he'd go, with another snuffle and a chuckle, which somewhat disconcerted Nurse Davis, though she liked Uncle Van; chiefly, because he seemed to be fond of me, which was certainly more than my aunt was.

"Com in ten," he'd say—ten standing for "then" in his imperfect English, "Com in ten—he-he-he—an' zee 'ow de noisy ones are all—he-he-he!" So saying, we'd enter together, when I'd be boisterously welcomed by my three cousins, until checked by the spectre-like apparition of Aunt Clym, who was one clear inch and a half above Uncle Van's head, and represented, in a general way, height without breadth.

Aunt Clym was of a serious turn, and used to read prayers, and sermons, to the household on Sunday evenings. Uncle Van generally scandalized my aunt horribly by snoring so convulsively, that it seemed as if nothing short of a fit could relieve him. His head would drop forward, jerkily, until his chin touched his second shirt button, when he would suddenly start up as though awakened by a violent blow, and stare about, wildly, for a few seconds, apparently in search of an invisible assailant. Becoming more collected, he'd appear surprised at finding himself where he was ; and after frowning at any one of the children who might be exhibiting signs of restlessness, he'd let his head droop gradually, and again allow himself to glide down the bank into the placid waters of oblivion. Once, awaking suddenly, he jumped up and said, as he shook himself together, "Hullo ! hey ? he-he-he ! Very good, let's join the ladies "—being under the impression that he had just been listening to a racy after-dinner story, instead of sleeping through some prosaic discourses on the prophecies. I got on my legs, too, with the idea of following my uncle. Aunt Clym glanced at him, but, with great Christian forbearance, said nothing to him . . . *before the servants.* No one except Aunt Clym troubled me about religion, and what I could learn of it, through *her*, did not favourably impress me.

Nurse Davis sometimes took me to church on a Sunday afternoon, but I always considered it a tedious affair, and in hot summer weather I opposed it, strenuously, and successfully.

While upon this subject of first religious impressions, so important in after-life, the only instance, in my own case, that I can call to mind, is, that one afternoon I went with my nurse and her nieces (whom I will not name here, as they will appear in their proper places in this history) to hear some friend of theirs accompany their eldest sister on the organ, during a service in a chapel somewhere in the city,—I fancy, belonging to the Catholics. Somehow I managed to stray, and found myself quietly walking down the centre, between two rows of pews, and with my back to all the lights and incense, which I ignored entirely; and of which, strange to say now, contrary to what would be expected, I have but the dimmest recollection. No; what struck me *then* was the earnest look of all the people. I was meeting their faces, but their eyes were fixed on something far away beyond me, and no one heeded me as I walked on. It was so different to the weary demeanour I had seen in similar congregations on my Sunday visits, that I felt inclined to stop at one of the pew doors, and request an explanation from the kneeling people within. Nurse Davis, however, had fortunately caught sight of me from her elevated position in the organ-loft, and, coming down, seized me, and bore me away somewhat hastily. Whatever I did I was not to mention this episode to my Aunt Clym, and this charge, as I was not fond of talking to her on any subject at all, I had very little difficulty in observing.

Indeed, on the whole, I was becoming reticent as to my usual occupations, which, though very much to my fancy, were, I felt, not suited to the tastes of my relatives. Aunt Susan was the only person to whom I ever talked on the subject. I took her into my confidence over a box of bricks, and told her a good deal, though not everything, about my nurse's relations who lived in lodgings out of Soho Square, and to whom, being thrown among them to a great extent, I was really attached.

They were poor people, that I knew; but they were very kind, and I infinitely preferred a dinner and tea there, where I was made much of, as well on account of my superior position as for Nurse Davis's sake, to the solemn dinners with either of my grandmammas, or the family-table at Aunt Clym's, where the children, my cousins, stared, or made faces at me, and where I couldn't get enough to eat. Besides, after dinner I was always forced to fight one of my cousins, and if I thrashed him I was complained of to Aunt Clym, and punished ; and if I didn't, I was set upon by the united family, and treated most unmercifully. I disliked the Clyms, and have never got over it.

But my reception at the Verneys was a very different affair. I was never welcomed but with a speech from Mr. Verney, who, though in the prime of life, was an old actor, a profession in which he had been reared.

"You like my cousin, Mr. Verney, don't you?" Nurse Davis asked me, after meeting him in the street for the first time, when he had, in most eloquent phrases, invited us to join them at their early repast. But from his manner it struck me, that, though he used such fine words as I had never before heard, and which caused me to stand and gape at him in admiration and amazement— whereat Mr. Verney, finding an appreciative audience, was highly gratified—I say, in spite of his high-flown words, I fancied that he didn't mean us to accept in earnest; and experience has since proved that he must have felt a little uncomfortable at the prospect of two good appetites being suddenly added to the number about his table, for which his little daughter, a bit of a child less than myself, was now carrying home some delicacies, from the à-la-mode beef-shop, in a piece of old newspaper.

Mr. Verney had a clear complexion, an aquiline nose, light-brown hair, showing signs of coming baldness, faded-blue eyes, of a vague and undecided character, and which were, I subsequently noticed, occasionally a trifle hazy, the effect, perhaps, of too much suppressed emotion. He wore turndown collars exposing his throat, and was closely shaven. With his invariably well-brushed hat very much on one side, and a chirrupy stereotyped smile, on his otherwise peculiarly inexpressive lips, he would have admirably succeeded in imposing himself upon the public as the most knowing, most Don Juanish, most reckless Lothario, and the gayest dog in existence, if everybody hadn't seen at a glance how thoroughly artificial was such an assumption, which never for one moment really concealed, except from himself, the hard-working professional man, for whom, and to whose family, the stage had no poetry to be equalled by the material fact of a certain "treasury" on Saturday.

"I like him very much, Nurse," I replied to her question. I daresay it wasn't strictly true, but I felt intuitively that my appreciation would please her. And it did.

"What is his name?" I presently asked.

"Well," said Nurse Davis, with some degree of hesitation, "he calls himself Charles Mortimer Verney. But his real name is William."

"Then," I naturally inquired, "why not call him William?"

"Because people who begin with William end with Bill for short: and he doesn't like it. Those who know him always call him 'Charles Mortimer.' And once," she added rather reflectively, "he called himself Montgomery."

"It's a long word Mont—gum—"

I was not good at spelling in those days, though, as my nurse informed my father on his return, "I had a great taste for it;" and having decided that the second syllable of Mongomery was "gum," I got as far as that, and appropriately stuck there.

I subsequently discovered that Nurse Davis was inclined to take Mr. Verney at his own valuation—an inclination which was, to a certain extent, shared by his wife and family. It pleased them all very much, and really, instead of doing any harm, it diffused a kind of halo of romance about their humble home, of which he was the centre, which not all the hard knocks of a plain matter-of-fact, workaday world was able to dispel.

It was on the occasion of this conversation with Nurse Davis that an idea suddenly occurred to me.

"There was a little girl with Mr. Verney," I remarked.

"That, dear, was my niece, little Julie."

"I like *her*," I observed decisively.

"We will go and see them one day."

"And have dinner there?" I suggested.

My practical experience of visiting up to this time had always included dinner. Wherever I had been taken to call, and my round of visits was, as I have before men-

tioned, limited, there I dined. Nurse Davis acquiesced
in this arrangement, which she seemed to think would be
highly pleasing to *her* relatives, though she cautioned me
against mentioning the subject to mine.   So when I dined
with my Aunt Susan, at Grandmamma Pritchard's I re-
frained from speaking about my new acquaintances, and,
indeed, a box of bricks and a caricature book so engrossed
my attention, that Mr. Verney and his little girl entirely
slipped out of my memory.

On going home that evening, I insisted upon stopping
Nurse Davis at a toyshop in order to invest a part of the
new, bright half-crown which Grandmamma Pritchard
had given me (in addition to a box of tooth-powder and
a brush to lay it on with), in the purchase of a small
cavalry sword, price sixpence, for myself, and an elegant
gold watch, price fourpence, with a real key, which would
set the hands at any hour you liked.   This was, I said,
for little Julie.   I remember it, not only as the first
present I ever made, but as marking what I may fairly
call, on looking back, the starting-point in my time.

I stayed awake that evening longer than usual, conversing about the morrow's visit with my nurse, who
was sitting at a small table near my bed.   I slept with
the cavalry sword by my side, and the watch under my
pillow.

CHAPTER II.

PRESENTED AT COURT.

THE day of the dinner-party at Mr. Verney's turned out
to be little Julie's birthday, so that purchasing my
present had been a perfect inspiration. Nurse Davis remembered it in the morning, and bought for her a little
silver thimble, and a case for needles and cotton. Little
Julie had completed her fifth year, and was such a mite,
that, on our being placed back to back, it was discovered,
that though I was only a year older, I had the advantage
of her by two years in height, and indeed was nearly as
tall as her elder sister Carlotta Lucille.

Mr. Verney at this time lived in the retired neighbourhood of Frampton Court, Soho. Three symmetrical iron
posts, looking exactly like three small cannons growing
out of the ground, each with a cannon-ball sticking in its
mouth, guarded the entrances at both ends of Frampton
Court. They were not wide enough apart to allow of a
boy, with anything like long legs, attempting the popular
gymnastic exercise of "overing" them. Hence, the court,
being protected from these rougher spirits, offered itself as
a suitable playground for the girls out of school hours,
and for such boys as might be contented to play at
marbles in the four corners, where they could enjoy their
amusement without danger to the upper panes of the
kitchen windows, which were on a line with the ankles.
The pavement of this court was so clean as to be like a
sort of irregular chess-board, with nothing but white

squares in it, marked out with very black lines. How it was kept in this state is a perfect marvel to me now. There was a lamp in the centre, which acted as an immovable sentry, in a queer sort of helmet with a round knob at the top, and with one eye that lighted up with intelligence at night, and, looking four ways at once, kept ward and watch over the sleeping denizens of Frampton Court. I don't know who Frampton was, whether the builder, proprietor, or architect of the court. But the central lamp-post was a really brilliant idea. The arrival of the lamplighter in the winter-time was quite the event of the day, except perhaps the appearance of the muffin-man. One represented necessity, the other luxury, and they were on excellent terms with one another. Having seen many courts in my time, I assert that Frampton's Court could (in a sporting way) give all others a mile in any direction, and beat them easily. As to the courts of the Temple, they're none of them to be compared with Frampton's as it was, and as, probably, Frampton designed it. And I'll be bound that there was more honesty and true charity in Frampton's than in most other courts, whether legal or regal. King Frampton if alive then, might have been proud of his subjects; and if he wasn't alive, he might have come out with the ghosts at midnight, and have been perfectly satisfied with this part of his property at all events. There were flowers and birds in many of the windows, and at the side of every front door were several little bright bell-handles, with, in most cases, small brass plates, underneath each bell, indicating whom a pull would summon.

We pulled, or rather Nurse Davis pulled, at Mr. Verney's knob; and when the knob had come out and gone back again, Mr Verney's head imitated its example, and having come out, rapidly, from the first-floor window, to see who it was, went back again satisfied.

Then Mr. Verney descended in his shirt-sleeves, bade us welcome in the passage, and congratulated me on my being presented at court (Frampton's), for the first time.

I was not, I remember, so struck with the difference between Mr. Verney's apartments and the houses of my relatives, as, perhaps, I should have been had not we two —that is, I mean, my nurse and I—been accustomed to lodgings, which, though in a better situation, and of a more aristocratic character (this distinction I *did* notice), were but very little, if at all, larger than those old and exceedingly well-proportioned rooms in Frampton Court. The floors were of stained wood, and the walls were panelled. There was something of a Caroline character about the carvings on the old mantelpiece; but whatever was on or about the mantelpiece did not interest any of us half so much as what was being prepared, in a gigantic saucepan, on the fire. Mrs. Verney, with a red shawl crossed in front over her shoulders and pinned down at the back, was busy between this and the table, where her daughter, the eldest, a handsome girl of sixteen or more (but her age has always been a secret), was arranging some flowers in small tumblers of water, and occasionly giving a few slight finishing touches to the knives and forks.

In two minutes we were at home and perfectly at our ease. I was seated in state on a wooden chair, which Mrs. Verney having carefully wiped for me with her apron, placed by the piano, a piece of furniture which caused me to make my first observation to Nurse Davis, to the effect that "*We* hadn't a piano at home." This easily led Mr. Verney—who never, I subsequently found, lost any opportunity of hearing himself talk—into giving us a speech about this piano, embellished with as many brilliant figures of rhetoric, and original and striking similes, as occured to him during its delivery. In these ornamentations he considered himself pre-emiment; and finding that in me he had obtained a ready and delighted listener, he skilfully used the piano by way of a step on to his oratorical platform, where being once fairly planted, he entered into such details of the family annals, as he considered most interesting to his audience.

"A piano," said Mr. Verney, standing by the window still in his shirt-sleeves, for which dishabille he had apologized to us, stating that in summer-time, when a room, on such an occasion as this, was used both as kitchen and drawing-room, it became a trifle hot: "A piano, you must know, my dear Jane "—this meant Nurse, and I was really quite surprised at his familiarity, and not a little jealous, especially when he subsequently kissed her, which startled me as a tremendous liberty— " a piano, you must know, is with us—not with some people, I grant you,"—this he put pointedly at me, as if I had objected; " a piano," he resumed, " is with us not the corollary of luxury and unexampled splendour, as beheld in the mansions of the wealthy, where, it may be, ignorance of the divine art is their most unblissful state; but it is with us, here in our humble abode, a matter of sheer, clear, and absolute necessity."

After this preface, with which he himself was mightily taken, he found that his pipe required some attention. Now whether it was for this purpose, or whether to make mental notes of his recent phrases, and so stereotype them for future use, I have not been able to determine. Be the motive what it might, the result was a pause in his address.

" Now then, dear," said Mrs. Verney in an undertone to her daughter, " get some more forks and knives ready, and you can finish the flowers afterwards." The young lady left the room for a few minutes.

" I suppose," said Mrs. Verney, looking in under the lid of the saucepan and shutting it down again, as if afraid of something jumping out; " I suppose you hardly knew Sally again ?"

Nurse Davis was about to reply, when Mrs Verney said gravely—

" Lætitia !"

" Well, Charles ?" answered his wife, whom he addressed.

" I wish you would not call our eldest girl Sally. She is Beatrice Sarah." Mrs. Verney sniffed, and saying something, quite in an undertone, about its being all " stuff-a-nonsense," continued her employment.

Nurse Davis replied—

" Beatrice Sarah ! Well, I really should not have known her again. It's some time since I've seen her."

She was a handsome girl, with fair hair and a decidedly aristocratic face. It was a refinement on her father's.

"Well," said Mr. Verney, "*we* seldom see her. But, as I was observing, the piano, which has charms to soothe the savage breast, and whose tones thrill through you like the soft caresses of a mellifluously gifted woman,"— this was such a happy expression, and pleased Mr. Verney so highly, that he repeated it, looking round upon us with a beaming smile, while Mrs. Verney threw up her hands in admiration, and controlled her feelings with a sniff.

"The piano, I say," he continued "is a necessity to us, as both Carlotta Lucille, and Julie Lucrezia, are getting on beautifully. They'll do great things one of these days, in some line; but, at present, I am not certain in what."

"How is it you so seldom see Sal—I mean Beatrice Sarah ?" asked my nurse.

"She is studying with the eminent Mons. Nemorin."

"Lor, indeed !" exclaimed my nurse reverentially, though, as I subsequently ascertained, she had no notion who this distinguished foreigner might be.

"Yes," continued Mr. Verney, while the subject of their conversation was assisting her mother in various ways; "'tis very odd that Beatrice Sarah should have shown an early and undisguised sympathy with— and, I may fairly add, has absolutely developed a genius for —the operatic line."

"Why ?" asked Nurse Davis.

"Because I had destined her for the stage. She was called Beatrice after Shakespeare's splendid character. I played Benedick to her mother's Beatrice just before the event took place—she was born at Slocum in Shropshire, when we were on that circuit; and she was named Sarah after the great Mrs. Siddons."

"It's a good thing to have a godmother who can do something for her," observed my nurse, simply.

Mr. Verney explained—

"I called her *after* Sarah Siddons; but Sarah Siddons not being in the land of the living at the time, was unable to preside over the educational studies of my child —a loss which no one could appreciate more deeply than one who, like myself, is thoroughly imbued with the artistic spirit"—here he waved his hand, as dismissing that part of the history. "As Beatrice grows up, she takes to music, and having an engagement at the Opera, I managed to hire a piano, and get her such instruction as lay within my means."

"At the Opera!" said Nurse Davis, evidently astonished; "why, that's singing, ain't it?"

"It is," answered Mr. Verney; "the muse of singing" —he was evidently not very clear on the subject—"is the goddess whom she is at present worshipping."

"And do *you* sing, Charles?" asked Nurse Davis.

At this there was a general laugh, in which I joined, entirely out of politeness, whereat they all laughed still more, and Mrs. Verney declared that "that *was* a good 'un," meaning, I suppose, what her cousin had just said.

Mr. Verney did not join in the merriment. On the contrary, he didn't seem to relish it, and, indeed, looked so cross, that I instinctively came over from the jocose side, though we were four to one, and took his view of the question.

"As it happens," he said, severely, "I am *not* singing, Lætitia,"—he addressed himself pointedly to his wife, as much as to intimate that he would now make an example of the chief of this conspiracy to laugh him down— "because Pacini"—here he mentioned a celebrated name in the musical world—"because Pacini said, 'Verney, you must come and help me; Verney, I can't do without you:' and so all the artists said too; otherwise——"

"Otherwise you'd ha' been at them concerts at night, and Freemasonries and Caves of 'Armony—I know 'em," says Mrs. Verney, with a wink at her cousin Jane.

"I had a first-rate offer, Lætitia, as you are very well aware." said Mr. Verney, warmly.

"Yes, Father," interposed Beatrice Sarah, "and you would have been equal to Mario, if you'd only had the chance."

"No," replied Mr. Verney, much molified, and in a deprecatory tone, "not equal to Mario, *that* would be too much; but if I'd had your advantages and your——"

"Here's your coat, Father," said Beatrice, insisting upon helping him on with it, "and Lottie and Ju will be here in another minute."

It was as if she'd uttered an incantation, for in walked Miss Lottie, dressed in the smartest possible style—in fact, before, or since, I have never seen so smart a child—and carrying under her arm a soup-tureen, and three plates.

"What has the child got?" exclaimed Mrs. Verney.

"I bought 'em, Mother, coming along, for the soup. Some of the pupils made me presents of money; and I saved them up, and bought these for Julie's birthday."

How we straightway admired them! how we went into ecstasies over them! how I begged Nurse Davis to remark that Grandmamma Pritchard had exactly the same sort of things; and how I kept falling in love, first with Beatrice, and then with Carlotta!

"Ned's gone to fetch Ju," said Carlotta; "she's at rehearsal, and he'll bring her back, as I didn't want her to see these things till she came."

"Carlotta is fulfilling her destiny, I believe," said Mr. Verney, with pride. "I called her after Carlotta Grisi, the celebrated dancer, whose step combined the grace of a Terpsichore with the fairy-like lightness of a Titania, and the skill of a rare artist with the piquant playfulness of a kitten. Carlotta Grisi painted, if I may be allowed the expression,"—here, as I fancied, he seemed to wish for my assent before continuing; I nodded my approbation, and he went on—"she painted with her toes."

This was so neat a discription that he, as usual, smacked his lips, and stopped to make a mental note of it. Having registered it silently for further use, he resumed—

"At this present moment Carlotta is apprenticed to the celebrated Madame Glissande, whom she assists in Calisthenics"—this was a beautiful word for him, and for the family generally,—" in Calisthenics, and dancing. They are all making their money."

"Yes," sniffed Mrs. Verney, removing her apron and tidying herself generally, as she said with brusque good humour, "No lazybones here. All got to work hard.

B

We ain't born with no silver spoons in our mouths, like some folks."

I fancied that there was somehow a covert allusion to me in this remark; and I determined to question my nurse afterwards on such a curious subject.

They all did work, too, with a will. Bread was cut in good stout slices, plates were put down to keep hot, glasses were put out to get dry, knives and forks came rattling on to the table in a heap, to be duly apportioned; and, finally, an assortment of spoons of various shapes and sizes, pervaded generally by a bluish hue, suggestive of having been engaged, for many years, in active tea-service. But everything as clean and homely as the most domesticated old maid could possibly have desired. "Homely" exactly describes the Verneys' apartments in Frampton's Court.

The appearance of the spoons caused me to recur to the mention of the silver one supposed to have been found in some unfortunate (as it appeared to me) baby's mouth. I informed Mr. Verney, in return for his previous confidences, that *I* was possessed of a silver spoon in a leather case lined with blue. That here it lay in company with a dull silver knife, intended for fruit, and an effemi-nate-looking fork, made, I believed, to assist the knife should the fruit prove too much for it, and offer resistance. Further, I appealed to Nurse Davis as to the existence of a silver mug, out of which I said "when I was younger, I used to drink at dinner;" but I would have him to know, that "I had grown out of that now."

I suppose at this age I must have been very old-fashioned; indeed, I remember my nurse applying this epithet to me. And this old-fashionedness seems to have strengthened my memory for events, apparently trifling, of my very earliest years. Of course I do not pretend to recount dialogues verbatim, but my recollection of their purport and tone is unclouded, while from the more intimate knowledge I have since acquired of the speakers' characters and peculiarities, I am able, without distorting the truth, or doing them injustice, to paint the portraits of those " of my time," in their true colours.

And here, once for all, it may be well to state, clearly, that where I myself relate events which I could not have witnessed, I have subsequently learnt the precise account of whatever took place on such occasions, of which the reader will meet instances in the course of this narrative; or, failing the evidence of eye-witnesses, I have ventured to infer words and actions, from motives, which were only known to me *after* the event.

But to return to our birthday party at the Verneys'.

All the information (whereof, I need hardly say, the foregoing explanatory digression formed no part) concerning such articles of family plate as had for me a personal and peculiar interest, I bestowed on Mr. Verney, who, smiling upon me benignly, hoped that I would not, on this occasion, object to the use of the ordinary, but serviceable, ware of Sheffield, and such metal as his poor table could afford in lieu of "metal more attractive," by which I supposed him to mean the plate above-mentioned.

"You will partake with us," he said, waving his right hand after the fashion of an old beau about to take his pinch of snuff, "of the succulent portions of the meat in a fluid shape, the nutritious joint, and a dumpling whose interior shall be redolent of Pomona, and whose exterior shall glisten like the virgin snow."

"Redolent of what," asked Mrs. Verney.

"Of Pomona," returned Mr. Verney, with the air of a man defying contradiction.

"Oh," said Mrs. Verney, with a sniff and a laugh, "I thought you said pomatum, and I was a-goin' to say——"

Mr. Verney showed himself so supremely contemptuous of the idea that by any possibility he could have, for one moment, mistaken pomatum for Pomona, that, for some seconds, he could scarcely speak. I broke the silence by piping out deferentially,—

"If you please, who was Pomony?"

"Pomona, my good young sir," replied Mr. Verney, condescending to my ignorance, "Pomona was the Goddess of Apples."

From that day to this, I never see a dumpling—an how seldom does one see a genuine dumpling—withou thinking of Pomona. Before, however, we could further investigate this important subject, little Julie—her name in full was Julie Lucrezia, in honour of Madame Grisi, in whose footsteps Mr. Verney had destined her to follow—little Julie had arrived, in her brother's care.

She was the loveliest little child, with the brightest grey eyes, and the darkest possible hair. If Beatrice Sarah, the eldest, was a perfect blonde, as she was, Julie —this little mite of a Julie—was a perfect brunette. Carlotta came between the two with her brilliant complexion, her violet eyes, and brown hair. Julie was such a mite, that I have known people seeing her in the street staggering behind a paper parcel, stop her to give her a threepenny bit, out of sheer pity for her being so small.

This very day she came in joyously with a sixpence, presented to her, she said gaspingly, by "Madame—at —the—theatre," where she was playing in a ball-room scene the distinguished part of the *Guest-in-perspective,* in which character she had (poor little trot!) to walk a *minuet de la cour* with another guest-in-perspective of her own size; the real guests, full stature, and out of perspective, being in front near the audience; but so vast was the saloon in the King's palace (where the fête was given) supposed to be, that to the spectators the nearest guest would be six-foot-one, while the most remote, up a set of handsomely-carpeted steps, would be one-foot-six. As for Charles Edmund—so called after the distinguished Kean, and Kemble—he had no turn for the stage, and, having enlisted in the railway service, was now what I believe is called a "Greaser" at the Great Western; whence he returned home generally uncommonly dirty, and, so to speak, slippery, until he had burnished himself with soap and a hard towel. After this operation he came out a triffle streaky, perhaps, but with nothing about him to be cavilled at, except his hands, whose condition he had always to defend to his father and sisters, while his mother, who said *she* knew what grubby work was, and shared his failure in this respect, stood up for him, and told him "never to mind."

On this occasion, he had taken immense trouble with himself, and was as clean as a railway whistle. But, unfortunately, the extra stickiness of his hair and the full flavour of its scent might have suggested the idea, that in a fit of absence, he had mistaken his head for his wheel, and had used the company's grease with considerable liberality.

He was so bumpy and awkward by the side of such bright creatures as his sisters, that I was not sorry to see him sent out for the beer, carring two jugs, "which," Mrs. Verney explained to me, "makes it come exactly one halfpenny cheaper." It was a very merry dinner. The soup was excellent—that's all I know about it. We had a quarter of a leg of mutton, that being, Mrs. Verney told her cousin, "half of the half as they had had—half to boil and half to roast," and so we had the roast. There were potatoes, and bread and cheese, and Pomona's dumplings, which we finished entirely, and which, by way of retributive justice, entirely finished us.

Then Charles Edmund went out and returned with something in a bottle, about which there was a good deal of joking between Mr. and Mrs. Verney and Nurse Davis. Then Nurse produced some oranges which we had bought coming along. Then Mr. Verney, with much unction, proposed Julie's health, and we all drank it, whereupon Mr. Verney considerately returned thanks in a sympathetic manner. Some of us cried, and I am sure Mr. Verney did. Then came tea and bread and butter, and we made merry again. Then the lamp of King Frampton's court was lighted, and the shades drew in around us. Our little Julie, who was wearing my present of the watch, took a chair by me, and gave me a kiss for it, and so we sat together while Mrs. Verney dozed, and Mr. Verney smoked, and Miss Beatrice Sarah sang and played; and then Carlotta Lucrezia played and did not sing; and the lanky Charles Edmund (called Ned by his sisters) did something with a chorus to it, which he sang by himself; and then they tried something together, and then the kettle was in requisition—not for tea this time, though, for the bottle reappeared, and spoons and sugar were brought out. Then, what with the heat and the excitement, I tumbled off to sleep on the old horsehair sofa, my arm round little Julie's neck, and hers round mine.

And so we slumbered, loving each other very much, and in our blissful ignorance of all misery and evil to come, very, very happy.

CHAPTER III.

MY PLAYTIME COMES TO AN END.

AFTER the memorable day recorded in the previous chapter, I became a constant visitor at Frampton's Court, and acquired a considerable amount of knowledge in theatrical matters. Whether my time up to eight years old might have been more profitably spent is scarcely an important question for me now; but of one thing I am certain, that no sort of education, however picked up, is to be despised. Skelt's books of plays adapted to the same ingenious person's "Scenes and Characters," in "Blue Beard," "Der Freischutz," and, of course, "The Miller and his Men," formed my first library, and of these with my little stage, oil-lamps, and blue and red fire, I was never weary. I was manager of a theatre where there were neither heart-burnings nor jealousies, a theatre whose expenses might be estimated at twopence per night laid out in coloured flames and oil, and which, though it never reimbursed the proprietor for the first outlay—herein resembling some other larger theatrical establishments that I have since known—gave the greatest satisfaction to everybody, both before and behind the curtain.

Our landlady, Mrs. Gander, of the Dairy, and her bouncing daughter Polly, who at sixteen looked as if she'd been brought up on the richest butter and most nourishing cream, were always ready of an evening to take their seats, in the back parlour behind the shop, and witness a performance of a thrilling melodrama. Somehow we were a little continental in our habits as regards amusements, and I am bound to record that our great night was invariably on Sunday, when Carlotta Lucille would bring little Julie to spend the day and be fetched by Charles Edmund, who, I fancy, had formed an attachment for Polly Gander, as he always took care to sit next her during the performance, and, also, at the early supper which terminated the entertainment.

Lottie had rather an offhand and supercilious way of interfering with the management, which, though she was my senior, I really could scarcely brook; but she was kept in check by little Julie, to whose opinion on stage effect her elder sister, being chiefly learned in the calisthenics and dancing, would generally defer. But little Julie at that age commanded the entire family, with the exception of the eldest girl, the *protégée* of Monsieur Némorin, who was always spoken of by her father as a real genius if ever there was one. As I paid return visits to the Verneys, I soon got myself mixed up with their domestic economy, and would often accompany Julie to the butcher's, where we purchased two or three pounds of "pieces"—which were the bits chopped off from the joints sold to richer customers—and thence we would go to the greengrocer's, where we usually bought three pounds of potatoes, which I insisted, in a polite and gentlemanly manner, on carrying for her; and thus weighted we would trudge back again to Frampton's Court as pleased as in later days I have seen childern coming out of Messrs. Shuger and Spyce's, at Christmastime, with ruinous bags of biliousness in their hands. How pleased the family physician must be with the last-named spectacle. If Messrs. Shuger and Spyce should ever fail—which calamity may the kind nymphs of the Christmas Tree avert—let a committee of medical men form themselves into a company and carry on the business: it must pay them, so to speak, in the reaction.

Talking of doctors, I cannot call to mind any illnesses about this time, save one, and that was the chicken-pox. I remember it solely by its pleasures, not by its pains. The doctor ordered me nothing but chicken in every sort of form, and Grandmamma Pritchard called, and left for me a beautiful book of the old, old fairy tales, with such pictures!—a delightful volume, which, I fancy, it is nowadays marvellously difficult to procure. Blue Beard, whom I had only known dramatically, was there, as were also the Sleeping Beauty, Graciosa and Percinet, the Beauty and the Beast—and oh! shall I, can I, ever forget those illustrations to my dearest Cinderella, whom I identified with little Julie, both because of her work at home, and of her two sisters being decked out finer than herself. And then her fairy existence at night at the theatre—where, you must know, I had actually seen her come out of a parsley-bed in a pantomime, on which occasion I attracted the attention of all our neighbours in the pit to our party, consisting of Nurse Davis and the Ganders, by exclaiming "There's Julie!" and by bursting into passionate tears on seeing her pursued by the clown, when indeed, as she afterwards confided to me, she had been as much frightened, on her own account, as I had been for her. And when one comes to think of it, it must be startling for a nervous child of five years old to be, suddenly, before a crowd of unsympathetic people, chased by a hideous savage, painted all over white and red, without any hair on his head, and with so fearfully wide a mouth as to threaten with instant swallowing any infant luckless enough to fall into his clutches. She ran, crying piteously, to her mother, who was waiting for her at "the wing," and who soothed her fears by informing her that the horrible ogre was only Mr. Grimes, the clown, who had given her a penny at rehearsal for sweets, when he wasn't dressed so fantastically as now, and had behaved in all respects like a reasonable being and a father of a large family, as indeed the poor man was.

So Julie and I used to con over this fairy book, when I assisted her in her spelling. How perfectly I got pictures and all by heart, may be gathered from the fact, that, after these many years—no matter perhaps how many—I can vividly recall the representation of a pink prince in white tights, and two sisters gorgeously arrayed in long dresses, feathers, and turbans—-pink and white again, with a touch of blue somewhere—and Cinderella herself also in pink, of which colour the artist must have had a good stock on hand, as he seemed to have used it liberally.

When next I went to my Aunt Clym's, a wretched time for me usually, I attempted to inoculate my cousins with my dramatic taste; and being full of theatres, I wanted them to get up a pantomime in a small room out of the day nursery. My preparations were made by closing the shutters and lighting a candle, this being a sort of morning performance, wherein I was harlequin, with Annette Clym, three years older than myself, for columbine, while Arty, her brother, my senior by a year, was told off for clown. Nellie, the youngest child, being thus put down for pantaloon, turned sulky, and told my aunt what we were doing, whereupon Mrs. Clym came upstairs, and we all of us "got it" all round, my nurse coming in heavily for her share. Not content with this severe reprimand, Aunt Clym informed Nurse Davis that she should consider it her duty to let her brother know how irreligiously his child was being brought up, and bade Mrs. Davis be more careful for the future, or she might find herself dismissed, without a month's warning, any one of these fine days. While I stood trembling, and the others dreadfully abashed—including the clown and pantaloon, the former in a nightgown over his day suit, and the latter with her small legs hidden in a pair of her father's Wellington boots, in which costume she bore a striking resemblance to "Hop o' my Thumb" in my book—Nurse Davis made bold to reply that "she was answerable for Master Cecil to Sir John, and that he was brought up as well and as religiously as were any of Mrs. Clym's children," whereupon my aunt, who could ill conceal her passion (a failing of the Colvin family), ordered her, and me too, out of the house, adding that she would have written to her brother forthwith, had she not expected him by the next mail from India.

This announcement somewhat startled us. We left Mrs. Clym's; and my unfortunate cousins had to learn some catechism, then be lectured and sent to bed, after a lively meal of bread and water. I believe Uncle Van used to try to obtain a mitigation of the sentence on such an occasion, as he liked to have them about him when he returned from the city; but Mrs. Clym was inexorable, and so my uncle sighed, chuckled, snuffled, and dropped the subject.

"She's jealous of your boy," said Mrs. Verney to Nurse Davis, "because if it weren't for him there's them as would come to the title, unless he were to marry again and have a family, which they won't let him do in a hurry, you'll see."

"Little Pitchers," observed my nurse, with a side glance at me; for becoming interested in their conversation I had looked up from examining a book of theatrical costumes, wherein Richard the Third's boots had immensely taken my fancy, and was listening intently.

I saw at once that either Julie, or myself, was a little Pitcher; perhaps both were intended, but, at all events, that conversation was there and then dropped—Mrs. Verney declaring, with a sniff, that she mustn't waste her time chatting, having a lot of things to attend to. She seemed to me to do the work of the house, Julie coming in as a junior assistant; and Carlotta Lucille, when not at calisthenics and dancing, occasionally lending a hand, with a scrubbing brush in it. Everything in the Verneys' lodgings looked tidy except Mrs. Verney; and everything was scrupulously clean, except, apparently, Mrs. Verney. What she did with her hair, it is almost impossible to imagine; I know that, from the first moment I met her, I never could help staring at Mrs. Verney's hair. It seemed as if she had got in a rage with it every morning at finding it still encumbering her, and had thereupon dashed at it with a brush, somehow—first on one side, then on the other, and had then twisted it up fiercely in knots behind, as though her head were a pudding-bag, and this was her way of tying it up. She was too, so Nurse Davis informed me, a martyr to asthma and spasms, for which reason she used to wear over her shoulders, and crossed in front, such a handkerchief as I have previously described, generally of some such quiet and unobtrusive pattern as red spots on a brilliant yellow

ground, which was pinned somewhere about the middle
of her back in so secret a manner that Mr. Verney—
feeling in a caressing humour, and putting his arm round
Mrs. Verney's waist—would suddenly withdraw it with
an expression of pain and anger on his face, which would
have frightened me into tears, had not the others only
laughed and said, "Hush father!" while Mrs. Verney
apologized for having forgotten to inform him where the
pin was.   My earliest impression of her was, that she
was always bustling about and sniffing in a lost-pocket-
handkerchief kind of way.   Indeed, that useful article
was invariably mislaid, and could never be found under
at least three minutes, during which time all the members
of the family were engaged in the search.   Then she was
perpetually "tidying up" the rooms, and cleaning something or other so indefatigably, that you'd have thought
no ordinary floors, chairs, or tables would have stood the
friction.   If life by warmth could ever have been put
into table legs and chair legs, Mrs. Verney's method would
have produced the phenomenon.   The wooden furniture
looked quite pleased and beaming after the operation;
and there's as much difference, in the aspect of a room,
between dingy, sombre, sullen chairs, which seem rather
inclined to kick than support you, and to have a positive
objection to being moved—generally making themselves
as heavy as possible—I say there's all the difference in
life 'twixt such as these, and the sharp, bright, highly-
polished, dapper-looking, though common chairs, without
leather or padding of any sort, but, so to speak, in a
state of nature, which seem ready to step lightly on
tip-toe toward you, saying, "Here we are! won't you take
a chair? do take a chair and make yourself at home."
Then there was the old arm-chair, whose framework had
been made any number of years ago, and which had been
covered and re-covered, and covered again after that, and
which, like a faithful old servant, wouldn't desert the
family upon any account, no matter how much it might
be laughed at and sat upon.   Mr. Verney smoked his
pipe in it at night when at home, which was not too
often, as he was a popular man at the "Kemble Tavern,"

and one or two other clubs of a professional and convivial character. It is on record that Mr. Verney would return home occasionally a trifle elated after these merrymakings, and would then insist upon arguing with such of the family as might be in waiting to receive him, on any point that might come uppermost, when he would use the longest words that could be found in a dictionary—experiencing no little difficulty in getting to the end of a sentence when once started. In these circumstances, Mrs. Verney, though perfectly alive to the fact that something-or-other-and-water was at the bottom of it, used to wonder at the command over the language which her husband possessed, though the command didn't include a perfect mastery, as Mr. Verney, having once brought out the long words, could not do very much with them —reminding one of a civil magistrate with power to call out the troops, but unable to manœuvre them when they'd obeyed his order. Godliness was somewhere after cleanliness in Mrs. Verney's creed, the object of which, I am convinced, was her husband, solely and only. For him she would have sacrificed everything and anybody, even the children. He was to be comfortable —that was enough for her. In return, Mr. Verney considered her as a good sort of useful wife, beneath himself in mental power, which he saw inherited by his eldest daughter, in whom he recognized Brain, and for whom he foresaw a mighty career, which should raise them all up, and whom, in consequence, he idolized. To him, she was Genius personified, and the lady of the family. She was going to be, he predicted, an authoress, a mighty actress—everything that was, in fact, within reach of a woman striving to be professionally great. He knew by heart all the actresses' names who had married noblemen; and on this fact he would dilate, generally after a social meeting as mentioned before, with such pathos and so many long words, as brought tears to his own eyes, and even overpowered his humble wife with something like a hope of a brilliant future, in which, however, the central figure, to *her*, was not her daughter, but her husband. Her elder daughters, Beatrice and

Lottie, having already perceived the necessity of respectability, insisted, on Sunday, upon her arraying herself in
her best, under the superintendence of one of them, who
would see her hair properly done and her bonnet placed
properly; and who would put in force certain sumptuary
laws of their own with respect to a fair restriction upon
vivid colours on her appearance, among her neighbours, at
the parish church. Nurse Davis used to take me there
now and then; and I have a distinct recollection of the top
half of Mrs. Verney appearing above a high pew, and I
remember how she reminded me of Uncle Clym by
awaking in the middle of the sermon, with such a snort
and start as frightened herself, electrified the slumbering
congregation, and considerably discomfited the minister.

Such time as could be spared for Julie's education was
found, as best it could be, out of the hours when she was
not at the theatre, earning her contribution to the household. Her school time had to be accommodated to that of
her rehearsals, and, thus, her learning anything at all
soon became a very haphazard affair. Being, however,
naturally quick, intelligent, and of the most amiable and
docile disposition, she not only made excellent use of such
opportunities as she possessed; but also picked up with
facility as many scraps of information on various subjects
as her elder sisters and her brother could give her.
Beatrice Sarah coming home occasionally from Mons.
Némorin, talked French and Italian to her, and from
her she learned something of singing and music. Lottie
instructed her in calisthenics, which she didn't care about,
and in dancing, in which she made rapid progress.

Beatrice Sarah professed an ambition, in accordance
with her father's estimate of her own powers and exalted
destination. His latest idea and hers too, was that she
was to astonish the world with a play which she had
already commenced to write, and of which occasionally,
and quite as a treat for us, she would read portions in the
presence of her admiring parents (Mr. Verney seated in
the arm-chair, and seriously deluding himself into the belief
that he was impartially critical) and a select circle, consisting of Nurse Davis and myself, in addition to the rest

of the family. There were no comic parts, I believe, but I laughed at the sound of some strange words and at Beatrice's declamatory action, which I thought very funny. Mr. Verney severely reprimanded me for this levity, which so frightened me, that on the whole I ranked Miss Beatrice's readings next after my Aunt Clym's discourse on a Sunday evening, and preferred a regular sermon in church.

I have dwelt at some length upon this portion of my career, as my relations with the Verney family were to be summarily suspended, owing to my father's arrival from India, as my Aunt Clym had already told us.

I had often asked Nurse Davis for a description of my father, but portrait-painting was not her strong point. I had attempted to get at the truth by such artful cross-examination as was founded upon comparison with Mr. Verney.

"Was he (my father) at all like *him?*" I inquired.

"Well, no, he wasn't," she had answered, after some deliberation; "Sir John's taller and more stouter."

"Does he wear a shiny hat like Mr. Verney? was my next "fishing interrogatory," as the lawyers term it.

"Well, Master Cecil," returned my nurse, "I dont know what he wears now, because he's in India."

"Where the tigers are?" I suggested pleasantly, as if that fact settled the fashion of hats in India.

I used to wonder to myself what he would be like, and what he had been doing. There was a book out of which Polly Gander, our landlady's daughter, used sometimes to read to me about some distinguished Indian, represented in the steel engraving as a very wild-looking person in a large white turban, and generally light and airy costume, who was turned into a mouse, an elephant, a bird of some sort, and several other things, one after the other. This fabulous individual—Indur was, I fancy, his name—was always shot, or somehow killed, in every new character; and the story pointed some moral in connection with these rapid changes, which, I suppose now, must have been that one ought to be content with one's lot, whatever it is, without wanting to be a mouse, or a bird, and so forth.

To this story I was indebted for nearly all my ideas of Indian life. There was, now I think of it, another tale in the same book, about a lady, on whom, while walking through a jungle, a tiger sprang out, when she immediately frightened him away by suddenly opening her umbrella. I think this was called *Presence* of mind; and so it undoubtedly was.

That my father would be tall, with mahogany-coloured face, very glaring eyeballs, and with a white turban, I had settled in my mind to my own entire satisfaction. Weeks went by, and, occupied as heretofore with Nurse Davis and the Verneys, I had ceased to think about him. One afternoon I was summoned to Mrs. Clym's drawing-room, where, standing by the fireplace with my aunt, I saw a gentleman with dark whiskers, and such thick eyebrows as gave a scowling look to his otherwise kindly brown face (not deeply browned as anybody from India ought to have been), and dressed much the same as any other gentleman I had ever seen. At first it occurred to me that he was a doctor, and I was considerately preparing to exhibit my tongue to him, when he exclaimed :—

"What a big fellow he's grown!"

Whereupon, as he left the hearth-rug and advanced towards me, Aunt Clym said in her sternest tone—

"Cecil, say 'how do you do' to your father."

I did say "how do you do."

That was all.

And so we stood, for a minute or two, regarding each other curiously.

CHAPTER IV.

"Why, Cecil, what a big fellow you've grown!"

Had I? This was the first I had heard of it, and I did not know exactly how to take the greeting.

It was either admiration or reproof. It certainly did not sound like the former, and it could not, evidently, be intended for the latter. The next minute he added, in a tone of disappointment "Not quite a man yet though, eh?"

Not quite, certainly. Sir John, I have ascertained, had been accustomed to speak of me during his absence as "My son, sir, who'se at home now,"—he quite forgot that I was not even out of petticoats,—"will be quite a companion when I return."

He was chagrined to find me a child, and his first salutation was only a complimentary tribute to my size *as* a child.

Thank goodness, I did not commence by crying. I was very near it however. I looked down and blushed: I looked up and smiled. I, what my Aunt Clym called, "fiddled" with my fingers, interlacing them in an awkward and nervous fashion.

"Don't do that, Cecil," said Aunt Clym. "Haven't you got anything to say to your papa?"

No, nothing.

Had we been left together, I should have had a great deal, but it required a preface of getting on his knee,

c

and accustoming myself to him, before I could repose confidence in my newly-found father. Whether there lurked iu my mind a doubt of his identity, or whether I was only a striking illustration of the truth of the proverb about a wise child, it is impossible to tell. I was abashed in his presence, and Aunt Clym's method did not go far towards conciliating me. My father, poor man, was disappointed. So was I. Neither put this into words. I seemed to experience a sort of feeling of having been imposed upon, and that this was not at all the father I had been expecting—in fact nothing like him.

After the first greetings were over, and I had come out of it all without crying, I was anxious to get back to the housekeeper's room, where my nurse was; but this was not permitted by my aunt, who seized the opportunity to point out to my father how fond I had become of certain associates, who, she was sure, were leading me astray.

My father heard her to the end gravely, and then observed—

" He must go to school at once."

This did surprise me. I do not know why, but such a course had certainly never entered into my head as one which was to be pursued with myself.

" You'd like to go to school ? " my father asked me.

I smiled and was silent. Intuitively I felt that he wanted me to say "Yes," and that he would conceive a very low opinion of me were I to reply "No." So I kept the latter to myself, for private communication, subsequently, to Nurse Davis, but I said " Yes " to my father, and thus it happened that almost the first word of any importance that I had had to say to my father, was an untruth.

His manner made me nervous and timid. I was afraid of displeasing him, and he had a way—I saw it in the first five minutes—of knitting his eyebrows, and twitching his nose, which served to indicate that the slightest contradiction would set him against me.

The Colvins are undoubtedly an excitable family,

impulsive and irritable in various degrees. Mrs. Clym was all this and more. She was a woman of stern determination and settled purpose. Not so my father; he represented the Colvin virtues and failings in full. To impulsiveness and irritability, he added vacillation. If you had asked him for his own opinion of himself— and he often quoted himself as an example to be followed on most matters—he would have shown you what a cautious, calculating man he had always been in business, how he had anything but a hot temper, and how he was invariably willing to hear both sides of a case, and to give a calm and impartial judgment, even where his own interests were vitally concerned. He prided himself upon being excessively neat and clean, as indeed he was, and upon his extremely polite and courteous bearing in the society he frequented, where, to do him justice, he was always welcomed, and where he flattered himself on shining as a wit and a *bon vivant*. That he did flatter himself, is certain, as he was neither one nor the other, though with a secret desire to excel in both characters. These are characteristics of the Colvins decidedly; but I fancy I have met others, besides Colvins, who have easily deceived themselves in such matters.

At eight years old I should have liked, in spite of Aunt Clym's presence, to have jumped on my father's knee, and to have asked him all about the strange country whence he had so recently come, and, especially, about the tigers. But such familiarity was out of the question. As we had begun, so we were to go on, and the next thing I had to hear was my good nurse complained of, and scolded, before my father, who, having his *rôle* given him by his sister, did not dare depart from it, but intimated to Mrs. Davis, that, after Master Cecil had been sent to school, her further services would be dispensed with.

That night my father made his *rentrée* into society, at a stately party given by Uncle Clym, who, being heartily glad to see his brother-in-law back again safe and sound, was for an extra bottle in honour of the occasion, after the retirement of the ladies and of the children. When I was brought in to say "good-night to Papa," I was uncertain about kissing him,—a doubt I had always entertained with regard to any gentleman, whether relation or not, to whom I had had, up till then, the honour of having been introduced.

Sir John seemed as confused and as timid as myself, and I believe his brown face coloured slightly, as he turned round to bid me good night, and kiss me. His was a rough chin, and I did not like it. Two or three gentlemen called me to them, and asked me my age, and when I was going to school. This was an unfortunate question, as it started a stout gentleman with a red face on the subject of " rods in pickle," and remembrances of a leather strap, and a peculiar birch rod when he was a boy (I was glad to think that *he* had suffered, at all events), which so affected my nerves, that, being over-tired and rather frightened, I began to cry, not noisily, but breaking into it, and suppressing it, all at one time— two opposite efforts that nearly choked me.

My father was, I saw it at once, considerably pained by my unmanly way of taking what was only meant in jest, but which, not seeing the fun in the same light as the stout red-faced gentleman, I had looked upon as very real and serious earnest, and had thus given way. Biscuits and fruit partially restored my equanimity. I accepted these presents in order to share them at home with Nurse Davis. My father observed that " I wanted to be knocked about a bit, and be among boys," which would have brought on another fit of tears, had not Uncle Clym's butler entered with a fresh bottle, to whose care (the butler's, not the bottle's) I was straightway confided, to be delivered to Nurse Davis, awaiting me in the passage. As I went out I heard Uncle Clym say " Now ten,"—meaning " Now then !"—which I have since learnt is the formula for the commencement of a jovial evening, the " Up Guards and at 'em " of a convivial commander-in-chief. Jovial that evening might have been for them; not for me.

At home in our lodgings, all our conversation was about school, and of the separation between Nurse Davis and myself; and though I did not understand much about either subject, yet of one thing I felt certain, and this I said as I sobbed on my dear old nurse's bosom, "that I loved her very much, and wished Papa hadn't come to take me away."

Then she hushed me, and set me to say my prayers, ending with "God bless dear Papa this night," which somehow seemed to me unnecessary now, when he had returned safe and sound from among the tigers in India.. And thus father and son met, and I fancy that neither of us was the happier for the meeting.

I fell asleep dreaming of the birch, leather strap, and rods in pickle with which that horrid red man had impressed my imagination.

One thing was clear at all events and no dream, namely, that I had come to the end of my play-time, and that, henceforth, school-time was to begin in earnest.

CHAPTER V.

SCHOOL-TIME. GLIDING ONWARDS.

THE Colvin baronetcy had a history, written and illumin-
ated, up to my great-grandfather's time; who, being a
fine old English gentleman of the sporting-squire type,
sold the library, sold the venerable portraits, combined
with his son to cut off the entail, and finally raised money
on everything that was worth a penny. There being at
length nothing left to live for, or to live on, he died at
Geneva, in the odour of bankruptcy, leaving his debts
and difficulties to his son. The Colvins of the Crusades
had once more to go to the East; for my grandfather
having settled in his own mind that a title was of small
use without money, brought his remaining capital into
Wingle's firm, started to lead a new life on the Stock
Exchange, and dedicated his son, my father, to business
from his very earliest years with all the enthusiasm of a
Hamilcar. Beyond this the old gentleman had no notion
of education, and my father was kept so closely at the
grindstone by his employers (a large mercantile firm,
dealing chiefly, I fancy, in silks, with a highly respectable
provincial connection) as to have hardly any time left for
recreation or self-improvement at night.

This firm, Owen Brothers, merchants, had a branch
establishment at Shrewsbury; and here my father was
sent for, I think, two years, to make himself thoroughly
acquainted with all the details of the business. This, it
seems, was about the only time he ever resided out of

London as long as he remained in England. Later in life
he quitted Owen Brothers. He revived the old Colvin,
Wingle, and Co. stockbroking firm, and, starting on his
own account, went on and prospered.

My father valued his title—reverenced it as something
quite apart from himself, and he had determined that
" he would give his son," as I have often heard him say,
" a first-rate education, sir ; and then he'll be fitted for
anything." Lacking this himself, he saw what an excellent thing it would be, although he had but very vague
notions of how to set about it. He heard of Holyshade
College as the first public school where all the nobility
sent their sons, and for this place he at once destined his
boy. After that would follow one of the two great Universities, and then the Church, or the Bar, as a profession.
Business was to be out of the question. Two Colvins
were enough for the city, and the time was fast approaching when the woolsack, or the episcopal bench, might be
graced by our name. The Colvin baronetcy was, whatever might be said, something in hand to begin with.
The Clyms, my cousins, were to be brought up to business—the Clym business being shipping insurance; and
henceforth, from the commencement of my career at the
private school, preparatory to Holyshade—I was taught
by my father to look down upon the Clyms, and, indeed,
upon any boy who was on his road to Cornhill. He
seemed to forget there might be some danger of such a
sentiment reacting upon himself, but then he looked upon
himself as the wisest, kindest, and best of parents; as I
believe my grandfather, taking his conduct from quite
another point of view, had done before him. People
were paid to educate me—that was all my father knew
of the matter, beyond the fact that these people, whoever
they might be, were paid by him. Business might get
better or worse, but he considered that his heir was
laying up for himself such a store of knowledge for the
future, as must achieve greatness by an easy and pleasant
way; and, as to the sinews of war, had he not already
provided for the improbable adversities of the future ?

He was fond of delivering oracular precepts for my

benefit, generally while he was dressing for a party, and I, ten years old, and seated on a chair, was intently watching the operation—being much interested in the watch and money, usually lying on the dressing-table.

"You must always," he used to observe, under the impression that he was enunciating some original philosophical doctrine, and deluding himself all the while with the idea that he was addressing a young man twice my age, "You must always look on both sides of a difficulty," —here he would fold his cravat twice round, and tie it in the nattiest bow possible. "One day I might not be able to do all for you that I intend."

I am sure he felt a sort of pleasure in saying this, as if the contingency were too remote to be even possible, and, therefore, one on which he could safely expatiate. He continued: "*Then* you'll have plenty of friends to help you, and you'll only have to get up in court and make a speech, and they'll say, Hulloa! here's a clever fellow, by Jove!"—here he got into his coat and gave his whiskers a last brush; "and then"—here his money and watch went into his pockets, and the chance of half-a-crown had vanished for that time—"you'll be Lord Chancellor or something"—here his brougham would be announced, and after saying, "Good night," he would sometimes, not often, stoop to kiss me—stooping not being an easy matter in such a stiff white tie as it was then the fashion to wear. Besides, to caress the child destroyed the illusion of my being his companionable grown-up son. As a child he treated me as an ideal man, without foreseeing that this would end in his treating the man as an ideal child. He always left home in more or less of a hurry, and after he had consulted his watch, and observed that it was past time, he would run downstairs and be driven off at a rapid pace, leaving me to my own devices for amusement. These I soon found in any books I could get hold of, and in my old friend the theatre, with Blue Beard and Co. (only on rather a larger scale, consistent with my increasing age and improved means), of which I used to give performances to the servants. My audience included the cook and her cousin—an enormous tall corporal in uniform—of whom I was at first very much afraid, but who really proved a most amiable person, and, considered as (in himself) the greater part of my "gentle public," most appreciative. My performances at this time were, for the most part, under the patronage of the cook and The Military.

After this came supper; and then the housemaid—to whose hands, during my holidays, I fell, in company with the grates and fire-irons—would intimate that it was time for me to retire for the night, "unless," she generally was obliged to add, "you wish your Pa to come 'ome and catch you hup."

She used to emphasize the "h's" very strongly. She had wonderful stories about her grandmother—who seemed to have been a sort of Mother Shipton, seeing strange forms in the sky. These stories I would get her to tell me with a view to inducing repose, but unsuccessfully, as I subsequently lay awake fancying all sorts of woes coming upon the earth in consequence of Anne's venerable relative having beheld a regiment of soldiers marching in a flash of lightning. This and a new Blue Chamber in "Blue Beard"—which I had lately purchased, and which was furnished with fearful skeletons in rose-coloured flames—impress my memory to this day so vividly and clearly, that, as I write, I seem to behold the bony creatures of my imagination dancing on the wall, as I had often seen them in those childish days when, unable to ring or to scream, I sought safety under the bed-clothes, where after a time I fell asleep.

I dwell upon these incidents—slight and valueless in themselves, but of great weight as bearing upon my future: of great weight to parents who leave children to form themselves as best they can; of great weight to those who look forward to their children's companionship in later life; who, neglecting to sow carefully, yet expect to reap profitably. It is, indeed, a wise child who knows his own father so thoroughly as to avoid his faults, and improve upon his good qualities.

When I have said that Sir John was weak and impulsive; when I have said that his only idea concerning his son was, that there were those whom he paid for their duty of attending the youth, until the time should arrive for him to be his father's companion—when I have said this, I have said all I have to urge against the parental policy. Between him and myself there might have been the strongest attachment, had not he, in the first instance, kept so far apart from me, that the cord of our natural love, strained to the utmost, was forced to yield to the force which, later on, was brought to bear upon it, and then it snapped in twain—but, thank God, not for ever.

Had my mother been spared, she would have had to suffer much, as this history will show, for what has fallen heavily on my father and myself would have fallen heaviest on her, and she would have been wounded through me, but by no fault or misdoing of mine.

No one could have been kinder to me than Nurse Davis. She was, certainly, for her station in life, a superior person, and before going to school I really possessed a very fair amount of knowledge, as far as reading and writing went, besides an intimate acquaintance with Oriental habits and customs as illustrated in "Blue Beard," on my stage, and the Eastern fairy tales in my dear old book; not to mention such an acquaintance with Germany as was to be met with in the play of "Der Freischütz," with Skelt's "Scenes and Characters," and in the legendary lore of the Brothers Grimm. So was it with Robin Hood and William Tell (whom I had seen in a pantomime, the first I ever witnessed, and who for years remained in my mind as a man with thin legs and an enormous head, who would pepper his son's nose and otherwise illtreat him at breakfast)—I say, with all these odds and ends, my knowledge-box was fairly stored, and, by the way, so was my school-box, wherein were a cake, apples, biscuits, and a small jar of mixed pickles, which Nurse considered a rare delicacy. At school my cake was divided among my new companions, as were also the apples and biscuits, everyone looking upon the distribution as a matter of course, calling for no expressions of gratitude towards the noble donor, who could not help himself, and what is more, could not prevent *their* being helped. As for the pickles, to the best of my recollection, I never set eyes on them after they had once been taken out of my box. I rather fancy I heard Miss Secunda Sharpe, the second sister, say something about pickles being very unwholesome, but I think this remark must have only applied to them as eatables for boys, as I am pretty sure that, on Sunday, I recognized some well-known favourites of my nurse's, such as very small but very strong onions, at the upper end of the dinner-table, on the schoolmistresses' plates. But what is not, in the goose's opinion, sauce for the gosling, may be a very excellent relish for the goose herself.

Nurse, who had quitted my father's service, came, with Julie and Mr. Verney, to see me one Sunday during the summer time. Mr. Verney, on this occasion, was peculiarly light and airy, and wore a countrified hat, and turn-down collars. He told me he took this opportunity of "courting the zephyrs which were trifling with the fragrant buttercups and the humble daisies in the luxuriant meadows." I did not understand him then, but I believe this to have been a mere poetical figure, signifying that having been deposited by the sixpenny 'bus at the corner, he had walked up the lane under the trees, and through the front garden to the school-house.

Julie was grown, and a little shy. I asked her if she'd like to come to my school, and she replied "No," which I considered at the time rather unkind. At parting, however, we cried a bit, all of us except Mr. Verney, who stood over us in the attitude of a benignant gaoler. He presently interrupted our sobs with an admonitory cough.

"Parting, Jane, as the bard has expressed it, is 'such sweet sorrow' that we shall be here till to-morrow, I'm afraid, unless we leave our excellent young friend to his scholastic duties, and catch the fleeting omnibus at the corner of the lane, where it will be within the next quarter of an hour. Farewell!"

When they'd gone, I didn't get over it for an hour or more, but sat alone, thinking of what they were doing now, and how happy they were in being free while I was

still a prisoner. I managed to secrete the cake which
had been given me, and shared it with a friend in the
bed next to me, eating it in haste as if it were a sort of
Passover ceremony, due regard, by the way, not being
paid to the necessary dress to be observed on such a
solemn occasion, for we ate it at night, when the other
boys were asleep, in our dormitory. We paid for it, in
medicine, the following day. This did not prevent our
repeating our gluttony on the occurrence of a similar
opportunity.

Of my time at this period I have very little worth
recording. I cried on the first morning after my arrival,
and was dazed by the formality of school prayers round
the breakfast-table. I remember that the first words to
impress me with anything resembling a sentimentally
religious feeling were in the collect commencing "Lighten
our darkness," which was always read at night prayers,
and imbued me with a mysterious dread of bedtime.
This solemn petition used invariably to make me feel
very sad; it seemed to be a sort of funeral service read
over us boys previous to storing us away for the night.
I fancy this impression had vanished by the time I had
got into bed, or I should not have indulged in such reckless dissipation as cake-eating after the light was out.

It took me a long time to master my duty towards my
neighbour in the Catechism, and I really do not think I
ever rightly succeeded in acquiring the proper order of the
sentences about being "true and just in all my dealings"
(which always reminded me of shopkeepers), and about
"hurting nobody by word or deed." In consequence of
the Catechism I suffered a martyrdom, not for any con-
scientious objections to its doctrinal statements, but for
the reason above mentioned; and it certainly was tiresome work on a hot Sunday afternoon, under the eye of
an irritable mistress, who often hurt somebody "by deed,"
and that somebody was myself. Our punishments were
various. One, of Chinese origin, was a stiff leather
collar, which kept your chin up, and forced you to assume
a proud bearing in spite of yourself, and greatly to your
own discomfort. The position of some people enjoying

an elevated social position and paying its penalties, has forcibly recalled to my mind this collar. Then there was the ruler for the knuckles of the recalcitrant, which extracted from me many a sob on a cold morning. Bread and water was not much of a punishment for me, as I was very partial to dry bread, if I could only have enough of it.

My holidays were passed at home, where, except my Clym cousins, with whom I occasionally spent the day, I had no companions, save the servants and the corporal afore-mentioned. I enjoyed their parties while my father went out to his. Of him I saw very little, except on Sundays, when he would send for me into the sitting-room (we were still in lodgings—on our road to a big house, my father having changed his intention on this subject several times—but no longer over the dairy), and would read two or three chapters "out of the Old Testament" to me—generally those wherein occurred the hardest and longest names, which he took great delight in hearing himself pronounce. He was proud of his reading, and considered the exercise as equivalent to a church service. Sometimes, of an afternoon, he would let me accompany him, in state, to a fashionable place of worship; of which all I remember is, that there was exquisite singing, accompanied by a great rustling of music-paper, and that the preacher, reader, and clerk were piled up one above the other, of each of whom only just so much was visible as can be seen of a punch-doll in the usual show. More often, however, he took me, on Sunday, to call on Grandmamma Colvin, and then to my other grandmamma, Mrs. Pritchard. He never came to see me at school, or asked me any educational questions. He appeared to be uninterested in me as long as I continued a child; it seemed such an age before I should be anywhere near manhood. Nothing short of my having been born a ready-made man would have satisfied him. It was clear that both of us must wait. But my father was impatient.

So far the stream of time bore me along, lazily, easily. Nurse Davis, Julie, and Frampton's Court I already seemed to have left far behind. Where on my voyage I might meet them again never entered into my head. The future gives a child no trouble, and the past but little pleasure. I had been happy with the Verneys, and I was happy without them. Be it remembered, I was alone, and therefore selfish. Our family archives record instances of selfish individuals among the Colvins. It is a theory that every man has in him some disease which will exhibit its fatal power if he live long enough for its development. Growing up within me was selfishness. I see, now, that nothing but the knife could have saved me. I know, now, that a true love had already taken root deep down in my heart, out of sight; and of its existence I should not be aware until the earth above should be broken by the strength of its first upward shoots.

My small boat was now to be delayed at a landing-stage, where I was to take in fresh stores and meet new characters. Already the pilots destined to betray their trust, to run both ship and boat upon the rocks, were awaiting us on this new shore.

CHAPTER VI

OLD CARTER'S ACADEMY—AS HINTED IN A FORMER CHAPTER,
ONE OF MY IMPORTANT PERSONAGES APPEARS FOR THE
FIRST TIME.

SOON the time came for jackets, and with a new suit I
was sent to a new school, near Bromfield, in Kent, which
I was informed was to be preparatory to going to Holyshade. This establishment was kept by the Rev. Thomas
Carter, a pompous clergyman of the Evangelical school,
who stood in great awe of his wife. Mrs. Carter ruled
him, ruled the ushers—who did their best to render themselves agreeable to her—and ruled the boys. Here, I
made the acquaintance of that diabolical instrument, the
cane. Mrs. Carter generally looked in at the door when
any chastisement was being inflicted, and would keep her
husband up to the mark by such words of encouragement
as "That's not hard enough, Thomas; make him feel it
my dear," so that Mr. Carter, one day losing his temper,
and getting very red in the face, cried out to her,
"Perhaps you'd like to do it yourself," to which she at
once replied that she wouldn't cane at all if she couldn't
do it better than that, adding that "she'd like to cane
him and the boys too," whereat the second usher put his
head under the lid of his desk and laughed, while his
senior smiled grimly, and took an enormous pinch of
snuff. She was a dreadful little, freckled, shrivelled
woman, and was quite my idea of a witch. With a
broomstick and a sugarloaf hat she would have been per-

fect: only I pity the imp who would have dared to get within reach of her broomstick; he would have had a Walpurgis night not to be forgotten in a hurry.

Out of the fifty or sixty boys, there were only two in whom I was interested. One was the captain of the school, Percival Floyd, whom I admired and feared. The other was Austin Comberwood, of whom I was very fond. The head boy—we didn't call him captain—was Percival Floyd. He was nearly seventeen, and in the general opinion quite a man, if it had not been for his still wearing jackets, which gave him rather a nautical appearance, especially about the legs, of which, as may be imagined, we saw a good deal. He had a magnificent reputation for strength and prowess at fisticuffs. It was just a question whether he could thrash Stephen Harker, who was about his own age, and had lately gone into stick-ups and tails. These appendages caused Master Harker considerable embarrassment, on account of his having been christened, on his return in this new attire, "Pussy Cat," by the drawing-master, who was a wag in his way; but if *his* pleasantry was tolerated, out of deference to Art, that of the juniors—who pretended to "miaow" when Harker's back was turned, and to be afraid of his tail coat—was visited with condign punishment whenever he succeeded in catching a delinquent, which was not often. Harker was strong in neckties of a rainbow pattern, and flattered himself that he was the admiration of a girls' school which frequented our church. He was the son of a Manchester manufacturer, reputed to be immensely wealthy, with mills and machinery in every direction. He was partial to sweet-smelling pomade, with which he used to plaster his black hair until it shone again, and his great amusement and delight was to watch the very gradual growth of some fluffy down on his upper lip, for which purpose he kept a small looking-glass fastened to the inside of the lid of his desk. This dark streak of down, looking like a smudge from a lead pencil, was as interesting to him as the first sprouts of a spring crop to a farmer. The drawing-master remarked that every pussy cat had moustachios, and this joke

lasted us for some time, until Fatty Bifford asked Harker
if he wouldn't like some cat's-meat, therewith imitating
the cry of the purveyor of that article ; whereupon, being
unable to run away as quickly as he had intended, he
was captured, and handled so severely, that we never
attempted to imitate the humorous Bifford, who, we considered, deserved all he had got, for his inability to escape
the consequences.

There were two Biffords—Fatty and Puggy—brothers
with so strong a family resemblance to each other, that
it seemed as if they'd been originally intended for twins.
They were not, however, and Fatty was the elder by two
years. They were never known to agree on any one
point, except that they should always be fighting, and no
question ever arose between them, which was not at once
decided by the ordeal of battle. Such a battle, too !
where all was fair, except a blow below the lowest waistcoat button, which Fatty Bifford could not, and would
not, stand. And this was the fatal blow that his brother
Puggy invariably gave him when affairs were becoming
desperate. Then Fatty, doubled up like a Punch doll,
would fall, protesting, with his latest and shortest breath,
against foul play, whereat the ring would interfere.
Then, in consequence of a difference of opinion having
arisen between Puggy and one of the interposing by-
standers, it became the younger brother's turn to have a
fresh encounter on his hands, when he, after some few
feints and guards, invariably succumbed, and spent the
remainder of his play-hours in tears and abuse of his
brother. Fatty was never known to speak well of Puggy,
and Puggy never had a good word for his brother. Fatty
would confide to the boys that there was no such sneak
as Puggy, and Puggy would confidently assert that there
never was such a cowardly bully as that Fatty. Yet
their attachment to each other was, strange to say, firm
and sincere, and has so remained through life. In their
conflicts at school, hair-pulling came to be considered
quite as one of the fine arts, while throttling and kicking
were managed with so great a dexterity, as, in more
sporting times, would have elevated their performance to

D

the rank of a science. Blows were seldom exchanged, except *the* one already mentioned. Nobody having authority ever interfered between them, except on two occasions, when I remember Mrs. Carter suddenly rushing in, having been at the keyhole for some minutes previously, and seizing them both by the hair, which she tugged impartially until they yelled again, she banged their heads together and took them off to be caned on the spot : and a very sore spot it must have been for a long time afterwards. This is the only instance within my knowledge of a satisfactory issue of an uncalled-for interference by a third party in the quarrels of relations.

As for the ushers, the senior was seldom with us in play-hours, having his own amusements and lodgings in the country town of Bromfield, within five minutes' walk of our school-house. Our second usher, as a rule, had scarcely settled down into the ways of the place before he was somehow or other sent about his business ; generally, it was believed, through Mrs. Carter's instrumentality.

It was a tradition at old Carter's that the second usher never stopped more than one half : if he did, he'd stay two years. When I first came, this post was occupied by a Mr. Daw, a little man with a large head, who ate garlic privately and smelt of it publicly. On wet afternoons he used to sing to us some rollicking songs with strangely worded choruses. Mrs. Carter came in during one of these performances, and as his music did not possess charms sufficient to calm her savage breast, he received notice and left.

To his professional chair succeeded a Mr. Venn. He was an unwholesome-looking man, whose complexion reminded me of a frog's back. His restless eyes, peering out of deep recesses, moved quickly and suspiciously, as though he were perpetually on the alert for the appearance of somebody from some unexpected quarter. I remember in the story of the fisherman and the genii how in the king's palace the wall suddenly opened and a Moor stepped out, much to the consternation of the · fisherman. Had our second usher been the fisherman, he would have been ready for him and waiting.

The way in which he would play with the ruler seemed to suggest the defensive, and he always dived down behind the lid of his desk, and brought up his head again to look right and left sharply, much after the manner of a thrush on a lawn, fearful of being surprised in his worming operations. In the place of eyebrows he had two irritable-looking red lines, with stumps of hair dotted about, as though they alone had been spared in a severe visitation of pumice-stone. His nose was trowel-shaped—that is, it fitted in a very broad and flat manner on to the cheeks, and tapered away to not too fine a point. His mouth was large; but he generally kept it shut, scarcely opening it to speak. He had no more smile on his face than has a man, with a strong sense of humour, suffering from sea-sickness. Easy-going, lounging Mr. Crosbie, M.A., the senior, who affected a sporting costume, and kept two dogs of doubtful breed (which curled their tails downwards when interviewed by other dogs, and pretended never to see any cat that happened to be quite close to them), was afraid of him, and in his presence was on his best behaviour. Old Carter spoke of Mr. Venn as a gentleman with the highest recommendations from the most learned, reverend, and respectable authorities. He trumpeted him before he arrived. After his arrival, old Carter saw less of the schoolroom than heretofore, and at dinner Mrs. Carter was far more civil to Mr. Venn than ever she had been to Mr. Crosbie. All the boys remarked the change, and wondered. Percival Floyd was soon on as friendly a footing as one ever could be with Mr. Venn; and Harker, being ignored, was left to Crosbie, who, it was whispered, knew Harker at home, and having actually stopped at Harker's mill, was, for reasons of his own, very lenient with his young friend over Horace and Homer.

One hot summer's day the boys were in the field playing cricket—a game which I never could summon up sufficient nerve to play. So much danger and so much trouble for nothing, seemed to me to be associated with this amusement, that I and the only other boy who shared my feelings on the subject, Austin Comberwood, were accustomed to retire to a distant part of the field, where he would tell me the stories of Scott's novels, wherein, as was natural, I was mightily interested; and were he compelled to leave off at a thrilling point of interest, I used to look forward with pleasure to the night-time, when, as we lay in our little room (we were the only two sleeping there), it would be "continued in our next" by him.

While he was recounting "Ivanhoe" to me, Mr. Venn came up, and sent Austin with a message across the field. Then he turned to me, and knitting the red marks which did duty for brows, asked—

"How old are you, Colvin?"

"Twelve last birthday, sir," I replied, for I was getting on by this time.

"Where's your father now?"

"In London, sir."

"Always in London?"

"Always, I think," I replied with some hesitation, because it struck me as quite a new idea that my father should ever go out of town. Then I added, by way of such an explanation as appeared to me necessary—

"We live in London, sir."

"You know Shrewsbury, don't you?" he asked.

I was never strong in English geography; and geography out of England would have at that time completely floored me. It occurred to me that Mr. Venn was taking a mean advantage of me out of school hours. However, I knew enough to reply confidently that Shrewsbury was the capital of Shropshire.

"Ah," he returned, "I don't mean that. Didn't you once live there?"

"No, sir."

It suddenly occurred to me that I might have been born there. I shouldn't have been sorry to prove this to my schoolfellows, as all the other boys had been born, they said, in the country; and they used to call me a cockney—a term I detested, implying, as it seemed to me, an ignorance of such matters as riding, hunting, shooting, and fishing, with which my companions, one and all, professed themselves familiar. Their derision was all the more galling on account of its being caused by what was simply the truth, and nothing but the truth. I knew no more of fishing, or indeed of any field sports, than I did of astronomy; and, as may be imagined, I was not much of a Newton at this period of my life. Not that I wish to infer that I have since attained any eminence in the science of the stars. No: such high flights I have left to Dædalian individuals. For myself, I am content to leave the solar system alone. It has worked remarkably well for some considerable time without any interference on my part, and I am not ambitious of being a Phaëthon, and getting the calendar into a muddle. I will accept alterations peaceably, but will not originate them. Make old May-day in December, and put Christmas-day in July, I shall not complain, but will celebrate the one with port and filberts, and the other with iced plum-pudding and cold mince-pies.

However, to come back to Shrewsbury, whence we started. The notion of its having been my birth-place, with its logical train of consequences, commencing with the certainty that I could no longer be upbraided with cockneyism—this notion, I say, seemed to me so brilliant, that I couldn't help suggesting to Mr. Venn that it was not impossible that I might have been born there.

"H'm," he said presently, after a pause, "you don't take after your mother."

I had always been told I was very like her, and I said so, adding, "I'm not like my father, sir"—of which distinction I was not a little proud; because, to my imagination, my mother had been the loveliest creature ever seen.

He had unwittingly struck a chord in my heart of infinite sweet melody. My mother seemed to me too sacred for him to mention; and as the tears welled up, and the green fields and landscape became obscured by the mist that filled my eyes, I replied—

"She is dead, sir."

"Dead," he repeated, softly, as if much shocked; "Yes; I forgot, or I should not have mentioned the subject."

The excuse sounded awkward, but kindly, and at that moment, in spite of my grief, I felt myself of considerable importance. I could not, had I been then asked, have put the reason into words, but I suppose that my personal vanity was flattered by having received a sort of apology from an authority so formidable as Mr. Venn. .

Being in this humour, I was quite willing to talk about myself and domestic matters. He smiled when, becoming confidential, I described Mr. Verney; and I thought he really must have known him, but he said that he did not; and he appeared considerably interested when I, wishing to impress upon him clearly the marked distinction between my Aunt Clym and my Aunt Susan, was forced to point out, as something to be remembered, that Aunt Susan was my mother's sister, and *my* Grandmamma Pritchard was my mother's mamma.

" Pritchard ?" he asked, in a tone that implied a doubt of my veracity. I assured him that it was so, and he seemed as puzzled as Fatty Bifford when thinking of the answer to a question in Proportion. Then he said—

" Have you ever heard the name of Wingrove ?"

I had some idea that he was laughing at me, but I saw by his face and manner that he was quite serious. I seemed to have heard the name of Wingrove, but somehow, if at all, in connection with the Verneys. The longer I thought, the more sure I became that I never had heard it before.

" Then," he said, with his peculiarly ill-favoured smile, " then, when you see your father, ask him if he knows the name of Wingrove ;" and as we looked at one another I laughed timidly, not being quite sure whether it was said in joke or earnest, and being uncertain as to how he might take it if I were wrong.

But he patted me on the back and laughed in turn, as the wolf might have laughed, when he was so tickled with the the idea of the practical joke he was going to play on little Red Riding Hood; and then as Austin Comberwood returned, Mr. Venn walked away. I asked Austin about Wingrove, and *he* didn't know, and, moreover, didn't think it was in any of Sir Walter Scott's novels (which put the matter in a new light to me), unless it might be, he surmised, in one of the books that he hadn't yet read.   This led to a discussion as to the number of books he *had* read; and just as he was commencing where he had left off, about the Black Knight (who *he* was going to be I couldn't make out), we were summoned into school.

I thought of Wingrove and the conversation with Mr. Venn, once or twice afterwards, but it very soon ceased to interest me—having no chance against Ivanhoe, as narrated in the dark, at bed-time, by Comberwood—until, later on, a slight incident recalled it to my memory. Mr. Venn's conduct towards me from this time forth was distinguished by so many marks of kindness (he once actually rescued me from old Mother Carter's hands, by moral not physical force) that this portion of my time at this school was, on the whole, very happily spent.   It is true I was dubbed " Venn's Favourite," but the boys soon dropped this when they discovered that, on the love-me-love-my-dog principle, to be the friend of Cæsar's friend was to be the friend of Cæsar.   The Biffords were the sole exception to this rule.   They were too deeply engaged in their own domestic broils to trouble themselves with the affairs of the outer world.   They left during my third half, and fought not only up to the last minute, but on the very steps of the fly which was to convey them to the station.   The last that was here seen of them (from Carter's dining-room, and looking through the fly window) was Fatty Bifford with both his hands tugging at and twisting Puggy's hair, freshly oiled for going home; while the latter had got hold of his brother's new necktie, and was trying to strangle him before they should reach the station.   As we soon after received news of them from Holyshade College, whither they had both preceded me, though the majority of Carter's boys used to go to Harton School, we had the gratification of knowing that their latest squabble had not ended fatally.

During my last two school-times I ceased to be Venn's

favourite, in fact, as I had long before ceased to be in name. As the circumstances which, I have since learnt, occasioned this change of demeanour have shown themselves to have been fraught with consequences of the deepest importance, not only to myself but to others, I must not now pass lightly over certain events which, trivial as they then seemed, did most undoubtedly mark an epoch in the history of my time.

CHAPTER VII.

WORKING ROUND—OTHER IMPORTANT PERSONAGES ON THE
SCENE—AN ILL WIND, AND SOME CONSEQUENCES.

ABOUT this time, my father, at the recommendation of
his greatest friend and constant adviser, Mr James Cavander, and in opposition to all that could be urged against
the scheme by Aunt Clym—on all occasions Cavander's
warm opponent—took and furnished a house in that district of Kensington which a Museum and a National
Portrait Gallery have since combined to render famous.
Business in the city—whatever that might mean—had
been good; "things" also in the city had been for some
time "looking up," and had enabled my father to purchase
the long lease of a residence which the auctioneer's
advertisement described as both eligible and desirable.
Mr. Cavander was probably correct in suggesting it as a
good investment. For my part I know very little more
about such matters now than I did then; practical
experience alone can endow me with such wisdom as is
necessary for matters which are, like the prices of Bel-
gravian palaces, too high for me, and as yet—that is up
to the present time of writing—I have not been able to
purchase another house on a similar site.

But this Mr. James Cavander—could I write this
history and omit all mention of him, I would.   Could I
show my love for my enemies by observing silence about
them, I would.   But it is as impossible to keep James
Cavander out of this veracious narrative, as it would be
to ignore the devil in the history of Christianity.

For you, my friends, who honour our family by perusing this addition to its past history, I have no disguise,
no trick; I tell you that at this particular point I introduce my arch-villain, so that you may sympathise with
me when I, as a' boy, first saw him, and intuitively disliked him.   Let us be in jackets and turn-down collars
again, and let us dislike him together, for the plain and
simple reason that we *do* dislike, and can't tell why.   My
instinct was right—I can say so now : and for the correct-
ness of first instincts, I will back children and women
against all others.   It was on returning to Old Carter's
that I first encountered Mr. Cavander, and felt as kindly
disposed towards him as I have above intimated.   He
was, so far, my Doctor Fell: the reason why I could not
tell; but this I knew, in less than two minutes, and
knew full well, that I *did* not, and never could, like Mr.
James Cavander.

Undoubtedly a handsome man, with the darkest hair,
whiskers, and eyebrows I had as yet seen; and I do not
think I have since met his equal in this respect.

His eyes were, so to speak, his face; for you got at
them and they at you first and foremost.   They faced
you out, steadfastly.   They bothered you like the light
of a dark lantern.   These eyes further gave you the idea
of their being the spies set at the windows to seize on all
that might furnish material for the brain within, whose
machinery was hard at work all day, and far into the
night, until the watchers should succumb to drowsiness,
and the busy thoughts should hie to their play-ground in
the land of dreams.

Cavander took you in as raw material through his eyes,
and turning you over and over, and round and round,
easily and pleasantly produced you in the form best
adapted to his purpose.   Cavander's mental steam hammer
could brush the dust off a fly's wing without disturbing
it, or could crush a boulder of granite.   This latter effort
was not to the man's taste, as requiring sudden violence.

He would have preferred treating Leviathan as a trout,
and bag him by tickling.   If you were of no use to him,
he forgot you, and it would be fair to say of him generally

that he only remembered you for your own disadvantage. Thus, he could forget what was not worth his while to remember, but he never troubled himself to forgive.

Do I suppose, looking back at this man, that when by himself he professed undying hatred of any human being? Undoubtedly not: I firmly believe that he considered himself no worse than those among whom he moved, and far better than many whom he heard parading their charitable sentiments. He despised both Pharisee and publican, as canting hypocrites. And, to do him justice, he neither professed too much with the one, nor abased himself abjectly with the other. I have seen his name attached to many a subscription for a good and pious purpose, and I have heard of his kind acts in gifts of money to certain poor people who had proved themselves to be deserving objects of charity. People mostly spoke of him as "a clever fellow," but at the same time they shook their heads knowingly, implying thereby that there are more ways than one of being clever, and that on the whole they'd rather not be called upon to explain precisely their meaning. Such remarks as these my father used to take as complimentary to his own sagacity, for in the city he and Cavander appeared to be inseparable. While I had been growing, Cavander had been becoming a necessary part of my father's business. My shoes were too small for him at present, but he had taken my measure for my boots of the future, which, made for me, he intended to wear himself. Somehow I had never met this gentleman at home. He said he perfectly remembered me as quite a child, and I've no doubt but that he was right. Perhaps his holidays coincided with mine, and so when he went away I arrived. Be this as it may, we met face to face when I was between eleven and twelve, and since that day in the city I have not had the opportunity of forgetting him.

I confess my sorrow at the personal appearance of the wicked genie of my story. I am annoyed that he should have been at once so patently proclaimed villain; and were it in my power to change, I would make him of Saxon type (when, you see, he would not be cursed with this conventionally villanous black hair), and would let him skip on to the scene, like a sheepish Colin to a pastoral symphony, without a vestige of the wolf popping out anywhere. But it cannot be. I am not painting a monster; I am only drawing a black sheep, whose dark wool is as glossy as the coat of a seal, and who is an ornament and not a blemish to the flock.

For his complexion, it was pale, lightly, yet healthily, browned by the sun. The heaviest part about his face was his chin: you almost expected to see it worked up and down behind the ears with pulleys. Sometimes I noticed that while ruminating he would let it drop, and so stand thinking, with his mouth open. When he had settled whatever it was that might be occupying his attention, he would bring his jaws to with a click of the teeth, which boded no good to an adversary. This habit of his was uncommonly startling to me, as also was his way of wetting his lips, which he often did when he had not quite made up his mind as to a course to be pursued, or whenever he permitted himself to show his annoyance.

He was altogether a man of striking appearance. His dress was exactly to his time of life, and within the fashion of the day. As a child I mentally compared him with my uncle, Herbert Pritchard, who, to my mind, was the gayest dressed man I knew; in fact he was all coloured shirt and patent boots. By the side of Mr. Cavander, Uncle Herbert might be considered as the wearer of a fancy dress. In the summer you would have thought, on seeing Uncle Herbert's light and airy costume in the city, that he had come thither in his yacht—or in somebody else's, which would have been far more probable. But Cavander's dress remained apparently very nearly the same at one season as at another—in perfect taste always; and you would never hear him, as you would Uncle Herbert, complaining of the excessive heat of an ordinary summer, or of the difficulty of keeping warm in a seasonable winter, at which time of the year Uncle Herbert's appearance was that of a man bound on an expedition to the northern regions, especially if you met him in a carriage—somebody else's, of course, never *his*—where he would have rugs and wraps enough to smother a whole orphanage asylum of babies in the Tower.

Herbert Pritchard was a favourite with Cavander, whom he used to consult on his "little matters of business in the city," whenever he came to see my father. Herbert's city speculations were to Cavander like the card-playing of old ladies for counters at two-pence a dozen. He had microscopic investments, too, in various odd things, all done, as it were, in threepenny bits. It amused him, however, and, as it gave him an interest in perusing the city article in *The Times*, it also added to his subjects of conversation. But as we shall see more of Herbert Pritchard later on, I will not stop to discuss him here.

Uncle Herbert had volunteered to see me safely down to Carter's, having to pay a visit in the neighbourhood. I was glad of this, as it meant half-a-sovereign more in my pocket—certainly five shillings, and on previous occasions I had been seen to the station by one of my father's clerks, and booked for my destination like a parcel. So Uncle Herbert took the city on his road.

The city puzzled me immensely, but as we were driven up to the office door in a close cab (hackney coaches had recently gone out, and hansoms hadn't come in) I did not on this occasion see very much of it.

We went up some stone stairs into a sort of gallery, dark and dirty. Had it been Mr. Cavander who had taken me, I might have suspected some mischief. I couldn't imagine my father having anything to do with such a dreary place as this.

We stopped before a glass door, on which I distinguished the word "Private." I suppose on this occasion we went in by a back way. The place has been so altered of late years—in fact, I rather fancy those old offices have been entirely pulled down—that were I to come upon it again suddenly I do not think I should recognize it.

The private room was empty, but in the front room, where some clerks were at a desk, behind a sort of screen of brass wires, like some sort of dangerous birds, and hidden from view by green curtains on brass rods, stood Mr. Cavander, leaning on the mantel-piece.

"How are you, Cavander?" said Uncle Herbert.

Mr. Cavander turned and saluted him with a nod, and then took me into consideration. There was not at this time much of me to take in, and he did it with ease at a glance.

"Your nephew?" he asked.

"Yes," replied Uncle Herbert, "this is Master Cecil Colvin, on his way to school."

I expected to be asked to shake hands with Mr. Cavander, but I wasn't, so I merely looked up at him and smiled, with an indistinct notion of corroborating Uncle Herbert's statement, which if acted upon by Mr. Cavander, I surmised dimly, and from the first with great mistrust, might lead to half-a-sovereign. A schoolboy's ideas are on these occasions generally mercenary. If Mr. Cavender had given me a shake of the hand and a tip, I wonder if my opinion of him would have been altered? I imagine that I should even now still have some lurking prejudice in his favour in consequence of this going-to-school gift, and would at any time have lent an unwilling ear to what might be said against him. However, he did not give half a sovereign or half a penny, and consequently not being bribed to vote for him as the real friend of the schoolboy, I was at liberty to resent any of his observations addressed to me.

"Have you been flogged yet?" he asked.

This was not a pleasant subject to begin with, and I *did* resent it.

"No," I answered shortly, "I've not."

"Ah!" he said, as if old Carter had been remiss in his duty on this point. "A boy's no good till he's flogged. You're going to Holyshade after this."

I said that I didn't know. From his tone of allusion to this great public school I augured the worst, and sincerely hoped that my father would abandon his intention.

"*You* don't know," he returned, eyeing me with

evident disfavour, "but I do. Little boys don't know what's good for them. They fag, and flog, at Holyshade. You'll be made to clean the boots and shoes. That's the thing to make a man of you."

I did not see at the time, and I have failed to understand since, how cleaning boots and shoes for other boys could advance me either socially or morally. I candidly said to Mr. Cavander that I did not want to go to Holyshade.

"Oh, don't you?" he asked ironically.

"No," I replied, with a smile that was so very like a threatening rain-cloud, that Uncle Herbert attempted to illuminate the view of Holyshade with a few rays of warm sunlight.

"He'll like it well enough when he's accustomed to it. Plenty of fun, boating, cricket, and all that kind of thing. I know a lot of Holyshaders. Jolly chaps. 'Gad, I wish they'd sent *me* there. Ah! here's John."

My father entered so busy and pre-occupied, that he scarcely took any notice of me beyond patting my cheek and referring to his watch, in order to see how close at hand the time for the starting of my train might be.

Then he handed some papers to one clerk, and told another to run over to somewhere (Capel Court, I suppose) and bring back the latest news. Then Uncle Herbert very much wanted to know something about "Turks," and the reply appearing unsatisfactory, he wanted to know something else about "Indians," and something further about "Rupees," and requested a few particulars as to the Polygon tin mine (in which he was interested up to the price of one share, value ten pounds) and the Antipodean Gas Company; and then, having, as it seemed, being unable to come to any conclusion on any of these subjects, he pulled up his collar and wristbands, and lounging back in a hard arm-chair, he laid himself out on an incline, and considered his boots, while my father early consulted Mr. Cavander.

I watched the latter closely. He never hesitated when he had once shut his mouth with a click. His teeth coming together settled the matter. I saw that my

father deferred to him entirely.   I saw that everything
he was doing in the city was at his friend's instigation,
and that without his advice he was doing nothing.   The
clerks coming in obeyed Mr Cavander's orders, or told my
father that Mr Cavander had already expressed his wishes
on some business affair, whereupon my father left it to
him, and appeared perfectly satisfied with his arrangements.

Clients looked in to see Cavander if they could, and
put up with my father if they couldn't, or they got Sir
John to speak for them, and presently they'd all .talk
together, while Cavander listened, and quarrel and get
excited, until a clerk who had been previously sent out,
would rush in and hand a paper to Mr. Cavander, when
all would suspend their arguments and listen to the
latest news and his advice.   No one took any notice of
me, except to ask Sir John " Whose boy—yours ?" when
my father smiled and nodded, as much as to say, " Yes,
he's of no consequence just now ; he's not a man yet:
only a child : but it does him good to let him listen, as a
man, to our conversation : don't mind him," and then
passed on to business.

Once a fat, foreign gentleman—an Italian merchant, I
fancy—coming in suddenly, and out of breath, thought
to interest Cavander in his behalf by pretending to
be enraptured with my personal appearance, and then
asking him if I wasn't his eldest.   Whereupon he answered
curtly, No, that I was nothing to do with him, and
handed the mistaken man over to the head clerk, and
would have nothing further to say to him on any subject
whatever.

A young clerk, a mere boy, was commissioned by my
father to see to my wants as to luncheon before I started.
The lad was not allowed to indulge in luxuries himself,
but was told to furnish me with whatever I liked best at
Birch's, where I prevailed on him to have some delicious
tartlets, which he put down to me, and we said nothing
about it.

On returning to the office, I found Uncle Van, who
had come in from Lloyd's, talking about the fearful gales,

which had resulted in serious losses to the under-writers.

"I never 'knew such a ting—he-he-he," he was saying, laughing as usual, but in a nervous, uncertain manner. "Such losses—my god-a-gracious!—ev'ry one is hit hart."

Were I to spell "every" thus, "evhry," it might give some idea of Uncle Van's way of pronouncing an "r." It didn't sound at all like one of the liquid family, but resembled a guttural that had lost its way in his nose.

"What is it, Van?" asked Cavander, smiling, for Uncle Van, in his way, amused him as much as Herbert Pritchard. My father was sitting at a small table casting up some accounts.

"The late gales?" suggested a long-legged gentleman, looking out from behind a newspaper. There were generally three or four nobodies in the office reading the papers, and imagining that they were engaged in enormously profitable transactions. They were somehow or other useful in the way of business, or they wouldn't have been encouraged.

"Gales!" exclaimed Uncle Van, "tey've been fearful. We—tat is Peter Hoskins, Heinz, and myself—hat written to *Prairie Bird* from Melbourne——"

"There was nothing risky in that," said Cavander, stretching out his legs on the hearthrug, and taking a cigarette out of his case. Smoking was not permitted in business hours to anyone except Cavander, whose health was supposed to require it, and he never used anything but cigarettes of his own private and particular manufacture.

"Risky!" exclaimed Uncle Van, "no, it was a certainty."

"And it hasn't come in?" said my father carelessly finishing his sum in arithmetic, and opening his desk.

"It's te vorst of to-tay, and tere are someting like tventy wrecks on te coast," replied Uncle Van, shaking the paper in his hand. "Zee 'ere! No salvage, notting at all. Zee tese telegraph account to te room. Zee, I reat you—um—um—'Total loss of te *Prairie Bird* . . . . the names of te five persons ascertaint to have been savet'

E

—tat's notting. I reat you tese accounts: it vas fear-ful . . . 'savet'—yes—" he was so agitated that he had some difficulty in picking out the part of the paragraph he required, and thus it happened that, involuntarily, he ran over the line containing the list of the people rescued from the vessel—"Jacob Furnival,—Penfold, Richard Varish (of Sunderland), Sarah Wingrove——"

A startled exclamation escaped my father as he sat with the half-raised lid of the desk in his hand, while Cavander, for one second, paused in lighting his cigarette.

"Eh ?" said Uncle Van, looking up; and the long-legged gentleman, emerging from behind his newspaper, observed that the storm must have indeed been awful.

Uncle Herbert remarked that it would have been nasty weather for a cruise, and requested, being nautically inter-ested, further particulars.

Uncle Van turned towards him, and commenced read-ing his account of it, including once more the list of names.

It was listened to with breathless attention, and I well remember noticing how my father, from time to time, cast a nervous glance at Cavander, who stood before the fireplace imperturbably smoking a cigarette.

Having made his effect here, Uncle Van, after nodding kindly to me, hurried off, to be the first with the news in another quarter.

Observing that my father was apparently disinclined to enter upon any business except his own that day, for he was still seated at his desk, and engaged upon whole rows of accounts on several sheets of paper, Herbert Pritchard rose to fulfil his promise of seeing me safely off by the train which was to take me back to school.

My father said, "Certainly, thank you," and shook my hand shortly and coldly. Suddenly it occurred to him that I should want some money, and he gave me a sovereign, for which I thanked him.

For an embrace, for a cheering smile, for one warm word of interest in my career, I would have sacrificed my gold piece then and there. In another moment my heart would have spoken, and I should have burst into tears, had not Mr. Cavander said, as I followed Uncle Herbert to the door—

"You'll be flogged when you get back for being a day late."

I replied surlily, "No, I shan't," but after this intimation I did not feel at all comfortable on the subject, and my dislike of my father's friend became intensified by several degrees.

As I went along the dark passage I lagged behind Uncle Herbert, in the vain hope of my father coming out and embracing me. This slow progression brought me opposite the inner private room, the door of which, marked "Private," opened on to the landing.

I was startled by a dull sound, as of some one thumping a table heavily, and then my father's voice anxiously addressing Cavander.

"You heard the name?"

"Yes," answered Cavander quietly; "what of it?"

"What of it!" exclaimed my father. "Why, heavens, Cavander, did you not tell me that she——"

Here Uncle Herbert loudly called to me to descend the staircase, and, as quickly and as lightly as I could, lest the man I most dreaded should come out, and accuse me of eavesdropping, I ran on, and in another minute was at my uncle's side and in the street.

CHAPTER VIII.

SCHOOL-TIME AND PLAY-TIME—A STRANGE VISITOR.

On returning to Old Carter's, where I wasn't flogged for being a day late, as Mr. Cavander had prophesied I should be, Mr. Venn, whom the holidays had rendered thinner and yellower, as they had made Mr. Crosbie larger, redder in the nose, and generally stouter, asked me privately,—

"Colvin, did you mention the name of Wingrove to your father?"

"Wingrove, sir?"

I had forgotten all about our conversation, and I thought he would have been angry with me for the omission.

"Yes; do you not remember what I told you?"

"In the cricket field? Yes, sir. But——"

I was about to stammer out an excuse, when it flashed across me that almost the last name I had heard in the office was this identical one of Wingrove.

"I didn't speak about it, sir," I therefore began, adroitly, "because I heard it read out."

"Read out! What do you mean?"

"From a newspaper, sir, by my Uncle Van."

"Van? Is that his name?"

"Not all of it, sir. Mr. Van Clym is my uncle. He has something to do with ships, and"—here it all came back to me clearly—"he rushed in—— "

"Where?"

"My father's counting-house, when I was coming down

here, sir, with my Uncle Herbert. Do you know my Uncle Herbert, sir?"

This was thrown in craftily, as if to establish a friendly relationship.

"No. Is *his* name Wingrove?"

"No, sir, Pritchard; but he took me up there, and Uncle Van ran in with a newspaper and told us all about some dreadful wreck."

"Well?" Mr. Venn was listening attentively.

"And he said that nearly everyone was drowned except I forget how many, sir; and then he said Wingrove."

"A Wingrove drowned?" he asked, rather sharply.

"No, sir, saved."

"A man?" he asked, scrutinizing me in a way that caused me to wish I had never fallen into this conversational trap.

"A woman, sir; Sarah Wingrove."

"*Sarah?*" he repeated emphatically.

"Sarah," I returned, almost defiantly.

I thought, as a long pause ensued, he was about to dismiss this witness, having no further questions to ask. I was mistaken. He laid his hand on my shoulder, and prevented my turning away.

"You've not made up—you've not invented this story?" he said, pointing, so to speak, his eyes at me with deadly aim.

"No, sir, indeed not," I replied with energy.

"H'm. Do you remember—remembering so much, perhaps you can—where the ship was from?"

I thought for an instant, and then ventured, "Africa or America, sir."

Perceiving my hesitation, for this geographical inquiry trenched on business, he suggested, smiling as much as *he* could smile, "Australia, perhaps, eh?"

I was much relieved. It was like being prompted in an examination, and being unable to catch the word. "Yes, sir, it was; I am sure of it. It *was* Australia."

"In the paper?"

"Yes, sir."

"And you came down yesterday. That'll do. Go.

Stay. If you are writing home, you need not mention my asking anything about it; do you understand, Colvin?"

I answered that I had not much to write about generally, and had no objection to omitting even this item from my scanty budget of school news.

He walked away thoughtfully.

As to my home correspondence, my father used once a week to send me a commonplace letter, which was so stereotyped in its phrases as to weather and health, as to be far more like a circular. As to what I was doing, what progress I was making, what books I was reading, or what might be my moral or religious training at Old Carter's, he never once inquired. They were paid to teach at Carter's, and he took for granted that what was bought and paid for was found on the establishment. As to a line in life for me, that had never entered into his head. His strong point was, that to be a gentleman was everything in this world, and probably in the next, though, at this time, he never ventured upon such *terra incognita* in my hearing, or for my benefit at all events.

" We've all been in business," he used to say, " and your grandfather made his name there. He wasn't a father to me as I am to you, and you'll acknowledge it afterwards as you get on in life. My father put me to work in the city when I was fifteen, and I never had an education such as you've got. *I* never had *your* advantages. You will be a gentleman and—and—one of these days you'll have your horse in the park, and your stall at the opera, and be able to go about with me."

This was the brilliant future held up to me by my father. He was somehow, he knew not how, fashioning a companion for himself, or rather he was employing others to do it for him, he supplying the material on which they were to operate, and paying for the labour.

At the commencement of this schooltime, however, my father for three weeks forgot the usual letter; and in reply to an inquiry (monetary of course), I received a brusque note from Mr. Cavander to the effect that my father was away and too busy to write. What affected me deeply was that the letter contained no enclosure.

However, I represented the case to Mr. Venn, who recommended me to go to head-quarters, where I applied with success, and returned with half a sovereign, to be charged in Old Carter's bill as twelve and sixpence.   But business is business.

I was never stinted; I had pretty well what I wanted, and more, perhaps, than any other boy at Old Carter's.   I was on an equality with them at school; but at home they most of them had brothers and sisters, and their mother was never out of *their* picture of home.   But for me, I had no companions of my own age, save the Clyms, my cousins, about whom I did not care, and no one to fill in anything like an adequate way the place to me of a mother.   What might have been done for me I have understood since, on learning that the Pritchard family, including Aunt Susan, had once offered to take me, but that this was resented, as an interference, by my father, who irritably observed, that, if *he* didn't know how to bring up his own child, no one else did.   It was a mistake on his part, and so they retired from the field: Grandmamma Pritchard limiting herself as heretofore to good advice and timely presents of tooth-powder, and a brush as before; and my Aunt to amusing me on my visits with illustrated books, and showing me what pretty pictures she herself could paint; while Uncle Herbert, lolling on the sofa, as usual, informed me where the best boots in London were to be obtained, and promised me that when I was old enough to appreciate a good fit, he would introduce me to his own tailor.

"Every gentleman," said Uncle Herbert, yawning, and then admiring his light-coloured trousers, tightly strapped down over his polished leather boots, "should be well dressed."

Uncle Herbert was the only one of the Pritchards who ever thoroughly got on with my father.   I fancy his view of clothes was one bond of union between them, and perhaps my father was really able to be of some little use to his brother-in law in the city.   But this opinion I formed later on, when I was, of course, far better able to judge of such matters—though I never understood, and never shall understand " business," on account of my having been so carefully trained to be nothing but an idle gentleman of fortune.

I used to hear enough of business though, on Sundays, during the holidays, when city friends were wont to call and talk over the affairs of the money market. Before I was fourteen, I had a parrot's knowledge of such phrases as " four to an eighth," " buying for account," and I was perfectly aware that " bulls " and " bears " on the Stock Exchange had no sort of connection with those which Nurse Davis had taken me to see in the Zoological Gardens.

None of the visitors at our house in town that I ever saw had any subject but one, and that was business. There were nervous men, who couldn't take Sunday as a day of rest, but were down on my father, to ask him what he thought Rothschild would do, and whether the Prime Minister had really sent such a message to the Turkish Government or not. There was a stout, bilious-looking German Baron, who became almost green under depression in the city, and took to his bed, I believe, in a panic. He always seemed to be considering what was his next move, on Sunday at least, aud perhaps on Monday he *did* move or changed his mind. My father looked over his accounts on Sunday morning, and spent the time, from breakfast to lunch, in his private room. I came to wonder why we at school should be taken to church when all the gentlemen I saw in the holidays, including my father, never went to church on Sunday morning, and as we invariably met them in the park on the afternoon of the same day, I concluded that they never affected a place of worship at all. It once occurred to me that, perhaps, they were taking their holidays too, like myself, and that when *their* work-time recommenced, they would perhaps have to go to church as regularly as Old Carter's boys.

When they were not speaking of city affairs, which was seldom, they had something to say about the singers at the opera, and the actors and actresses at the theatres. Uncle Herbert was strong in this line generally, and there was a jovial, pleasant, fat-faced young stockbroker, who used to give us (I was always of the party, receiving the visits with my father) choice anecdotes of the previous night, which at first astonished me. For though my father would ignore me on a visit to the counting-house, in strict keeping with his notion of my having nothing to do with his business, only with his pleasure, yet I was being educated to enjoy myself, and to do with others as I saw others doing. Thus, at an early age, in my father's drawing-room, and at his dinner-table, I was "one of themselves."

These were my models, for they were my father's chosen companions, and for this position I was being brought up. What was classical learning—what were Latin and Greek, and modern languages, by the side of such pleasures as I heard about from these gentlemen, who were all, it struck me, as happy as the day was long, always excepting the German Baron, who suffered in the chameleon-like manner I have before mentioned, and nervous Mr. Twiddingly, who never could get his money satisfactorily invested, and who was always buying when he ought to have been selling, selling when he ought to have been buying, and ruining himself, gradually, at the rate of a hundred a year, deducted in small losses.

I have since come to appreciate the nuisance I must have been to these *convives*. They were obliged to talk round me, so to speak, and my father often looked at me, covertly, to ascertain whether the conversation was intelligible to me. He was decidedly pleased to find, on occasions, that it was. This showed the kind of sharpness which gratified him, and proved that it would not be long before my intellect, if not my age or growth, would make me a fitting companion for himself. I leave my readers to pass judgment on this mental measurement and this paternal system. I say nothing here.

"Ha, vell! so!" said the German Baron, pinching my cheek; "I tell you vat it is, dey starve you at school, do they? So? no?" And then turning to my father, he'd go on, "He look ver vell—ver, such a col-lor. But "—here his voice sank to a whisper, and his whole manner

evinced deep earnestness of purpose—" tell me, my dear
Sir John, vas dere anoder rise in de Bonozares, eh ?" and
forthwith they would slip into business.

One thing had much struck me at school. The boys'
parents often came to see them, or sent for them into the
town where they were putting up for a day or two, to
spend a Wednesday half-holiday. Old Bifford—about
whom, in consequence of his wearing a huge muffler, and
taking prodigious quantities of snuff, there were various
mysterious reports as to his daily avocations—used often
to run down (which is a figure of speech, as old Bifford
couldn't have run had even an Andalusian bull been
behind him), and walk about with his boys one on each
side of him. Thus placed, fighting was impossible; and
as old Bifford didn't care about talking, and each was
afraid of uttering a word in his presence, lest it should be
contradicted by the other, and so lead to what the Ameri-
cans call a "difficulty," their enjoyment of the afternoon
must have been of a peculiarly placid character. Indeed,
so remarkably gloomy did the trio appear, that Mr.
Bifford had more the air of the wicked uncle, taking two
overgrown Babes in the Wood out to be killed, than of
an affectionate father devoting himself to the amusement
of his two children. They afterwards made up for the
temporary truce, by having a regular set-to for the possession of five shillings, of which sum each had been the
recipient of half-a-crown.

Harker's papa and mamma, from Manchester, came
once a half to see how he was getting on, and left an
"h" or two in Dr. Carter's drawing-room, to be picked
up by the servant, or by anyone in want of an aspirate.

Comberwood, my companion and evening reciter of
Scott's novels, used to depend upon a visit from either
his papa or mamma, accompanied by his married sister,
as a certainty, about the middle of the half. I should
have often liked to have exhibited my father to the boys,
walking with his hand on my shoulder, and enjoying the
sports going on in the playground. But I never saw any
of my relations during school-time, except once Grandmamma Pritchard, and once Uncle Van. Uncle Van

didn't call; I met him quite by accident, as we were out for a walk, and I was allowed to fall out of the rank and talk to him. He was startled at seeing me, and after exclaiming "Hullo!" he laughed and chuckled in so high a key, and with such a nervous manner, that Mr. Venn and several of the boys turned back to look. He recovered himself, however, and invited me into a confectioner's.

"Will you 'ave zum zoop or zum buns? he-he-he!" he asked, laughing. "Take what you like. It is all goot for boys, eh, ma'am?"

This question he addressed to the elderly female at the counter, who replied that her pastry was made with more than maternal care for the welfare of her youngest patrons. I remember selecting two Bath buns, half-a-dozen ginger cakes, for which this shop was celebrated, and a tin of acidulated drops, wrapped in red paper. This choice seemed to delight Uncle Van, whose chuckles and laughs were so catching, that the elderly person couldn't refrain from smiling and nodding at me, by way of congratulating me, personally, on the possession of so kind and good-tempered a relative.

"Will you write 'ome, an' zay you've zeen me, hey?" he asked with a laugh, expressive somehow of considerable anxiety. I know that it struck me at the time that something was wrong somewhere. It turned out afterwards that he had been enjoying a little holiday, without Aunt Clym, and he was afraid lest I should be writing home to my father an account of our meeting, and so let the cat out of the bag. I answered that I was not going to write, but I would do so if he wished, when he brightened up, and told me that I needn't do anything of the sort, as he would himself see my father, and bear to him any message I might want to send.

"I have none, thank you, Uncle Van," I replied after some consideration.

"Your love, hey? he-he-he! and 'ope he's sholly," Uncle Van suggested, by way of a dutiful formula, in the absence of anything better.

I said, "Yes, that would do," and thanked him for his

kindness; but I really had nothing to say to my father —nothing that at least would, as I knew from experience, interest him.

Uncle Van insisted upon seeing me safely restored to Mr. Venn's usherly care, being perhaps fearful of my affection for him overcoming my discretion.

"Mr. Venn, this is my Uncle Van," I said.

"Mr. Van Clym," returned Mr. Venn bowing.

"Yes," chuckled Uncle Van, "he-he; I 'ave come tese way to tese part of Kent, as I make a 'oliday wit my business."

"Shipping, I believe, Mr. Van Clym," said Mr. Venn, politely. I had never seen him so affable.

"Oh! he-he—yes! ships and shippin'. I like to zee for myzelf some time. It is zad tese large wrecks. Dese gales and tese losses—he-he! Well, we must have losses —eh—he-he?"

"I am afraid so. There have been several sad mishaps at sea lately."

Uncle Van adjusted his spectacles and chuckled. Whether it appeared to him, so generally ready to chatter with anyone, a waste of time to talk to an usher on shipping insurance, it is impossible to do more than conjecture. He only answered "Yes," and chuckled again, but this time more dolefully. I fancy he had overstayed his leave granted from home by my aunt.

The boys had passed in, and we then were standing at the back door of the school-yard, which opened on to a dull and dreary road, where an occasional tramp or beggar might be seen, but unless he had some eatables for sale he could expect nothing from the pupils at Old Carter's.

Where the wall of our school-yard ended, another had been begun by some enterprising builder, who, becoming depressed, had given it up, and left it to tumble down as soon as it liked. It had commenced tumbling, and our boys had assisted in making a breach, where we occasionally divided ourselves into military parties, and stormed and defended in turn.

While we were conversing, my attention was attracted to a woman apparently hiding behind this fragment.

Once she looked out, but on seeing that I was watching her, she quickly withdrew.

I only wondered whether she might not be the old woman who dealt in unwholesome sweets, boot-laces, hand-glasses, stationery, and pocket-knives, and who had been forbidden to come within bounds. If so, I could not mention the fact to Mr. Venn.

If not, it was of no importance to me, or to anybody. In the meantime, Uncle Van Clym, who had allowed the cork of his unnatural reticence to be drawn by our usher's skilfully applied screw of inquiry, was now bubbling over with details about losses in general, and the loss, mentioned by Mr. Venn, of the *Prairie Bird* in particular. He had by this time heard from him the full corroboration of the account which he said he had recently read in the papers.

So, I thought, he doubted me, and got the newspaper himself.

Uncle Van had himself seen, he said, and talked with the chief officer, and relief had been afforded to all the sufferers, with the exception of one person, a woman of notoriously bad character, who had left the Refuge where she had been hospitably lodged, and had not been seen since. As for the cargo, nothing had been recovered, nor was it likely now that they would hear any more of it.

Mr. Venn, looking at his watch, said he must be going in to lessons, but gave me permission to accompany my uncle to the end of the road, where I could point out to him the shortest way to the town.

After parting from Uncle Van, I turned back leisurely, and seeing that I could not be observed from the school windows, I ventured to stop and look about for the person whom I had supposed to be the old woman with her forbidden tray.

As I approached the breach in the wall, she stepped out. It was not the one I had expected, and I was rather startled by her strange excited manner,—a middle-aged woman, of slatternly appearance, a face that had been handsome, and eyes that were still fine, though wild and roving.

"Come here," she said, addressing me harshly.

I stopped where I was, fearful of advancing towards her.

"I shan't hurt you," she said, with a half-drunken laugh.

I did not feel at all sure on this point, and was ready to take to my heels. I was not the Napoleon's Old Guard. I would not yield, but I would run.

Seeing me undecided, she came close up to me.

"Who was that man you were talking to?"

"Which?" I asked, summoning all my courage.

"The one who went in at that door," she replied, indicating the spot with a hand that I could see was well shaped, even in the ill-fitting black glove.

"That,," I said, "was our usher, Mr. Venn."

"No," she answered, rudely, "that won't do."

"That is his name."

Before I could utter another word, she had pounced upon my wrist, and was pulling me towards the door.

"In there I mean," she said, stopping exactly opposite.

At this moment the door opened, and Venn himself appeared.

Seeing us, he recoiled one step.

The woman released me.

"Mr. Venn?" she inquired, in a tone of mock politeness.

He recovered himself quickly.

"Yes. Go in," he said, turning to me; "I was coming in search of you. Go in, and wait for me in the school-yard."

Then the door was closed behind me, and locked on the outside.

I listened, and heard their footsteps as they walked slowly away, along the road, in the direction of the town, together.

CHAPTER IX.

I RECEIVE AN INVITATION.

PRESENTLY the key turned in the lock, and Mr. Venn entered. Quite blithely for *him*. " A poor mad woman," he explained cautiously; take no notice of her if you ever see her again. You'd better not say anything about her to the boys, or the small ones might be frightened. Besides Dr. Carter would punish you for speaking to her. However, I shall not mention it to him.

So we went into work. He was rather cheerful that afternoon, I remember.

At bedtime I told Austin Comberwood all about it, and he asked me if she was anything like Meg Merrilies in " Guy Mannering."

This started our usual evening's entertainment, and I was soon deeply interested in Walter Scott.

We looked out for the mad woman next day, but saw nothing of her.

Austin Comberwood used to tell me how he spent his holidays, and it was quite a treat to hear him talk of his sister Alice, his brother Dick, and his mother. I told him that I had no mother, which seemed so odd to him, that he was silent for some time, and then he questioned me about *my* holidays, and I was able to tell him about the theatres and the London amusements that I had been to, that was all. But he, too, knew of these, so that his enjoyment of the country far outbalanced anything within my experience.

Thus it chanced that I was lonely in the holidays, when I had only servants for associates; but happy at school, for I got on well with the boys, and Austin Comberwood was my very dear friend; but I really could have saved up my pocket-money with pleasure, and paid an uncle to visit me regularly, just to show my companions that I had some friends in the world worth knowing.

There was one excellent creature who never forgot me, and that was Nurse Davis. She called at Old Carter's, but the grandeur of the house, the corpulency of the butler, the haughty condescension of Dr. Carter, and the snappishness of his wife frightened her off the premises. She did not come a second time. I was not sorry for this result. I confess it as against myself, and a fault of the snobbishness of boyhood, that I had grown out of Nurse Davis, as I had out of pinafores.

When I returned to the schoolroom, and was asked who had been to see me, I coloured, and refused to answer. Then, somehow, it got about, through the boy who cleaned the boots, who had heard it from the butler, I think, that it was my nurse, and I was so teased and bullied on the subject, that nothing short of a fight with the two Biffords both at once, which ended in their pitching into one another, and a declaration of active war against the whole school, could settle the question. When they found she had brought me a hamper, and that there were cake and wine and apples inside, sentiments of the utmost friendship towards me were expressed by every boy in the school.

When Nurse called I was very shy, and found some difficulty in asking after the health of the Verneys, politely singling out Julie for special mention.

"Good-bye, dear, and God bless you," said Nurse Davis at parting; "if you're not too proud to see me when you come home for the holidays——"

I protested against her thinking that I should be proud. But somehow I felt that there was truth in it.

"——And," she continued, "if you ain't yet ashamed of seeing your old Nurse——"

Again I protested, and again I felt that she was right.

"Well, dear, I hope you never will be either too proud or ashamed to speak to those as loves you, and as has brought you up and known you from a child; and if your Aunt Clym only takes as much care of you as I've done, and as I'd ha' done still, if I'd been let alone, I shall be glad to hear of it."

She always disliked Mrs. Van Clym, and so, I said, did I, and positively scorned the idea of their being any comparison between her and my nurse. For this I was rewarded with an embrace, after which the hamper was shown to me in the hall; then repeating her blessing, and with tears in her eyes, she gave me a last kiss, and, without disturbing His Corpulency, The Butler, I let her out of Old Carter's front door.

I sat down in the hall and cried when she had gone. At night too I awoke suddenly, and thought of her; and as it crossed my mind that I had been hard and unkind in my reception of her that day, I burst out crying again, silently, though, on account of my companion, and dropped so many heavy tears on one side of my pillow, that I was obliged to try the other, as dry, cool, and refreshing, and finally, as a stroke of genius, to turn it altogether, and begin my slumbers afresh.

One night, just before Austin Comberwood, who was really quite a Scheherazade in his story-telling, had commenced the recital of "Guy Mannering," which had reached its third night's entertainment, he said, from under his coverlet,—

"Cecil."

"Well, Austin."

"Would you like to come home with me next holidays?"

"Very much." My first invitation.

"Mamma wrote to tell me to ask you if your papa would let you."

"Oh, of course he will," I replied warmly

"And you're to stay a long time."

"What fun!"

"Dick will be there, and Alice. You'll like my sister Alice so much."

I was sure I should. I should like everybody and everything down at—what was the name of the place where he lived ?

"Ringhurst Whiteboys."

Whiteboys! how we laughed at the name. In itself it was full of promise of amusement. Who were the Whiteboys ? Were they ghosts ? This was a dangerous subject in the dark, and Austin set me right at once.

"No," he told me, "they were monks who had lived there a long time ago (I will tell you next Scott's 'Monastery' and 'The Abbot'), and who used to dress in white. They were called the White Friars, and Friars in French meant brothers, and so the people came to call them the Whiteboys."

Austin Comberwood, who was better informed than any boy of his own age whom I have ever met before or since, had answered my question with the gravity befitting the subject. He was older, too, than most boys in his ways, and was looked upon by most of us as a bookworm. His memory was excellent, as I have shown; and not being so robust as his companions, he was allowed to bring one of his favourite books out of doors to read, while others played. There was something so gentle, so feminine about him, that I entertained, it seemed to me, towards him much the same kind of affection as I should have had for a sister. I felt, too, when he mentioned his sister, that I was prepared to love her deeply and at once. I say "at once," as the Colvin failing is impulsiveness. It may be directed for good or for evil, and so be a blessing or a curse; a strong point in a character, or its weakest. I remember, as well as I remember anything, our conversation on this night, and my great desire to see Alice Comberwood.

"We're going to have some theatricals," said Austin.

"What, with a stage and lights, and dressed up as characters ? " I inquired, thinking of my early successes with Der Freischutz and Co.

"We dress up," he answered; "and Dick, who can carpenter and paint, he makes a scene. We often act—

Alice and I and Dick, and sometimes our cousins. Nelly plays the piano for us."

"Who's Nelly?"

"My eldest sister. She's married now, and her husband's a clergyman."

"I may act, mayn't I?" I asked, with some diffidence.

"Oh yes. Alice says in her letter that if you come you shall be Blue Beard."

I was delighted! "And who was to be Fatima?"

"Oh, Alice, of course."

Alice Comberwood Blue Beard's wife—mine in fact! In imagination—I was then thirteen—I had already, as Blue Beard, allied myself to the Comberwood family.

So we fell to talking over our dresses and our scenes, and I ventured to confide to him such theatrical knowledge as I possessed, and said how I could depend upon Nurse Davis and Mr. Verney to help me with a dress; and then I told him as much about them as I could, consistently with my own dignity and importance as the future Blue Beard, possessor of his sister Alice; but I kept silence as to the details of Frampton's Court, and the Verney's mode of life, and absolutely did not once mention little Julie.

Then we dropped off to sleep, without "Guy Mannering," and only thought of the play-acting, which no doubt entered largely into our dreams that night.

CHAPTER X.

CHRISTMAS INVITATION—ACCEPTED—HIDE AND SEEK—A
MYSTERIOUS MEETING—SILENCE IS GOLDEN.

A MEMORABLE Christmas. Not the day itself, though
that was always a pleasant time for me. I rejoiced in
new shillings and sixpences fresh from the Mint, coined,
I supposed, purposely for Christmas presents. My father
seemed to be worried and annoyed about something, and
he and Mr. Cavander were now seldom apart.

Just before Christmas Day came a formal invitation
from Austin Comberwood addressed to me, to be referred
of course to my father. This proposal he bade me accept
at once. I was to leave on the Saturday; he had already
arranged to depart on some urgent business the day before. Had I not been thus comfortably disposed of, I
should have been sent to Aunt Clym's during my father's
absence, for he expected to be away a week or a fortnight.

At my father's request, Uncle Van no doubt would see
me into the train for Ringhurst. Uncle Herbert was
away.

Our house was not so far from Kensington Gardens but
that I could be trusted to roam about there alone, and
report myself safely to the housemaid and cook at dinner-
time. Kensington Gardens, therefore, had, during the
holidays, become my playground, and I was on intimate
terms with the park-keepers, the refreshment-stall people
and the waterfowl. When my Clym cousins came to
spend a day with me, I took them, by way of treat, to

my gardens, and introduced them to the acquaintances above mentioned.

Now it so chanced, that while my father was turning over in his mind in whose custody I should be sent to the railway station on Saturday, labelled for Ringhurst, Uncle Van appeared with two of my Clym cousins, whom he had brought to see me, and for whom their mamma was to call in the afternoon.

My father told Mr. Clym he was just the man he wanted to see, whereat Uncle Van adjusted his spectacles, stared, chuckled, and asked what was the matter. Whereupon my father, looking less anxious than I had seen him since my return, took him by the arm and walked him into his brougham, which was waiting to transport him to the city.

On their departure I proposed Kensington Gardens. Thither we went, adjured and admonished, but unaccompanied.

Robbers and brigands among the trees were our favourite games. There were no rules except those of a fair start to be given to whoever was to assume the lawless character, generally myself. These games were inspired by that love of frightening one another common to all children. To hide anywhere, even though it be in the same place day after day, and then to rush out suddenly, or even to be caught when the surrender itself would be of a startling nature, seem to be among the first notions of juvenile amusement.

Exulting in my superior knowledge of the domain which I had well-nigh come to look upon as my preserves, I was not only able to hide without much chance of detection, but could follow them, after they had passed my place of concealment, and harass them in the rear.

On this day I chose a large tree not far from the boundary railings, and well in view of one of the summer-houses in the walk beyond; that is, in Hyde Park.

I was deliberating whether I should occupy my time in purchasing refreshments at the gate, or should await my cousins' arrival, when a gentleman and lady walked within a few yards of me towards the entrance to the

Park. They were not following the beaten track, but crossing the grass. Neither figure was strange to me, except so far as it was strange to see either there. One I could not mistake, and when he turned round, as if looking out for some one to meet him, I said to myself distinctly, "Why, it's Venn!"

Mr. Venn decidedly. And with him I recognised the odd woman who had stopped me opposite our school-door.

He was too much associated with school for me to be inclined to welcome him in the holidays; and for his companion, once of *her* had been more than enough for me. So I held my tongue, remained in ambush, and waited for them to quit the Gardens, as they were evidently on the point of doing.

I watched them out by the gate. They had been conversing earnestly; now they stood still without saying a word, but each turning from the other to explore the distance.

Evidently whoever they had been expecting was disappointing them.

They walked towards the Park slowly.

A carriage pulled up at the rails, close by the bridge over the Serpentine.

The door opened and out stepped Mr. Cavander.

He met Mr. Venn and his companion; then with them he returned to the carriage, which the three entered, Mr. Venn and the woman first, Mr. Cavander delaying a second to give the coachman some directions.

These being ended, he too got in, closed the door himself, and in another minute or so the carriage was lost to my view.

This meeting seemed to me, then, to have something to do with me at school. Flogging perhaps. I did not know what to make of it. My cousins came up and caught me for the first time in their lives in my hiding-place.

They did not know anything about Mr. Venn or Mr. Cavander, and only cared for my playing with them. So at it we went again till dinner-time. In the evening I thought of mentioning it to my father, but he returned home with Mr. Cavander, who was dressed for dinner, and after making his toilette they left together.

I said good night to my father in the hall, and in answer to a request, whereunto I was prompted from the kitchen, he told me that if I liked to go to a theatre in company with one of the servants I could do so. " You will soon be able to go about with me," he added. But this was quite a formal phrase with him. Mr. Cavander was already in the carriage, and he did not hear the remark. I was glad of this, as, disliking him intensely, the prospect seemed to be a bad compliment to Mr. Cavander, and calculated to make him more my enemy than ever.

The theatre intervened, and I had enough to talk about to my father next morning, though he did not prove much of an audience, being apparently nervous and fidgety. His pormanteau was packed, and he was leaving.

He gave me five pounds, and hoped that that would be sufficient for me at Ringhurst. I stared, and, perversely enough, was not profuse in thanks. The amount had paralysed my gratitude. I did not understand then that I was about to represent him at Mr. Comberwood's, and the ambassador's uniform ought to be something more than ordinary. I had in view various investments for my five sovereigns, and a wish to show them to Austin Comberwood all at once. Also it seemed to me that I should appear before his sister Alice as a gentleman of more weight with my five pounds than with one."

" After next half-year," observed my father, "you will go to Holyshade, and then when you come back for the holidays you will be quite a man."

Always the same burden to his song. Then he said good-bye to me, observed that he should certainly ask Mr. Comberwood to dinner (as a reward, I suppose, for having invited me for a week) on his return to town, and so left me ; and all that for the time remained to me of my father, so to speak, were my five golden sovereigns jingling in my trouser pocket.

CHAPTER XI.

UNCLE VAN had looked in at the last moment to under-take the charge of me for Saturday, as proposed to him the previous day.

Uncle Van knew Mr. Comberwood as a solicitor often employed by certain shipping firms, and was pretty sure about his going down to Ringhurst every Saturday after-noon. To his care he promised to confide me. Indeed he had been, he said, commissioned by Mr. Comberwood to help him on this occasion in the theatricals.

" Are you going to act ?" asked my father.

" No, no ; he-he-he," answered Uncle Van, spanning his spectacles, and fitting them into his eyes with his finger and thumb. " No, I can not acts "—he sometimes varied his broken English with plural terminations—" and I am not as-ked. I should not go—he-he-he—if I was as-ked —he-he-he,"—here he chuckled and spluttered—" because Eliza toes tink all wrong such tings, and she woult not 'ave accept te invitation."

" She never goes to any public amusement, does she ?" asked my father.

" No. Ven I goes I goes alone," said Uncle Van, making a noise in his throat resembling a weak watch-spring gone suddenly wrong. This sound was expressive of his intense delight.

" I think the Comberwoods know Herbert," observed my father, meaning Herbert Pritchard.

" I tink zo. P'raps he goes town tese time, but I ton't know. I vill ask Combervoots; I shall zee 'im tomorrow. Cecil, you comes to me on Saturtay morning, and we go to te zity togeters—kee-kee-kee."

Kee-kee-kee is the only way I can invent to represent the peculiar watch-spring chuckle in Uncle Van's throat.

If he could have made my father's trust an excuse for staying away from home all Saturday, I know he would gladly have availed himself of the opportunity.

Saturday was to Uncle Van worse than Sunday. Sunday was a decided day. It was one thing: and Monday and all the other days up to Saturday were another. But Saturday was neither one nor the other, with the disadvantages of both.

It had not always been so. He had not been brought up to it: on the contrary, he had been gradually brought down to it by the power in his house, against which revolt was impossible, because so evidently impolitic. As a boy—that is, as a Dutch boy—he had been accustomed to take religious duties in as easy a way as his father, with his long, big-bowled pipe, had done before him. They worshipped with their hats on, in a frigid manner, and sat in a plain, undecorated building, fitted up apparently with loose boxes, or, more devoutly speaking, sheep-pens for the fold. In Dutch devotion there was no outward show, and not much inward fervour. When he had married Miss Colvin she had been moderately Evangelical to begin with, and ultra-Evangelical to go on with. She considered, that, however clear-headed her husband might be on business, "out of it he has," she said, "no more mind than a jelly-fish." Now a jelly-fish is not remarkable for intellect. She constituted herself his director, but not his confessor. There is a marked distinction between the two. A director may advise and shape a course: but a confessor must have a penitent, or his office is a sinecure.

Uncle Van was willing to abide by her directions as long as he was allowed to remain in peace and quietness, which meant as long as he had a good dinner at a reasonable hour, and was not interrupted in his doze, and his pipe, after it. Mrs. Clym had long ago conceded the pipe. After all, it was not a point of doctrine but of practice, and might perhaps be gradually given up. It led to no excesses, as Van, though of a generally fishy nature, was not troubled with thirst. So he was permitted to smoke-dry himself like one of his own country's herrings, and he was happy.

But Mrs Clym was a reformer, and she was bent upon reforming her household's Saturday. She determined to commence Sunday on Saturday, as the Jews begin their Sabbath on Friday at sunset.

"But te Jews," said Uncle Van, " leave off teir Sabbat on Saturtay, and at zunzet—he-he-he! and she *ton't.* Bezite, vat 'ave her relishion to toes viz my tinner?"

He complained to his friends, not to her.

Aunt Van had commenced her reforms. She had abolished Saturday dining—or rather, dining *late* on Saturdays.

There was, to her mind, something more devotional in tea than in dinner. There was an unction of solace to the spiritually-minded in buttered toast; and an incentive to heroic virtue in hot tea. Late dinner was of the world, worldly. Tea was, somehow, more congenial to piety. It never occurred to her that the only thing celestial about tea was the heathen empire whence it came. Mrs. Clym never admitted into her presence anything in the shape of a joke. Uncle Clym kept such as he knew to himself. He pronounced jokes " jox," with a short vowel.

Before dinner he would say, " I vill tell you some goot jox when my vife's gone to te drawn-room."

When he did tell them, they were very mild : always such funny harmless things as one oyster might tell another, and slobber over afterwards. But on Saturday nights there would be, henceforth, no more guests, and no chance for his " jox."

"I cannot come 'ome to colt meats ant tea," exclaimed poor Uncle Van, in my father's presence.

Sir John wouldn't interfere between man and wife.

At the first of these reform dinners Mr. Clym very

nearly burst into tears. He meditated a peaceful solution, with his pipe in his mouth. He slept on the subject, but could make nothing of it. The servants, he was told, found it so convenient, the children liked it; his wife, of course, did. He represented the government in a minority. He appealed to the country; the country couldn't help him. There was only one thing to be done : *not* to take the goods the gods had provided. He would stay away on Saturdays, and dine elsewhere. But then, how to explain this absence from home ? Would Madame believe that he merely stayed away to dine ?

Suppose he obtained permission first ? An honest idea, and worthy of a well-regulated husband. But how ?

To get round Mrs. Clym was a hazardous proceeding. She was so angular, and perpendicular, and she offered so small a chance of a footing, that the first pointed prejudice, sticking out abruptly, would knock you back into the water.

I do not believe in Hannibal's receipt for getting through an obstacle. Sweet oil sounds more like the thing than vinegar. .

Clym thought of emollients. With other wives diamonds are the best diplomatists. Mrs. Clym was not to be bought : that is, at *that* price.

Uncle Van would have, hopelessly and helplessly, gradually settled down to like it, as untravelled Englishmen, abroad for the first time, pretend a pleasure in becoming accustomed to the greasiest foreign cookery, had it not been for a friend, who showed him that to succumb was to eat the lotos and be lost.

This friend's name was Pipkison. I cannot pass him over with bare mention of his name. Pipkison was one of the most popular men in London.

He was a Worshipful Brother, with a company of letters after his surname in single file ; he was a Fellow with nine letters of the alphabet, every one of them pregnant with meaning. He was a Merry Shepherd, an Ancient Druid, a Redoubtable Buffalo, a Knight of something or other, a Mystic of the Rosicrucian Order, and a number of numerous other social, fraternal, and professedly levelling-up societies, whose bond of union is common subscription for a dinner, whose acolytes are publicans, and whose stoutest supporters are husbands, ready to welcome a solemn excuse for dining out periodically. Their charity begins in conviviality, and is co-extensive with it.   Their hymn is "And so say all of us."   Their aim, dignified by high-sounding titles, and disguised under cloaks of moralities and mysteries, is to establish jolly-good-fellowship, among Brothers of the Bottle, all the world over.

But apart from being all these worthies rolled into one, Pipkison was the kindest-hearted and most good-natured bachelor to be found in or out of a Government office, where he laboured from ten to four, and spoke on deep subjects with high officials face to face, and with clerks and underlings through speaking-pipes, which instruments he performed on with much ease and elegance, and great conciseness of diction, arrived at by long official practice.

Pipkison went everywhere worth going to, and knew everybody worth knowing.   He also knew anybody, and was to be met, like a geranium on a bleak cliff, when least expected.   He was of no particular age : and as far as conviviality went, he was for all and any time.   He was never too buoyant ; he was never over-fatigued.   He fitted into all sorts of society, like a master-key into every kind of lock.   He knew everything, and did a little of it well and unobtrusively.   He never got himself, or anyone else, into trouble.   He received as many communications as a letter-box, and kept them till called for legitimately.   All his acquaintances were equally dear to him.   He had one friend : just one—an invalid, bedridden in the prime of life, by whose bedside he would sit and chat regularly every Sunday.   He never allowed any engagement (save absence from London, which was rare, and then he wrote his friend a cheery letter, full of gossip) to interfere with this duty.   This poor fellow's name was Yennick.

Did Pip, in passing through Covent Garden on his morning's walk to his office (under Government), see flowers fresh and · beautiful, and fruit in its season, it straightway occurred to him that poor Yennick couldn't get at those luxuries for himself. In another hour fruit and flowers were at Yennick's door, with Mr Pipkison's compliments. The kindest-hearted creature, Pipkison, and no scandal-monger, which is a marvellous thing when said of a man, the life of whose conversation was small talk, and who was perpetually being questioned by every-one as to how everyone else was getting on.

Half the world doesn't know how the other half lives. Best not, if one half is to be called, French fashion, the *demi-monde.* Pipkison lived between the two halves, and knew all about both, without really concerning himself about either. Pipkison was this Pip when I was a boy. He is this Pip now, unchanged.

Being such an one as I have shown him, it was only in the natural course of things that he should know Uncle Van, as he knew everybody. Stopping my uncle in the Exchange, as he was moodily walking, frowning at the pavement, jingling his keys in one pocket, and balancing them, as it were, with their value in halfpence in the other, Mr. Pipkison called out—

"Hullo, Van! Woa, Van!" which was Pipkison's waggery.

"He-he-he!" laughed Uncle Van, with his usual jelly-fish way. "Always your jox—eh? He-he-he!" and he laughed again, taking one hand out of his trouser pocket to fix his spectacles on, so as to have a better look at Pipkison. Then he said—

"Vell?"

Pipkison answered him—

"Where shall we dine to-day? I'm not speaking like an advertisement, but I mean it."

"He-he-he! I vas tinking tat moment. You zee my wife—he-he-he!—she's a deucet goot voman, but I tink only tea at six o'clock on Saturtay von't do. Il faut dîner."

"Of course," replied Pipkison; then with a wink, and indicating Uncle Van's ribs with his forefinger, "How about the Burlington Baa-lambs?"

" Hey ?—He-he-he ! Vat ?" asked Uncle Clym. He laughed because he thought Pipkison had made one of his "jox," which he had missed.

"Burlington Baa-lambs, Van! You must be a Baa-lamb!"

"He-he-he!" snorted Mr. Clym; "te Baa-lamb—vat is he?"

"The Baa-lamb," replied Mr. Pip, "is a gregarious creature who dines on Saturday at two o'clock, in company with others of the Burlington flock, which, meeting in a pleasant pasturage in the neighbourhood of the Burlington Arcade (whence this name), make a circuit of other grass lands, returning on the last Saturday of the year to their ancient inclosure as aforesaid. That is the poetical account. That is what the gods call us. Mortals would denominate our society a social club, dining out every Saturday early, and not going home till evening."

"I coult get home by seven, eh?" asked Uncle Van, much interested,

"By six if necessary."

Uncle Van thought he could manage this. He would dine with the Baa-lambs and return home to tea. He would run with the hare, and hunt with the baa-lambs.

"Are there many?"

"Baa-lambs?" asked Pipkison: then answered, seeing that Mr. Clym had intended this; "yes, there are Barristers qualified as members of the Baa—you observe. Bar—Baa——"

"He-he-he! I zee. Yes. Bar," said Uncle Van, nodding like a loose-headed toy figure on a Christmas bon-bon box.

"Then there are literary men, Baa-lambs of the Pen."

Mr. Clym thought over this. "Pen, eh?" He didn't see it.

"You begin well as a Baa-lamb," said Mr. Pip, "as I see you are a ruminating animal."

"He-he-he!" Uncle Van in fits. This joke had really tickled him. Recovering his seriousness and his spectacles, which were slipping off his nose, he announced his determination thus—

" I say—he-he-he!—I'll be a Baa-lamb."

Mr. Pip solemnly grasped his hand, and appeared to invoke a blessing on the neophyte. Then he, in a deeply tragic manner, addressed Uncle Clym.

"Meet me here at two precisely. At half-past we must to the meadow. Come dine with me and be my love. By the way, Comberwood told me about wanting some professional person to drill them in their theatricals. I've got the very man. He's an eminent Baa-lamb, and you'll meet him at dinner this afternoon. Good-bye." And off he went.

"Funny fel-low—he-he-he!" said Uncle Van to himself; "vat tit he mean by 'pen,' and 'ruminate?'" He considered a bit, then shrugged his shoulders. "Vun of his 'jox.'"

He saw at once that for this Saturday, at all events, he had obtained a fair excuse. He had "to see a professional person on behalf of Mr. Comberwood, solicitor," and this, without further explanation, would be quite sufficient for Mrs. Clym when he returned home in the evening. Besides, he needn't be late. He could dispose of me by a mid-day train, dine with the Lambs, and be back for seven o'clock tea at home.

This being settled, we proceeded to Mr. Comberwood's office in Gray's Inn.

His clerk informed us that Mr. Comberwood had intended going by the two o'clock train to Ringhurst, but had changed his mind. However, if I were to travel by that train, I should find the carriage waiting to meet me. This was enough for Uncle Van, who forthwith took me to the station, and having, by giving me in charge to the guard, labelled me, as it were, for my destination, he hurried off to keep, as I learnt afterwards, his appointment with Pipkison—whereof we shall meet an important result later on.

I did not like to move about much, or take my eyes off the guard, who seemed to have plenty to do without troubling himself any further about me.

While I was wondering whether I should ever get to Ringhurst, a slouching young man, in an oily green velveteen costume, touched his hat to me in a bashful sort of way, and hoped Master Colvin was quite well.

"Why, it's Charles Edmund!" said I, recognizing little Julie's brother.

He had grown enormously, and spread out into hands and feet. I felt that I ought to shake hands with him (three of my hands would have slipped into one of his easily), and that if I didn't, he'd think I was proud. So I held out mine to him, and rather hoped that nobody saw us.

"Thank ye, Master Colvin," he said; "I'm quite well, an' I'm getting on. I ain't a greaser now."

"No, indeed!" I returned, being vaguely glad to hear this on account of my own position in society.

"No," he continued, "I'm porter now. I'm workin' into it, and I'll be a guard in time. Inspector p'raps."

"I hope so, I'm sure. How's your father?" I was becoming atrociously patronising. He was ever so much taller and bigger than I was, being, indeed, by my side quite an ogre.

"Gettin' on capital lately, Master Colvin," he replied. He evidently liked calling me Master Colvin, and was rather pleased and amused by my patronage. "Little Julie's out of an engagement now; she was in the panto-mime at the Lane last year. Sally—Beatrice Sarah, you know—she's coming out in the Op'ra, I b'lieve, at Paris; but we ain't seen her for a long time. Lottie's still helping Madame Glissande. Father would ha' gone with Julie to Portsmouth for a week to see Aunt Jane——"

"Nurse Davis?"

"Yes, Master Colvin, she's very well, thank you; I'm sure she'd be glad to hear as I've seen you. I'll tell her; she's a comin' up soon."

"Is she? I should like to see her." I said this partly out of politeness, and party because I really meant it. Children can be as snobbish as their elders. Master Cecil Colvin, standing on the platform talking to Charles Edmund, was unconsciously developing snobbery. It was new to him, and he was hot and uncomfortable in the performance.

"Yes, mother—she's very well, Master Colvin, thank you"—for I had not asked after her—"said as it would do father good to go for a little fresh air, and take a holiday while he was doing nothing; and so he'd ha' gone, but just then a friend told him as there was something for him to do as 'ud give him the fresh air and put money in his pocket, along with some ammytoors in the country, so as he's to meet the——"

Here he was suddenly called off by my guard—under whose eye I did not feel justified in shaking hands with him again. However, after he had finished his job he returned to me, looked carefully after my luggage, put me in the right carriage, and finally reappeared just as the train was starting with a bottle of lemonade opened, two oranges, and two sponge-cakes in a bag.

This was so kind of him, and I was so much affected by it, that I had scarcely time either to thank him or to ask him to take some refreshment himself, when the engine, snorting, puffing as hard as if it were quite out of condition for a long run, pulled us away from the platform, like an impatient companion insisting upon lugging you off in a hurry, and Charles Edmund disappeared.

"I wish Julie had been with him," I said to myself. We were on our way to Ringhurst.

CHAPTER XII.

THE COMBERWOOD FAMILY—ALICE—FIRST IMPRESSIONS—A
WORD ON HANDS—NEW WORLD—THE ARRIVAL OF AN IM-
PORTANT PERSON—DESCRIPTION DEFERRED.

A VISIT to Ringhurst was a great change to a town boy
like myself, whose only acquaintance with country-houses
was what I had made with such exteriors as I had seen
during our walks on half-holidays.

Between twelve and thirteen I was man enough to
travel alone, with my five pounds reduced to four pounds
ten shillings, and to like my independence. With delight
I hailed Austin and his younger brother, Dick, who
wasn't at our school, as they in turn waved their hats to
me from the platform. There was a beautiful carriage to
meet us, with which I mentally compared my father's
brougham, wherein I very rarely had the pleasure of
riding. We drove—it was a crisp winter—between small
plantations of young firs, which looked like Christmas-
trees met together for a party, only without the gifts
hanging from their frosted branches.

Through a lodge gate, and up a wide road, in view of
more plantations and far older trees of various sorts, until
at the doorway of a gabled house the carriage stopped.
Then such a bell sounded, the like of which I had never
before heard out of church, and men-servants came to see
to my luggage. My luggage was only a small portmanteau, and the man easily slung it off the foot-board of
the driving-box, where it had been hidden by four stal-

wart calves. That was all. And the stately vehicle disappeared, and might have turned into a bumpkin without
astonishing me very much; everything around was so
new, and yet, oddly enough, so familiar.

We stood in a grand old hall. Old pictures, fitting into
old panels; a huge fire-place, with fantastic carvings on
and about it, and fantastic logs ablaze, as they lay across
ancient dogs, between which were feathery ashes, that
looked as if grey parrots had been plucked there. Foxes'
brushes, trophies of arms and armour on the walls, doors
in four recesses in the four corners, looking just the very
places whence persons of a mischievous turn might rush
out suddenly and say " bo " to the goose they wished to
frighten.

" We're at home now," said Austin, helping me to take
off my coat and wraps. The remark was unnecessary;
but it sounded so kindly in my ears, that I thanked him,
and then replied, that " I was so glad."

" They're all in here," cried Dick, touching the handle
of the door farthest from me on our left.

" Come in and see my mother," said Austin. " She's
here with Alice."

I entered the drawing-room. I felt, and I believe the
Colvins experience generally the same feeling—that I
was, there and then, in love with Alice Comberwood. No
matter what her age, no matter what her looks, I was,
without setting eyes on her, devoted to her as soon as
Austin had mentioned her to me.

I had not been long in the world, and had shown
myself very tender-hearted wherever the sex had been
concerned. So had my father and my grandfather before
me. Of this I was not then aware. I note the fact now,
and beg that it may be remembered. I had not forgotten
my nurse, my first school-mistress, my Aunt Susan; nor
Beatrice Sarah, Carlotta Lucille, nor Julie, of Frampton's
Court. My heart was large enough to hold them all, it is
true, but it resembled a child's play-drawer, where the
old dolls and tops are stowed away, when the new one
makes its appearance.

Mrs. Comberwood, a handsome lady in the sleekest

black velvet, resembling one of the portraits in the hall, welcomed me in a motherly manner.

"I am glad to see you, Master Colvin; I have often heard of you from Austin."

Here we shook hands. I could not say that I had often heard of *her* from Austin, and so all I could do was to look at Alice sheepishly. It must have been sheepishly, for she, standing with one foot, of which I could only see the shoe's point, resting on the steel bar in front of the ancient fireplace, turned towards me and smiled a welcome.

I advanced towards her.

"This is my sister Alice," said Austin, by way of introduction.

I *had* heard of her several times before he had mentioned her name just now. Cecil Colvin, my friends, was deeply impressionable at this time of his life, and, as on soft wax, the image of Alice was forthwith stamped on my heart. Images and superscriptions in soft wax are very soon effaced. Heat the wax once more, bring a different die, and the former image will, at a touch, have disappeared utterly, and for ever. But Alice had, in consequence of Austin's night recitals of Scott, got mixed up in my mind with Sir Walter's heroines, and then I had understood from her brother that we were down there to act something which she had composed for us. I valued authorship, and Austin had read something of his own to me privately, and as a great favour, which struck me as very clever, because it reminded me so strongly of "Ivanhoe" and "Guy Mannering."

Let me recall this first meeting with Alice Comberwood.

Alice Comberwood, seventeen, the real ruler in her father's house, regarded by all with that imperfect love wherein there is an admixture of fear. Yes, Alice Comberwood, I will set you before me once again, after these many years, as with your mother's admiring gaze fixed on you, you stood smiling upon the gawky, awkward boy, whose silent tongue and speaking eyes told you of the admiration with which you had inspired him. You took it, as a queen, as your right; you took it from me as you would have taken it from anyone, but you secretly prized the homage of a simple, straightforward boy, as the real metal of truth, free from the alloy of flattery.

She had been standing in a meditative attitude before the fire, her fingers interlaced. Now she unclasped her hands, and stretched forth one to me.

I have ever been inclined to judge of female character by the hand. Not as the fortune-teller, who, from the lines engraved on the open palm, predicts a destiny; but, by the whole hand, and the hand's movements, I will warrant myself, if going by first instincts only, to be right in my appreciation of individual character. As to prediction of results, to that I do not pretend. To predicate of a firm character, that in certain circumstances it will act firmly, is to ignore inconsistency. Allowing much for accident, you must allow more for inconsistency. So, on thinking over this matter of hands, I conclude that I have an inclination towards hands, and when called upon to pronounce judgment at all, would rather form my opinion of a woman by her hand than by her face. I do not say this of men. I do not care for men's hands. There probably is great character in them, but they have never interested me, and never will. Alice Comberwood's hand looked best against a clear, sharply-defined white cuff, turned back over a tight sleeve. I will tell you what it was not. It was not a ghostly, transparent hand, that would have appeared in a Vandyke portrait, with long, tapering, pointed finger-tips, which seem as though they were only formed for bird-like staccato passages on the pianoforte.

Nothing unreal about Alice Comberwood's hand, as there was nothing unreal about Alice Comberwood. It was a firm, solid, fleshy hand, of even temper, soft in its mesmeric caress, truthful in its decided grasp.

Her gloved hand piqued curiosity like a veiled Venus. It was a positive pleasure to see the glove withdrawn, and then you wondered how you could have ever admired the glove which lay lifeless (and what so helpless and lifeless as a crumpled glove?) on the table beside her, suddenly dead and dull as the skin shed by the water-snake on the bank.

Most women appear to advantage in a riding-habit, Alice to more advantage than most. Logically you can infer how a habit became her.

Something more on this hand, and I have done. It was a hand that would write a plain, straightforward, yea for yea, nay for nay letter, in unangular characters that bear little resemblance to the ordinary meagre regularity and pointed-Gothicness of a school-girl's style.

She had never been a satisfactory pupil. Ordinary persons are satisfactory pupils. Ordinary girls could copy with exactitude : Alice could not. To copy led her on to fanciful additions. She saw, intuitively, what she wanted in a book or a picture, and adapted it, after her own fashion. She unconsciously imitated, and a certain sort of originality grew out of her imitation. Later on she would have called this eclecticism, and have wondered at herself for her wilfulness. Facts were to her only the foundations of romance. She mentally dressed up anybody who was presented to her, just as, when a child, she had insisted upon undressing a dressed doll in order to clothe its sawdust-stuffed body in the costume that pleased *her.* She would ride a tilt for those whom she had chosen to call her friends; but was inclined to scarify such as were obnoxious to her. Religion moderated her eagerness to scarify ; and her attempts to reduce the precepts of charity to social practice, resulted either in silence or commonplaces. With her large, bright, inquiring eyes, clear complexion, and dark wavy hair, she could have passed anywhere for a genuine Irish beauty. But her parentage was pure Saxon.

"I am sure you must be very cold," she said to me; " come to the fire. Why, your hands are like ice."

Thereupon she made way for me, and I began to feel myself of some importance. Mrs. Comberwood asked after my father, Sir John, whom she hadn't the pleasure of knowing, and requested some details about the Colvin family, with which I willingly furnished her.

"You have no brothers or sister ?" said Alice. "You are the only one, are you not ?"

"Yes, I am the only one."

" You and Austin are great friends ?"

Her brother put his arm round her waist affectionately.

" Yes," I replied, " very great friends."

" We have a room together, you know," said Austin.

" Yes, I *do* know," returned his sister, " and you keep Master Colvin awake with Scott's novels."

We both laughed. Then Alice said to her brother,—

" What do the boys call him at school ?"

" Nickname ?" asked Austin.

" No, nothing rude ; I won't hear it, Austin." She held up her hand to warn him.

" It is nothing rude. You know they used to call me ' Owl in the Ivy-bush,' because, when I first went, I had such long hair."

" Owl in the Ivy-bush, indeed !" repeated his mother, quite annoyed at any child of hers bearing such an appellation.

" He," Austin went on, alluding unceremoniously to me, " was called ' Elephant.'"

I didn't like this before Alice, and I coloured. Alice smiled. This made it worse. I think I should have been angry, for I wasn't much given to tears, except when anger was abortive, if she hadn't remarked,—

" Well, I don't see why he should be called Elephant."

No more did I.

Austin informed her : " Because, when he was a new boy, he was so big and awkward, and had such large ears."

" You shouldn't repeat such things, Austin, at all events, of your friend," said Mrs Comberwood.

" He doesn't mind it," answered her son. " Do you ?"

I replied that I didn't mind it, of course, from *him*, but that I disliked it from others. Now was my opportunity for explaining to Alice that the title had fallen into disuse by this time, and that in point of fact I was no longer the " Elephant ;" but there was a boy whom they called " Rhinoceros," and two others, the Biffords, whose names, up to the time of their leaving, were " Fatty " and " Puggy."

Alice thought these vulgar.

" I hate anything vulgar in names," she said ; " and I

don't think I like funny names ; they ought to be stopped,
unless they're exactly suited to the people."

"Nelly's a funny name," observed Dick, who had now
joined the party.

"Nelly's my eldest sister," explained Austin.

"Elder, Austin, not eldest. The comparative must be
used where there are two, the superlative where there
are more."

"Dear me !" ejaculated her mother, pretending to perk
herself up. Elders who are unacquainted with the process of extracting the yolk of an egg by suction, do not
like being instructed on the subject by juniors, even when
the instruction is conveyed obliquely. A ball striking
you just as it glances off an angle of a wall hits hard.
Besides, flesh and blood feel the blow ; the wall, first
struck, did not.

"We're very particular," she added ironically.

"If we *are* to learn grammer, let us speak it," said
Alice.

"And what," I asked, becoming bolder, "is your elder
sister's name ?"

"McCracken," answered Alice, with a sparkle of fun in
her eyes.

It was impossible not to laugh. We all laughed, except
Mamma, who begged us to consider what an excellent
housewife sister Nelly was ; and what a good man Mr.
McCracken.

"Ah !" exclaimed Alice, moving to the table, "he's so
dreadfully low."

"Low ! my dear Alice !" cried Mrs. Comberwood, quite
startled : "I never heard you say such a thing before, and
I hope I never shall again. Of your brother-in-law too !
Low ! he's a perfect gentleman—and a clergyman—and
you who say you have so much respect for the clergy——"

"So I have, Mamma. For all clergymen on account of
their office, not for their individual opinions. I was
speaking of Andrew McCracken as a clergyman. Of
course he's a gentleman, or Nelly wouldn't have married
him. As a gentleman, he is what he ought to be. As a
clergyman, he is what he ought not to be."

"But you called him 'low,' Alice," Mrs. Comberwood reminded her.

"Well, dear, I thought you would have known that 'Low' meant Low Church—Evangelical."

"He has a right to his opinions: though, as far as I go, and I go quite far enough, I'm sure, I think Nelly might manage to have the service more cheerfully conducted."

"She gives in to him," said Alice, with a toss of the head.

"Ah !" said her mother, thinking, perhaps, that at this point it would be as well to drop the subject. Alice was sharp enough, she was perfectly aware, to have seen long since that Mr. Comberwood's wishes were not quite law in his own house, any more than they were in the courts where he professionally appeared as solicitor instructing counsel.

I found myself in a new world. What did I know of Low, High, Evangelical, Anglican, and such terms at that age ? Nothing at all. I just remembered having heard Dr. Carter telling the senior usher how, on being invited to some clerical meeting in the neighbourhood, he and two friends had appeared in their black gowns, while the others were all in surplices and hoods. Mrs. Carter denounced this as tomfoolery, and we boys (at dinner) unconsciously imbibed her notion (if any at all) on this subject. The matter was one in no way interesting to me. Had I not been invited to take a part in some New Year's festivites, and to pass a merry holiday-time at Ringhurst ? Undoubtedly.

Between seven and eight the steam of a great fuss pervaded the house. There was bustling among servants, fires were suddenly and savagely attacked, logs were piled on recklessly, chamber candles were reviewed in a line on the hall table, where they appeared in heavy marching order, armed with their burnished extinguishers and their snuffers by their side. Then the family mustered in the hall.

The master was expected every minute.

In point of fact he had already passed his usual time. Mamma's anxiety showed itself in the various reasons she gave to prove that there was no cause for it. Nor was there.

"He's not a bit later than he was last night," said Dick.

"Rather earlier, if Papa comes now," observed Alice, walking to the door.

We heard the wind threatening outside, as much as to say boldly, "Coming! Of course he's coming; only mind I'm against him to-night, and the more I try to keep him back the more urgent will he be to press forward." Then the voice was lost among the firs and larches, as with a sharp gritty sound, the sharper, and the more gritty as it neared the hall door, came the wheels of the dog-cart, broken by the horse's slinging trot, like the conductor's bâton beating common time on a wooden desk to the opening of the overture to "Semiramide." The last *fortissimo*, the last bar, and the bell was rendered unnecessary, though rung, by the rapidity wherewith the butler threw open the front door.

First came Mr. Comberwood's voice.

Then some of Mr. Comberwood's parcels; for he was of that order of pater-familias which looks upon fish in a straw-plaited basket from London as a peace-offering for venial sins.

"Now, Stephen, *do* come in," urged his wife.

Then Stephen Comberwood came in.

As, however, he is a very big man, and a person of some importance, I must beg leave to reserve his description for the commencement of the next chapter.

CHAPTER XIII.

MR. COMBERWOOD ENTERS—SUNDAY AT RINGHURST.

HE was an enormous man, every way. Over six feet, and stout out of all proportion. The dog-cart horse, specially purchased for this work, could do nothing more in a day than take his master to and from the station. In London all omnibuses were closed against him at the price, and cabmen suddenly became singularly short-sighted when hailed by Mr. Comberwood on the pavement. Once he was in the same situation as the famous Irishman who, being taken in a sedan-chair whereof the bottom was out, remarked that "but for the look of the thing he'd as lief have walked"—that is, Mr. Comberwood's legs appeared as auxiliaries to the wheels: fortunately without accident, and without either a summons or an action. You can't expect an ordinary vehicle, intended for ordinary persons, to carry an elephant; and an ordinary driver, obliged to take up a fare whatever his size, can't bring an action against his customer for exceeding a certain weight.

Mr. Comberwood's practice was therefore chiefly in chambers, where Mahomet came to the mountain, the mountain being a necessity to Mahomet as a client.

He had a bald head, bordered from temple to temple with hair, as evenly and exactly as if he had been measured for it by a village barber, with an inverted wooden basin, and this hair was as curly and neutral-tinted as the Astrachan trimming on a lady's jacket. He spoke quickly, and repeated his sentences, in part, or wholly, as might be necessary. His countenance was capable of three expressions, and three only. The first was humorous, the second irritable, and the third blank incapacity. He appeared at his largest when wearing the last expression; it was the one that came naturally to him after dinner, when he spread himself out over a stalwart arm-chair and stared at the fire, which must have seemed to him like the glow of the setting sun illuminating the outline of his waistcoat's horizon. The first and second expressions merged into one another. When humorous he became suddenly irritable, and when irritable he became suddenly humorous. Also if his wife were inclined to be irritable, he became immediately humorous. She herself had no humour, nor appreciation of it.

He kissed Mrs. Comberwood and Alice (which I did not like), and told the boys to help him off with his great coat. It *was* a great coat with a vengeance. Judiciously parcelled out, it would have clothed a deserving family of eight.

He was very glad to see me.

"Hullo!" he said; "Master Colvin, hey? What's your name? what's your name?—hey?"

This was said so fast as to be almost unintelligible to me. I paused, and smiled. I did not like to ask what he had said. He did not, however, give me time to think over it, as he went on hurriedly, wearing his humorous expression,—

"Not got a name—hey? No godfathers and god-mothers—hey? What did your godfathers and god-mothers do for you—hey?"

"Papa!" said Alice, reproachfully.

"They gave him a name—hey?"

"Cecil, sir."

"Cecil—hey? Cecil. Here, Dick, take that fish to the cook; don't tumble down with it now—hey? Do you hear?"

"Yes, Papa."

"Now then," he went on, "hands washing—'what no

soap, so he died '—hey." To me: "Did you ever hear that story, Master Cecil. 'No soap—she bear—and the Great Panjandrum with the little round button at the top '—hey ? "

I had not, and hoped he would tell me.

Mrs. Comberwood now thought it time to interfere.

"Dinner is already very late," she said, with the precise certainty of a person who knows what o'clock it is to a minute, "so I do beg you will get ready at once, Stephen."

We passed that evening, a very short one, with the weight of the coming Sunday morning on us. This was to be the first Sunday I had ever spent away from home in the holidays. Miss Alice was generally for straying into theological discussion, while Austin read, and Dick taught me the game of Fox and Geese with draughts. Mr. and Mrs. Comberwood talked about the people who were coming, and who were not, to their party. Alice joined them in this, and my attention was drawn towards them twice by the mention of Herbert Pritchard and Mr. Cavander.

"How's Uncle Herbert—hey?" asked Mr. Comberwood; "you didn't know he'd be here. Yes: come to look after you and give a good report to your father—hey ? What a good boy am I—Horner in the corner—hey ? "

Then he resumed his part in the conversation.

On Sunday morning he read family prayers. Kneeling was out of the question with him. He did it vicariously, through Alice, who was devotional enough for the whole party, enjoying it so evidently, that, not being accustomed to outward piety, and knowing nothing at all of inward, I wondered mightily.

During the morning, all mention of the coming theatricals and party was banished. Mr. Comberwood did ample justice to the breakfast in the true spirit of a holiday-maker who has the entire day before him. On week days he scarcely knew what breakfast meant: it was a hindrance, which very often had nearly caused the loss of his train. But on Sundays, this, and luncheon, were novelties to be thoroughly enjoyed.

We did everything to the sound of the bell, so much
so, that I soon began to derive the name of the place
from this practice. A bell got the servants out of bed,
and us out of our sleep. Bell number two ordered them
to breakfast. The third bell was to inform us that they
could not go on any longer alone, and "their betters"
must get up and help them. The fourth bell invited us
to breakfast. This was an economical bell, and did duty
for prayers too. Then came the church bells, running
after one another merrily ever so many times, then taking
breath, then coming out at intervals in pairs, then the
laggard by himself was peremptorily stopped by the
church clock striking the hour. Then on our return,
there was bell number five for us to prepare, so that the
announcement which would have to be presently made
should not take us by surprise; then number six, which
let out the secret of luncheon, and number seven to
summon the servants to dinner in the servants' hall. Tea
had another bell, being the eighth. The ceremony of
dressing for dinner was celebrated with a good rattling
fantasia, number nine, on the bell. Dinner itself was
the occasion for the tenth, the servants' supper for the
eleventh, and evening family prayers the twelfth.

We walked to church slowly and comfortably. Alice
had plenty of questions to ask poor old women, tottering
old men in slate-coloured smocks, and shy children.

The church at Whiteboys was the first village church
I had seen, that is I mean with a purely village congregation. It had its Christmas decorations, chiefly done by
Alice Comberwood. It was an old Norman church, and
one of the few objects of interest in the neighbourhood.
It had been patched up and restored, and its massive
pillars were half hidden by the high pews. The pews
indeed were so high that had a stranger suddenly entered
during the lessons, or the sermon, he would have thought
he had come upon a clergyman rehearsing his part in an
empty church. Looked at in perspective and on a level,
the tops of the pews seemed like a sea of fixed waves,
between each of which, when the heads popped up, you
suddenly beheld the bathers.

This discription could not of course apply to Mr. Comberwood, and *a-propos* it now occurs to me what a magnificent *Suisse* he would have made in a French church. I could not help remarking Mr. Comberwood during service. He was short-sighted, and took a long time to find and fix his eye-glasses. He generally got hold of the wrong psalm, when he made the responses, in a rather husky, but very audible voice, and so quickly, that he had finished his verse before the rest of the congregation had got half-way through theirs, when, having done his part, he would look round from under his glasses (he always viewed everything from a point either above or below his eye-glasses, never straight through them), as though inquiring irritably, "Why the deuce don't you get on—hey?" When his wife, or Miss Alice, would point out his mistake to him in a whisper, he replied aloud, "Hey—what?"

Having ascertained the nature of their communication, his legal training rendered it compulsory on him to verify their assertions by reference to the calendar, when, having arrived at a right and proper conclusion, and found the correct psalm, he had to wait some seconds in order to adjust, as it were, his ears to the new sounds, and test the accuracy of the congregation's responses by the text of the Prayer-book. When the hymn time came, he put his whole voice into it, and shot ahead of organ, choir, and everybody, until the antagonism got so fierce as to threaten the peace of the worshippers. He led them whether they would or not, that is to say he was first, the organ a good second, and the people last, following sulkily. When on coming out of church he observed, "That was a beautiful hymn to-day—hey? very fine hymn—hey?" you might be certain that he had had quite a field-day of it, all to himself. Occasionally the choir skipped, by arrangement, verse number three, an omission of which Mr. Comberwood took no notice, singing it right through without faltering, and commencing verse number four just as the clergyman was commencing his short pre-preaching prayer, and the congregation were settling into various praying attitudes, of which the one

considered most reverential at Whiteboys was a compromise between kneeling and sitting, which was neither
one nor the other, and very little of either.

Alice knelt.   She had a beautiful book in Gothic
binding, the printing being in red and black.   She was
enthusiastic at lunch-time about her pupils for the choir
of boys which she had begun to train, and spoke with
deep regret of the sentiments and opinions of the parish
clergyman, who, she said, was fast asleep and wanted
waking.

In the evening we had sacred music, when Alice sang
sweetly, and I was enraptured.   Bedtime was at an early
hour, and when I had tucked myself carefully up for the
night, Mrs. Comberwood entered, and bending over me,
said, "Good night, Master Cecil.   You have no mother,
poor boy.   You shall be one of my boys.   Good night.
God bless you."   Wherewith she pressed her lips on my
forehead with another loving motherly kiss; and I have
seldom fallen asleep as happily, and in such sweet peacefulness, as on that first Sunday night at Ringhurst
Whiteboys.

CHAPTER XIV.

MR. COMBERWOOD went up to town on Monday morning early. He breakfasted hurriedly, keeping his eye on the clock and his watch, as though suspicious of some collision between these two to prevent his catching the train. The dining-room clock was two minutes in advance of his watch, corroborating the latter's evidence, and volunteering additional statements. Then, everything necessary for his departure, although displayed in perfect order under his very eye, on the hall table, had to be requisitioned hastily.

"Where's my coat—hey—my coat ? Now, then, Dick."

"Yes, Papa."

" Ah !"—here the butler assisted him on with his overcoat. "Now, let me see—where's my umbrella ? Can't go without my umbrella." Umbrella produced. "Ah ! gloves—hey—no gloves ? Alice—where——" Gloves shown to be waiting for him. "Ah ! now then—there—there hey ?"—this to me, with a humorous expression. "Nothing you want me to do in town ? No"—this to his wife—"Very well—I shall hear about the professional person you know—all right." Then with a vast amount of puffing, he hoisted himself on to the driving-box of the dog-cart, adjusted the reins, called out to the groom "Rough shod ? no stumbling ? Hey ?" to which the man replied that it was a thaw, the snow lying only in long

H

strips about the country, as if rows of white linen had been left out to dry on the ground; then on Mr. Comberwood crying out, "Let her go! ky up!" the groom released the horse's head, dashed after the trap, clambered up and took his seat behind in all the stern composure of folded arms, the evident representative of ignorant Prejudice turning its back on Progress, with which it is compelled to be carried along in spite of itself, and looking only to the traditions of the past.

The performances at Ringhurst had been long ago projected by Alice Comberwood for the stirring up of the neighbours generally.

"No one ever does anything here," she said, in the course of the morning, complainingly to Mrs. McCracken, her eldest sister, who had come to stay over the festivities.

"You're better off for amusement than we are, though, Ally," replied her sister, who was providently knitting worsted stockings.

Miss Comberwood had married a Norfolk clergyman with, it was said, "prospects." In a certain sense this was decidedly true. There was already a family of three. "Prospects," unqualified by any sort of adjective, command a wide range. To make up for the omission of an adjective, old ladies talked of Mr. McCracken's prospects with pursed-up lips and graduated nods, whose movement, beginning briskly, died away imperceptibly, like those of the China mandarin's head in a grocer's, which are becoming as rare as politeness.

Mr. McCracken's prospects consisted in reality of little more than what he surveyed from his kitchen window, in the rear, and from his drawing-room in front. How poor country clergymen manage, not only to exist respectably on two hundred and fifty per annum, but to send sons to the university, was, at one time, as great a problem to me, as ever it must have been to them. But when I met the sons, when I knew what they had learnt at home, what they could turn their heads and hands to, and how—what with scholarships and odd prizes, such as, hidden away from sight in dusty old collegiate corners, do exist for the benefit of honest lads like these—they contrived to lighten their father's burden, while improving their own position, then I understood it all; and if ever I require a couple of heroes for an epic, I know where to find my models. Much to the disappointment of my friends, I take this opportunity of stating that I have no intention whatever of writing an epic.

And the only use of the above disquisition is to present you with a fair estimate of Mr. McCracken's prospects, which had not improved since his marriage, and were not regarded in a hopeful light, privately, by Mrs. McCracken, who, however, was as blithe, cheerful, and contented as, I believe, she would have been with half the sum, or double.

"Ah," said Alice, "you don't care about amusement. You've got your own at home."

Mrs. McCracken smiled, paused, looked at the fire-place with the air of having forgotten something, and resumed her knitting. Then she observed—

"I don't care for theatricals, if that's what you mean, Ally. You know I never did."

"I know you were always Little Mother, weren't you, Nellie? Always staid and quiet, and ever so many years older than you really are."

"Nellie has a good deal to occupy her time," said Mrs. Comberwood, who was rather reserved in evincing her own admiration for her second daughter. She was afraid of her.

"Yes, of course she has. She was cut out for a clergyman's wife." Then she added, as if fearful of having said something unkind, "Dear Andrew! I'm sure there's not a better brother-in-law in the world."

"Nor husband," said Nellie, sedately.

"Yet I *do* think," cried Alice impulsively, "that clergymen ought not to marry."

"My dear Alice!" exclaimed Mrs. Comberwood, who had caught a whisper of this before among the "new-fangled notions."

"Then all the young curates would be licensed to flirt on the premises. Very dangerous!" laughed the elder sister, speaking as one who, from her experience, could afford to ridicule such a notion. In her old-fashioned and well-regulated ideas, a clergyman was, necessarily, a marrying man.   If it was not good for man, of the laity, to be alone, much less was it for man, of the clergy.

Alice saw matters in a very different light, and was in a heat directly.

" I don't see why they should flirt."

" It is their nature to," said Mrs McCracken, still laughing.

" Nature, dear !   There is something more than nature required for a clergyman," replied Alice, warming with her subject.

" Something more than nature?   Well good-nature, I suppose."

Alice did not approve of this levity on so serious a subject; or rather on a subject which she had chosen to make so sacred.   Yet she had given herself a mission, which was to convert her family—from their own views to hers.   The service, at Andrew McCracken's church, was as unpalatable to Alice as the informalities of a meeting-house; and she thought that could she influence Andrew in the direction of ornate devotions, and just a trifle more surplus and stole to begin with, what a great thing it would be for—for what ?   Well, she would not hesitate to reply—" For the future of Anglicanism."   This I heard her say to Austin, who seemed to ponder her words, as he caressed his favourite sister.

They dearly loved each other.   Austin was two years her junior, yet his grave countenance and generally delicate appearance, gave him an air of seniority which was much increased by his calm demeanours and thoughtful way of speaking.   He was a born student.   Alice sipped books ; Austin drank them to the dregs.   Alice was easily daunted by uncut leaves ; Austin faced them knife in hand, and conquered.   Alice peeped at the last page of a novel to see how it ended ; then she skipped all the descriptions, and alighted only on points of dialogue, or action.   Her bent was dramatic.   Austin trudged through the book-country bravely, taking it as it came—heavy plough, marsh, shady lane, or hard, open road.   He paused to admire, or to reckon up matters between reader and author.   He missed nothing, and, having once read any passage of more than ordinary merit, he remembered it, sometimes literally, but always its proper sense.   I have already said how he told me most of the Waverley novels. It is a great tribute to the skill he brought to this kindly, self-imposed task, to record that when I came to read " Ivauhoe," " Guy Mannering," and the " Talisman," I was, in a manner, disappointed.   Austin's voice was wanting, and he had made reading a trouble to me.   It had been so delightful to lie in bed, gradually sinking to rest, to the delicious music of romance and chivalry.

Austin had now joined them, having entered the dining-room in search of me, and the conversation took a new turn.

" Alice."

" Well, Austy."

" The carpenter is here about the arrangements for the stage in the drawing-room.   You understand these matters better than I ; will you see him ? "

" Yes, at once."

" Does Mr. Cavander come home to-day ? " asked Austin of his mother, as Alice was leaving the room.

She stopped at the door.   I was naturally interested in the reply, and looked from Alice to Mrs. Comberwood, and then back again.

" Yes.   He will come down with your father this after-noon."

" I know some one who'll be delighted to see him," observed Mrs. McCracken, slyly.

Alice blushed.   At that minute I knew some one who would *not* be delighted to see him.   That some one was myself.

Alice, mind, was just on eighteen ; I was thirteen and a-half.   Mr. Cavander's youth, or age, was of no con-sequence to me : I was jealous of him.   I disliked him already : now, I could have challenged him with the greatest possible pleasure, and should have disposed of him with rapture.

I think I must have blushed deeply on this occasion, as Mrs. Comberwood and Mrs. McCracken both laughed.

"Well," said Alice, still at the door, as if the subject had so great an attraction for her that she must speak on it, "I do like him. He's very clever; isn't he, Austy ?"

Austin smiled. He only asked if Mr. Cavander was going to take a part.

"No," said Alice, "that's the worst of it. He's coming to be among the audience. I know," she added, in despairing accents, "I shall never be able to do anything before him."

Oh, I could have demolished him there and then. Afraid of *him!* Whatever his cleverness, I despised him. I rather fancy I expressed myself so strongly to this effect, as to cause them all, including Alice, considerable amusement.

I wished at that moment that the drama could have been "Blue Beard," with Cavander as the celebrated polygamist, Alice for Fatima, and myself as Selim, to rush in just as his scimitar was coming down, and—whish —run him through the body. The theatricals with which I would have amused the company, should have been the kind of entertainment that upset the Danish court, and made the wicked King go supperless to bed.

The preparations occupied Alice and her brother Dick the greater part of the morning, and at luncheon Cavander was again mentioned.

"He's rather like a Jew," said young Dick, boldly.

"Have you ever seen a Jew ?" asked Alice, colouring.

"Yes, at school. A chap very like Cavander—— "

"*Mister* Cavander," interposed his mother, correcting him.

"They do not learn manners at school," said Alice.

"And they don't teach 'em at home," retorted Dick, who had a hot temper.

"Hush, Dick," said Austin, gravely.

"Oh, humbug!" cried Dick, who had somehow got thoroughly out of temper with everybody. "Cavander's a fool, and Alice makes such a fuss about him."

I could have embraced him.

He went on:

"Yes, you do, Alice; and you look at him when you're talking, as if you wanted to know whether you're saying your lesson right—and—when he's here you never come with us—and——"

He couldn't fire off his revolver quick enough. But before he was stopped—as he was with spirit by Alice, who was immediately backed by her mother's authority —I think one bullet had certainly gone straight home. In a half-apologetic, half-sulky tone, Dick continued, giving a last shot as he retired,—

"Well, you know you do. You're always talking with him about churches, and that sort of thing."

Alice brightened up, and the two other ladies smiled. The absurdity of Alice's attempting such a conversion as Mr. Cavander's had often, ere now, been a subject for their quiet merriment.

"It's a fancy she has at present," was Mrs. Comberwood's opinion; "she'll give it up as she gets older."

In the afternoon Alice and Dick went out riding. I was offered a pony, but did not feel quite certain of my capabilities, although I should have liked to have accompanied Alice.

Later on Mr. Comberwood arrived, bringing down a heap of packages from town, and appearing, as Mr. Verney might have described him, "in his character of Izaak Walton, on the threshold of the honest alehouse, where he was welcomed by the buxom hostess"—that is, with the usual basket of fish. Having seen his parcels all deposited, and kissed his wife, he said, briefly, "Here's Cavander," rather as if he had counted him among the packages, and after the turbot.

"Anyone else?" inquired Mrs. Comberwood, after welcoming her visitor.

"Let me see—let me see," said Mr. Comberwood, fumbling about in all his pockets, one after the other, as though he had mislaid a friend or two in an odd corner. "No, not to-day—not to-day."

He chorused his last words in his fussy way, walking about, and sniffing suspiciously, in a fee-fo-fum and ogreish fashion, and then stopped to stare at me, with an expression of comic surprise at seeing me before him on that particular occasion.

"I've seen your Uncle Van, to-day—hey? Yes——"

"Any message for me, sir?" I asked, with an air of importance.

"Yes—of course—he said bad boy—whip him—hey?" Then he followed his wife into the library.

While we were all here, Alice returned.

She came in from her ride the very picture of full bloom. The sweet scent of the fresh country air was upon her: its fragrance about her. As she walked into the study amongst the old musty books, it was like letting the bright light of a May morning in upon a closely curtained chamber.

"Miss Alice! how well you are looking!" said Cavander, advancing to take her hand, in evident admiration.

Ah! she had not seen him at first: "it was so dark," she said, "coming out of the open air."

"Shall we return to it, if you are not fatigued with your ride?" he asked, and his voice was so sweetly modulated, and yet so strangely to *my* ears, that it was like the effect of a commonplace tune, set by a skilled musician to the most perfect harmonies.

"Yes, I am a little tired," returned Alice. "Come and see Bess before they put her into her stall. She was a favourite of yours, you remember. She's so much improved, you wouldn't know her again."

"That's unkind, Miss Alice. I'm not a George the Fourth. I never forget a favourite."

So chatting, they left the room. He had taken no notice of me, beyond saying, "Ah, you again," when he first entered.

Cavander classed boys with toy dogs—expensive, useless, stupid, dirty, and always in the way.

Master Dick's behaviour towards him was consistently sulky, and to my mind Cavander was less of a Doctor Fell than heretofore, as now I had positive and clear reasons for disliking him.

Had I been asked what harm could possibly come from Alice's partiality for Mr. Cavander and his liking for her, of course I should have been utterly at a loss for an answer. I was in a minority, without even the shadow of a right to an objection. Dick was with me to a certain extent. Austin tolerated him on his sister's account, and committed himself to no opinion on Cavander, except as to his cleverness, which he admitted. Indeed, with Alice, he was fond of listening to him talking on most subjects. The family generally appeared to be proud of their visitor. I was ignorant of evil, but I was jealous. Being jealous, I was suspicious of there being a great deal more than met the eye; but as to the nature and extent of what I feared, I was totally in the dark.

Ignorance is the best soil for suspicion, and, therefore, mine flourished prodigiously.

CHAPTER XV.

THE piece to be played by our elders in the Ringhurst
Whiteboys back-drawing-room was a French *proverbe,*
with which a grateful English public had already been
made acquainted by the help of a kindly version rendered
into language understanded of the people. Alice had
read this aloud one evening to her parents, and had suggested "getting it up." So it was got up, and to avert
hostile criticism, and to keep the evening's entertainment
to its original domestic character, Alice arranged a little
after-piece, as already described, wherein, however, her
brothers would not play unless she joined them, as
authoress and actress. So she consented, and stooped to
the pigmies in order to disarm the giants. Her appearance, in *Naughty Little Blue Beard,* seemed to introduce
the reality of children's make-believes, and the freshness
of innocence among such otherwise overpowering vanities
as were those of costuming, painting, and directing and
ordering at rehearsals.

And what to all well-regulated minds, let me ask, is
the attraction to us seniors (we do *not* go to the back of
the box always, or if we do, we push ourselves forward
into priority when we think there's something we haven't
seen, though we know we shall pooh-pooh it afterwards)—
what, I ask, is the attraction to us, at Christmas-time, in

the heated, noisy theatre, if it is not the sunny smiles of
the children making the gas-light garish? To see them
all in a row, gloves, oranges, and playbills—a ripple of
laughing waters—it does your heart good, and warms you
towards the oldest jokes, clumsiest tricks, and stalest stage
devices. But, understand me, even in this retrospect I
say distinctly to *see* them, *not to bring them.* I once un-
bosomed myself sweetly on this subject at a table where,
it being Christmas-tide, the hospitality was profuse, and
there were olives to the wine, and olive-branches round
about; and the good hostess exclaimed, " You love children! Ah!"—here she turned up her eyes, and thanked
heaven for a man, and not a brute—" I will give you
a treat. *Will you come to the pantomime with us
to-morrow week?"* I was ravished, I was enchanted, I
would look forward to it with rapture. The day came
—so did the evening. Dinner was provided at five, that
we might be in time. In time for what? For the first
piece before the pantomine, which is, I am aware, played
by the most patient and energetic artists, amid howls and
execrations from the upper and uppermost galleries. It
was a tea-dinner, too, such as I have already described as
having fallen to the lot of Uncle Van. In fact, it was
not a dinner at all, considering what I *had* had at that
house. Papa was obliged, he artfully said, to leave us on
business, but would join us at the theatre. The sneak!
He deserved his amiable wife's cutting sarcasm, wherein
she drew the happy comparison between the bachelor
who doated on children (me), and the husband who
avoided them (him). But oh, the miseries! I had to sit
on the box of the fly. I had to hold everything; argue
with everybody; pay anybody who preferred a claim.
Finally, I was put right at the back of the private box,
where I leaned my head against the side, like a disjointed
punch-doll, in the vain attempt to catch even a glimpse
of a dragon's tail. The next day I had a cold and a stiff
neck. But, even on this purgatorial occasion, their
infantine hilarity came to me like a message from
heaven; for assuredly it told me of good things going on
in an unseen world (I have said the stage was invisible to

me on account of my position), concerning which I could only guess, or take their statements.

The announcement, then, that the lesser Comberwoods were going to play a little piece written by their elder sister, drew (so to speak) a house, and many wrote for permission to bring friends—a free-and-easy way of increasing a party to any extent, much practised both in town and country, and often taken as the discharge of an obligation. In this sense, as asking costs nothing, except perhaps the trouble of polishing up a certain amount of brass, the practice is valuable, on economical grounds.

The party had grown into something like the proportions of a county ball, and had begun to frighten Mrs. Comberwood. At this time Mrs. McCracken was most serviceable to her, and undertook the general direction. As for Comberwood, he, for his part, would have had all England invited, and would have " taxed the costs," severely, afterwards.

The county people liked the owner of Ringhurst, and were inclined to be gathered together round his board, as often as he liked to invite them. There was a jovial geniality and warmth about him, which was as attractive as sealing-wax after friction. When they entered Ringhurst, they felt, instinctively, that there was a round of beef, and a chine, and a pasty, and a Tudoric flagon, in the refectory—that, in short, they had not been asked merely to heat the house with their breath, and save the fuel.

No, Mr. Comberwood blazed out on his guests, and welcomed all without distinction. He had secret corners, though, for choice spirits who cared for oysters and stout (from London) in preference to all the champagne and chicken you could give them; and he knew, too, having concocted them himself, which were the cups to make you wink, and gasp, but clutch the handle all the more firmly for such expressions of emotion : and these cups he would recommend to his gossips.

However, much had to be done before we arrived at the supper, which to some of us boys was not by any means the least portion of the evening's amusement.

I had to work for my meal for days before—that is, I had to study Baron Abomelique, be perpetually called into the housekeeper's room to try something on (for our dresses were home-made), and to be ready at any moment to hear Austin, Dick, or Alice, if required by them to lend them my ears, in return for theirs, occasionally.

Mr. Cavander lounged about, and when the important business of the morning was over—which was, of course, our theatrical preparations—Dick would be called upon to ride with his sister Alice, who was invariably accompanied by Mr. Cavander. Dick sulked and wouldn't, but Alice told him it was unkind, and then he obliged her. He often anticipated their return, riding back alone.

When evening darkened the house, Alice, who loved the fire-light, as being "thinking-time," would sit in a low chair, and hold silent communion with the glowing logs and coals.

Mr. Cavander was never far from her at this hour; and, sometimes, Mamma and Mrs. McCracken would consent to take their refreshing cup of tea in the dark. This predilection for comparative obscurity was unintelligible to the practical elder sister.

"You can't read, you can't sew, and really there's something, to my mind, so oppressive in it, you can hardly talk," said Mrs. McCracken, who did not approve of everyone giving way to Alice.

"I do not always want to read, I do not always want to sew, and I think we all talk a great deal too much," said Alice, whose face was thrown into a Rembrandt-like shade, by the red light on her dress, from her knee downwards.

"It *is* nice to be quiet sometimes," observed Mamma, trying to find a safe place for her tea-cup, "only why not be quiet with light. I really cannot see at all."

"We should see much better were we to rest our eyes oftener," said Alice, sententiously.

"Close them, then," said Dick, at full length on a settee.

"Dick's right," observed sister Nellie, quickly, in order to save him from consequences. "We go to bed too late as a rule."

" For my part, I love this time of the day at this season. Indeed, I am not sure if I do not prefer it far above all other times and seasons throughout the year." Alice thought over her own proposition, and then continued: " The fire is such a companion, and such a superior being too."

" Miss Alice is verging on the doctrines of the Parsees," said a voice, whose owner was now part and parcel of the sofa.

" Better than the Par*sons*," exclaimed Dick.

"Dick !" said Mrs. McCracken, reprovingly.

" Beg pardon, Nellie, only fun," Dick apologized ; " but Par*see* is like Par*son*."

" Not in sense," said his brother Austin, gravely. "The Parsees are disciples of Zoroaster, and worship fire."

" It is very natural, since they begin with the sun, of which fire is the offspring, and the living image. I worship the fire—in winter. I agree with Miss Alice. The fire *does* seem to have a sympathising heart; a warm, glowing heart; a living heart, with a placid pulsation."

" We can hear it beat, can we not ? " inquired Alice, approving the simile.

" Yes !—Listen ! Calmly : now excitedly, as though it had great things to say. Now there is a change in its constitution. No, it recovers, is brilliant for a second, so that all around catch the ray at different angles, but are helpless to return it, only showing up our own dull-headedness against the fire's wit."

"There certainly is nothing so cheery, or cosy, in a bedroom," said Mamma.

" Or so roaring, noisy, and eager in a kitchen," added Mrs. McCracken, who had been thinking it out.

" Look at it in a blacksmith's," cried Dick.

" In a study," said Austin.

" In a drawing-room," I suggested, vaguely, but with some remembrance, too, of one cold, steel, and highly-polished fender at my father's. I would rather have quoted Mrs. Davis's nursery fire, or that of the Verneys' at dinner-time. I felt that we were playing a sort of game of How do you like it, When do you like, and Where do you like it, of which I had not as yet filled up the blanks in my formula.

"No," said Alice, planting her elbows on her knees, and stretching both hands out towards the fire, as though imploring its inspiration for her on its own behalf. "See it in a sick-room. How quiet, soft, and purring! How comforting to the invalid is the mere sight of it, telling, as it does, at once of human sympathy, of unremitting care! As long as there is a fire, there must be hope. Fire is necessary to life; it can be of no use to the dead."

"Alice!" said her mother, shivering. There was a pause. We seemed to have drawn ghosts about us, as the shadows grew upon the walls, higher and higher, like spectral creepers.

Mrs. McCracken was for coals, or a log, at once. Alice prayed her to stay her hand.

"Don't bring the servant in," said Alice; "all the ghosts will run away if Bale comes in with the candle. Don't!"

"We prefer," said Cavander, identifying himself with Alice, "we prefer darkness rather than light."

"But *not* for the same reason, I hope," returned Mrs. McCracken, who did not feel quite sure whether Andrew would have countenanced this sort of conversation. The Rev. Andrew had once preached strongly about "idle words," and *she* had not forgotten that sermon. In fact, she had occasionally turned the weapons of that homily against the worthy Andrew himself, when he had been stupidly irritating, as husbands will be sometimes. However, he wasn't there to explain himself; and had · he been, his explanations, out of the pulpit, did not carry conviction to her mind on all subjects. Besides, Mr. Cavander was, everyone said—and she could testify to it, too—a very superior man, who (everyone said this also) wrote in some philosophical magazines, and even in *The Times*, and was shrewd, too, in business. Who was she, Mrs. McCracken, out of her parish, to sling at this champion? No; if it pleased Alice to essay his conversion, why it was a fine employment for Alice, and she might hear some plain truths from a man who was not only clever, but commonly sensible. So she reseated herself, and joined in letting Alice have her way.

"Certainly not," said Cavander, answering the last speaker, "although we do wish to propitiate the shades."

"I wish there were fairies," observed Austin, quietly, preferring these to ghosts. "I mean Pucks, Titanias, and Oberons. I have a book of stories, with pictures of goblin faces in the fire, and elves twisting about in the smoke. If they are in the sick-room, they must be very good spirits, unless they take to make the kettle boil over, or pulling off the lid."

"Mediæval writers," said Mr. Cavander's voice, for he had by this vanished altogether, "spoke of a spirit behind all forms of life. The spirit of fire was to them as real as to a Parsee; perhaps more real in proportion as their credulity was stronger."

"Their faith," Alice suggested, with some show of nervousness in her voice.

"A synonym in this case," replied Cavander, quietly.

"No," she answered quickly, "faith cannot be credulity. I am not credulous because I believe."

"Credulous is derived from *credo*," said Austin, to whom a new line of thought had occurred.

When in after-years we have arrived at a sure and calm haven, how almost hopeless is the search back again over the trackless waters to find what breeze first caused our shifting sails to swell in its direction.

"I think," said Alice, speaking cautiously, one is bound, or almost bound, to believe in the existence of disembodied spirits."

"But the popular notion of a ghost," replied Cavander, "is an embodied spirit. If I hear a human voice uttering words, I know that certain organs must be in exercise. I know that I am near nothing dead, but something living and human. I am bound to believe this by common sense: there is no other compulsion."

This was not at all what Alice wanted, and both Mrs. Comberwood and Mrs. McCracken were secretly delighted at this very reasonable answer as to ghosts.

Alice felt that she was called upon to assert her belief

in the supernatural, and on the strongest and plainest grounds.

" There is the Witch of Endor mentioned in the Bible."

Here, at least, it occurred to her that she should have the Rev. Andrew McCracken's better-half and her mamma with her. She was doomed to disappointment.

" I trust," said Mrs. Comberwood, " that you don't rank the Scriptures with ghost stories, Alice."

She had a mind to say something severe on new-fangled notions, but, for her, she had gone far enough.

" No, Mamma, of course not," replied Alice, somewhat pettishly.

" Miss Alice meant that she was willing to accept as fact an improbability, if it came to her on such undeniable authority as that of the Bible."

From which it will be seen that Mr. Cavander could adapt his conversation to his company. Alice felt grateful to him for the rescue. It is dangerous to the well-being of a weak state that it should be obliged to accept the voluntary services of a powerful ally, who, may, at no distant date, imperiously dictate, where once it deferentially advised.

" I should think it is nearly time to dress," said Mrs. McCracken, rising.

The dignified Bale entered with candles, and finding us all thus sprawling about as if we had fallen on to the sofas and chairs through the ceiling, expressed facially no astonishment, but, guarding himself carefully, and in the best-bred style possible, against treading on any other people who might be strewn about at haphazard on the carpet, he placed his lights, while his attendant drew the curtains with a sharp, decided click, as though there were spectators outside who hadn't paid their money for the show; and having, officially and distantly, answered some questions as to "time," and "his master," withdrew.

" Are the thingummies to come to-night?" cried Dick, suddenly, jumping up into an erect position, and shaking himself into his clothes.

" Thingummies?" repeated his mother, who preferred to hear spades called spades, if there were reasons for so doing.

I

"Yes: you know what I mean,"—which, by the way, is peculiar to boyhood, which generalizes and trusts to chance—"I mean the fellows who are going to play. Mr. Longlegs——"

"Mr. Langlands, Dick," said his mother, fearful of her son calling her guest this to his face. "Why, he will think that we have been speaking of him as Longlegs behind his back."

"Their rooms are ready," said Mrs. McCracken, "Mr. and Mrs. Jakeman, Mr. Langlands, and Mr. Dothie."

"And we shall have a rehearsal this evening," said Alice.

"May I be prompter, or call-boy, or something?" pleaded Mr. Cavander; "if you have nothing to employ my talents, what shall I do?"

"Talk to Mrs. Jakeman," said Alice; "she's very nice." And she swooped down before the fire.

"Thank you. She will be watching her husband's rehearsal the whole time, and expatiating on its beauties. No; do let me be prompter."

"Austin's going to prompt on the evening itself," I remarked.

Cavander took not the slightest notice of me.

"In the first piece," said Austin, "that's all. The person whom Papa brings from London is to prompt and do everything in that way while we're getting it up."

"Then," said Mr. Cavander, "I shall constitute myself a *claqueur*, and shall rehearse when I am to laugh, cry, applaud, and throw a bouquet. Come, Miss Alice! I may be of use to you, may I not?"

She turned round, smiling on him; and their eyes met. In a second hers were lowered before his, as the vanquished ship salutes the victor on the high seas. It was a lesson in silent eloquence; but it was the master in the art instructing his pupil.

The bustle and the bells all over again. To-night we sat down a large party to dinner, for Mr. Comberwood's two carriages had arrived with the *corps dramatique*, consisting of the guests above mentioned.

Then came the Rector of Whiteboys, the Rev. Mr.

Tabberer, and his daughter, who was to take a part in the first piece. The whole talk was of the stage; and the gentlemen-amateurs spoke like Olympian demi-gods on a visit to men, telling good and racy anecdotes of a life higher than ours, and freely and honestly expressing themselves refreshed, and revived, by the incense of praise offered at their shrines, by the devotees to whom the Olympians knew they could be uncommonly useful. What is the use of being on friendly terms with a demi-god if he can't get you into Olympus? A fico for your outsiders—these lovers of the drama for its own sake (which soon came to mean for their own sakes; but once in their early days it was not so, but then they were not demi-gods) accepted sacrifices of houses turned topsy-turvy at their word, and libations of champagne at the hands of those who yearned for even the acquaintance of a cloud in Olympus. These demi-gods of the sock and buskin, invited right and left, introduced left and right, ordained where civility should end, and where begin, and graciously put Christopheros Sly at my lord's supper table, asking my lord in turn to the theatricals *chez* Christopheros, which honest Christopheros, once a cobbler in a stall, now a millionaire in a mansion, was only too pleased to give.

Mr. Comberwood was in no need of these demi-gods but if your theatricals were to be the thing, and as good (at least) as your neighbours', then it was as necessary to success to reckon on Messrs. Jakeman, Dothie, and Langlands in the night's programme, as to secure the name of Serjeant Blyster on the brief for the defendant in an action for libel. Percival Floyd, late of old Carter's, and now a big hulking fellow, reading for the army at a private tutor's in the neighbourhood, had been invited to fill some minor character. His legs were still his difficulty, but were gradually assuming a military character, a result, probably, of the direction of his studies.

I remember liking them all very much. They were very kind to me, and Mr. Langlands condescended to call me "an infant Roscius." They were vastly polite to Miss Alice and attentive to Miss Tabberer, and appeared to appreciate Cavander highly, having been, it seemed, all of them, well acquainted with him in London. They confirmed his mysterious literary reputation, and put such questions to him as were intended to show the by-standers how much they themselves knew, and to draw some corroborative information out of Cavander. Directly after breakfast "the young uns," under Miss Alice's direction, were to rehearse for an hour, which we did, with as much regularity and precision as if we had been at lessons.

At the end of that time the stage was to be occupied by the "professional person" from town, to whom Uncle Van had been introduced by Pipkison at the "Burlington Baa-Lambs," and who, having already arrived and taken up his quarters at the "Old Whiteboys Inn," was to have the stage to himself to arrange for our elders, with whom he would then spend the greater part of the day rehearsing.

Having finished my task, I was crossing the hall, when I stumbled upon a gentlemen in a grey countrified suit, removing a comforter from his throat, and by his side a young lady most elegantly dressed. Her back was towards me, but at that instant she turned, and the sunlight fell full upon her. Had she come suddenly through the wall on that golden ray, I could not have been much more astonished.

"Julie! Mr. Verney!" I exclaimed, and pulled up suddenly with my hand out—the group looking uncom-monly as if we were playing at some eccentric game of Partridge and Pointers, in which they were the birds and I was the dog, marking them down.

133

CHAPTER XVI.

A CHANGE COMES O'ER THE SPIRIT OF MY DREAM—A COLD
FAREWELL.

IN some old Irish tale, the peasant who has been spirited
away into a sorceress's castle, suddenly takes up a pipe
that he finds lying near him, and commences to play a
lilt. At the first note, Devildom had vanished, and he
was at his own peat fireside, clasping his dear Norah
round the waist. One note of home had done it.

Frampton's Court had been a home to me. Julie represented its good fairy, Mr. Verney the—the—well, I
don't know what he represented except himself, unless at
Frampton's Court he might be considered as a sort of Don
Wiggeroso Pomposo, the comic Chamberlain, who gives
up his grandeur to dance with the King. As a man has
indelibly impressed upon him the stamp of his public
school, or university, like a hall mark, so I had the impression of Frampton's Court on me strongly, and no
desire to be rid of it. It was, to me, to belong to a secret
lodge, a confraternity. I fancy I could pick out a
Frampton's Court man now, could I see one. If a queen
has died with "Calais" written on her heart, can I not
live with "Frampton's Court" engraved on mine?
Whether I can, or not, or whether the material fact be
true (which in any case I doubt), is not to the purpose
here, seeing that Frampton's has been in my heart for
years, worn by time, but not erased. In an instant
Ringhurst Whiteboys had vanished, and I was once more
in my old home.

Mr. Verney himself was the first to break the spell.
While Julie stood by his side, smiling so prettily, he
welcomed me to Ringhurst Whiteboys. Having, in
imagination, previously taken possession of this baronial
residence, it might, from his manner, have been the
property of his ancestors for generations.

"My dear Master Cecil Colvin," he said, waving his
hand gracefully, as if pointing out the beauties of the
place to me, swaying his body gently meanwhile,—" My
dear Master Cecil Colvin, how lovely is this scene! This
is indeed rural and yet baronial, from cottage to court!
and without, what more lovely spectacle to a mind
capable of appreciating the physical beauties which a
Watteau might people, and a Claude depict,"—here he
took breath, recovered his theme, and continued—" Yes;
sir, what can be more thrillingly entrancing than the
ancient face of ever-bounteous Dame Nature, smiling
upon us through her tears, and with the pearl-powder of
last night's masque not yet brushed from her dumpling—
I should say dimpling—cheek ?"

He meant that the snow was still on the ground in
places. But his *lapsus linguæ* had recalled to my mind
Pomona the Goddess of Apples, in Frampton's Court.

"In patches, yes," he returned, for I had asked him if
this were his meaning. "Powder and patches. Dame
Nature in powder and patches, with the trimming of the
flow'ret crocus on her mantilla, and a faint sniff of the
last rose of the previous summer wafted to us from the
somnolescent Flora."

"Have you come to stay here ?" I asked.

"No," he replied in an off-hand way. "I was asked to
superintend the rehearsals of the drawing-room comedy,
in which I have myself taken a part, and know all
Madame Vestris's business in it, from flirting her coquettish
little fan, down to the pointing of her delicate, pinky-
tipped, satin slipper. Your relative, Mr. Van Clym—I am
correct in his nomenclature, I believe—for though I
think I may safely trust myself not to err in any word of
purely Saxon character,—and it is astonishing how the
best educated people mispronounce their own mother

tongue,—yet I am not so certain when I cannot, so to speak, feel my feet—I mean, for example, on the soil of Holland, to which country your worthy uncle—uncle is he not?——"

"Yes."

"Your worthy uncle no doubt belongs. Ahem! I was about to say"—recalling his own attention to his original theme on noticing a desire on Julie's part and mine to start a conversation—"I was about to inform you that I had the pleasure of making Mr. Van Clym's acquaintance at one of those convivial meetings to which your youth yet renders you a stranger—where the voice of jocund melody delights the ear—where the pathetic song gives you *hysterica passio* all down the back, like a flash of lightning on a finger-post—where the feast of reason is enlivened by the play of wit and fancy, with Mr. Pipkison, our mutual friend, in the chair, who introduced me to your Dutch uncle—I mean no offence—and instructed me to the effect, that, if I would not mind running down—metaphysically, for I came by train—to Ringhurst White-boys, I should confer an obligation, increase the circle of friends, and add another five years to my life; by sharing with the feathered warblers the pure breezes toying with the thatches of our English homesteads. Apart from this, they have made it sufficiently worth my while to enable me to bring Julie with me, after a consultation with her mother, who is of opinion that this brief change will vastly benefit our child. The others, thank you, are doing well, and——"

Here he was stopped by a sneeze, so sudden and so powerful, as to have all the effect of a violent shock from a galvanic battery. There was a tremendous report, and then his whole frame vibrated, after which he stood for some seconds, clutching at the wrong pocket for his handkerchief, and struggling as it were with a fiend of sneezing, which had been exorcised, and was now doing his worst, and last, on quitting Mr. Verney's human form.

The noise brought out nearly everyone to inquire into the cause, Mr. Langlands among the rest, who, proud of recognising Mr. Verney as an old theatrical acquaintance

whom he had known " behind the scenes," and who would
assist his own reputation by corroborating his theatrical
experiences, seized upon him at once, and insisted upon his
recovering his equanimity by means of a glass of sherry,
or other refreshment.   Floyd lounging in at this moment
was introduced to Mr. Verney, and then stood staring
heavily at little Julie.   Floyd was, at this time, something
between a raw recruit and a middy.

I was still in wonderment at little Julie—little no
longer, and yet she was not so tall as I—she looked so
much older than she ought to have looked ; and the secret
of this I have since discovered, though, when at this time
she told me the reason herself, I was not sufficiently
experienced to understand her.

" Do you still play in pantomimes," I asked, " and come
out of flower-beds ? "

She was quite indignant with me.

" Oh dear, no ! " she answered, " I haven't done that for
ever so long.   Why, last two seasons I've been in the
opera."

" The opera ? " I exclaimed.

Floyd stroked the down on his upper lip, and regarded
her attentively.

The notion I had of the opera at this time was not in
any way founded upon what I knew of a theatre.   The
opera (I remember this fancy so well) was, to my mind,
some enormous building like the Colosseum at Rome, of
which I had seen pictures, with singers and music and
dancers, somehow, all about, with the irregular regularity
and inconsistent consistency of a dream.

That little Julie, who had played with me, who had
looked over my picture-books, and received some instruction at my hands, who had, moreover, only, it seemed to
me, quite lately been small enough to go into a theatrical
cauliflower or a parsley-bed ; that this little creature
should be, in a long dress of the fashionable style of the
day, with bonnet, and the neatest wristbands, and gloves
to match, telling me of her prowess at the opera, was a
greater puzzle, far greater, than if Mr. Verney had
announced his appointment to the see of Canterbury, and

had walked in dressed in a shovel-hat, knee-breeches, apron, and gaiters.

" The Italian opera," said Julie. " I was one of the pages in the ' Huguenots ' and in ' Favorita.' "

" What ! " exclaimed Alice's voice. She had advanced with Austin unperceived, and had overheard the conversation. Floyd was still caressing the fluff meditatively. No one seemed to take any notice of him. And, after all, he was only a supernumerary in the theatricals.

Stranger still. Comparing Alice with Julie, there seemed to be but little difference. Both were, in my eyes, young women, only that I knew Julie's age.

Little Julie's life, hard work at home, and the necessity of working for her livelihood, had nearly made up the interval of years between them. As I looked from one to the other (for I was confused, and did not know exactly what to do), Julie became less and less ; dwindling away, in spite of her dress and bearing, to the little Julie with whom I had gone marketing to the *à la mode* beef-shop—my Julie, in fact, of Frampton's Court.

" You accompanied Mr. Verney ? " Alice inquired, with some *hauteur* in her tone, while Austin appeared interested in the new-comers.

" Yes," answered Julie, pleasantly.

She was not a whit discomposed, but as much at home, and as unembarrassed, as though she had lived in palaces all her lifetime.

" This is Miss Alice Comberwood, Julie," I explained, blushing.

I loved Julie, but Alice was older and grander. Had the choice been then given me between the two, I should have taken Alice, but should have requested Julie to wait until she was eighteen. In my own estimation I was two years ahead of anyone of whom I had become enamoured. My love gave me the superiority, and, somehow or other, the notion that, in carrying off Alice, I should be a successful rival of Cavander, was at the bottom of it, I believe.

Poor Cavander ! had it remained with me to banish him to the mines of Siberia when I was just on fourteen, or to let him stay in the city, Cornhill would not have seen much of him for some years to come.

" You act ? " Alice asked little Julie, rather abruptly.

" Yes, every night."

" What in ? "

" The first piece."

" Where ?   I mean at which theatre ? "

" The Portico," answered Julie, naming one of the largest metropolitan theatres.

" Do you like it ? " asked Austin.

"Very much.   I have never done anything else."

" I wish I were an actor," he said, regretfully.

Julie smiled. She knew Frampton's Court as well as the Portico theatre.

Alice was annoyed with Austin.

" An actor, Austy ! how can you say so, when you've set yourself on being a clergyman."

It was Alice's pet idea of his future. Austin said that he did not really mean it, which pacified her ; but I could see by her manner that there was something deeper than mere annoyance at her brother's thoughtless wish, when, on being summoned to attend the rehearsal, she left us, and called her brother to accompany her.

"You remember going to the opera last year, Mamma?" she asked her mother, in the front dining-room, a while later on, when I was then watching the performance, and Julie was sitting by what were to be " the wings," talking to Mr. Jakeman.

" Yes," returned Mrs. Comberwood, " we heard—dear me —something new, wasn't it ?—yes : my memory is so bad for names."

" Les Huguenots," said Alice.

" Ah ! of course."

" Do you remember where the queen comes on ? "

" No—yes—let me see—in a sort of barge . . . ? "

" I mean where there are steps, and some women dressed as pages ? "

" Oh, quite well. There were four or five very hand- some young women, and Mr. Langlands pointed out what beautiful diamonds one had on, and told us that there was quite a story about it." Mrs. Comberwood went twice to the opera during the season, and forgot nothing.

" Yes. Well, that's one of them sitting there."

"Where, Alice, dear ? "

"There," answered Alice, inclining her head towards the spot where Julie was seated.

Mrs. Comberwood was vexed. I could not then understand why she should have been; but I remember the fact, as, having overheard the conversation, I felt it incumbent upon me to assist with such information as I could bring to the subject.

" Does your father allow you to associate with—with—these people ? " Mrs. Comberwood asked me, raising her eyebrows.

I was bound to reply that my parent knew nothing at all about it. Whereupon Mrs. Comberwood was of opinion that she ought to let Sir John know. This distressed me. I saw there was something wrong with the Verneys, at least in the eyes of Alice and her mother, and I determined to ask Austin what it was.

Mr. Verney was very great at rehearsal, especially with the ladies, Miss Alice and Miss Tabberer, whom he had to direct. With the gentlemen he was affable, but firm ; with the ladies equally firm, but overpoweringly courteous. When he wanted to show the practical bearing of any stage-direction, he would request Julie to assist him in giving the lesson.

"Stage-management," he said, stopping to lecture, " is an art—an art, I regret to say, almost entirely lost. Thalia and Melpomene may do their best, Apollo may give us his most sparkling tunes, and, to come to modern days, a Garrick or a Kemble may conquer by the force of a genius which would sweep all before it, like Niagara over a dust-bin, and absorb every moving creature in its own exhaustive vortex with the irresistible succulency— I should say, the tremendous suctional power—of the Northern Maëlstrom." Here he paused, expanded his chest, which was swelling out, as it were, with the great notion of the last simile, and beamed on us all round. "But," he continued, "without the stage-manager, what is the use? *Cui bono?* I repeat, *cui bono?* Hamlet may be perfect, but if he be lost in the crowd, or if Rosencrantz and Guilderstein are brought too prominently forward, where is the opportunity for the gifted Roscius? No, sir—pardon me"—this to Jakeman, who was beginning to be a little impatient—"whether it be low-comedy, which I take to be your line, sir "—to Jakeman, who was standing as if waiting his turn to advance in a quadrille—"or light touch and go, Charles Matthews' line, as I take to be yours, Mr. Langlands "—whereat that gentleman gave a mock bow, but was really highly flattered — " no matter whatever it be, stage-management is as much the necessity to our art as the light of heaven to a Michael Angelo at work on his immortal frescoes. Stage-management is the generalship of our art, ladies, and we make our successes as the noble Roman warrior made them, by strategies, which are to the ignorant like a truffle to a bumpkin. The finest picture and the merest daub of a signboard are of equal value in the dark; and Hamlet put out of sight in the Play scene behind Ophelia, instead of in front of her, might as well be in the sixpenny gallery sucking oranges over the brass rail as in such a position as would ruin the chance of the greatest dramatic genius in the world. I beg your pardon, sir. Now let us proceed."

From this specimen it may be imagined what time the piece, which was to last an hour in performance, occupied in rehearsal.

Mr. Verney and his daughter were obliged to leave early, in order to catch the train for town, their engagement at the Portico necessitating their presence there soon after six.

Julie asked me—

"Don't you think me much grown ?"

"Yes, Julie, ever so much."

"I'm not," she answered; "only Papa makes me wear heels, and he will have me dress like a grown-up girl."

"Why ?"

"Because then they give me small parts, and when

you've once played those you don't go back again, and you get more ? "

"Get more ? "

"Yes ; higher salary, I mean.'

She stopped suddenly. At that moment a vague sense of the line of demarcation between us occurred to her. She changed the subject abruptly, and asked me whether I would not like to see her Aunt Jane again.

"Nurse ? " I asked. The word returned to me most familiarly.

"Yes," said Mr. Verney, who was now wrapped for his journey. "She is still a nurse. Head nurse, too, in a very large family. She is superintendent at St. Winifred's Central Hospital, near the General Post Office, where she cheers the pallid invalids like a blooming Aurora smiling on a sickly swede in a kitchen garden." Mr. Verney's similes smacked of the country atmosphere. He asked, "Shall I tell her that you will do yourself the pleasure of paying her a visit ? "

"Yes, please."

" I will. We must make haste, Julie." At this moment Langlands and Floyd entered, and Mr. Verney emerged from the upper fold of his comforter to bid them farewell, and do something in the way of an advertisement.

"We shall see you at the Portico, Mr. Langlands, one night after the Convivial Lambs, where Mr. Floyd will give us the honour of his company." Floyd bowed, and said he should he very happy to renew the acquaintance of Mr. Verney and his daughter.

"Julie, Mr. Langlands, now plays Dolly, in *The Wish*," continued Mr. Verney : "a soubrette's part of considerable responsibility ; something between the Humby and the Vestris in, of course, quite the early days. You will go and see her play one night, I trust. She grips the part, sir "—here he extended his right hand and suited the action to the word—" she grips on the part, sir, with the nip of an irritated panther. You'll be astonished, I assure ye. There's an intellectual grasp about her, sir, that makes you sit tight in your stall, and yet turns you over like a crocus in a whirlwind. Come, Julie.

Good-bye for the present, gentlemen.   Good-bye, Master
Cecil."

"Good-bye; and good-bye, Julie."

When we had last parted, we embraced.   But now, I
was a guest at Ringhurst Whiteboys, and she was playing
a chambermaid in a farce, a page in an opera, and wearing
heels to her boots in order to obtain some addition to her
week's salary.

It was not a parting as of old.

The next day Mr. Verney's visit was repeated, but he
was out of spirits.   His conversation was pitched in
a minor key, his similes were dull, his instruction tame,
and he did little more than merely his stage duty.   He
spoke to me occasionally, and disappeared earlier than on
the previous day of rehearsal.   I asked for Julie, but she
had not accompanied him, and "would not," he added,
"be again required on this scene."   Her absence threw a
gloom over my day, as I somehow felt that I had, indirectly, been the cause of her banishment.   I was for
putting this question to Alice, who, I fancied, knew more
about the matter than anyone else, but, just then, her
attention was fully taken up by the theatricals, and Mr.
Cavander.

CHAPTER XVII.

RINGHURST THEATRICALS—THEATRICALS IN GENERAL—MRS.
CAVANDER—A HAPPY COUPLE—THE PERFORMANCE FINISH-
ED—ANOTHER YOUNG LADY ON THE SCENE—A FAREWELL
TO AUSTIN—I RETURN TO OLD CARTER'S—PREPARATION
FOR HOLYSHADE—MY PROGRESS.

THE theatricals at Ringhurst (for which Mr. Verney was
unable to stay, being summoned to town professionally)
were merely a good specimen of what I have since known
private theatricals to be, everywhere, without exception.
Bustle and hurry; everyone wanting assistance from
everyone else, and wondering at everybody's selfishness.
Laces that have been strong up to within a minute of being
wanted, suddenly snap. Gum, from which, at any other
moment, there would have been no escape, now playing
the unfortunate cavalier false in the matter of moustaches.
The handsome young gentleman, who has to "make himself up" for a lover, fails signally in an attempt to give
himself a beautiful complexion with carmine and bismuth,
and comes down looking uncommonly like a clown. The
agitation of the hand which is to make a delicate line of
black, causes a smudge on the cheek, as if you had commenced a cartoon there with charcoal. The experienced
amateur, who has selected the part of a hoary-headed
veteran, whose grey hairs are during the piece well-nigh
brought down with sorrow to the grave, and who has a
vast amount of stirring sentiment and manly pathos to
deliver himself of in consequence, suddenly, and at the

last moment, appears on the scene with his entire head
apparently fresh from a plunge into the flour tub, with
just so much of it wiped away as will enable him to see
with occasional blinking, which spasmodic movement of
the eyes, however, might be taken for a sign of suppressed
emotion.   The audience, at first, recognize in this extraordinary character neither the experienced amateur, nor
the venerable papa of the misguided youth (a young
gentleman addicted to card-sharping), but laugh heartily
under the impression that it is the comic man disguised,
for some reason or other, as the baker, and salute him
accordingly.

Dresses supposed to be "all right," and therefore allowed
to pass muster without being tried on, are suddenly discovered to be all wrong.   The impossibility of playing
the Young Pretender in the costume of Francis the First
has, somehow or other, to be got over.

Ingenuity comes to the rescue.   Pins are in great
request, and oaths plentiful, with apologies.   Nobody's
drink is secure from anybody who is thirsty.   All are
thrsty.   Everybody wishes everybody else out of the way.
Books have been mislaid, and the Prompter, who has
craftily secreted his, is now waylaid, and has it wrested
from him by some unfortunate amateur, who, in piteous
tones, cries: "Do let me have it, I'll give it you back
directly, *but I have to go on first.*"

Everyone doubts his own appearance, and is full of
congratulations for everyone else, with a view to being
congratulated in turn.   All excitement.

Then the voices won't pitch themselves properly, everybody being more or less inaudible, with the solitary
exception of the Prompter, whose every word can be
heard, causing irrepressible titters among those of the
audience most remote from the stage.   Mr. Boanerges,
whom, ordinarily, you have to request not to speak quite
so loud, comes on to say ten lines of dialogue, and for all
one can hear of him, from the front, he might as well be
performing the part of a dumb slave in a ballet of action,
only that he has about as much action as the old-fashioned
flat wooden doll, with hardly chiselled features and a

black beard, whose arms and legs are moved by one string.

The best memories fail: the over-zealous Prompter gives the word twenty times when the unfortunate actor has only paused for dramatic effect; or he has lost the place in the prompt book, or is giving directions about the lights, just at a critical moment, when the whole *dramatis personæ* have come to a dead lock. These things will happen even in the very best regulated Private Theatricals, and so, I suppose, those at Ringhurst were no exception to the rule. I thought them perfection.

Alice looked lovely as a marquise, and Cavander attended her in the green-room, on the pretence of holding her book, and hearing her her part up to the last minute.

There was a lady looked into this green-room, and, fearing lest she might be on forbidden ground, withdrew, but, as if acting upon a second thought, looked in again to say—

" James—I beg your pardon, Miss Alice—how charming you look—I only want to speak to James a moment."

" Oh, come in, Mrs. Cavander," said Miss Alice, graciously.

Mrs. Cavander had arrived that evening. I did not remember having heard any mention of her before this. At first it occurred to me that it might be Mr. Cavander's mother; but her appearance at once dispelled this notion. Cavander himself seemed to be a little annoyed. I could not recognize, at that time, that Mrs. Cavander resembled the stage-coach, which was very useful in its day, but has been superseded by steam. When James Cavander, years ago, was on the look-out for a lift along the road of life, this heavy vehicle had picked him up, and had helped him on his way.

She was a fluffy woman, with dumpy nails. A bolster tied round tightly with a string, would have had as much pretension to figure as Mrs. Cavander. Her portrait, taken when she was a girl, represents as comely and buxom a lass as any yeoman's daughter need be.

She worshipped her husband, and the object of her

K

idolatry thought her a fool for her superstition.   If she talked of his faults to her confidential friends, it was only to palliate them, and excuse him.   If she came to her intimates with a tale of her being hardly treated, or neglected, she would tell the fact as a fable, whereof the moral was, that James was not to blame, and that she was treated according to her deserts.   At first her friends pitied her, but before long lost patience with her.   She complained, and would hear of no remedy.   She had expended all the spirit she had ever possessed, when she had insisted upon marrying in obedience to the dictates of her own heart.   So she had her money, and went her way. Her father washed his hands of the affair.   She was entitled to a certain sum at her own disposal; but not one penny more would the old man give her.   She invested her property in James Cavander, and Mr. Griffiths, a well-to-do country solicitor, did not approve the speculation.   Betsy, however, was obstinate.   Fluffy people when obstinate are hopeless.   You can't break pillows.   Glass offers formidable resistance, and retaliates cruelly.   A pillow yields with the feeblest opposition. You do not hurt yourself, or it, by offering violence. After a contention in which your pommellings are active and the pillow pommelled is passive, both remain as before —the pommeller having the worst of it.

So Betsy Griffiths insisted placidly on being Mrs. Cavander, and ran away with him: or rather *to* him, for he did not go out of his way to fetch her.   What was the use, if she was determined?   Evidently none; only a waste of time and money.

Mrs. Cavander was now as obstinate as ever.   Not that she was not pliable as fresh putty in her husband's hand, for whom she would have done anything; but this was the effect of her obstinacy, and her obstinacy was the effect of her infatuation.   She persisted in loving him obstinately, with a dumb animal kind of attachment, which is not reasonable affection.

Mrs. Van Clym was a friend of hers.   My aunt congratulated herself on having brought Mrs. Cavander over to her own particular way of thinking in religious matters

This Mrs. Clym called " conversion." She was wrong about Mrs. Cavander, who would agree with any friend, on any religious question, as long as she herself could obtain a listener and a temporary confidant for her own sorrows. At Ringhurst she was mildly charmed with Alice's talk about Gothic churches, altars, vestments, and her sort of enthusiastical mysticism. Alice, in her turn, thought her a convert to High Churchism, and began to see an additional reason for her husband becoming a believer.

Mrs. Cavander with a Wesleyan would have been, negatively, a Wesleyan, with a Catholic a Catholic, with an Irvingite an Irvingite ; in fact, all things to all women, only let them in turn listen to her tale of woe.

" Bah !" said Mrs. Clym, after some experience of her, " she has as much real religion as a pudding."

The truth was Mrs. Cavander had no vacancy in her little mind for such matters. The object of her worship was James Cavander. The cause of her sorrow was James Cavander. She was devil's advocate against him, and then she refused to admit her own testimony, and, finally, canonized him.

" I do hope, Miss Alice," said Mrs. Cavander in the course of conversation this evening, " that you will keep your promise of coming up and staying with us."

James Cavander smiled.

" Then," he said, " we shall be able to continue our arguments. You must come and stay with my wife, as a missionary."

Alice would be delighted, she replied, only Mrs. Cavander must obtain Mamma's consent, for which this amiable wife promised to ask at once. Then, on her husband's arm and satisfied with having done her duty, and at all events pleased *him*, Mrs. Cavander returned to the drawing-room, where the audience were impatiently awaiting the rise of the curtain.

The performance of the juniors went off with great satisfaction to themselves, and we were allowed to come to supper in our costumes. Fatima was considerably taller than her Bluebeard ; but this difference exhibited, in the strongest colours, the mysterious moral ascendancy which Baron Abomelique had gained over his unhappy spouse, and I waved my wooden scimitar over the kneeling Fatima's devoted head (who begged me to content myself with cutting off her locks) with a bloodthirsty air. There was something soothing to my wounded feelings (for since Cavander had appeared I had had scarcely a word from Alice) in having her at my mercy, even in a play, for a few minutes. If Garrick in a rage was six feet high, I, in this scene, was conscious of at least seven years, and eighteen inches, having been added to my life, and my stature.

As for Alice, she was the centre of attraction. After the performance, everyone crowded about her, and compliments were showered on her from all sides.

Cavander simply congratulated her, and left her to be worshipped.

He knew that the morrow was for *him.* Our party staying in the house had been swelled by our theatrical friends, who were to leave on the day after the performance, and by the Cavanders, who were to stop on for some little time. The Cavanders were Mr. James, his wife, and sister. The last was a brown-haired, mild-faced girl, many years younger than her brother, whom she only faintly resembled in her eyes. She had not been long away from school, so Austin told me, and, but for her brother's success in the City, Miss Cavander would have had to turn her education to some account, perhaps as a governess. Indeed, I have since heard that, for various reasons, which I should not have understood then, but do now (as also will those who peruse this record of our family), Mrs. Van Clym had, at one time, entertained the idea of engaging James Cavander's sister as governess for my cousins. Cavander himself had heard of the offer, and had not forgotten it. It was, of course, declined, with such expressions of good will, and esteem, as ordinary civility, and the relative positions of the parties, required.

Miss Cavander played the piano with great skill, but without much feeling. There was just that difference between her style and Alice's. Alice played partly from ear, partly from notes, never for show, always from liking. Miss Cavander performed as if she were invariably playing something that no one else could attempt, which, faultless in execution, should create about as much sympathy in the hearers, as a schoolboy's Greek declamation on a speech-day. Her finger-tips turned upwards, and her nails always seemed as if they had just come from under the scissors. She dressed neatly, and appeared homely, which, interpreted by society, means more or less stupid; though Miss Cavander was only apathetic, until she thought her own interests involved, and then, somehow or another, she managed to have her own way, without getting off her chair, or allowing her ordinary occupations to be for one instant interrupted. To sum her up once and for all, Miss Cavander was an Influence, all the more powerful because unsuspected. Once admitted into a family she seemed to mingle with the atmosphere, and impalpably to pervade the entire household. And this description will be found to hold good when Miss Cavander shall be encountered once more, later on in this story. As she had nowhere else to go, she lived at her brother's, where she was a check upon Mrs. Cavander, and of considerable assistance, for domestic purposes, to Mr. James.

The time at last came for separation. Austin was not returning to Old Carter's. I was going there for one quarter more. Holyshade was then my destination, and Austin, whose health was delicate, was to be accompanied by a private tutor to the south of France.

We cried bitterly at parting, and promised to write frequently.

Carter's had changed. Mr. Venn had gone, some of the elder boys had left, and so had some of the younger ones.

This roll-call after an absence is repeated throughout life; and when the next long vacation is over, whose place at the desk will be vacant? Through whose name shall the black line be passed? What expectant junior shall occupy the position that was so lately ours? There were plenty of empty places now at Old Carter's, and I looked forward, with pleasure to the end of my time at this ill-managed school, where I had learnt little, except the stories of most of the Waverley Novels from my dear Austin Comberwood.

My attention was now given to what I was told I should have to do at Holyshade. The two Biffords had preceded me by more than a year, but they were far more advanced than I when they left. Carter's, however, did not profess to prepare for Holyshade especially, so, as it subsequently turned out, what I had managed to pick up was of very little use to me, when I came to take my place in one of the upper forms of the great public school.

My father had made all the necessary arrangements, and I was to board at the Rev. Mr. Keddy's. Thenceforth my father considered me a man. He gave me a watch, and allowed me, as by right, to dine at late dinner with him and his friends.

Now commenced my education in earnest. In my father's idea to be a Holyshadian was to be privileged. It was, to his thinking, who knew as little about Holyshade as he did of Oxford or Cambridge, a sort of degree conferred upon a boy, giving him a certain kind of status in society, which could be generally described as "making a man of him." It was a sort of esquireship leading to knighthood.

The bachelor parties were frequent, but my father spent two nights a week regularly at the Cavanders. Cavander and he were inseparable; but though I saw more of this gentleman, I did not dislike him less, nor, as I have reason to believe, did he me.

CHAPTER XVIII.

I ADOPT A FASHION—ASSISTING IN MAKING A MAN—SELF-IMPORTANCE—THE VERNEY GIRLS—TO ST. WINIFRID'S—A VISIT OF CEREMONY—MR. SWINGLE AND THE CRUMPETS—THE ACCIDENT WARD—I COME ACROSS SOME OLD ACQUAINTANCES IN A STRANGE WAY—I SEE ONE FOR THE LAST TIME.

I NOW began to disdain jackets. I knew that many years must elapse before my plumage would develop into a tail. Being possessed of liberty to roam London at will, and money to spend at pleasure, I used often to saunter up Oxford Street and admire the garments in a ready-made clothes shop, where I had seen a pea-jacket, on which I had set my heart. It appeared to me to be a compromise. It was not a tail, nor was it a short jacket. So in the process of making a man of myself I bought this garment for seven-and-sixpence, and walked home in triumph with it under my arm. I was a trifle nervous of meeting any member of my family. The next day I waited until my father had gone into the City, to put it on; and in order that I might run no chance of his seeing me in the course of the day, I cunningly inquired of him at what hour he considered his return probable. To this he answered that Mr. Cavander was going to dine with him at home earlier than usual, in fact at half-past five o'clock, as they were going to see some *new* play, to which if I chose, I might accompany them: only, if so, I must be

back, and ready dressed at the same time as the dinner.
With this offer I at once closed, and made up my mind
to forestall their arrival by half an hour, so as to get out
of my new jacket, and into my ordinary one, before they
should come in to dress for dinner.   My time for return
I therefore fixed for half-past four.   I turned up my
collars to represent stick-ups, and tied my sailor's knot
in a large bow, and feeling that, somehow or other, I
was trying to make a man of myself, experiencing at
the same time a half-conviction that I was probably
making an ass of myself, I determined to brave the
world's opinion as far as the top of Oxford Street and
back ; and so, with no particular object in view, except
that of seeing how I liked, and how other people might
like, my new clothes, I sallied forth.

I crossed the Park, and came out at the Bayswater
end of Oxford Street.

At this moment I saw two young ladies most elegantly
dressed.

A Colvin is, as I have before hinted, a sort of lightning
conductor, where the glances of fair women are concerned.   " It was," as the song says, " ever thus from
childhood's years."   The two young demoiselles who
had attratcted my attention turned out to be Miss
Carlotta Lucille and Julie Lucrezia, who scarcely recognized me in my nondescript costume.   I blushed considerably on meeting them, and devoutly wished myself
back in my own proper dress; that is, at first, as they
seemed to speak to me with some slight coldness and
reserve, as though perhaps they considered me in the
light of a Boy Detective, in disguise, for the purpose of
taking juvenile delinquents.   I do not know whether
detectives are thus educated from childhood, but I should
say not.   Yet if the office be an important one to the
safety of the community, surely a Training College for
Detectives might be capable of valuable development.
Julie informed me that they were just returning from
a visit to their aunt, my Nurse Davis, at the hospital,
which, if I felt inclined to call, I should find not very
far off, and thereupon they gave me full and particular

directions. They were glad enough to be quit of me; at least Carlotta Lucille, who was magnificent, certainly was, as she did not care to be seen walking about with such an absurb bundle of clothes as I must have seemed. Carlotta was still with Madame Glissande, and, as a matter of business (for Madame taught all the best people in town), was attired in the height of fashion.

I determined to go and show myself to Nurse Davis, who, I felt sure, would be as proud of me as I was of myself. Besides, I should be able to tell her about my having to go to Holyshade at the end of the holidays. So I said good-bye to Calrotta and Julie. I should have liked Julie to have come with me, but as that could not be, I strutted off alone to St. Winifrid's Central Hospital, which I found without much difficulty.

There were a number of steps up to the front entrance, and it seemed to me like going into a show. I remember experiencing a feeling approaching awe on first visiting the Polytechnic Institution, where, I know, I for a long time considered the lecturers as representing the highest scientific attainments of the English nation. I, perhaps, had my doubts as to the exact chair, in this learned body, which should be occupied by the Professor of Dissolving Views, whose voice sounded awfully from nowhere particular in the surrounding gloom; but from the first moment of my witnessing a startling experiment with a glass jar, some hydrogen, and some oxygen, out of which (I mean the experiment, not the jar) the Professor issued cool, calm, and triumphant, I placed the Chemical Lecturer on the highest pedestal, and mentally elected him to the Mastership of the Polytechnic.

I fancy that what brought the Polytechnic to my mind, at St. Winifrid's Hospital, was a kind of beadle, in a chocolate-coloured overcoat, with a gold band round his hat, who was on duty, behind a glass window at the entrance.

"What do you want?" he asked, opening a small pane and looking out suddenly, probably under the impression that I was an accident of some sort, rashly taking care of myself until I could obtain surgical aid.

"Does Mrs. Davis live here ?" I inquired mildly.

"Mrs. Davis," he repeated, dubiously, either on account of the name being strange to him, or because there were so many Missuses at St. Winifrid's as to make the selection of one particular Missus a considerable effort of memory, or because my pea-jacket and stick-up collars did not inspire a man in his position with much confidence as to my ulterior objects in asking for a respectable matron on that establishment. Whatever might have been the reason of his hesitation, he considered for a few seconds, and then asked cautiously—

"What do you want her for ?"

"I want to see her," I replied, innocently, resenting such unwarrantable curiosity on his part.

He touched a bell, and then whispered into what seemed to me to be a thing like an elephant's trunk sticking out of the wall.

The elephant's trunk snorted something by way of reply, whereupon the beadle, turning to me, said—

"What name ?"

"My name ?" I asked.

"Yes," answered the beadle sternly, frowning as though he had all along suspected me of some attempt at introducing myself into the hospital under an *alias.*

"Master Colvin," I replied.

"Master what ?" he asked, still frowning. He was evidently of opinion that, in my next answer, I should manage to contradict myself, and so expose some deeply-laid plan for robbing the donation-box, which his sagacity had been in time to prevent.

"Colvin," I repeated, and I am sure he was disappointed.

The beadle told this as a secret to the elephant's trunk, and in return the elephant's trunk conveyed the information that Mrs. Davis would be "with me directly; would I step in and sit down ?"

I had scarcely time to avail myself of this polite invitation, and to ingratiate myself with the gradually thawing official, before Nurse Davis, in a grey dress, with the neatest possible cap, wristbands, and collars, entered by a side door, took both my hands, and gave me a kiss.

The kiss, which made my cheeks tingle for a second, partly because I did not like to be treated as a child before the chocolate-coloured beadle,—who, the moment previous to my nurse's appearance, had been on the point of handing me the paper in order that I might read the political questions of the day,—and partly because I had been, for some time, unaccustomed to this mode of salutation, completed the beadle's thawing, and warmed him so much that he unbuttoned his coat so as to let the human sympathy in his breast have freer play, put his hands into his trousers pockets, and allowed his features to relax into an approving smile, expressive of his approbation of the proceedings, so far, generally.

"He's my boy, Mr. Swingle, he is," said Nurse, proudly stroking my hair. "I've always called Master Cecil my boy; haven't I, dear?"

I nodded, and she continued, just to show my importance in the world, and her own position with regard to the aristocracy, "How is your good father, Sir John?"

The beadle raised his eyebrows, and became deeply interested.

"He is very well," I answered.

"Not married yet?" she asked.

"Married!" I exclaimed, almost indignantly, though I really did not know why; "no, of course not."

"Of course not," she returned. "It would not be fair. If you should ever have a stepmother as was not inclined to be as kind as she ought to be, you'll know where to come to, won't you?"

"Yes, Nurse," I answered, understanding her to mean that I was to seek her for consolation. The beadle seemed to wish to be comprehended in this invitation, but said nothing.

"Now you will come and see my room, and if you're not above taking tea with your old Nurse——"

I stopped her at once by laying hold of her arm. Mr. Swingle ventured to make a suggestion.

"If a crumpet would be any assistance," said Mr. Swingle, "I've a couple here, and can send Jim out for a cake, Mrs. Davis.

"If you can spare 'em," said Nurse Davis, "and it won't be robbing you."

Mr. Swingle assured her that in his attitude towards muffins, crumpets, and such like articles of tea-cake confectionery he was a perfect Gallio, inasmuch as "he cared for none of these things," and that therefore he was in no way to be credited with the merit of a bounty in presenting them to Mrs. Davis's tea-table, where they would be thoroughly appreciated, and, he sincerely trusted, perfectly digested. Not that he expressed himself in this form; he simply said—

"You're welcome, Mrs. Davis. I don't hold with such things myself, except occasionally, as being a trifle puffy. They agrees with some," he added, "but what I say is, wholesome is as wholesome does."

Whereupon we took the crumpets, and Jim, an errand-boy, having answered the summons, Nurse Davis gave him a shilling, for which he was to bring back a pound-cake flavoured with citron, to which Nurse remembered me to have been, in bygone days, peculiarly partial.

"I'll just see to the tea-things, for I didn't expect a visitor, and come back, Master Cecil. You won't mind staying here with Mr. Swingle, will you?"

"No, I'll stay," I answered, whereat I fancied Swingle quite brightened up. Had I left him to accompany Nurse, I am convinced that man would have become a misanthrope: he would have ceased to believe in gratitude, and would have lost all confidence in the sincerity of youth, and the purity of its motive.

"Plenty of life here," said Mr. Swingle, putting a chair for me, so that I could kneel on it, and, placing my elbows on the window-ledge, could look out on to the busy thoroughfare. "Plenty going on all day: 'busses, cabs, carts, carriages, all sorts. Wonderful few run over, considering."

"Run over by carts?" I asked.

"Yes," he returned, "by carts, or some vehicles. 'Orrid careless most on 'em is. Casuals come in circles, so to speak. At one time there's a run on broken legs, then on arms, then heads. It's a head's turn now."

He stood behind, looking over me and propounding his theory quite cheerfully. It was the widest part of the street opposite the hospital ; and in the middle of the road, like an eyot in a river, was a small paved piece, in the centre of which was a lamp-post surrounded by four ordinary posts at the four corners, bearing altogether some resemblance to the arrangment of skittles, the lamp being the king. It was an island of refuge for old ladies, a breathing space for the adventurous, a place of observation for the cautious, and a sort of Roman camp for a policeman.

Across the road, on the farthest side from my window, stood at the edge of the kerb a flauntingly dressed woman. She had but just arrived, and her extraordinary actions were attracting the attention of the bystanders. She was evidently addressing them, and waving her parasol to the crowd already increasing rapidly.

Suddenly running towards her, came a respectably dressed man, who on approaching, began to remonstrate with her, and tried to induce her to enter a cab which he had hailed. She refused, and, scarcely able to walk steadily, made a dart forward into the road, right in front of the cab, with a view as it seemed to gaining the paved refuge. At that same instant, a horse, whose reins had been dropped by the driver on his jumping down from his cart, suddenly took fright, and dashed towards the very spot for which the unfortunate woman was already making. A shriek of horror arose, audible in our room, as the wretched creature, in her struggle to free herself from the man who had frantically seized her arm in order to drag her away, fell sideways, in a heap, right under the cart, the wheels of which passed rapidly over her head and legs, as the horse, maddened by the yelling and shouting, galloped headlong towards Oxford Street, and the man, who had in vain tried to avert the catastrophe, fell forward, unhurt, on the pavement of refuge.

In another minute the insensible form of the woman, crushed and mangled, was borne into the accident ward of the Winifrid Hospital. A crowd hung about the steps, and were disposed to resent any attempt at excluding them from the building, as an infringement of their rights as citizens, and as unfair to those who had found her, and had helped to carry her in.

Nurse Davis passed anxiously down the plain unfurnished passage, carrying a bottle and glass. I followed nervously, and entered the casualty ward. Two young surgeons were examining the wounds, and I heard the dull, heavy sound as of a person groaning in sleep.

"No hope?" inquired a man's voice that struck me as familiar.

"None," was the surgeon's reply. "She may live half an hour; she may live half a day. It is improbable that consciousness will return. You know her?"

"Yes," the familiar voice replied in a hard tone. "I regret to say, yes." After a pause it said, "I should like to send a message."

Nurse Davis indicated the writing-table.

I was standing by it, unable to obtain more than a glimpse of the dying woman, and feeling very sick and nervous. Towards this table the man with the familiar voice turned quickly.

It was Mr. Venn.

We stared at one another. It all at once occurred to me that I had seen him with this woman twice before. *Now*, in encountering him, I recognised her. It was she who had stopped me at school: it was she who, with Venn, had met Cavander in Kensington Gardens. I was not, therefore, so surprised, as I otherwise should have been, at his first question to me, which was—

"Do you know where Mr. Cavander lives?"

"Yes."

He thought for a second, then he said, "Is he likely to be at your father's?"

All that I had intended as to my return home flashed across me.

"Yes," I answered; "he will be there to dinner at five. He dresses there."

"They may be back before that," observed Mr. Venn,

hastily writing a few lines and enclosing them in an envelope. " Take this at once and return."

Mr Swingle saw me into a cab, and carefully gave the necessary instructions.

Neither my father, nor Mr. Cavander, had as yet arrived. They were expected every minute. In the midst of all this hurry and excitement, I remembered my jacket, and changed it for my ordinary attire. Understanding that Mr. Venn expected me to return, I left the note on the hall table, and was driven back in the cab to the hospital.

On reaching it I found my father's brougham already at the door, and in the casualty room stood my father, with Mr. Venn and Mr. Cavander, besides the surgeon and Nurse Davis, whose arm was supporting the heavily breathing, helpless figure on the mattress.

Once—it was the only time I could look at her—I saw her head roll slowly, from side to side, as if in mute agony ; I saw her glassy eyes open on to the hopelessness of life for the last time. Then from her heaving breast came forth a deep sigh, heavily laden with the weariness of sin and misery, a sigh, pray God ! of the poor soul's contrition, a sigh of eternal gratitude from the penitent, laid at last to rest in the arms of Divine compassion.

Dead.

I heard Mr. Cavander saying, that, having known the poor woman in better circumstances, he would be answerable for any expenses that might be incurred. This was to Mr. Venn. My father sat apart for a while, pale and motionless, with his eyes fixed on the covered corpse. He did not seem to notice my presence. Nurse Davis placed a glass of wine before him, but he only inclined his head slightly.

An official book was in Mr Swingle's room on a desk, in which the name of the deceased, and whatever particulars were requisite, had to be entered. The man whose duty it was to make such entries put one of these necessary interrogatories to Mr. Venn, who appeared lost in thought. Mr. Cavander touched his elbow, to recall him to himself. Mr. Venn, as if he had not understood the inquiry as addressed to him, looked up, and the question was repeated.

He answered, with a strange sort of nervous hesitation—

"I beg your pardon. The event has shocked me considerably. She was a connection of mine by marriage. I had not seen her for years. She was, latterly, occupying apartments in the same house with myself." Here he gave his address.

"Her name ?"

"Her name ?" repeated Mr. Venn, as if putting the question to himself.

The window of the glass screen of the porter's room was open, and before it my father paused for a second, as Mr. Swingle opened one of the front folding doors leading on to the steps.

The man's pen hovered above the page as he looked up, over his shoulder, at Mr. Venn, awaiting his answer.

My father turned his head quickly towards Mr. Venn. Their eyes met, and were withdrawn instantly. Mr. Swingle pulled open the door, and as my father was passing out, Mr Venn, in a firmer tone than he had hitherto used, answered—

"Her name was Sarah Wingrove."

CHAPTER XIX.

HOLYSHADE AND THE HOLYSHADIANS.

THE incident mentioned in the previous chapter closes, as it were, the first book of this present chronicle of the Colvin Family. To retrace my pathway through My Time, and to note carefully what I have done with it, has been a task forced upon me by circumstances, with which, in due course, my readers will be made acquainted.

We are now arrived at the second part of my narrative, which commences at Holyshade College, the most celebrated of our public schools.

To be a Holyshadian is to be impressed with the guinea stamp of currency for life. Enrolment among the glorious band of Holyshadian youth has in it, not to speak it irreverently, something resembling, what is termed, "the character" of Orders.

Once a Holyshadian, always a Holyshadian. Boy and man, the Holyshadian is supposed to bear the indelible mark of the grace conferred.

For to be a Holyshadian *does* confer some special grace; —the grace in question, as far as I am able to ascertain anything certain on this matter, being that of an easy, gentlemanly deportment. This grace then, if my presumption is correct, is of the exterior, visible to the world. It remains, as a rule, even to the most interiorly graceless Holyshadians. The disreputable Holyshadian is, in comparison with other disreputables, as Milton's Lucifer, Son of the Morning Star, to the other fallen angels. A

L

swindler who has had the advantage of a Holyshadian education, has in his favour far greater chances than all other
swindlers.   A Montmorenci may cheat you out of five
pounds, where a Muggins couldn't do you out of a brass
farthing.

The pride of Holyshade, as a public school, is to produce—Gentlemen.   Scholars if you will, Christians if you
can ; but, in any case, Gentlemen.   Yet the veritable
aboriginal Holyshadian is *ex officio* a scholar.   He is on
the Foundation, which means that his education is
bestowed on him by way of charity ; and, in order that
the aboriginal may never forget this, he is clothed differ-
ently from those who are not on the Foundation, wearing
a coarse sort of college gown winter and summer, and
being fed and boarded according to certain ancient rules.
These birds of like plumage flock together, and do not
consort with the noble strutting peacocks, called Oppidans,
save occasionally, and then on sufferance.

These veritable Holyshadians have for their nest the
grand old rookery called The College.   The Oppidans
have built without the precincts of its walls, but within
the bounds of its domain.   The number of the Collegers
is limited.   The Oppidans are to them as seven to one.   It
seems as though the Collegers, like the Indians of South
America, had gradually yielded to the advance of the
white skins : the white skins representing the aristocracy.

A barbarous and uncivilized set were at one time, and
that not so very long ago, the aboriginal "Tugs," as these
poor Collegers were called, in allusion to the sheep whereon
they were, traditionally, fed, and which they were supposed, being half famished, rather to "tug" at and tear,
like hounds worrying, than to eat soberly and quietly, by the
aid of those two decorous weapons of well-fed civilization,
the knife and fork.   The epicure who invented the knife
and fork must have been well able to wait for his dinner.

Yet, theoretically, this Tug tribe holds the post of
honour.   Their chief is *the* Captain of Holyshade ; the
chief of the Oppidans having but a brevet rank : being,
like a volunteer, only Captain by courtesy.

The Collegers are, by right, Royal scholars, just as the

actors at Drury Lane are Her, or His, Majesty's servants. In consequence, there were privileges. One of the inestimable privileges enjoyed by the aforesaid comedians, was, I have been informed, the right to a dinner at the Royal Palace daily; and Messrs. Clown and Pantaloon, if only *bonâ fide* members of the Drury Lane Company, would be only in the due exercise of their prerogative, were they to walk down to St. James's Palace, call for the chief butler, and order chops for two to be ready hot and hot with mashed 'taters and bottled stout at half-past four in the afternoon, so that they might be in good order for performing in the evening's pantomine. Such privileges as these have fallen into desuetude : actors are no longer the monarch's trenchermen; they have suffered loss with many another institution; and Holyshade in its old age, like the faded mistress, once Queen by a royal caprice, can boast only of favours, which, in time past, she was wont, so regally, to confer. There still are some privileges, but of late years they have been sadly, but tenderly, shorn of their glory, and the gates of even their particular paradise, St. Henry's College, Cambridge, once for the entrance of only the Holyshadian elect, are now thrown open to all the world. True, there are yet some reservations for poor Holyshadians, as there are for a few nobly connected, at the aristocratic College of All Souls, which, by recent enactment, due to a liberal policy, has well-nigh passed into the hands of All Bodies.

Of all such matters of schools, of colleges of All Saints, and Universities of All Sinners, my father knew nothing. All he had to do was to send *me* to some place, or places, where they would "make a man of me;" which in his view was, as I have said, a sort of degree.

Had he mixed with his equals in rank, who would have been ready enough to welcome him, I should probably have benefited by his enlarged experience. But he preferred his own pleasure, in his own way, his own sociable gatherings of City friends, and his own circle of family relationship. Left to himself, Sir John Colvin, of an old title, might have played an important part in society. But he was no more his own master than is the vessel

obeying the turn of the helm.   Whose object it was to
sail him round and round this wretched pond, letting
him think that he was making progress on the sea of life,
will be gradually evident, as it is to me now, in the course
of this history.   My father worked for my future, and for
the best, as *he* viewed that future.   He had been brought
up in a money-making school, to consider a good per-
centage the one thing necessary.   From this bondage he
had emancipated himself so far as to have started me with
very different ideas.   From one extreme he went to the
other.   Business had been everything to *him;* it was to
be nothing to *me.*   Yet, in his inexperience of all walks
of life which were not within the City Labyrinth, he
imagined his son taking the highest position to which a
commouer could rise, by such mere sharpness and quick-
ness as might serve for answering a conundrum, or for
uttering the flippant sort of jest that, at that time, passed
for true wit among the *habitués* of Capel Court.   Labori-
ous study, or application to one particular line, never
entered into his vague scheme for my preferment.   He
knew nothing of the existence of scholarships, fellowships,
the attainment of high degrees, and other similar in-
centives to the study of the various branches of learning,
and, consequently, he was unable to question with my
instructors, or to go over the ground with myself.   He
showed himself not in the least interested in my schooling,
and so I came to look upon school-time only as a pleasant
enough interval between the vacations, my one aim and
object being to devote these intervals to the cultivation of
as much enjoyment as my supply of pocket-money would
permit.

The cuckoo places its egg in another bird's nest, being
ignorant of the art of hatching.   By a cuckoo-like instinct
my father placed me in nest after nest, belonging to other
birds, in the hope, perhaps, that I should turn out an
eagle.   Alas! hatched and fledged, he found me still of
his own brood.

My new nest was not in the College Rookery at Holyshade, but among the fine Oppidan birds.

Not having been specially trained for Holyshade, as I

have before said, I had to begin at the beginning. The beginning was the Fourth Form Lower Remove.

After, what I may call, my Comberwood Christmas holidays, I went to Holyshade. I did not anticipate meeting any friends there, except the Biffords, who had been with me at Old Carter's. I was an utter stranger to the boys of the place, and found myself isolated.

It was a raw, dull day, and wretchedly cold, when my father took me to Holyshade, and introduced me to my tutor, in whose house I was to board.

The Rev. Matthias Keddy was a lanky disjointed-looking person, with a clerical white neckerchief, so untidily twisted as to give its wearer the appearance of having been suddenly cut down in a stupid attempt at hanging himself; an idea which his way of holding his head very much on one side, and his nervous, confused manner generally, tended strongly to confirm. On seeing me for the first time, he grinned, always with his head askew, as if focussing me in a favourable angle, laughed, and rubbed his right hand through his toused-looking hair, by way of preparation, before offering it for my acceptance.

"Well," he said, squeakily, "how-de-do? Hope we shall be good friends."

I hoped so too; but neither of us seemed particularly sanguine as to the future. His voice bore the sort of family resemblance to that of Punch, that might be expected to come from Punch's nephew on the Judy side.

My father surveyed us both benignly. He had nothing to say as to classics, or mathematics, as to school hours, training, or, in short, as to any subject connected with my educational course. He had brought me down there himself, and, I imagine, felt himself somehow out of place, beginning, perhaps, to wish he had confided me to a clerk, a butler, or an uncle, or to anyone who would have relieved him of this responsibility. After politely declining Mr. Keddy's proffered hospitality of sherry and biscuits, my father was about to take leave of me, when Mr. Keddy, who had been staring at the tip of his own boot, as he rested his foot on the fender, suddenly squeaked out—

" Would you like to see your boy's room, Sir John ? "

" Thank you," said my father, with an air of great satisfaction.

My poor father! he had been troubled about many things just at this time, whereof I was then, of course, profoundly ignorant, and he was too glad to be quit of me, for a time, to be at all critical as to the lodging provided for me. I think, too, he was as much puzzled by this first view of Holyshade as I was, and, on the whole, was confusedly impressed by the atmosphere of the place.

An elderly maid-servant conducted us to a passage on the first floor. On both sides were ranged the boys' rooms, looking like a corridor in a miniature model prison.

The third apartment, on the left, was to be mine.

It was neatly furnished, with a small table, a turn-up bedstead, a cabinet, containing in the upper part two or three bookshelves, in the middle an escritoire, while its lower part was divided into three drawers. In a corner stood a common wash-stand. The room looked, with its bright fire lighted in joyful celebration of my arrival, snug and cheerful enough, and I was so highly delighted and taken with the notion of having a room, at school, all to myself, that I was really only half sorry when I saw my father drive off in his fly, in order to catch the express for town. He was going to spend the evening with the Cavanders.

I felt a choking in my throat and a difficulty in bidding him farewell, which I was fearful of his noticing, lest he should set down this ebullition of emotion to cowardice, and should depart hopeless of my ever being made a man of, and despairing even of the efficacy of Holyshadian treatment. Uncle Van has since told me that he talked of me and of Holyshade, for several days after, whenever an opportunity occurred ; from which I have inferred that the choking sensation at the moment of bidding adieu was not solely confined to *my* throat. My father loved me in his own peculiar way ; and as all the Colvins will insist in doing everything in their own peculiar way, so neither of us at this time at all events was any exception to the rule. By his example I was brought up to under-stand that any show of affection was childish, and had better be restrained in its very commencement. Such a check is as dangerous to some constitutions as is a sharp frost in May to the promising fruit-trees.

Only some of the lower boys had returned. This information I received from my tutor's butler, a jolly, round, and red-faced man, with a square-looking nose, named Berridge, who always seemed to me to smell more or less of oil, and was perpetually in his shirt sleeves cleaning glasses. After him came George, a livery servant, a good-natured lout, who looked as though he had been torn from the plough and shoved into a swallow-tailed dirty-yellow livery coat, with flat metal buttons, in which costume he bore a striking resemblance to a very big bird.

These two carried my boxes upstairs, and assisted to cheer me, not a little. I took possession of my cupboard-like apartment with a new feeling of proprietorship. It was all mine every inch of it. Here I could do what I liked: just exactly what I liked. As a commencement, I made myself free of the place by the simple, but expressive ceremony, of poking the fire. The fiery coals answered to the poker, like a fiery steed to the spur. The fireplace and I warmed to one another, and Mr. Berridge's face reflected the glow, and beamed on me, encouragingly.

"You'll want," said Mr. Berridge, thoughtfully, while I was laying out my wardrobe, "some candles and a lamp for your room."

Of course I should. I had not brought them. I had overlooked this, as well as various other necessary articles of furniture.

"That's no matter," said Mr. Berridge, kindly; "you can get 'em all here easy enough. You'd better have 'em of me. All the young gentlemen does."

Certainly anything that every other Holyshadian did, must, I concluded, be right.

"A candle-lamp is what you want," continued Mr. Berridge, decisively, "with a nice glass shade."

I thanked him for his consideration. I had seen a candle-lamp in Old Carter's study.

"You won't want it just yet," said Berridge; "I'll bring it you in a *hour's* time about."

That would do. In fact, at that moment anything that would have suited Berridge, even a cut-glass chandelier, would have suited me.

"I'll put a candle in for you," he said, "and you'd better have a packet o' Palmers besides."

By all means. This was my first venture in lamps and candles. I felt as if I were about to give a party.

"Then that's all at present," said Berridge, looking round, cheerfully. "You don't want nothing else, I think, just now. Sarah, that's the maid, will bring you your kettle and tea-things, roll and butter. When the other young gentlemen come back, you'll mess with some one."

He gave one look at my small hamper, wherein our cook at home had stowed away a tongue, a cake, and a pot of strawberry jam.

There was such pleasure in anticipation of a meal all by myself, *in my own room*—an idea I could not sufficiently enjoy—that, at first I really had no wish to go out of doors.

Mr. Berridge returned, in about half an hour, bringing with him the lamp, candles, and a box of matches. It was a very bright affair, of slightly gingerbready material, I'm afraid, with a ground-glass shade.

To one unaccustomed to its use it was comparatively dangerous, as, if in attempting to put a candle in, you didn't screw the top on, which struggled and resisted on its own account with quite remarkable power, the candle flew out, as if discharged from a catapult, and either broke something, or smashed itself against the wall, or ceiling, greasing the carpet in its fall. It was, therefore, some time before I mastered this firework. It was a deceptive thing, too, as the candle always appeared the same length, and when you were in the middle of a most exciting story, there was a sudden click, a sharp vicious sputter, and, the next instant you were in darkness.

However, as a commencement towards housekeeping, it served its purpose, or rather it served my tutor's excellent butler's—Mr. Berridge's—purpose, who, being a chandler by trade, and having a lamp and candle shop "down town," was naturally disinterested in recommending this admirable invention to my notice. I paid Mr. Berridge five shillings and threepence for it, and he, condescendingly, gave me a receipt.

Berridge's only chance of profit was, I subsequently found, with the new boys. When the old ones returned, and we became acquainted, one of the first questions was, "Got one of that old humbug Berridge's lamps?"

Berridge must have taken a secret and peculiar pleasure in these transactions, as, in spite of their having done considerable harm to any future dealings, he never omitted a chance of passing off one of these lamps on a new boy, apparently in preference to doing a steady and regular business with us throughout the year. The master and townspeople, however, dealt with him largely, I believe, and this, therefore, was only, so to speak, a little "fancy retail trade."

I suppose it was my loneliness at first at Holyshade— and I was the more solitary on account of no longer having such a companion as Austin Comberwood had been to me—that developed in me a taste for diary-keeping. I was then in my fourteenth year, and, until I had friends to talk to among the Holyshadians, my great amusement was to keep accounts of time, doings, and expenditure, to write to Austin, occasionally too receiving and answering a letter from Miss Alice, and making up for Austin's absence by applying myself to the study of the best novels within my reach.

I soon got accustomed to all the miseries of the Lower Fourth Form. The candle-light dressing, the raw mornings, the shivering little wretches in the old oak-panelled school-room, dimly lighted by guttering tallow candles stuck in iron sockets, the master as irritable as he was drowsy; in short, the whole sickly farce of half an hour's duration, at the end of which, the great clock struck its welcome note, and we tumultuously rushed forth to throng the pastrycooks' for coffee, hot buttered buns, hot rolls, or rusks and butter.

I have no doubt, now, but that the coffee was gritty, thick, and, with the unwholesome greasy buns, not worth the matutinal outlay of fourpence.   But of all refreshments whereof I have partaken at all times and in all places, I do not remember—with the single exception of the hot soup and the *demi-poulet-rôti,* at Calais, after the sea-voyage—anything so acceptable, or which so thoroughly served its customer's purpose, as those same buns and coffee at Bob's, Poole's, or Stepper's, in the old Holyshade Lower Fourth days.

When, afterwards, I had attained a higher form, we took our coffee later, and patronized, chiefly, Stepper's, which was frequented by the fastest and biggest Holyshadians, on account of such luxuries as hot sausages, grilled chicken, and ham and eggs, being served up in the back parlour by the fair hands of the two sisters, Louey and Dolly Stepper; the latter being what we used to consider a "doosid fine girl," and a great attraction to the more adventurous among those who wore the manly tail and the single white tie.

Apropos of costume, stick-up collars were never worn. I remember one innovator who came out with them.   He braved public opinion for a day, attempted to lead the fashion, but, finding tradition and custom too much for him, he gave in, and followed it with the rest.

Our dress was black jacket and black tie, in a sailor's knot for small boys; and black coat and white tie, without collars, for the big ones.   All wore hats.   A Holyshadian Fourth Form boy's hat would have made Christy rejoice: the necessity for a new hat would have been so evident to that eminent tradesman.   It was to my hat I owed my sudden leap from the status of a nobody into that of a popular celebrity.   How this chanced I will forthwith proceed to relate.

CHAPTER XX.

SHOWING HOW SOME HAVE GREATNESS THRUST UPON THEM—THE EPISODE OF MY HAT.

HOLYSHADIAN initiation begins with hat smashing.

When I appeared in the cloisters for the first time, well-nigh friendless among all the boys (for, as yet, I had only made a few acquaintances at my tutor's), waiting the egress of the masters from their solemn conclave in chambers, I was surrounded by some not much bigger than myself. They gradually swarmed. Never before did I see so many boys all at once; and of so many sizes too. Such a humming and buzzing about me, as though I had been a drone trespassing at the entrance of a hive. They came upon me one by one, two by two, threes, fours, as birds do from all quarters to a large crumb, and then began pecking.

"What's your name?" asked a boy.

"Colvin," I answered, peaceably.

"Calvin!" shouted a bigger idiot, wilfully mistaking my pronunciation.

"Hallo!" cried a third. "Here's Luther!"

At this witticism, there was a burst of laughter, in which I feebly attempted to join, just to show I was equal to taking a joke, even at my own expense.

"*What's* your name?" inquired another earnestly, as if really asking for information.

"Colvin."

"Then take that, Colvin," he returned, illogically, smashing my hat over my eyes.

"How are you, Colvin?" shouted twenty different voices at once, and while struggling to set my hat straight, I dropped my book, and was hustled from one to another, being passed on with a kick, a hit, a pinch, or a cuff, as occurred to the particular fancy and humour of the boy to whose lot I happened, for the moment, to fall.

"Where's your hat, Curly?"

I did not know. Scarcely had I placed it on my head, and begun to take breath, than at a blow, from some skilful hand, it disappeared into the school-yard.

"Bully! Bully!" was then the cry.

I perfectly agreed with the sentiment. I considered that I *had* been grossly bullied, but I could not understand why those who were shouting so loudly "Bully!" should be *the* very ones to run viciously at my unfortunate hat, and treat it like a football.

In another second I saw it sky'd up into the air, when, its line of descent being suddenly inclined at an acute angle by a playful breeze, which could not any longer keep out of the sport, where a hat was concerned, it comfortably fell and settled itself, in rakish fashion, over the crown which adorned the head of the Royal Founder's statue, that stands, with a ball and sceptre (it had better have been a bat) in its hands, on a pedestal in the centre of the College quadrangle.

This incident was greeted with such an uproarious shout, as brought the masters out of chambers sooner than had been expected. Aware of this result, a malicious boy in the crowd, pretending great sympathy for my exposed situation, offered to give me a back over the railings which surrounded the figure. This I accepted, and had scarcely got myself safely landed inside the barrier, when a fresh sort of hubbub arose, and I saw the boys shuffling off in gangs towards different doors in the cloisters, while most of the masters, all in academical costume, an entire novelty to me, were standing in a corner, apparently puzzled to account for the recent extraordinary disturbance, which had not yet completely subsided.

One of these was an old gentleman, something over the middle height, with white hair brushed away behind the ears, and bulging out at the back from under his college cap. His face was of a somewhat monkeyish type, for his forehead receded sharply, and his upper jaw was heavy and protruding, his features being as hardly cut as those of the quaint little figures carved out of wood by a Swiss peasant. He used golden-rimmed eye-glasses suspended round his neck by a broad black ribbon. He wore a frill which feathered out in front, suggesting the idea of his shirt having come home hot from the wash and boiled over. His collar and cuffs were of velvet. He invariably stood, and walked, leaning to one side, out of the perpendicular, as if he had been modelled on the plan of the Tower of Pisa.

This was Dr. Courtley, Head Master of Holyshade.

"Bleth my thoul!" lisped Dr. Courtley, holding up his glasses, and almost closing his eyes in his efforts to see distinctly. "Bleth my thoul! Whath that?"

He pronounced his "a" very long and very broadly, giving it the sound it has in "hay."

"A boy, I think," said a squat, sleek master, with a mouth like a slit in an orange. I subsequently learnt that this was Mr. Quilter, the most severe of all the tutors, the development of whose smile varied in proportion to the magnitude of the task which he might be setting as a punishment. He was a rigid disciplinarian, but strictly just, and never accused of favouritism.

"It is," chirped a third, a dapper little man in such tightly strapped trousers that walking seemed almost impossible. When he had uttered his opinion he sniffed, put his head on one side like a feloniously-inclined magpie, and having smiled at his neighbour, and been smiled upon in return, he appeared satisfied. His name I found out in time was Mr. Perk; he was familiarly known among the boys as Johnny Perk.

A stout, ruddy-faced, clean-shaven master, with a very low vest, and a college cap right at the back of his head—purposely put there on account of his great display of forehead—stepped from the group, and shouted brusquely—

"Here! hi! you sir! Come here, sir!"

"Please, sir, I can't, sir," I replied from my prison.

I was very unhappy.

"Can't!" exclaimed the brusque master. "You got *in* there. Eh?"

"Please, sir, I came in for my hat."

"Come out with your hat, then," retorted the master impatiently.

"I can't get it, sir," I urged, plaintively. "Please, sir, the statue's got it on his head."

All eyes were now turned upwards. In another second they were all grinning.

"Bleth my thoul!" said Dr. Courtley; "I knew the proper place for a hat wath over a *crown*—but—he! he! he!—hith Maathethty in a lower-boy'th hat—an inthtanth of *thub tegmine fagi*—eh!"—he looked round at his companions, as, in uttering the quotation, he made the penultimate syllable short, and the "g" hard, for the sake of an academic pun. His assistants were of course immensely tickled. Three or four groups of boys, still hanging about their schoolroom doors, waiting the arrival of their respective masters, passed round the joke about "faggy" and *fagi*, and Dr. Courtley was gratified by youthful appreciation.

In the meantime the Doctor's servant, Phidler, of gouty tendencies, and a scorbutic countenance, was shuffling towards me with a ladder.

"You get up," he said, gruffly, when he had fixed it, firmly resting on the railings, and reaching up to King Henry's head.

I obeyed, and fetched down my hat. I heard a slight cheer, which, as in a court of justice, was immediately repressed.

"Come here, sir," called out the portly master with the intelligent forehead. As I was approaching, I heard him saying to his dapper companion, "Like Pat Jennings—'regained the felt, and felt what he regained,'"—whereat the Mr. Perk smiled, and moved off, being followed into a distant room by a troop of boys.

I had some idea that I should be expelled, or at least flogged there and then.

" What part of the thchool are you in ? " asked Dr. Courtley.

" Lower Fourth, sir."

" Take off your hat," he said ; for in my nervousness, and forgetful of the presence in which I stood, I had quietly replaced it on my head.

" Who threw your hat there ? " he went on.

" I don't know, sir," I answered, adding by way of satisfactory explanation, " I've only just come here this half, sir."

" Whatth your name ? "

" Colvin, sir," I answered, almost expecting him to make a jest of it, and perhaps some further rough treatment from the three masters who were still with their superior. To them he turned, saying, in a tone of genuine annoyance—

" It'th iniquitouth ! really motht iniquitouth ! It'th an old barbarouth cuthtom I thould like to thee abolithed. You will if you pleathe ekthpreth my opinion thtrongly, motht thtrongly, on what I conthider to be thith motht ungentlemanly conduct—motht ungentlemanly—and I thall ekthpect whoever had a hand in thith to give themthelvth up, and come to me in Upper Thchool before twelve o'clock."

The masters bowed, and walked away to their several departments. Dr. Courtley then beckoned to a big boy, who, with a slip of paper in his hand, was going from one door to another.

" Præpothtor ! "

" Yes, sir," answered the boy so addressed, advancing hat in hand.

" Thow thith boy, Mathter Colvin, where the Lower Divithion Fourth Form ith athembled, and then go round to all the Divithions and thay that I ekthpect every boy who wath contherned in thith motht ungentlemanly, and motht unjuthtifiable, protheeding, to come to me in Upper Thchool by twelve o'clock."

" Yes, sir."

" You can go," said Dr. Courtley, dismissing me ; and away I went at the heels of the Præpostor, along the cloister, through a dark archway, and up a broad flight of stairs.

"Do you know who knocked your tile over the rails?" asked the boy, stopping when we were out of Dr. Courtley's sight and hearing.

"No."

"What's your name?"

"Colvin." I began to wish I could vary the answer.

"Where do you board?"

"Keddy's."

"Oh, Punch's. Old Keddy's called Punch," he explained.

"Oh!" I said, pleased to find that such liberties could be taken with a master's name.

"My name's Pinter," he continued, "Pinter major. I'm in Upper Remove. My minor's just come. In your form."

"Your minor?" I repeated, humbly, for I had'nt an idea what he meant, and really thought it was some allusion to the mining districts, or perhaps to some young lady, whose name being Wilhelmina had been abbreviated to Mina, of which I remembered an instance in the case of the sister of one of Old Carter's boys. It puzzled me, however, to think how Miss Mina Pinter, if there were such a person, could be in my form at Holyshade. I was too frightened to ask him any questions.

"Yes," he replied, not appreciating my difficulty. "You'll be next to him, most likely." "Him" meant his minor, and certainly of the masculine gender.

He now opened a large door and removed his hat. I followed his example. An indistinct hum of voices fell on my ear, with a strong one occasionally predominating. We were in Upper School, in the first division of which, cut off from the next section by heavy red curtains, sat the Lower Fourth Form boys, engaged in construing to a tall master.

The præposter pointed out a seat to me, but before I took my place the master asked—

"What's your name?"

"Colvin, sir," said I, very hot and uncomfortable. Whereat there was a titter.

Then the Pinter major (Pinter minor *was* next me, and was his younger brother—I soon discovered that, by boldly asking him *his* name) delivered Dr. Courtley's message, which was frankly announced by the master to the boys.

At this there was no titter. On the contrary. Only a quarter of an hour more schooltime remained (the eleven o'clock school commenced at ten minutes past, and lasted till a quarter to twelve and sometimes till twelve), and nearly ten minutes of this was occupied by an official inquiry into, what might now be termed, "Colvin's case."

So many had had a hand in, or a foot at, my hat, that, on Holyshadian principles of honours, everyone feeling himself affected by the charge, offered himself on this occasion.

This happened in all the Upper School forms from the Middle Division Fifth downwards, until the story of My Hat began to assume the form of the familiar alphabet which recounts the history of "A was an apple-pie." B had bumped at it, C had cut it, D had danced on it, E had egged others on, H had helped them, I had injured it, J had jumped on it, K had kicked it, and so on.

Thus, by twelve o'clock, at least sixty or seventy boys were waiting, with me, to hear what the Head Master had to say to them.

They were summoned to the furthest part of the school-room, where Dr Courtley, standing in a sort of reading-desk, received them.

He was very strong on the "barbarity and brutality of thith protheeding, and athtonithed that any Englith gentlemen could have been guilty of thutth a blaggaird—yeth, he would thay thutth a blaggaird acthun. He withed it to be clearly underthtood that Mathter Colvin had named nobody"—no great merit on my part, by the way, as I was unacquainted with a single name, except Pinter's and the Biffords', whom I had not yet seen—"and therefore," continued Dr. Courtley, with severe emphasis and with considerable dignity, "I trutht there will be no mean or bathe attempt at retaliathun; but I intend to

M

mark my thenthe of thith ungentlemanly conduct, by an impothithun. You will write out, and tranthlate——"

What it was to be I lost, as Pinter major, who was attending, officially, as the præpostor charged with the delivery of the Doctor's message, whispered to me that I should at once ask old Smugg (Good heavens! even Dr. Courtley had a nickname!) to remit the punishment. He urged me so strenuously, that plucking up a prodigious amount of courage, I stepped forward, and addressed the Head Master in a husky and tremulous voice.

" If you please, sir——"

" Hey, What 'th that ?" said Dr. Courtley, putting up his glasses in utter astonishment. He could not at first ascertain exactly whence the voice proceeded. Having satisfied himself on this point, and focussed me by squinting down his nose, he asked as if impatient at the interruption, " Well, what ith it ?"

" Go it !" whispered Pinter major, prompting me behind.

I felt that all eyes were on me, and I did more than warm with my subject; I glowed with it into quite a perspiration, and, adopting Pinter major's whispered advice, I determined to " go it," or, as it were, die on the floor of the House.

Looking up at the Head Master, I made this remarkable request :—

" If you please, sir, will you let them off ?"

Dr. Courtley considered. I was trembling with agitation.

" Well," he said, slowly, " it'th a noble thing to athk. It'th the part of a gentleman and a Chrithtian. I conthent."

As if by inspiration a hearty cheer was given.

The Docter held up his hand. " But mind," he went on, " never let me hear of thith again. If I do, depend upon it, ath it'th a dithgrathe to the thchool, it shall be motht theverely punithed. Now you can go."

No sooner had he disappeared, which he did by a side door as rapidly as possible, than the delighted boys insisted upon "hoisting" me, a peculiar Holyshadian fashion of celebrating the triumph of anyone of their boating heroes, and closely resembling the old ceremony of chairing a member, or an Irish crowd's method of elevating, on their shoulders, a popular counsel, after the successful issue of a State Trial.

I had begun that day at Holyshade without a friend; before the night I was hand and glove with the whole school.

But I made no friend here like Austin Comberwood, from whom I heard about the middle of the half, informing me that he was leaving England for his health's sake, and was to be accompanied as far as Nice by Mr. Venn,. who was to act as his private tutor for some months to come.   Austin added that he thought Mr. Venn had obtained some appointment abroad, and intended to live on the Continent.   I was more interested in reading that Alice was, just now, the guest of the Cavanders, than in any news about Mr. Venn.

CHAPTER XXI.

LIFE AT HOLYSHADE—AN ESTIMATE—HOLYSHADIAN MORALITY
—ENJOYMENT—AIDS TO LEARNING—A HOLYSHADIAN BOY'S
DIARY—FAGGING—THE ORDEAL—A PROSPECT.

I HAVE no hesitation in recording the fact, that, if I was
not the best boy at Holyshade, at all events I was not the
worst.   Like Lord Nelson, I could say primly, as far as
the Holyshade code went, " I have not been a great
sinner."   But I am equally bound to add, that I do not
hold in high estimation the Holyshadian code of social
morality, unless I am called upon to admire the justice of
a thief who shares his plunder with his companion in the
theft, and refuses to compromise his honour by turning
Queen's evidence.

It was said by them of old time, that no Holyshadian
would tell a lie, and that, therefore, any master could rely
upon a Holyshadian's " honour as a gentleman."

I say that the honour depended on the circumstances.

When Tulkingham major, who could fag me, ingeniously
branded my new bureau with my initials, using for that
purpose the red-hot pocker, did I give up his name to my
tutor when he demanded it ?   No.   Why ?   Because I
thought I should get the worst of it with Tulkingham.

The boys themselves, with a keen sense of humour, had
a graduated scale of honour, which was represented by the
following formula :—

" Will you take your oath he was ten feet high ? "
" Yes."

" Will you take your dying oath ? "

" Yes."

" Will you bet sixpence ? "

" *No.*"

The Holyshadian youth was taught to pay some deference to authority in the hours of study, but he was likewise taught, that, in play-time, this same authority is a half-sleeping dog, which, as it is dangerous to approach, it is necessary to avoid.

Thus the Holyshadian learnt that there were bounds beyond which he might not venture.

He was told, for example, that boating on the river, beyond these bounds, was permitted, nay encouraged.

To be on the river was allowable ; to be caught going *to* the river was punishable. Therefore the object of the boy, bent on enjoyment in a boat, was to get out of the way of any master whom he might happen to see on his way down to the river. The boy had to " shirk," that is, to dodge into a shop, or behind anything, anywhere, out of sight of the master. The latter knew it to be all nonsense ; the former knew it too. Like the augurs, they would have laughed had they met. The Holyshadian Moral Code was easily summed up in one commandment, " *Do what you like as long as you are not found out.*"

But I shall presently state a case which roused all Holyshade at the time, and not Holyshade only, but the municipal authorities of the City of London, and two boys, two Holyshadians, whose guilt was known but to a select few, held out in the face of rigid examination and cross-examination, were proof against surprise, and thus it happened that, finally, Falsehood triumphed, and Vice was triumphant. Of this later on.

For my part, I took Holyshade as it came ; and for me, after the first year, it came pleasantly enough.

My father never seemed to expect any learning from me, and was perfectly satisfied with my improved appearance in the holidays, when at Easter and Midsummer he took me to the Opera, which was an enormous treat. I did my best to prove myself worthy of this advancement.

If Holyshade can do anything for a boy, it can do one thing, and that is, make him independent.

Whether this be for his advantage 'or not, is for the consideration of the Holyshadians generally. I answer, that, as the system was in my time, this independence was a disadvantage.

Practically, out of the actual schoolroom, the Holyshadian boy was his own master, and could do, within certain limits of time, just exactly what he pleased.

I am told that Holyshade is improved now-a-days. I am glad to hear it. It needed improvement. From what I have been able to gather from present Holyshadians, however, I am inclined to think that, in spite of some studies having been rendered compulsory, and official encouragement given to novel athletic sports, the *morale* of the place is very much the same as it was twenty-five years ago, and as it was twenty-five years before that, and as it will be, while the circumstances of its present existence remain unaltered, to the end of its time.

Only Holyshadian masters ruled over Holyshadian boys. They knew therefore by experience what was going on under their very noses, but satisfied with results which had placed them where they were, and provided for themselves and their families for life, they did not intend to open their eyes to the fault of the system, or to own themselves wrong, where they had the credit, from outsiders, of being in the right. They pointed with pride to the names of Holyshadian worthies, but were loth to admit that each Worthy would have been worthier under better moral guidance. That these have become great men is no proof of the system's excellence; that they have, in some instances, been good Christian men is certainly irrespective of it.

I remember busts of some of these Worthies arranged along the walls of the Upper School. Ghastly objects they were, with their dirty white faces, blank eyes, and dusty double chins, stuck up on brackets as though to warn the thoughtless youth against following in their footsteps, along the road to fame, which would bring them to this complexion at last.

Clerical Holyshadians, of the Tory High Church type, used to point with pride to a modern Holyshadian Worthy in the person of a Missionary Bishop, whose energy of character and physical capacities would have stamped him as remarkable in any profession. He was invariably spoken of, with much shaking of heads and uplifting of eyes and hands, as "Apostolic." The Holyshadians, who used this term, being pressed for an exemplification of its appositeness to this eminent Worthy, usually fell back on tales of the hardships and fatigues endured by their schoolfellow, and were never weary of narrating how his Holyshadian training had been of the greatest use to him in—swimming rivers. I do not think it was ever said that he received his strongest religious impressions from Holyshadian teaching.

I soon discovered that the Colvin nature was admirably adapted to the Holyshadian constitution.

Money was no object, apparently, not even to the tradesmen, who were kind enough to allow an almost un-limited credit. This was generous on their part, as it involved a risk. The tutors signed orders for clothes and books with the openhandedness of those liberal spirits who have *carte blanche* to deal with others' money.

I found myself in a new world, with a paper currency, and means at hand of obtaining present enjoyment, without the drawback of immediate outlay.

There were clubs, there were social gatherings, there were, in fact, all the appliances at hand for forcing the young ideas, and turning growing boys into men before they were half through their teens.

The Holyshadian was, at a very early stage, initiated into the wary use of those miserable short cuts to know-ledge known as "cribs." Better to have plenty of time for breakfast and tea, and five minutes for the preparation of lessons, than a few moments for either meal, and half-an-hour of careful, painstaking study. It was a simple plan. One boy took the "crib," and read from it slowly, the others seated about the room following him with the utmost attention, and each writing down with a pencil in his own book, any word which there was a chance of his forgetting.

As to the science of making Latin verses, why, it was clear that, as every Holyshadian, in my time, was compelled to make verses, whether he had any taste for the employment or not, anyone, stupid or clever, could make verses. If stupid, he would do stupid verses; if clever, clever. After a year and a half of this, a boy would be indeed a dunce if he had not mastered the knack of treating any theme in Ovidian metre, from the Birth of Minerva to the Reform Bill. Was there not a *Gradus ad Parnassum,* with a perfect store of epithets, which you could pick and choose at will, and fit in to measure? But, for the Holyshadian too stupid, or too busy with any of the various amusements, boating, billiards "up town," cricket, and so forth, to have any leisure for prose themes or Latin verse, what was he to do? Nothing—but to come to an understanding with someone to perform these learned exercises for him. In short, with a few honest, hardworking exceptions, mainly among the Collegers, the whole school was employed in getting the maximum of enjoyment with the minimum of work, out of Holyshade. They were fine dashing fellows, placed there to commence an acquaintance with those with whom they would either have to mix by right of birth and position, or with whom they might hope to be associated by good luck; and as to learning—well, if they picked up enough of it to pass creditably among some who knew no more, and others who knew less than themselves, that was sufficient, provided only they were gentlemen, and, this being granted, they might be what else they liked compatible with respectability.

Mathematics and modern languages were beneath a Holyshadian's notice. They were included among the "extras," as were also music and drawing. My personal and peculiar acquaintance with the properties of a triangle was limited to what I had seen of it as a musical instrument in a regimental band, or in the orchestra of a theatre.

The religion of Holyshade was a dull Respectability,

hallowed by the external surroundings of antiquity. It was a "made" wine in a genuine cobwebby bottle.

Chapel-time on a whole holiday took the place of school-time. It had this advantage, that it required no preparation. It had this disadvantage, that it effected nothing for individual benefit.

How impressed has any visitor been on seeing that grave old Mediæval Chapel for the first time. What Holyshadian has not delighted in the sweet strains of the anthem sung by fresh young voices, and felt his heart throb at the rejoicings of the Hallelujah resounding beneath that glorious roof? Yes, for a moment he has seen the stones instinct with life; for a second, he has heard the echo of the past, and has mistaken it for the voice of the living. Another minute, and the grey stones are again inanimate, the momentary throb of life had ceased, the clanging doors are shut, and the echoes are once more homeless.

The time-mellowed colours of the venerable stained glass window, over the spot where once stood the altar, dye the sun's rays as they pass through to fall, in richly-toned patchwork, upon the chancel floor,—a variegated woof as unreal as the mere sentimentalism of religion. Save for this the chapel is cold and drear: for all that made its glory and its life in the past, left it three hundred years ago, and all who gave it animation but half-an-hour since, are in the play-fields, or on the river, rejoicing in their liberty. Well,—in after life the majority will find out how they have been educated only to enshrine Respectability, and, seeing, that, in the long run, this worship is the least irksome, and the most generally accepted, they will contentedly bring up their children in the practice of the same rites and ceremonies.

Apart from the highly instructive sermon in chapel, which those boys who had watches were accustomed to time anxiously, the sole approach to anything like a religious moral training, was, that on Sunday afternoon, or evening, a class had to read an abridgment of Paley's "Evidences of Christianity" in "Pupil-room" to their tutor. Paley's, in fact, were the only evidences of living

Christianity in the place: the chapel and the College itself were monuments of a defunct Faith. It can be easily imagined how interesting this study was to a set of boys, from fourteen to sixteen, who would have willingly sacrificed to Jupiter (being on familiar terms with the heathen deities) for the sake of the hour's leisure, whereof Paley had deprived them.

Austin Comberwood wrote to me frequently, and through him I commenced a correspondence with Alice.

Deprived of my friend's recitals of Scott's novels, I developed a taste for light literature, and, inspired by Alice's " Blue Beard," I composed a drama on a story in a book of romantic legends, called "Chess with the Devil." About this time I began to keep a diary, and though separated by distance and by age from Austin, our friendship grew stronger and stronger. I told him everything concerning myself in my letters to him, a confidence which he was not slow to return. Alice, too, honoured me beyond my years with letters, which in after times were important, as voluntarily conferring upon me a sort of fraternal right to assist and advise, where assistance and advice were possible from one so much her junior in every way.

I find an entry in my diary, dated September 19, after I had been a year at Holyshade :—

" *Whitledge came for subscription to the Chapel Window. Humbug. Wrote to Governor for one pound. Will give less if I can. Subscribed to the Football and Field. No letter from Alice. Nor from Austin. Bad. Not heard from Governor for an age. Finished Charles O'Malley. Capital.*

" SUNDAY.—*Hot and fine: went for a walk with Bifford mi. Met Uncle Herbert. He said he was only down for a day. Gave me seven and sixpence. Glad of this, as I am rather low in pocket. Thompson ma. offered me five shillings for my buttons. Shan't sell them till I am very hard up. Old Jugson's not quite so strict as he was.*

" MONDAY.—*Had a magnificent game of football. Worked like bricks. Got one shin. No letters again to-*

day : horrid bore that. Put in a lottery for a set of camelian (West's) buttons. Bill got 'em. Sarah came to put my light out. Baited her by lighting it again. Good night.

"TUESDAY.—*No letter from Governor. Letter from Austin, at Boulogne in France. He begins to speak French. I don't. Hate extra work except for going out at night. Lark.*

Another day :

"*No letter. Pulled up to Squigley after four. Hunted swans coming back. Nearly swamped in locks in Bill's outrigger, and so obliged to go in Parry's tub. Left Bill in the lurch, and hunted swans coming back. Dead tired.*"

Here is a sequence :

"*So tired from yesterday's events I overslept myself, and went into school late, for which I got sixty lines of Long Ovid. Came back. Letter from Alice. Fryer came to-day for music lesson. Bore. What with fagging, music, and work for my tutor, I could only get five minutes for breakfast. Not much play for me to-day. Go to my tutor at a quarter to seven, and after twelve, and do a pœna after four.*"

Another extract :

"*Pulled up with Hipworth mi. Hall steering. We've taken a chance boat.*"

This meant paying a certain sum to the proprietor of boats for the month or the week, and taking the chance of getting any sort of boat. It was a popular method with those who had not had boats built for them, especially towards the end of the boating season.

Extract continued :

"*Pulled up in three-quarters of an hour, then coming back hunted swans. Fun. Must get order for jacket and things to pay Small's bill. Capital dodge. Alpaca overcoat to be cut into smoking coat and in-door coat. Amalekite and coral studs at Dick's. Small will let me have onyx buttons for ten shillings. Reading Devereux. Bother, here we are at the beginning of another regular week. No letters.*"

The "regular week" meant one without a whole and a half holiday in it.

As to the fagging, how I remember crying over the first toast I ever made in obedience to my master's command. I had not got a toasting-fork, and so was obliged to stick the roughly-cut piece of bread on a knife, and having wrapped a pocket-handkerchief round my hand, I knelt down before the fire to do my best. I roasted my face, and in changing my attitude dropped the slice into the ashes. Finding that I was unobserved, I picked it up, dusted it, replaced it on the knife, and continued the operation. To my disgust it suddenly became charred in the centre, while the bread remained perfectly white, but very dry, around the one black spot. One side being a comparative failure, I turned it, and hoped for a more successful result. In changing its front, however, it perversely glided off the knife, and fell once more among the cinders. Having carefully dusted it with my pocket-handkerchief, and blown off such specks of coal-dust as would have been fatal evidence against me if called on to assert that no accident had happened to it, I rather impatiently began again. To secure it from further tumbles I rested the point of the knife on the second bar, and anxiously watched the browning process, which was very slow.

At this moment Gulston, a boy about my own age, ran in to say that all the fags had been dismissed, and that Leigh, our master (a boy in the Upper Fifth, to whom with other young slaves I had been allotted) had said I was to be sent to him at once. Thinking that the toast might help itself in my absence, I piled a dictionary and a lexicon on the fender, which supported the handle of my knife, while the point of the blade remained on the bar of the grate. I should not be absent long, and doubtless it would be ready on my return. I went into his presence trembling.

His "mess" consisted of three : himself, Dampier, and Crossland ma. They had each two fags, and so their table, at breakfast and tea, was admirably served by six boys, who made the tea, the coffee, the toast, and cooked such delicacies as could be got out of sauce-pans and frying-pans in the way of a kind of washy omelette, excellent fried eggs, and buttered eggs (a superb dish by the way), fried ham, and chicken. Fags learnt something which was of considerable use to them when they arrived at that no-man's ground known as the Lower Division of the Lower Fifth, where there was rest at last, where the Holyshadian could neither fag nor be fagged; where, having served his time, he could enjoy himself, attending to his own luxuries and necessities.

" Where's the toast ? " asked Leigh, who was waiting with some potted meat on his plate in anticipation of a choice finish to his tea.

" Not quite done," I replied, trembling.

" Bring it," he said sharply, while his two companions eyed me suspiciously.

I returned to my own room where I had been experimentalizing. There was a strong smell of burning. The toast was smoking, and in another minute would have been unfit for human food. I rushed at it, landed it on my table, ingeniously scraped it with my knife, dusted it once more with my pocket-handkerchief, and tried to flatter myself that Leigh would be too glad of the toast to scrutinize details. So I stuck it on the knife, and reappeared before him.

" Hullo ! " he exclaimed, while the two others laughed. " What's this ? "

" Toast," I answered.

He did not attempt to touch it.

" You have been scraping it," he said, looking first at it, then at me, with the eye of one experienced in such matters.

" Scraping it," I echoed innocently.

" Yes. Don't tell a lie about it. Haven't you.

" I did—just—only—a—little," I replied, feeling that the supreme moment had arrived when I should be immediately ordered off to be tortured and executed.

" It's been in the cinders, hey ? "

" No, not in the cinders," I answered, wishing to be very particular as to the exact truth.

"Then what did you scrape it for?" he asked, naturally enough.

"Because it did not fall in the cinders—only in the fender," I replied, with an attempt at a conciliatory tone.

"Oh, indeed!" said Leigh.　Then turning to the others, he asked, "Is it to be the Chinese punishment, or the ordeal of the fork?"

They voted for the latter.　I did not know what was in store for me, and so my pent-up feelings gave way, and I burst into tears.

"Oh, don't—please—I—couldn't—help—it—I never —toasted—before!"

My supplication was unheeded.

"Put your hand on the table, palm down, spread your fingers out," said Leigh, sternly.　I obeyed convulsively.

"Now," he went on, "the ordeal of the fork will teach you to toast properly in future."

Then he took a fork and jobbed it down four times in rapid succession in the four spaces between my fingers, spread out on the table-cloth.　It was exciting, and I must say he exhibited considerable skill and dexterity in performing this feat about ten times, only prodding me, and that purposely, on the last occasion, when I cried out sharply, and was immediately told that in consequence of this ebullition I must receive the toasting-fork bastinado, which consisted of three thwacks from the prong-end of that switch-like instrument.

This I bore with Spartan courage, and, at its termination, I was about to quit the room, when Leigh called out, "Now, then! I didn't tell you to go, did I?"

"No."

"No fag can go without being told.　Stop where you are."

"Let him do another bit on the toasting-fork for practice," suggested Dampier.　Crossland ma. cut a slice off his loaf.

"Go and do it properly," said Leigh, presenting me with the toasting-fork, and taking care to give me a cut across my hand with it.　Whereat I winced, but grinned.　Thus was I being educated, socially, by the martyrdom of fagging.

Once back in my own room I gave way. I thought of home, of Ringhurst, of Austin, of Alice, of what they were doing at this time, and of the happy days I had spent there. I thought of Nurse Davis, little Julie, and the dear old days past and gone, of Frampton's Court, and it seemed to me as though my friends and acquaintances were one and all standing around me, bemoaning my suffering and degradation. Then, suddenly remembering the ordeal and the bastinado, and fearing lest the mysterious torture, alluded to as "the Chinese punishment," should be in requisition for my particular case, I braced myself up to the work, and produced such a highly finished work of toasting art, as sent me back to my master with an air of conscious pride. They had ended their meal, and paused in discussing some project of amusement to examine my *chef-d'œuvre*. It was so satisfactory, that Leigh informed me I might have it for myself, and forthwith dismissed me.

And this was my first experience of fagging at mess. I have nothing to say against the system. On the contrary, I praise it on the whole, as practised at Holyshade in my time. Its abuses were rare, and were resented at once by the upper boys, themselves masters, on a fair representation of the state of the case being made to one of their leaders by the injured party.

I remember only one instance of cruelty. One of the Sixth Form, a Colleger, maltreated a small lower boy, Oppidan. Immediate action was taken. The Oppidans about six hundred, invaded College in a body, headed by the Oppidan Captain, and demanded the surrender of the bully, who, however, had effected his escape by a back staircase. In the meantime, the masters, having got wind of what seemed to be the commencement of an insurrection, assembled for rapid consultation, and strategically cut off the return of the forces, by posting themselves at the head of every landing in College, where, the doors being only opened wide enough to admit one at a time, no boy could pass without encountering one or two authorities in their official dress, to whom he was obliged to render up his name and address.

Dr. Courtley summoned the whole of the Sixth Form, and himself, having heard the details, undertook the punishment of the offender. The school returned to its duties, and all went on as peaceably as heretofore. But it had been an awkward time. The boys were in the right, and the masters were, fortunately, sensible men: but one overt act, on either side, might have seriously affected the gravest Holyshadian interests.

Pleasantly enough, and carelessly enough in all conscience, my time now passed away at my tutor's, until an incident, of a rather sporting character shortened my career at old Keddy's, and was the cause of my being thrown once more among some old friends, of whom for some considerable time I had lost sight, and of my being present on a certain occasion, which was of more importance to me, in the future, than at the time I could have imagined possible.

CHAPTER XXII.

WHAT WE DID TO A SWAN—WHAT THE SWAN DID TO US
—SOME HOLYSHADIAN CHARACTERS—A CHANGE—A VISIT
—SOME OLD FRIENDS—A FRESH STEP IN THE STORY.

IT occurs to me at this point to ask myself whether a child should be carefully blind to his grandmother's faults, as so many Holyshadians appear to be to those of their Alma Avia ? For if the University be their Alma Mater, Holyshade College must be thus dignified.

Am I, as an Englishman, whose boast is that he lives in a free country, to protest that there is no better system of educating youths than that adopted at Holyshade ? Britons "never, never, never, and never, for ever, will be slaves;" and the Holyshade plan leaves them to themselves, as I have already shown. If enslaved at all, they become slaves to themselves, to their own wills, to their own pleasures. My father was perfectly correct in his instinct as to this public school "making a man" out of the materials furnished by parents. But what sort of a man was to be turned out ? Formed in the Holyshade mould, they were "men" of fifteen and sixteen, among whom there might, at rare intervals, be found a youthful Daniel living as if in the midst of Babylon, a Tobias in Nineveh, or a Thomas of Aquinas in the school at Naples. But the representatives of Daniel, Thomas, and Tobias, at Holyshade, were the objects of practical joking and derision. And they certainly were not lively boys, nor did anybody give them credit for genuine piety. They

N

were only taken notice of to be kicked, or ignored contemptuously as sanctified humbugs. We, as boys, took much the same view of such pietists, as was the fashion among the luxurious pagans of the old Roman Empire, *en décadence*, in regard to the austere early Christians.

Had Austin Comberwood been at Holyshade, I am certain he would have been the true model for a Holyshadian; for, he was religious without cant, ready to sympathize with all amusements, though not strong enough to take an active part in them himself; he was cheerful without being boisterous, and to the literary tastes of a scholar, he added the application of a student, while his natural sedateness was tempered by a sense of humour sufficiently keen to enable him to avoid anything approaching eccentricity. What Austin knew to be right, his will was strong enough to perform. He distinguished black from white, in whatever light it came before him, and, in morality, he recognized no such colour as grey. I think *he* would have passed through the Holyshadian furnace unscorched. Yet, having experienced those fires, I am glad, for his sake, and remembering the after part of our career, for my own, that he was not my schoolfellow at Holyshade.

At Midsummer, the public school week in town, was the realization of all our wildest and fastest dreams. They were days and nights to be recalled next schooltime, when we compared notes as to our London life, with all the zest of the heroes in that eminently delightful and morally improving, but now, alas! somewhat antiquated book, "Tom and Jerry."

I had well-filled pockets, and, unlike most others boys, who rather preferred school to home on account of its freedom, I was entirely my own master in London from morning to night; for I saw very little of my father, except on a dinner-party night, or when we went to a theatre, or the opera. Between fifteen and sixteen I was able to act the part of cicerone to Holyshadians, who, visiting the metropolis for that rollicking cricket week, wished to see as much of the amusements of the town, as their means would permit. I soon made myself acquainted with all that was worth hearing or seeing, between the hours of eight in the evening and two next morning. The footman, who used to stop up for me on these occasions, was generously fee'd, to keep his eyes open as long as possible, and his ears on the alert for the first touch of the bell. My father heard from me of the aristocratic company I was keeping (which was perfectly true) and appeared highly satisfied with this portion, at all events, of my education.

About this time I had partially overcome my antipathy to Mr. Cavander, who, in his turn, seemed to entertain a more friendly feeling towards myself. My sore point now was my resemblance to a Manx cat, inasmuch as I was still untailed, and I yearned for the day when I should assume the virile toga and stick-ups. I was perfectly aware that for such scenes of enjoyment as were the glory of Lord's week, the absence of tails placed me at a disadvantage. At the end of my second year I came back in stick-ups, a sadder and a wiser boy; but much had happened ere that epoch arrived.

It will have been noticed in my diary that I had developed a decided taste for swan hunting. This predilection was shared by another boy, and led us into a difficulty.

Not being satisfied with the pleasures of the chase, we purchased a pistol. It was of antiquated make, and might have been exhibited as a curiosity in the armoury of the Tower. We bought it for half-a-sovereign, including a bullet-mould, lead, and an old powder-flask. My companion, Parry, who was not at my tutor's, shared the expense and the privileges appertaining to the possession of this formidable weapon. That we could not use it, while the boys were on the river disturbing our game, was clear; so, on consideration, we matured a plan which we carried into effect on the first whole holiday.

After twelve, we took our "tub," and hid it among the bushes, in a creek to which access could be easily gained from a neighbouring meadow, without going through the town. We kept our scheme to ourselves, as there was only pistol enough for two.

At three o'clock we were in chapel, and when the service was nearly half over, Parry and myself were, one after the other, seized with a sudden bleeding at the nose, which necessitated our immediate withdrawal, with our handkerchiefs up to our suffering organs.

No sooner were we out, than we rushed up a lane into the meadows, and thence to our boat, in which we immediately embarked, and, unseen by a single person, sculled across into the very home of the swan, among the rushes on the other side of the river. We were not dressed in our boating costume, as to stop for this would have been to court detection. Parry carried the pistol, I the powder and bullets, and, after loading, we tossed for first shot. I won it, and sat in the stern. As we glided swiftly into the tall rushes, the swans, aroused from their *siesta*, took fright, and scuttled away left and right. This panic was only momentary, as in another minute they had wheeled about, poking up their heads, wagging their tails angrily, and swelling out their feathers in evidently increasing wrath. One, which might have been a model for Jupiter metamorphosed, took the lead, and, hissing furiously, came right at us. I was now facing him in the bows, while Parry was backing the sculls towards him.

" They can break an oar," said Parry, in alarm.

" And a man's leg," I added, feeling anything but comfortable.

" You must shoot him," cried Parry. " If you're afraid, let me ! I've often shot at home."

This was, as it were, a taunt which a Colvin could not stand. I knew it was the first shot I had ever had in my life, that this was the first pistol I had ever been trusted with, loaded or unloaded, and my heart thumped as I grasped the handle with one hand, the trigger with the other, and with my head on one side looked at the swan out of my right eye. In another second, both my hands were firmly screwed up, so as to render my aim in shooting perfectly impartial, and with a convulsive contortion of the mouth and a nervous grasping of the trigger, I fired my first shot, and then stood amazed, and anxious as to the result. The report had almost stunned me, and the kick of the pistol had been like a powerful galvanic shock. I was puzzled and dazed; so were the swans.

"Now, then," cried Parry, excitedly, "let *me* load."

I handed over the weapon to him, feeling rather abashed at the result of my ineffectual experiment. In the meantime the swans had recovered from their astonishment, and were recommencing hostilities. Parry, who was older and stronger than myself, now took so sure an aim, that, by good or ill luck as the reader may choose to deem it, he wounded the largest bird, just as it was breasting my scull, so severely as to render a second shot absolutely merciful. After a few convulsive struggles the swan was dead. And here I beg to inform all poets that this swan, previous to its quitting life, did not sing one note. He uttered a sort of rasping sound, like that produced by a bow when scraped on the above-bridge part of the violin-strings. But as to any sweet melody, this particular swan had no more pretension to it in his dying moments than a pig under the knife. We did not stop to discuss this question, but, having lugged him into our boat, we pulled into the stream and made for a quiet nook in dead-water, where we two guilty ones could talk over the best method of disposing of our victim. The Ancient Mariner was not more exercised in conscience, than were we, now, by our unexpected success.

"They're royal birds," said Parry, lifting up one of our jackets, and regarding the lifeless mass as it lay at the bottom of the boat. "They're royal birds, I've heard, and for killing one, I forget what a fellow gets, but its something awful."

"Is it?" I replied; "then we'd better bury it."

We had no spades, we had no picks, and saw no way of hiding it on the island where we were moored.

"Sink it with stones," said Parry.

This was evidently the very thing. We managed to unscrew the iron chain at the bows, and after a long search we found a stone sufficiently heavy for our purpose. We succeeded in binding the carcase to the stone with rope and chain, and then, looking this way and that, to be

sure we were still unobserved, we plunged it into the middle
of the stream.   It disappeared with a dull plash, but it
did disappear, and we regarded each other as though we
expected to see its ghost.

The rest of that "after four" we spent in watching the
spot where the swan *had* gone down, and we came away
with misgivings as to the result of this day's sport.

We kept our secret to the end.

The third party to the secret, that is, the swan, could
not rest in his watery grave.   Murder would out, and
two mornings after this I hurried off to Parry's room, to
tell him what I had heard from one of the "men at the
wall," of whom there were four privileged to sell sweats,
fruits, and cakes to the boys in the open air in front of the
school-house, and one of whom (Spiky) had the odious
reputation—perfectly undeserved, I believe—of being a
spy in the pay of the masters.

Spiky was a character.   His short thick neck seemed
to have sunk in between his high shoulders, as though
overburdened by the disproportionately big round head it
carried.   He was fresh-coloured, with little piggy eyes,
and the sliest smirk imaginable.   He carried a tin box,
divided into trays, filled with cakes below and apples
above.   He was always tidy and clean, and his boast was
that he knew everything about every boy's pedigree in
the school.   Directly a new boy appeared, he addressed
him in an unctuous tone, and in a sing-song style, with
his head much on one side, thus—supposing myself the
boy—

"Well, my little Colvin, son of Sir John Colvin, of the
City, stockbrokers, Colvin, Wingle, and Co., and of Langoran House, Kensington.   How do you do, sir, this
morning?   What can I do for you, sir, this morning?"
Then turning to a very small boy, about twelve years old,
in a very much damaged hat, "Well, your grace, what for
you this morning, your grace?   This is his grace the Duke
of Chetford ; his noble mother the Duchess was one of the
most beautiful ladies ever seen, and often have I had the
pleasure of serving his noble and excellent father, when
he was a boy, on this very spot."   Whereupon his little

grace would invest in a tart or whatever luxuries Spiky might have in his portable store.

"Well, my little Colvin," he said to me, on the morning in question; "did you go a shooting of the poor swan as they've picked up by the bridge?"

I was very nearly surprised out of my secret. Had I been thinking of it less, I have no doubt I should have confessed on the spot. As it was, I asked ingenuously—

"What swan?"

"What swan, my little Colvin? Why, the swan as was shot a day or two ago, and as belongs to Her Majesty the Royal Queen, and the Mayor and Corporation of the City of London, where Sir John Colvin has his office. It ain't quite a hanging matter, but very near it."

"Who'll be hung?" I asked.

"I don't know, my little Colvin; no, sir, I don't, sir; but there'll be a nice to do, sir, if they catch 'em, sir, whoever it was, sir. What for you this morning, my little Bifford minor?"

"What have you got, Spiky?" inquired Bifford minor, who was getting fatter than when he had been at Old Carter's. After inspection, he said, hesitatingly—

"I haven't got any money."

"That don't matter, Minor," replied the accommodating Spiky; "you take your banbury now, my little Bifford, sir, and you pay me another time, sir."

Leaving Bifford to the enjoyment of his banbury, I hurried off to Parry.

"We shall be discovered," I said.

"We shan't," said Parry, quietly. "We can't be if we don't tell. Who's to know?"

"Perhaps somebody saw us," I suggested.

"Well, then, somebody will tell of us. *We* won't," he answered.

We kept our own counsel. There was a great disturbance, and boy after boy was questioned on suspicion. Once Gulston, a friend of ours, was nearly convicted. Then I went to Parry.

"Look here," I said; "we can't stand by while he's punished."

"We won't," said Parry, phlegmatically, "when he *is* to be punished."

"But if they prove he did it—" I began.

"How can they prove *he* did it, when *we* did it?" asked my partner in guilt.

The force of this argument as a poser was evident. I was still uncertain as to our course, should they examine us separately.

"Supposing," I put it, "your tutor sent for you, and asked you if you shot the swan, what would you say?"

"I should say I didn't," returned Parry, "because it would be jolly unfair to ask such a question. I'll own it when they've found it out. Not till then."

After a while, when the excitement had worn off, somehow or another everyone suddenly knew all about it. My tutor, Mr. Keddy, sent for me privately and lectured me.

"Your conduct, Colvin," he said, in his shrillest tone, rubbing his hair irritably, "has been abominable; most abominably bad. I have written to your father. I don't know whether I shall keep you here or not."

I retired rather crestfallen. Parry was in any case going to leave at the end of the half. To be sent away was unpleasantly like expulsion.

However, the cards were to be played in my favour. The Rev. Vickers Raab, one of the senior masters, and the best scholar of Holyshade, was at feud with most of the authorities, from Dr. Courtley, whom he delighted to mimic, down to Mr. John Smoothish, the lowest master of the lowest form, and he indulged in many a jest at the expense of Mr. Keddy, of whose acquirements he entertained a not very exalted opinion, and at whom personally he had laughed from the time they had been both Collegers together at Holyshade. It was sufficient for Mr. Keddy to think something uncommonly right, in order to convince Mr. Raab that it was most egregiously wrong.

Now, Mr. Raab having some business to transact in the City, went to Colvin and Cavander for advice, and, in the course of conversation, heard from my father of my being at Holyshade.

Sir John therefore consulted him on this affair, and

being really terribly afraid lest I should have incurred some indelible disgrace, was delighted to find that Mr. Raab viewed the whole thing as a joke, and considered me perfectly right in not having confessed to the death of the swan.

"I'll take him into my house," quoth Mr. Raab disinterestedly; and thus it happened that I changed my tutor.

Mr Raab's house was the easiest, pleasantest, and most carelessly managed of all the houses in Holyshade, and his boys were the readiest, smartest, laziest, larkiest, and merriest of all the boys in that great school. We all liked him as no other set of boys liked their tutor. We did not reverence him in the least. He was outspoken, bluff, bold, and intolerant of affectation in any shape, but especially clerical affectation. He was hot-headed, and quick tempered; of a mercurial disposition. He was fond of giving his pupils an occasional treat, on which no one save himself would have ventured. He had an absurd nickname for every boy in the house, and for a great many out of it. He was partial to theatrical entertainments in any form, from the solemnities of the Greeks down to the frivolities of the Londoners in his own time; and whenever the little theatre of the neighbouring town was opened for a short season, he would make a point of taking us to see the performance, and treating us, on our return, to supper in his dining-room. On these occasions he invariably went behind the scenes, and gave any children, who might be playing, a kindly pat on the head, and sixpence for their pockets.

On the second evening of one of these seasons, Mr. Raab took us to see—I forget exactly what piece, but I fancy it was called *The Field of Forty Footsteps*. The two Biffords were of our party, and quarrelled for a bill, which, on its falling between them, I picked up, and, to my surprise, read that the two principal characters were to be played by Miss Carlotta Verney, and Miss Lucrezia Verney.

For the moment I was puzzled by the latter name, having forgotten that Julie possessed two. But the play had scarcely begun, when I recognized her, though she did not appear to have seen me.

Both the sisters were looking remarkably handsome, and I actually began to boast of my acquaintance with this couple of charming young actresses. Not being afraid of confiding this to Mr. Raab, he promised me that I should accompany him after the first act behind the scenes. I noticed that Carlotta's eyes were fixed for the greater part of the time on the private box at the side, where sat three officers, with whose faces I was perfectly familiar, as they were *old* Holyshadians, though very young officers, having recently joined, and were frequently mixed up in our cricket matches and boat races. I could not avoid following the direction of Carlotta's eyes, and I found that they invariably rested upon a handsome, brown-complexioned man, with very small features, bright eyes, and dark, crisp, curly hair, who seemed to be watching the performance intensely, as he never once, as long as Carlotta was on, took his eyes off the stage. He did not talk much to his companions, and, on the fall of the curtain, he rose at the same moment as Mr. Raab and myself. When we came on the stage, we found him engaged in conversation with Carlotta, who was beaming with pleasure at his marked attention, and my tutor saluted him briskly by a name that seemed to me like Mr. Herby. It turned out that this had been his sobriquet at Holyshade, his real title being Sir Frederick Sladen.

"How do you do, Master Cecil?"

It was Julie's voice, and in another minute I was talking to her and Carlotta, who, I thought, did not seem best pleased at the interruption.

CHAPTER XXIII.

IN public scholastic life the Holyshaders were divided
into Forms. In private life the Holyshaders had divided
themselves into Sets. Being at Raab's, and being an independent boy of fortune, my lot was cast in a fast set,
whose ranks were recruited from all other sets. It was
especially fast by reason of its being a monied set. Its
chiefs were, in my time, at Raab's, where, as I have
already shown, we enjoyed more liberty than fell to the
share of any other house in the College. We played cards
in our rooms, and during our school-time held an imitation
Crockford's at The Chichester Inn, where also we had
breakfast and dinner parties, the former, on Sundays,
being remarkable for a profusion of grilled chickens,
boiled ham, and poached eggs, when what was, in the
school slang of my time, known as "hot sock" was forbidden in our own rooms.

We had among us the best "Wet bobs," as the boys
were termed who were addicted to amusing themselves
with "Aquatics," and the foremost "Dry bobs" of the
cricketers. We were a fortune to Mrs. Frizley, the stout
proprietress of a small cigar-shop, where there was a
"counter attraction" in her florid and far from ill-looking
niece who served the youthful customers. Bifford major,

who, though neither a wet nor dry bob, was a noted billiard player, had been for some time "one of us," before my admission into the select circle, and with him and his invariable antagonist at the game, little Lord Pilchard, who was seventeen, and a head shorter than any other Holyshader of his own age, I used to frequent Disey's billiard rooms "up-town," whence, if they were occupied, we would proceed to the barracks, where I soon found myself quite at home. In these quarters I met Sir Frederick Sladen, and Percival Floyd, whom I had last seen at Ringhurst, on the occasion of the theatricals.

Floyd had developed into a tall, large-boned man, with such a sheepish expression as quite toned down the ferocity of his drooping blonde moustache. I was puzzled by this moustache, and, at first, had some difficulty in believing in its genuineness, as it seemed, after all, such a short time since Floyd had been the biggest boy at old Carter's. Sir Frederick was loquacious. Floyd was bashfully silent. I was not surprised, after our meeting on the stage, at hearing Sir Frederick Sladen full of the praises of Carlotta Verney, while, from the eloquent badinage of which his quieter companion was the object, I gathered that Floyd entertained a liking for little Julie.

Finding myself a person of some importance as a friend of the Verney family, I was easily induced to give such particulars as I considered likely to interest my military acquaintances, throwing in, I am afraid, a considerable dash of romance in order to suit the picture to the taste of my audience, and give myself the air of a thorough man about town invested with the privileges of the *coulisses.*

That I was, at this time, a thorough little coxcomb, I need not, after the foregoing candid admission, point out to my readers ; nor will it be necessary to show, that, in no sort of way, directly or indirectly, was there any moral or religious influence, in the *vie intime* of Holyshade, to counteract the great benefits accruing to the individual from this admirable system of almost uncontrolled liberty, which was, and perhaps is now, the proud boast of this great school. My time was, within certain pleasant limits, my own, and how well I was learning to make use of it, the student of these records will have already noticed.

Having ascertained the sentiments of undisguised admiration for my two fair friends professed by these warriors, nothing would satisfy me but I must acquaint the young ladies themselves with their great good fortune. At the same time I conceived a personal dislike for Floyd, which I had never entertained for him when he was Captain of Old Carter's school. Then, I feared him; now, I did not. He had not had a public-school training, but had entered the army with all his blushing gawkiness still upon him. A Holyshadian, five years his junior, was a better man of the world than he. He was a Goliath, I a David; but as it was the fashion to learn boxing (we had gloves at my tutor's for our evening recreation after "lock-up"), I took it into my head to master the noble art of self-defence, with a view to ascertaining the exact scientific blow which should, on an emergency, lay the giant at my feet. To see Floyd prostrate before me, to rescue and to fly with Julie—I do not in the least know where I intended to take her—was the melo-dramatic tableau that presented itself to my imagination.

The two sisters lodged in a cheerful little house, on the outskirts of the town, where—Julie having given me her address—I went to pay them a visit, and make an offering of flowers; for Holyshadians are noted for their love of bouquets, and the sellers of the earliest violets, and lilies of the valley, make a good thing out of their sweet merchandise.

When I entered, Julie was seated at the piano, and Carlotta was standing at the window with some needlework in her hand.

They were in the midst of a discussion.

I presented my flowers, without compliments, and then felt that I had arrived at an awkward moment.

Carlotta was frowning, and Julie was thoughtfully reclining in her chair, while her left hand was going through a system of fingering on the notes without producing any sound.

"I've been talking about you," I said to Julie, jumping in *medias res* with a vengeance, "to Floyd. I was at school with Floyd."

Carlotta looked at her younger sister somewhat sharply, and smiled. Her smile was meant to be sarcastic. I saw *that*, and concluded instinctively that something had gone wrong, and that the something in question was not wholly unconnected with the two military heroes.

"And what had you to say about me?" asked little Julie quietly.

It was quite astounding to me as a boy to see what a thorough woman she was. Not the sort of woman of my barrack-room romance. Far from it. Whatever I might have said to Floyd and Sladen, I felt that she exercised over me so soothing and gentle an influence, as to make me, for the time, less of a puppy or a coxcomb (which you will), and to transport me to the pure atmosphere of our childhood. Her large, soft grey eyes seemed grave and calm as if reflecting the certain light of the Spirit of Truth. Sweetly persuasive, a good and sensible little woman at sixteen was Julie, and, in after life, years have but intensified her sterling character.

"They were speaking," I replied, craftily evading a direct answer, "more about Lottie than about you, Julie. Sladen was chaffing Floyd about spooning,"—this I said with malice aforethought, and again I noticed Carlotta's smile as she glanced at her sister,—"and then the other fellows said they supposed there would soon be a Lady Sladen, and asked him for wedding-cake."

My report of what had been said in my hearing was, after all, not far from the truth. I suppressed details. I wanted to hear what the girls had to say.

Julie rose, with a very serious air. Lottie's head was turned away from her, towards the window. Presently Julie spoke, tenderly but firmly.

"Lottie."

"Well."

" You were wrong to go out walking with Sir Frederick Sladen without me."

" I'm older than you are, and suppose I know what's right and what's wrong. *Allons donc,*" replied Carlotta, in a sudden burst of temper.

In the dancing academy where she had hitherto been employed, French was the language of the principals, and she had picked up scraps, which, when at all angry, she threw into her conversation, in an off-hand manner.

" Yes, Lottie, you are older, but you have not seen so much, or anything like so much, of this sort of life as I have. Remember, dear, I have been on the stage since quite a baby, and I know well enough what fools girls can make of themselves."

" Thank you, Julie, for the compliment," returned her sister, making a mock curtsey. " I don't see why I'm a fool for talking to Sladen "—Carlotta was too impetuous to stick at titles—" any more than you are for talking to Floyd."

" Mr. Floyd," said Julie, calmly, " knew Papa in London, and we had met him in the country, when we were at those theatricals," she explained turning to me.

" Ringhurst ? " I said.

" Yes," returned Julie, " and he reminded me of that after he had asked Charlton to introduce him again to me." Charlton was the manager's name. " I have merely been civil to him, and, as you say, I am not so old as you, and he considers me, perhaps, only as a little girl. After he had spoken to me the first time, I really do not think he has said another word. But in spite of my begging you not to allow Sir Frederick Sladen to come here when I was out, he has been."

" I could not prevent his walking in when he was passing," retorted Carlotta ; " and as he said he should like nothing so much as a cup of tea with us, I couldn't tell him to go, *n'est ce pas ?* And then you came in."

" We met Floyd at Mr. Comberwood's," I remarked at this point, by way of distinctly corroborating Julie's previous statement.

" I don't see that makes any difference," said Carlotta.

"Well, Lottie, promise me you won't see Sir Frederick alone again while we're here."

"I won't promise nothing of the sort,". said Carlotta, colouring, and throwing her work down on a chair. When Lottie doubled her negatives, she was obstinacy itself,—for the moment. "I am quite old enough to take care of myself."

"Then," replied Julie with determination, "I shall write again to Mother, or Aunt, and ask her to come down."

"You may do what you like, and I shall do what I like," said Carlotta, tossing her head. "I'm sure I don't care. *Ca ne fait rien.*"

"Yes you do, Lottie," said Julie, going up to her sister caressingly.

Lottie resented this.

"Don't smaul and carney me about, Ju," she said, inventing, in her impatience, a word of her own for the occasion.

Julie, standing quietly by her side, continued: "If you fell in love with him"—again Lottie blushed, but shrugged her shoulders with affected carelessness—"what would happen, dear?"

Not a word from Lottie.

"Whatever he may say," Julie continued, pointedly, "whatever he may *say*, do you think that he really means to ask you to be his wife?"

"Why not, I should like to know? I s'pose we're as good as him and his any day, ain't we?" Carlotta said, indignantly, her feelings getting the better of her grammar.

Carlotta was a thoroughly downright girl. She spoke out all she had to say. It did not occur to her that others could be reticent, or were capable of saying one thing and thinking another. Language, for her, was made for expressing her thoughts, not for concealing them. A man who could look her full in her handsome face, speak without faltering, would be trusted by her, even though he should utter deceit. Open and straightforward herself, she was only to be duped by a manner made to resemble, superficially, her own. Sir Frederick Sladen possessed this art, unconsciously.

"I don't mind," said Julie, emphatically, "how much you see him if Papa, or Mother, is here, and they know all about it. One of them will be down to-morrow."

"You've written and told Mother?" asked Carlotta, frowning.

"No," answered Julie, "I have only written and asked Aunt, or Papa, to keep their promise of coming to see us from Saturday till Monday."

Carlotta was silent for a few minutes. Looking at my watch, I found that my visit would have to be brought to a close, so that I might get back in good time for five o'clock school.

Julie now proposed to her sister that they should accompany me, a little way, as far as a certain green-grocer's, where they were in the habit of buying such luxuries as watercresses for their tea, which they took about two hours before the opening of the theatre at seven.

They occupied but a few seconds in their simple preparations for the walk, and we were soon in the High Street.

Mr. Floyd on horseback, turning the corner at that moment, saluted us with, it appeared to me, the utmost respect. He was, as I have said, an awkward, loutish-looking creature, with very little to say for himself; and on this occasion he looked, I thought, as if he regretted his equestrian position, which prevented him from joining our little party. The truth was, as I discovered afterwards, that he could not make out from little Julie's manner whether she wished him with her or not, and his modesty getting the benefit of the doubt, he contented himself with looking wistfully after Julie's receding figure, rather expecting her, or her sister, to act like Lot's wife when flying from danger, and then rode slowly onward in the opposite direction.

"What a lolloping fellow that old Floyd is," said Carlotta, with just a sparkle of mischief in her bright eyes.

Julie smiled slightly.

o

"I dare say," Carlotta presently continued, by way of making reparation, "he's not so bad when you know him. *N'est ce pas?* But he makes me die o' laughing to see him sitting at the theatre and staring at you, Julie, as if he was a stuck pig. And when he come to tea, he upset his cup and didn't say a word."

Genius is above rule. Where grammar was concerned, it will have been already clear that Lottie was a genius.

She evidently wanted to hear Julie defend her admirer. Whether Julie would have spoken on the subject, or whether she did subsequently speak on it, she has never told me (though she has told me many things, and from her I have been able to obtain many of the connecting links of this record), but at that instant I perceived Mr. Karfax, the master of the Upper Middle Division, fifth form, only a few steps in front of me, engaged in conversation with three ladies and a gentleman. The latter was Sir Frederick Sladen, and the tallest of the three ladies was evidently, by the likeness, Sir Frederick's mother. Being out of bounds, I was forced to "shirk" into a shop until the danger (Mr. Karfax, the strictest master at Holyshade, with one exception, being the danger) had passed. Luckily for me, he and his party turned and came up hill, not in the direction of Holyshade, and they went by the window of the shop into which I had retired, meeting Carlotta and Julie, the former blushing deeply, the latter looking very sedate.

I was astonished to see that the only sign of recognition of the sisters made by Sir Frederick, as he passed them with an elegantly-dressed young lady on his arm, was a familiar and half-patronising nod, evidently intended to be unseen by his fair companion, who regarded Lottie and Julie with supreme disdain.

This movement of his caused me to obtain a glimpse of her face, when, surprised out of myself, I exclaimed to the shopwoman, by whose counter I was taking refuge—

"Why, its Alice!"

It was. Alice Comberwood on Sir Frederick Sladen's arm.

As I could not without personal risk, on account of Mr. Karfax, issue from my concealment, I was obliged to let this opportunity slip of greeting Alice, and inquiring after Austin.

I had not time now to bid good-bye to Julie, as Karfax had quitted his party and was fast approaching behind me *en route* for the school, where he was as much wanted at five o'clock as I. Only with a difference.

I fled before his face, and reached my tutor's in time to fetch my books.

As I was running out of the house, the butler, whom, by the way, it occurs to me, we used to call Trusty Jim, I forget why, but I think because he used to inform my tutor of anything going wrong in the house that was likely to get himself personally into trouble—Trusty Jim called out—

"Two gents come to see you. One a furriner, and a stoutish, fine-looking gent, with a message from your father *has* is werry important; and they must see you 'mejutly."

"Where are they, Trusty?" I inquired, anxiously.

I foresaw an excuse for leave out of five o'clock school.

"They're about somewhere," replied Trusty Jim, vaguely. "I told 'em *has* you'd be out again at six, and they said *has* they'd call again, and I warn't to let you go without seeing 'em."

A most important message from my father! My curiosity was aroused. Fortunately I was not called upon to exhibit my knowledge of my lesson, for, what with furtively looking at my watch, straining my ears to catch the very first stroke of the hour by the old school-yard clock, and trying to see if there might be two strangers walking about outside, I could bestow but very little attention on my book.

At last the hour struck.

Pell-mell we hustled one another out of school (being punctual to a second in leaving), and, detaching myself from the crowd, I hurried to my tutor's.

"The two gents," said Trusty Jim, "*har* now in your room."

My heart beat fast as I ascended the staircase, for I had an undefinable dread of some misfortune.

CHAPTER XXIV.

IN my room, to my utter surprise, I found Uncle Van, and, of all persons in the world, Mr. Verney. This room was a very small one, of an unassuming simplicity. Uncle Clym seemed to be quite at home in it. Not so Mr. Verney. He was cabin'd, cribb'd, confined by my four walls, and was expanding his chest, and breathing with as much difficulty, apparently, as he might have experienced in a diving-bell.

I never yet saw the room that was not too small for Mr. Verney, or for which he was not too big. Yet in any new place his manner was courtly in the extreme. He bowed, so it seemed, reverentially to the easy chair, politely saluted the ordinary chairs, was affable with the table, and would, on no account, ignore the presence of the fire-irons. The furniture were his audience, as was everything animate, or inanimate, in his world. In a looking-glass he was not himself, but himself in a new character, to be apostrophized, addressed, and appealed to. This reflection of himself in a mirror was, invariably, to Mr. Verney, the creation of a sort of " Charles his friend," the confidant of the hero in a drama, into whose patient ear the sorrows of his chief have to be poured, and who represents the medium through which all the mysteries of the plot are to be made known to the spectators.

Mr. Verney, in my little room, reminded me of the Genie in the yellow copper vessel fastened with Solomon's seal. He was still more like the Genie when he subsequently emerged into what he styled "Heaven's own pure unadulterated air," and expanded his chest in the College quadrangle, or, as we called it, the School-yard.

Thus, astonished as I was at the presence of my visitors, I was quite prepared for Mr. Verney's entire appropriation of the room, of Uncle Clym, and, in fact, of Holyshade College in general.

"Kee kee, kee," snuffled and chuckled Uncle Van, shaking my hand, or rather letting me shake his, which then dropped helplessly at his side, like a broken pump-handle.

Mr. Verney saluted me in his most Louis Quinze-ish style, giving his back the graceful outward bend of a shoe-horn, and advancing his left leg in such an attitude as suggested, either that he was about to display pinions and soar through the ceiling, or that he was but waiting for the music, in order to walk a *minuet de la cour*.

" I am so glad to see you," I said, being in fact uncertain as to whether I was more puzzled, or pleased, by their visit.

Were they come to take *me* out, or were they expecting me to show them over the College ? Lastly, when they had subtracted themselves from my company, would the remainder be one sovereign in my pocket? I knew I couldn't expect this from the exchequer of Frampton's Court, but I thought I might calculate on Uncle Van.

A schoolboy's table of relationship is graduated by a pecuniary scale. A father is worth so much per annum. A grandmother, or grandfather, so much a-piece ; or the pair together a lump sum down, and have done with them. Bachelor uncles, and spinster aunts, are " safe tips ;" while married ones are not to be relied on for a sixpence. Every relation can have his sovereign's worth, or half-sovereign's worth, of a schoolboy's affection, just as the schoolboy can go and have his fourpenn'orth, or twopenn'orth, of luxury at the "sock" shop. 'Tis a mean-spirited world at best, and money is *the* power after all.

You can buy guests, as you can buy dolls; you can buy opinions, you can buy friendship; in short, what is there you cannot buy, from a penn'orth of nuts to an Act of Parliament, if you have but sufficient money?

I am bound, however, to say that I liked my two visitors, apart from any valuable considerations into which Mr. Verney had never for a moment entered; but I should have liked Uncle Van more, could I have looked upon his bidding me " Good-bye " as equivalent to twenty shillings, or half-a-sovereign.

" I tought tat I vouldt come to zee you—he-he-he," said Uncle Van, nervously playing a jingling accompaniment with halfpence and keys in his trousers' pockets, " because ve 'ave a leetle tinner 'ere, ant ve go avays aftervarts. Your aunt——"

" Is Aunt Clym here? " I asked, rather astonished.

" He, he, he—oh, no," chuckled Uncle Van, " she is at 'ome, but as te Baa-lamps—it is our clup—come 'ere to tine tese evenin'—I tell your aunt tat I vill take te occasion te zee 'ow you get on, and vat you tink of it all."

" Thank you, uncle."

It occurred to me that he had not satisfied either himself, or his nephew, by this account of the origin of his coming down to Holyshade. Why with Mr. Verney as a companion? Not at my aunt's request, I should imagine. My countenance betrayed my question, which Mr. Verney. proceeded to answer. Before he spoke, he waved his right hand in his most elegant manner, as though clearing the air of a cloud of objections, which might be floating about, like dust motes in a sumbeam.

" Your uncle and myself," he said, " belong to a society called the Baa-lambs, whose aim and object——"

" I know," I interrupted, rather rudely. Then, remembering what was due to my guest, I added—" I mean I recollect your telling me all about it at Ringhurst. You dine together and sing. So do we. We go up the river to Sulky Hall——"

" A place or a person? " inquired Mr. Verney, who could not, all at once, recover his accustomed suavity, after having his address thus ruthlessly mutilated by me.

A sharp frost seemed to have suddenly nipped the flowers of his oratory in the bud, leaving nothing above ground but jagged and stunted stems.   Where he had been diffuse, he now demanded precision of others.   This was a momentary phase in his conversational life, but it showed that he had been as completely upset, as would have been a lame man, whose crutches had been unexpectedly kicked away from under him.

"Sulky Hall is a place," I answered, "up the river. We pull up to there.   Sometimes we dine, and have songs; but there's not always enough time for that.   I'll get leave, and take you up now."

"No, tank you, ve 'ave not te time now.   Te Baa-lamps vait at te 'Otel.   Mr. Verney is going to stop, and zo to-morrow, if your father does not send for you—he-he-he, you could take him to—he-he-he—Zulky 'All—he-he-he."

"I should indeed enjoy a blow on this lovely river," said Mr. Verney, who had now regained his usual manner, "especially in such a neighbourhood, where we are on classic and historic water, which meanders through the verdant pastures like a silver-backed serpent in a basket of mulberry leaves.   My daughters Carlotta and Julie, who are here fulfilling a professional engagement, would enjoy such a trip amazingly, and we could halt at some little inn by the riverside, take our modest refreshment, a draught of home brewed ale, with a head like the full bloom of a cauliflower, and the scent of the hop still lingering in its bubbles, served in a neat brown jug, with a handle fit for the grasp of a sturdy yeoman; then, on the table, covered with a cloth as white as snow, and as sweet as lavender, would be laid the clean old willow-pattern, a white wheaten loaf, a bright cheese as glossy as a new hat, and, perhaps, a plateful of last year's pippins, wrinkled, but pleasant as the physiognomy of a virtuous maiden aunt.   Yes," said Mr. Verney, coming to the end of his part, as it were, and drawing a long breath, just to give himself the chance of going on again easily, should any fresh simile occur to him, "yes, I shall enjoy it very much, and so doubtless, will they."

During Mr. Verney's speech, I had been considering Uncle Van's remark as to my father sending for me, and having concluded that this was not one of my relative's "Jox," but the prediction of an event which, for some reason or other, evident to him, not to me, was far from improbable, I determined to examine him on the subject.

For my father to send for me was so very unlikely. I never had had, during my schooltime, any holidays, save at the regular times. My father had never been to see me, even on our Holyshadian Festival Days, when boys, in knee breeches and buckles, made speeches in Upper School, using their arms like those on the railway signal posts, and with about as much grace; and other boys, dressed up in boating costumes, drank bad gooseberry wine at Sulky Hall, cheered Catherine-wheel rockets, and other features of the pyrotechnic art displayed on the Eyot, and returned more or less the worse for the liquor and the excitement, to answer to their names at "lock-up"—on neither of these Festivals, there were only two, had my father, as yet, honoured me with his company. Yet all the world and his wife were there, and fathers and mothers, and brothers and sisters, and aunts and uncles, were about all day with Holyshadians. · The boy who had no friends on this occasion was a melancholy exception. The exceptions, unless invited out by more fortunate companions, became cynical, retired to the river, hid themselves in the playing fields, murmured at the giddy throng, or lounged into "tap," and consoled themselves with what Mr. Verney would have probably styled "somniferent malt."

Perhaps Uncle Van meant that my father was coming down, and would want me to meet him at the station. "Was that it?" I asked.

Uncle Van elevated his apologies for eyebrows, took off his spectacles, and stared at me, blankly.

His conduct was so odd that I really began to think the society of the Baa-lambs, and the companionship of Mr. Verney, had had some effect on his watery brain; had made it boil perhaps, as he seemed to be steaming gently, like the outside of a silver urn at the first breath of the heat below, and was obliged to use a pocket handkerchief to his forehead. Then he replied—

"He—your father—come 'ere ? Oh, no. Vy shouldt he ? He cannot."

"Cannot, Uncle ?"

"No, you know zo well as I. He vouldt not go avay now ; he is zo busy."

"In the City ?" I asked.

"No—tat is nothing—Cavanter toes all tat now : it is ott, very ott." He meant "odd."

I thought it was too, for we seemed to be talking at cross purposes.

Mr. Verney referred to his watch.

"We have," said the last-mentioned gentleman, "only half-an-hour to walk to the hotel, to prepare ourselves for the conviviality of wine, with a libation of water—and soap, which we should find at its best in the neighbouring Royal town, whence this most useful commodity derives one of its most honoured titles." Here he took up his hat. "We must not keep our worshipful Bellwether Pipkison and the Gregarious Lambs waiting. Perhaps Master Colvin would accompany us some way upon our road."

Uncle Van appeared so embarrassed by my questions, and so glad to be relieved from further conversation, that I did not acquiesce in Mr. Verney's suggestion.

I accompanied them only as far as the bounds in that direction would permit, and for once, and only for once, I took advantage of their existence, and my uncle's ignorance of their unimportance, to excuse myself from going into the town. As we were quitting my tutor's, Uncle Van said—

"You 'ave not ten 'eart from your father ? No ?"

"No. Nothing particular. I had a letter three weeks ago, I think."

"Um—kee—" here he made a noise which with any other person would have resulted in a whistle, expressive of being utterly perplexed. Uncle Van's noise bore a closer resemblance to the swearing of an angry kitten, than

anything that I can call to mind, only without any
of that intensity which a kitten throws into this peculiar
sound. But I knew what it meant. He was bothered.

"Tit he say noting ?" he presently inquired.

"Nothing."

"Verrry ott. Ten per'aps I am wrrrong to mention it.
I vill not. It vill come in time."

"What will, Uncle ?"

"Te news—he, he, he—" here he laughed nervously
and snortingly, but seemed to be putting himself more at
his ease, as the prospect of parting from me grew less
distant.

"He vill sent for you, ant you vill 'ave a holiday.
Scholly, eh ? I vill not tell noting. Only your aunt
tought tat you—" here he checked himself and laughed
—"he, he, he—I shall not let te cat out of te back.
Atew."

"Good bye, Master Colvin. I shall see you to-morrow,"
said Mr Verney waving his hand to me.

I stood looking after them for some time, then revolving
many things, I slowly walked back towards College. What
could I be wanted at home for ? I felt I should not be
sorry to go, although I was enjoying myself to the full at
Holyshade : which means that I was spending my time
and my money with small profit to myself, though I have
no doubt as to the benefits which my openhandedness conferred on the Holyshadian tradesmen, small and great. I
was rather more my own master at home than at school ;
a state of things which was, I found, reversed in the case
of most boys of my own age. Therefore, the prospect of
a holiday in London, with the theatre, or perhaps even
the opera, with which to finish the day's amusements,
was something to boast of to other boys, whose parents,
being less anxious than was my father to force their
manhood upon them unreasonably, treated them at home
during the holidays, on the principle, properly applied,
that "boys must be boys," to be dealt with accordingly,
and not to be allowed the licence of their elders.

On the evening in question, I should have expatiated to
my companions on the subject of my probable leave, had

I not received a letter from Austin Comberwood, who was still abroad, and who had filled several sheets with a graphic account of his recent tour. He said he had written to his mother and sister at Ringhurst, and had told them that they must invite me for the summer vacation, as he was sure I should tire of London. He told me about the peasants of Brittany, their quaint customs, their ancient churches, and the striking scenes of various religious solemnities he had witnessed. "I do not understand much of what I see, nor I believe does Mr. Gwynn, my tutor (an M.A. of Bulford, to whom Mr. Venn, on leaving, was charged to resign me,) though he attempts to explain them to me. I miss our dear English Sundays at home, and the old church at Whiteboys, where nothing is done as Alice would have it. I write to tell her she should be here and see what I have seen; I fancy she would be less anxious for show and prettiness in church. You know I am intended to be a clergyman, and if I get quite strong and well again I shall go up to Bulford in another year. I don't think, Cecil, you ever cared much for these things. We like much in common, but I'm afraid that, as we grow up, we shan't see so much of one another. Your letters have been very short, but I suppose you have so many amusements, and so many friends at Holyshade, that you can scarcely spare time to remember your old story-telling companion. Do you read Scott now. I do always." And so the letter went on. Austin forgot no one of our former schoolfellows whom there might be a chance of my meeting. He would be remembered to the Biffords, and asked if I had seen Percival Floyd, of whose going into the army he was evidently unaware. It was a coincidence this letter of Austin's, on this very night when I had seen Alice, without being able to speak with her, and had met Floyd.

I began a reply to Austin, but bed-time, and the removal of the light, put an end to my scribbling, and the next morning, on my return from school, I received a letter from my father briefly requesting my presence in town that same afternoon. I was to come ready dressed for dinner (which sounded, my tutor said, as if they wanted to eat me), and with a portmanteau supplied for a few days' stay in London.

A Holyshadian obtaining leave has generally several very important necessaries requiring his instant attention. He must see that his "going home things," his hat, his tie, his gloves, and so forth, are a credit to himself, and his school. In the middle of a half there is generally a falling off in these respects; and therefore, instead of being able to go up to town not only for dinner, but for the best part of the day, I was obliged to pass part of the forenoon, and the afternoon, in getting myself properly rigged out, for this evidently very exceptional occasion.

These things, though, could not ᐧbe collected at a moment's notice, and the tailor, who had had certain indispensable articles of clothing in hand for the past week, now protested that it was as much as he could do to let me have them by four o'clock. Such was the wretched state of my wardrobe (from my London Rotten Row and Piccadilly points of view) that I could not have ventured to appear in the metropolis in any ordinary school suit. I was sensible of the fitness of things, and so was the tailor where they were made.

Waiting anxiously about Tom Jubb's, the tailor's, and looking in, every quarter of an hour, to inquire after the state of my trousers, I came upon Mr. Verney, or rather Mr. Verney came upon me. He had been suffering, he said, all day from headache, owing, he fancied, to the Baalambs having, on the previous evening, lighted candles rather earlier than was necessary, which, he explained, threw a glare down upon his eyes like the sun on a snowball, and the effect of which was, invariably, to make him very bilious next day.

"Jane, too," he added, removing his hat and pressing his hand to his forehead, "suddenly took it into her head to appear on the scene, and when I returned to my daughters' lodgings last night, she let me in. We sat up talking for some time, which didn't do me any good."

"Nurse—I mean Mrs. Davis—is down here?"

"Yes. I think little Julie wrote and asked her. There's

been something going on, but domestic affairs are seldom interesting to a third person. I have just stepped down here in fulfilment of my promise to visit the College to-day. Perhaps you were proceeding to the river when I met you ? "

I explained how matters stood with me ; and on Tom Jubb's assurance, that, if I came back in two hours, he would be ready for me, I accompanied Mr. Verney to the raft where our boat was kept, and here we met Carlotta, Julie, and Nurse Davis, about to go out in a waterman's wherry. They had a basket of eatables with them, and were going to make a sort of pic-nic.

" Why, Master Cecil, what a man you have grown, to be sure ! " exclaimed Nurse Davis, who was only a trifle stouter than heretofore, with the same good-natured brown face that had tenderly bent over me night after night, years since, and had smiled on me with a mother's smile.

" I suppose," she said, " you're too big to give me a kiss now ? "

Too big ! not a bit of it. There was only Shiny the boating cad looking on, and Ben the boatman, but there were Julie, Carlotta, and Mr. Verney, and though I blushed at the notion of Master Cecil Colvin, getting on in years, his own master, and a man about town, stooping to kiss his old nurse, yet I am glad to say (not having much good to mention of myself generally), that I did salute her heartily, and what is more, having done it once insisted upon a repetition of the ceremony.

" Go along, do ! " she exclaimed, pushing me away, " he's becoming quite obstreperous ! which highly pleased Mr. Verney, who otherwise seemed to be strangely out of sorts with himself and everyone else. This I attributed to the Lambs' candles, though I knew enough about Sulky Hall dinners and similiar convivial gatherings not to be aware that a mixture of champagne cups, and other liquids, had, perhaps a trifle more to do with Mr. Verney's complaint than the whole contents of the largest chandler's shop.

After the first greetings, indeed, we were all more or less gloomy.

Presently the reason became evident. I was to be treated as one of the family, and as Nurse Davis would have no further opportunity of speaking to her brother-in-law, she would do it, on the spot, and have done with it.

It occurred to me, then, that Mr. Verney, having fore-seen the outbreak, had craftily sheltered himself under my mantle as it were. He knew Jane Davis would be only too delighted to see me, and in that emotion he saw his way to the introduction of a more charitable frame of mind with regard to himself and his misdoings. To Mrs. Verney he would not have listened; before Mrs. Davis, his sister-in-law, he was dumb.

I have frequently noticed this in families. The un-married sister-in-law is the peacemaker, the adviser of husband and wife, and the best friend of the children. The sort of divinity that, as Shakespeare says, "doth hedge a king" seems to envelop the person of a sister-in-law. I never knew an instance where this relative by marriage was in the wrong. Mr. Verney, away from Frampton's Court, with the fragrance of the Baa-lambs' tobacco-pasturage still pervading his coat and hair, at once unpleasantly self-conscious and very bilious, could only hold up his hand in the dock, plead guilty, and beg to be dismissed, with only a claret stain on his shirt front, and a gentle reprimand.

But, not for the first time in his career, Mr. Verney was on a false scent. Conscience had made a thorough coward of him for the moment, and as he sat in the cool shadow of a bush, watching the vain efforts of the boat to escape from its moorings (we were landed in a creek running into one of the little eyots off the Thames), he had very little anticipation of what vials of wrath were about to be emptied out on his aching head. Not a word about the Lambs, but on a subject which, as it concerned the present and future welfare of his family, and especially of little Julie, was no less interesting to me to listen to, than it was absolutely necessary for him to hear.

Without more preface than might be conveyed by her
decided way of talking, Nurse Davis, after eating some
pickled salmon spread on a slice of bread and butter, and
taking the slightest taste of some corrective mixture out
of a stone bottle, commenced emphatically,

"William ! "

Carlotta and Julie looked up from their plates, frightened ; so did I.

As for Mr. Verney, he seemed so scared at being thus
addressed, that he positively looked about as if to ascertain whence the voice had come, it being impossible for him
to realise the fact of anyone styling him "William," after
so many years of happiness as Charles Mortimer.   I fancy
he still hoped that his sister-in-law might, by chance, be
addressing herself to the boatman.

Nurse Davis having produced this effect, spoke again,
and this time there was no question about it ; she looked
straight at Mr. Verney (the boatman had wandered away
to search for nothing in particular, and observe the stream,
which was a delicacy on his part hardly to be expected
of him at eighteenpence an hour), and said,

"William, I have something to speak to you about, and
for once I beg you'll not talk, but attend.   If you don't,
it may be the worse for you, and them as are your own
flesh and blood."

We were all attention.   Julie sitting next to me, pale ;
Carlotta flushed.   Their father held his breath, and stared
from me to the others.

"What is it about, Jane ? " he gasped.

"It's about your girls, William.   It's time to speak."

"Do you mind calling me Charles ? " he asked humbly.

"No, I don't.   I'll call you Charles.   Only I think, as
William, you're yourself, with sense about you, and
as Charles Mortimer you ain't.   But you've woke up now,
and are likely to mind what I'm going to say."

Mr. Verney raised his eyebrows and waved his hand
with as little of his usual majesty as I had ever seen
him reduced to.

He was evidently at a loss to know on what charge he
had been thus solemnly arraigned.

Not to keep him longer in suspense, Nurse Davis proceeded with what ought to have been his indictment, but which turned out to be his sentence, his case having been previously heard, and a verdict arrived at in his absence.

Both Carlotta and Julie seemed somewhat embarrassed, as their Aunt commenced her harangue.

CHAPTER XXV.

"CHARLES," Nurse commenced; whereat Mr. Verney,
hearing himself thus professedly styled, already appeared
to be considerably relieved; "I don't often interfere in
any family matters whatever, whether yours or anyone
else's."

Mr. Verney bowed acquiescence, and evidently wondered, more than ever, what on earth was coming
next.

"When my sister and you had a tiff, years agone now,
about a subject which shall be nameless before present
company, no one to be excepted in this present instance"
—Nurse Davis interpolated this remark under the oppressive consciousness of there being a proverb somewhere
about which she had somehow failed to introduce correctly
—"I made it up atween man and wife as I would ha'
done, if I'd ha' been asked, between any two others as I
should be loth to see quarrelling; and now and then I've
set you right when you was wrong, and done the same by
Letty too, and with a little sweet oil for local irritation,
applied when required, I've on occasion made things go a
bit smooth and comfortable for all parties. I don't mean
to say as you've had exactly an easy life of it altogether,

P

as who has I'd like to know? and I don't mean to say as
you haven't had difficulties to contend with not of your
own making; but so far you've done well, and your girls
are getting on well in the station as you've seen fit to
call 'em to, though whether better might not have been
done I'm not altogether so sure, and at all events it's small
matter now, when they're so far on the road."

" I've done all I could for them," Mr. Verney began, but
Nurse Davis cut him short.

" Let me go on and finish."

Mr. Verney bowed.

" You've been fortunate in getting them on.   Beatrice
is provided for, at least so you say——"

" So I understand," interposed Mr. Verney.   " We
seldom see her."   Mr. Verney was gradually reviving as
it became more and more evident that he was not brought
up to receive judgment on any Bacchanalian charge connected with the Baa-lamb festivity.

" Well," continued Nurse Davis, " she's provided for by
Mons. Nemmyrang, or whatever his name is," she added,
in order by anticipating correction to prevent interruption; " and I sincerely hope it will turn out well, though
for my part I'd rather not have trusted her to foreigners
—but that's done, and she's getting on in her profession—
and what I've to say is about these two here, Lottie and
little Ju, whom you seem inclined, Charles, to let take
their chance in life haphazard, anyhow, the good with the
bad, and they to pick and choose for themselves."

" Aunt! " cried Carlotta, blushing, yet impatiently
shaking her hand free from Julie, who had taken it
imploringly.

I looked from one to the other, with a kind of guilty
feeling stealing over me, which, had I seen so much as a
tear trickling down Julie's cheek, would have resulted in
weeping.   There being at the moment no demand upon
this expression of my sympathy, my attention became
fixed on a party of flies executing an intricate quadrille
figure about Mr. Verney's head.   One of these insects I
noticed occasionally sat out, as dancers term it, and rested
on Mr. Verney's brow, thus momentarily diverting his

attention from the subject in hand, and relaxing his nervous tension.

"You have let these two girls come down here alone, and neither you nor their mother has ever been down to stay with them, or even to look after them. You'll say you couldn't, and that Letty couldn't. And I say you could—that's my answer"—here Mr. Verney missed one of his tormentors, and hit his forehead—"and if you couldn't, then you oughtn't to ha' let 'em come here, two young, good-looking, simple girls like this, without sending to me, and if I couldn't ha' managed it, then you oughtn't to ha' let 'em come at all. There."

She threw down her "There!" as though it had been a champion's gauntlet. Finding that her brother-in-law evinced, as yet, no disposition to take it up, she, having become uncomfortably heated with her discourse, shook her bonnet-strings loose, and after a brief but general ruffling of her plumage, thus continued:

"There's a regiment quartered here, Charles, or some part of it—how much ain't no matter—and the young officers—and *you* know what that means, Charles—naturally find the theayter very amusin' in the evenin'; and where's the young girl that don't like being flattered and made a fool of? Carlotta, my dear," she addressed her elder niece, who seemed to be nearly as much surprised as Mr. Verney himself at the turn the lecture was taking, and far less able to control herself, "it's for your good I'm speaking, or I shouldn't say out what I have to say, and what has to be said had better be said out once and for all and have done with it. It's not your fault if you listened to a parcel of nonsense which a gentleman—and he ought to have found something better to do, I think, and I only wish he could hear me"—she added, raising her voice, apparently under the impression that the object of her indignation mightn't perhaps be so very far off after all, there was no knowing these snakes in the grass, they were so cunning,—"I'd let him have a bit of my mind, and welcome. Of course, Lottie, you thought yourself all that Sir Frederick Sladen chose to tell you you were."

"Julie!" here impetuously broke in Carlotta, her eyes flashing, and turning on her sister, "this is too bad. You've told aunt this."

"I have, Lottie dear," answered Julie, calmly.

"I don't thank you to meddle with my affairs," Carlotta went on excitedly. "I don't tell of you. And it's not true. You know it isn't. It's a shame! It's—it's—"

Her passion had been most violent for a second, and had utterly scared Mr. Verney, who witnessed such an ebullition as this for the first time; domestic broils having generally taken place in his absence. Now she burst into a fit of almost hysterical sobbing and threw herself on the grass. Julie was kneeling by her side in an instant, bathing her temples with eau-de-cologne from her little scent-bottle.

"Dear Lottie," she whispered, "I only acted as I thought was right and best."

"You didn't!" sobbed Carlotta. "Don't touch me!" and she pushed her away. Julie sat down, waiting patiently.

"Now," said Nurse Davis, quietly, to Mr. Verney, "you have seen, and can judge for yourself."

Now this, at that particular moment, was the one thing of all others that Mr. Verney was totally unable to do. He was incapacitated for action: he couldn't lift his hand to a fly. He was as dazed as if he had just been shot out of a baloon into a new world. A wasp on his knee aroused him. I believe that, but for the insects, which were certainly very troublesome, Mr. Verney would have lain down, put his face under his pocket-handkerchief, slept on the affair, and awoke to let matters right themselves as best they could. But Nurse Davis was on the spot as well as the flies, and Mr. Verney was not allowed time for deliberation. He clearly felt that now was the opportunity for his appearing in the character of a venerable and highly moral parent, and to speak with a dignified gravity befitting the occasion. It was probably with some idea of this kind, and as a protection against any interruption on the part of the flies, that he put on his hat, fitting it carefully to his head as though it were a new one, and then, with a deft shake, giving it that peculiarly knowing cock, which of itself would have been sufficient to destroy the influence of the most saintly patriarch.

"I am really most pained and grieved," he commenced, "at what has just come to my ears. Your mother was able to take care of herself when she was a girl and playing the lead in the Northern Circuit, with a pair of eyes, not unlike Carlotta's now, which went right through you like a bradawl, and such a style, and such a firm and beautifully rounded leg—which she displayed with the most perfect modesty and the utmost grace when she played Rosalind in 'As You Like It,' and Viola in 'Twelfth Night,'—that when she first walked on, like an Amazon among the pigmies, and came down to the flote, the conductor of the orchestra, a very sensible little fellow of the name of Jackson—Puffy Jackson we used to call him—was so completely electrified by her appearance, that he gave one shriek, threw up his bow, and tumbled off his seat in a sort of ecstasy. Lætitia pitied him, for he was ill for weeks afterwards; but when Jackson— Puffy Jackson—recovered his equilibrium, and reason once more resumed her seat in his brain, and he his in the orchestra, he found himself doomed to disappointment, for your sister Jane and myself were joined together for worse or for better, for richer, for poorer—in fact Puffy was nowhere in the final tableau of that little domestic drama, and we were man and wife."

"Well," said Nurse Davis, "I don't see what that's got to do with Lottie and Julie."

"Excuse me, Jane," returned Mr. Verney, deprecating the interruption, and showing signs of having perfectly recovered from his recent shock. "Excuse me. I was going to say that their mother had admirers everywhere. She was always called in the bills by her maiden name, and I had to explain, with the most thorough politeness and good breeding, to several gentlemen, that the talented young actress at whose feet they were ready to pour out their choicest flowers, and most costly jewellery, was my wife: but she had offers from—well, I'm afraid to say how many of the nobility and gentry, and might have been a duchess now, had she not preferred plain Charles Mortimer Verney—with a head, mind you, on his shoulders —to all the brilliant coronets that might have adorned her brow."

"Sladen has given me a ring," blurted out Lottie. "He said it was because he thought so much of my acting as Leyolin, in 'The Idiot of the Glen.'"

"You should not have kept it," said Nurse Davis, decidedly. She had not had much experience perhaps, but she felt she was right.

"Why not?" asked Mr. Verney, to whom a ring was a ring. "Why not? If a gentleman entertains a high admiration for the work, whatever it may be, of an artist, why shouldn't he testify it by a present? And why should the artist return it? No, I do *not* see it. I remember when I played Mercutio for the first time at Melbourne, Australia, all health and fervour, with a wide, open shirt front, a pink silk fall, and a property pin that shone with the brilliancy of the genuine article, a lady sent me, the very next day, a massive gold ring, with a diamond in the centre, like a dewdrop on a buttercup, expressing, in a neatly turned note, written in a gentlewoman's hand,— none of your pothooks and hangers begad—the great gratification she had experienced, and——"

"You returned the present?" asked Nurse Davis.

"No, I did not."

"It was very indelicate on the part of the lady, who-ever she was, that's all I've to say," observed Nurse Davis; "but we're not here to talk about what we did in Australia, and the less of that said the better——"

"My dear Jane," interposed Mr. Verney, but with, apparently, decreasing confidence.

"Never mind that *now*," continued his sister-in-law, emphatically; that's done with and gone. I want to hear what you know of Mr. Floyd in London, and what he's said to you about Julie; for she wrote to me chiefly about herself, and most about Lottie I've learnt afterwards. Now."

Thus interrogated, Mr. Verney replied:

"Mr. Floyd called on me at 'The Portico." He said he'd taken a fancy to Julie; that he was probably going abroad on foreign service, and in his absence would I allow her to be educated and brought up at his expense, so that when he came back, or at all events after two or three years, he might make her his wife."

"He said this, did he?" said Nurse Davis, nodding.

"Yes," answered Mr. Verney. "He seemed to be quite in earnest. He will be a Baronet one day."

"What did you reply, Father?" asked Julie.

"Well," answered Mr. Verney, looking as wise as he possibly could, "I said—I said—we'd see about it."

"Mr. Floyd told me this," said Julie in a low voice. "I asked him whether, supposing I had such an education as he meant, he really thought I could be his wife? He answered that he loved me very much; that he had done so since the first moment he saw me; that during his father's lifetime there might be some difficulty—'as to your marrying me?' I asked—and he replied, with hesitation, 'Yes.' I then told him that I had only asked him these questions so that I might judge of his sincerity, and that I had never for one moment any idea of accepting his offer, as I was too young to know my own mind. He told me he spoke by your permission," she said, turning to her father, who had appeared very uncomfortable during Julie's speech, "and I begged him never to mention the subject to me again. I learnt from him that Sir Frederick Sladen was engaged to be married to the young lady we saw at Ringhurst—you remember, Father, don't you?"

"Alice Comberwood," I said, proud of assisting at so important a discussion.

"I saw him for a few minutes last night at the theatre," said Julie, firing up, "and I gave him something that he will not forget in a hurry. He won't come pretending to make love again and be so glad to take tea with us, I'll be bound."

Lottie was silent. Julie had been so entirely the little mother, had shown herself so prudent, so good, so strong for herself and others under temptation.

"You recollect," Julie went on quietly, addressing her

father, but evidently for her sister's benefit, "you recollect the Birkets who used to be in Frampton's. The four girls were in the ballet at Covent Garden, and were all so dirty and so untidy at home. I remember one after the other they're coming out in such dresses; and when I walked up to Madame Glissande's with Lottie, I saw two of them, Loo and Fanny Birket, in a carriage and pair with a coachman with a cockade, and we thought it so grand."

"Ah!" said Mr. Verney, shaking his head seriously, "they were a bad lot. But they hadn't got a father and mother who could look after them as you have."

"Very good," said Nurse, coming to the practical point of all this conversation; "then let it be understood, Charles, that when they go in the country again, their mother goes with them if *you* can't: and if neither of you can manage it, then they must have their engagement in town."

"There's the difficulty," observed Mr. Verney.

"Is it? Well then, when they're out of an engagement, they can come to me. I'm saving up a bit, my dears," said Nurse Davis, "and its all for you and yours, as I've none of my own, and I think it proper to tell you this," with a look at Mr. Verney, who waved his right hand, and shut his eyes, as though to intimate that he, personally, could have no sort of interest in this financial statement, but thought that possibly the younger ones might, "just to show you that you won't be in want, even though things should not go altogether so well as one could wish in this haphazarding sort of profession."

Becoming at this point anxious about my clothes at the tailor's and about my own domestic affairs generally, I interrupted the debate to observe, that I must now return as quickly as possible, so as to catch the train without showing myself at my tutor's.

It was arranged that Nurse Davis should stop there that night, and that Mr. Verney should accompany me to town, whether he was summoned by his professional duties.

My tailor was faithful to his promise,· and within

less than two hours I was on my way to London, being entertained, during my journey, by Mr. Verney, who soon entered, in an affable and slightly patronising manner, into conversation with the four strangers sharing our compartment. Though at the time much occupied with my own wanderings, I remember noticing the apparent ease with which Mr. Verney opened up such general subjects as the state of the country and the crops, the probabilities of the weather, and the advantages of being a Holyshadian.

Somebody looked up from his book to ask him if he had been brought up at Holyshade; whereupon Mr. Verney admitted that "he himself had not," as though he wished it to be conveyed, that, having been unable to go himself, he had sent a substitute, and had been educated by deputy. However, Mr. Verney's interrogator with the book, was not, from that time forth, allowed to renew its perusal. Mr. Verney fixed him, talked him down on education, allowing him to say just so much as served Mr. Verney for a text, whereon he went to work, and slid, naturally into questions of elocu· tion as a part of the educational system; thence into the drama, theoretically, then into it practically, finally introducing himself and family to his audience, descanting upon the genius of his eldest daughter, whose play some London manager would, no doubt, soon produce; bringing me in, too, occasionally upon collateral issues, and giving my name, address, prospects, and present position of my father, with whom Mr. Verney seemed to imply, he was himself remotely connected.

We smoked all the way, and I fancy I remember offering one of our fellow travellers a cigar. I don't think I cared much about the taste of tobacco, but it was a free, independent, and manly sort of thing to do, and it kept up the Holyshadian character.

"There," said Mr. Verney, on descending at the terminus, "we've passed a very pleasant three-quarters of an hour —cheerful companions, and an interchange of the amenities to beguile the journey. That gentleman in the corner appeared to be possessed of considerable information."

Mr. Verney must have judged of this by the size of the book. The poor man had begun by asking a few questions at starting, but had not had an opportunity of uttering a syllable when once Mr. Verney had fairly commenced ; and, indeed, none of his audience stood a chance of throwing in a word, unless one among them was showing signs of weariness, when he was at once appealed to by Mr. Verney, and his answer cut short and twisted into the thread of Mr. Verney's conversation, which thereupon ran on again with fresh vigour.

"Our roads lie in different ways," said Mr. Verney, wishing me good-bye, " but we shall meet anon."

He shook my hand stretched out to him from the cab window, as I was starting from the station.

CHAPTER XXVI.

IT was more than half-past six when I reached home. As I had expected, there were all the signs of a large dinner party : a much larger one than any at which I had as yet been present. My father was evidently considering me as having become much more of a man than formerly, and I felt gratified at the implied compliment.

There was after all something "jolly" (this was then our Holyshadian word) in being summoned for such a festivity. Besides, I should perhaps go to the Opera the following evening, and not back to school again for three days.

In the hall there were our own servants, and many new faces shining with recent soap, and representing respectability, and gaiety, in their clerical white ties, and second-hand white waistcoats. There was a stir on my arrival, and our brave Pemdale (a butler who had the air of a retired corporal of the Life Guards with his moustache off—not altogether unlike the cook's cousin in uniform who used to applaud my performances of Der Freischutz) welcomed me with much impressiveness, informing me that my room was all ready, and I'd better get dressed at once, as dinner was to be on table in half an hour.

"Sir John," he added, "is engaged just now. You were expected before this, Master Cecil."

I ran up the back stairs, so as to avoid some ladies, with whose brilliant toilettes, my rumpled hair, dusty boots, and grimy hands (the effect of travelling by train) would not, I felt, be at all in keeping. Besides, I did not want strangers to be asking "Who's that boy?" in our own house. As for ladies, at that time of my life, unless with true Colvin impetuosity I fell in love with them, no matter what their age, I preferred, in a rude, shy, hobbledehoyish way, their room to their company, and in this instance, had I met Aunt Clym on the staircase, her nose would have detected the tobacco (it had settled upon me as if I had been bathing in it, and I was haunted by it myself), and she would have made the commencement of my holiday a little unpleasant.

In order to free myself entirely from the tobacco I had recourse to my father's dressing-case. I stole into his room. It was on his table. I took out the eau-de-cologne bottle, and, as I turned, I found myself under the sweet influence of my mother's eyes, as they seemed to regard me, from the picture over the mantel-piece. I have before alluded to the effect of this portrait on me. This night it had a mysterious attraction for me, for which I was utterly unable to account. It was with difficulty I withdrew myself from its influence. I crept from the room, as though fearful of waking a sleeping person, and found myself murmuring softly, "Dear Mother," as on quitting the apartment I gazed once again, with a yearning heart, upon her picture.

In another five minutes I had finished dressing, and Pemdale, knocking at the door, summoned me to attend my father in the study.

This was unusual, and not at all the preliminary to a festivity.

"What for, Pemdale?" I asked.

He didn't know, only I was to come quick, as dinner was just ready.

This solemnity made me feel very nervous. I descended the staircase, passing the drawing-room, where I heard reassuring laughter, and the buzzing of the guests, like that of flies round a cold joint in summer.

What had I done ?   Ought I to have come up earlier ? Had Dr. Courtley, or my tutor, heard of my remaining at Holyshade, and avoiding school when I was supposed to have gone away on leave ? and had I been sent for by special messenger—perhaps Phidler, Dr Courtley's own body-servant, had been charged with the mission ?   If so, this was serious, and—but here my imagination failed me.   It never could be that the murder of the swan had cropped up again ?   Impossible.

The daylight had now been excluded, and on entering what was called the study (a small room at the back fitted up with some nearly empty bookshelves, a writing-table, and a few chairs), I found several gentlemen gathered about the table, apparently deeply engaged in examining by the aid of a couple of wax candles, some object of interest laid out before them.

At that moment I felt far from certain that it was not the body of the murdered swan which they were in-specting.

At first I did not see my father, who was leaning over the shoulder of an old gentleman seated at the table.

My Uncle Herbert Pritchard was the first to observe my presence, and announce me.   I was always glad to see Uncle Herbert, and I felt that if I had been summoned to receive a lecture (and again it occurred to me, more forcibly than ever, that it might be the old charge about the swans turning up in London after a twelve months' oblivion) he would stand by me.

"He-he-he!" snuffled Uncle Van, emerging from the shadow like a flabby ghost; "'ow are you, eh?   Shust come ?   He-he-he!"

There was a forced heartiness in the manner of both my relatives that I could not help remarking, but it was nothing compared with that of my father's, who now called me to him, shook my hand warmly, and clapped me on the shoulder.

Mr. Cavander was here too, and stretched out *his* hand to welcome me.   I took it, and, as it were, made for

a time a truce with him, for I was puzzled by the proceedings.

Mr. Comberwood, too, was there in an arm-chair; he
nodded at me in the middle of some good story which he
was telling to a long-legged gentleman with weedy
whiskers, whom I recognised as one of the *habitués* of my
father's office.

"And how do *you* do, sir ? " said a little wizen old
gentleman with a high waistcoat, a frill, spectacles, and a
large ring on the third finger of his right hand. He was
seated close to the table, and before him, spread out
was a formidable-looking parchment, ornamented with
quaint characters, flourishes, seals, and little bits of
riband.

It was round this strange document, and not the swan,
that the party was gathered, and catching sight of it for
the first time, the meeting seemed to me to be a modernly
dressed representation of King John surrounded by his
Barons, signing Magna Charta.

"This is Mr. Crukley," said my father, indicating the
little wizen old man. I had a vague recollection of his
name as connected somehow with my mother, with law,
and the Pritchard interest generally.

"Very like his mother," said Mr. Crukley, regarding
me under the shade of his hand. "Very. Takes after
you, too, Sir John. I remember your mother, sir,"—this
to me—"when she was—ah, let me see—very little
taller than you are. Eh, Mr Herbert ? "   .

" Yes," returned Herbert Pritchard, in a light and airy
manner; "and *you* don't seem to get any older, Mr.
Crukley."

This pleased Mr. Crukley immensely, who looked
at his watch, and remarked that he was afraid the
dinner was waiting.

The introduction of my mother's name in this manner,
sounded once more the chord that had been already struck
upstairs.

Again the tears rose. I bit my lip, and luckily, the
urgent appeal to the gentlemen to "sign here, as we're
keeping dinner waiting," had the effect, at all events,

of diverting their attention, specially my father's, from me.

What they were doing I had not the smallest idea, and even now it would puzzle me to give such an exact account of the proceeding as should satisfy a lawyer.

Mr. Crukley called on me cheerfully to sign.

"I needn't read it, I suppose," he said, looking dismally at the parchment, and referring to his watch.

"Oh no," replied my father; "he may be quite sure that I shouldn't ask him to sign anything to his own disadvantage, eh Cavander?"

"Of course," chimed in Cavander.

Uncle Herbert and Mr. Comberwood were of the same opinion, for dinner was quite ready, and ought to have been served fully half an hour ago. If Esau sold his own birthright for a meal he would not be likely to use much delicacy with regard to anybody else's inheritance. It might have been mine that we were all signing away so comfortably. Heaven help me, I did not know, and as long as my father was pleased, it was all one to me.

My Holyshadian bringing-up had made me far too much of a gentleman, to trouble myself about business in any shape, and as this parchment evidently came under that head, I laughed as cheerfully as my nervousness would allow, and wrote my name in the space left for it, surprised to find that my signature was of any value whatever.

There was no time for questions as dinner was immediately announced, and the gentlemen, led by my father, ascended the staircase to offer the ladies their escort. I wanted to get at Uncle Herbert, or Uncle Van, and ask them about the transaction in which we had all been engaged. But each was occupied in making himself agreeable to his companion, and I saw no chance of approaching either of them. I was standing at the foot of the staircase as they descended.

My father came first, with Miss Cavander on his arm.

She was looking her best, and, on seeing me, nothing would satisfy her but she must stop, shake me by the hand, ask me if I would not give her a kiss, and pay me so many compliments on my growth and appearance, as to cause me to feel quite abashed, and really very comfortable in the presence of such a party.

Besides, Miss Cavander had been, whenever I had hitherto seen her, so very mild and unenthusiastic.

My Aunt Clym, who was on Mr. Comberwood's arm, looked, I thought, as sour as if she had been tasting bitter aloes, and I began to be afraid I had done something to offend her.

On coming up to me, however, after the van of the procession had marched into the dining-room, she was peculiarly gracious, and addressed me in such kindly tones as I had never before heard her employ, not even towards her own children.

Mrs. Cavander was on Uncle Van's arm, and recognized me good-humouredly. The pair resembled a fatuous codfish taking an amiable dumpling into dinner. Mr. Comberwood took down Mrs. Van Clym. I was placed next to her at the bottom of the table facing my father, on whose right was seated Miss Cavander, sharing the head of the table with him. This arrangement struck me as unusual, but I had never yet, when at home, met the entire Cavander family at our house.

As the remainder of the guests consisted of my father's most intimate city friends, with their wives and daughters, all of whom I had known since I was eight years old, the party, on the whole, assumed the aspect of a family gathering.

We were accustomed to annual meetings of this sort at Christmas time. But this was not Christmas time, and as it was neither my father's birthday, which I never remember being kept as a festival, nor mine (which I was accustomed to celebrate by writing to, or calling upon my relations to remind them of the happy event), I was not a little puzzled to know why all these familiar faces were gathered together, and why I had been specially summoned. Also Uncle Van's mysterious manner on the previous evening recurred to me, and I determined, that, when I could conveniently engage Aunt Clym's attention, I would ask her to satisfy my curiosity.

By way of opening the conversation, I took the first opportunity of inquiring of Uncle Herbert (who was on my left), during a pause in his conversation, how my Aunt Susan and Grandmamma Pritchard were?

He replied that the latter was far from well, that Aunt Susan had been lately married, and was now out of England.

"Married!" I exclaimed, for somehow, even at that age, I could not realise the possibility of my favourite aunt having married anyone except her favourite nephew. Though I had not seen her for a year, yet there was that traditional feeling still remaining from my childish days.

"Married, yes," returned Uncle Herbert; "she's Mrs Shenbrook now. You've got a new relative—Uncle Shenbrook. So you see you're adding to your relations in more ways than one."

I noticed that this answer of Uncle Herbert's seemed to interest some of the guests on the opposite side, who began talking about me (I was conscious of its being about me) in an undertone. Generally, at odd times, I became aware that I was the subject of conversation. I felt that I was turning red, and becoming hot and uncomfortable.

Herbert Pritchard was again occupied with his fair companion, to whom he was expatiating upon the pleasures of yachting in somebody else's yacht, of riding somebody else's horses, and on living without anxiety or responsibility, when it struck me that his last phrase required explanation.

Aunt Clym was disengaged and sitting silently.

To her I turned with the query, "What did Uncle Herbert mean by saying I was adding to my relations in more ways than one?"

"Well, aren't you?" answered my aunt, interrogatively.

"No," said I, "I haven't any new relations."

"Not yet," replied my aunt, severely, "but to-morrow you will have. Tell me," she said, stooping down and sinking her voice, "how do you like her?"

"Like *her*?" I replied in the same tone, for I saw that secrecy was demanded. "Her? Who?"

Q

" Miss Cavander," answered my aunt, with a searching glance at me.

"Oh pretty well," I returned, carelessly. I don't know her much."

"But you ought to like her more than pretty well *now*," said Aunt Clym, still in the same subdued voice.

" Why, Aunt."

"Why," she repeated, with an air of extreme astonishment. "My dear Cecil, how can you ask *why?*"

My blank look evidently puzzled her considerably, as she leant towards me sideways, so that no one should see her face, or hear her question save myself, and asked me, slowly and impressively,

"Do you mean to say that John—that your father has not told you?"

"Told me what?" was all I could say, for her manner began to frighten me. It occurred to me suddenly what a dreadful thing it would be were Aunt Clym to go mad, there and then, and bite my ear.

She sat up suddenly, looked about, caught Uncle Van's eye, who was sitting four places from her, raised her hands in most expressive pantomime, regarded her neighbours right and left for a second, then exclaimed, in a voice audible only to those immediately about her,

"Good gracious! He's never been told! He doesn't know anything about it!"

Such guests as were thus appealed to, smiled wonderingly, said "indeed!" looked at me, looked at my aunt, seemed not quite at their ease, and resumed whatever conversation my aunt had interrupted as quickly as possible.

Then she turned once more to me.

" Don't you know why you've been sent for ? "

" No. Except to dine here : for this party."

"And don't you know why we, the family, are all here, and why Miss Cavander sits at the head of the table, next your father ?"

" No, Aunt." And indeed I had not the faintest shadow of a suspicion.

"Why," replied my aunt, moving her words as

cautiously as though they were pieces on a chess-board, "she is to be your—*belle-mère.*"

French was not a Holyshadian accomplishment, and I was as wise as I had been previous to this information. Being unwilling to exhibit my ignorance, I said "Oh, indeed; is she?"

This seeming apathy on my part was evidently a fresh puzzle for Aunt Clym, who, however, went on—

"That is a prettier name than stepmother."

Suddenly, as if by a shock, I awoke.

"Stepmother!" I exclaimed, startled out of myself.

"Hush," said Aunt Clym, satisfied that my surprise was genuine. "Don't you know Miss Cavander is to be your stepmother?"

"No!" I replied, indignantly.

"Yes she is; and you are asked here to-night, so as to be present at the wedding to-morrow."

"Papa marries Miss Cavander to-morrow!" I gasped.

"Yes. You must be very great friends with your step-mother—*belle-mère* we'll call her; it is, decidedly, a prettier name."

Call it what you would, that woman sitting there was to be my stepmother. I had, I think, at that moment some vague idea of rising to protest against the marriage, and forbidding the banns there and then. I had always had a dread of the word stepmother: at that moment I detested it—I detested *her.*

My holiday had lost all its pleasure. It seemed to me as if I no longer had a place in my own home: hence-forth I could only be there on sufferance.

It seemed, too, so hard and cruel of my father to be laughing and joking with his friends, and with the lady who to-morrow was to be his wife, while he had not a word or a smile for me.

Why had he not told me in his letter? or why had he not visited Holyshade and informed me of it pleasantly? No, I had been counted for nothing, my self-importance was wounded, I had been treated as of no consequence in this new arrangement—I who of all should have had the most to say to this!

Well, I had been' brought up to be selfish, and so on this occasion it never occurred to me to ask what was best for my father's happiness, I only considered how it might affect that of my father's only son. Of any mercenary consideration, however, I entirely acquit myself.

And she, too—she was alienating my father from me. I should cease to be regarded as his son. I should have neither part, nor lot, in his future, nor he in mine. He would not care for me any more : I should be snubbed and controlled at home——

At this moment, as I sat at table and heard for the first time that I was to be presented with a stepmother, such confused thoughts as these—of anger and malice, and yet of a kind of pity for my father, who, it seemed to me in some vague way, had been duped by those whom I hated—whirled through my brain, suddenly to be checked by the remembrance of my mother's picture, which had arrested my attention that same night, and then—I could no longer withold the great, big, burning tears that oozed slowly from my eyes, and trickled down my cheek.

I struggled fiercely with myself, and hoped I was unnoticed. I need have had no fear on that score. I was almost unnoticed ; I was entirely unheeded.

My father was in high spirits. He ushered the ladies from the dining-room. Miss Cavander stooped to kiss me as she went out. I felt that this show of affection was the merest artificiality—I knew, instinctively, that she must dislike me, and I only hated her the more for, what seemed to me, her hypocrisy.

I would rather have heard her say to me, defiantly, as she went out " I hate you," that I might have returned her defiance with a will. But to be obliged to accept a caress from a person whom at that moment I absolutely loathed, of whose deadly enmity I felt assured, was revolting to a boy whose disposition was impulsive, frank, and open, who liked, and disliked, with equal warmth, and who, where "self" was involved, was inclined to speak his mind without reserve.

Could I have prevented that marriage that night, I would have done so.

I stole towards Uncle Herbert as towards my only friend in that company. I mistrusted them all, save him.

He talked to me of boating, of Holyshade, of our fun and amusements, and used all his tact to interest me, and revive my spirits. He saw at once that I was sad and unhappy.

My father apparently was not troubling himself about me. He knew he had procured me a holiday, and was of opinion that his marriage, somehow or other, was for *my* benefit. I had not entered into his calculations. I was being "made a man of," and I was provided for. So he was gay and happy, and laughed and talked; and Cavander, too, was livelier and more brilliant than I had ever seen him. The party broke up late. My father saw his *affiancée* to his own carriage, which he had lent the Cavanders for the night.

I noticed our coachman, an old friend of mine, on the box, and this excited in me fresh feelings of anger, for it seemed to my excited imagination that even the servants had turned traitors.

A gentleman whom I had seen in the City at the office (and have here previously described as being remarkable for legginess and luxuriant whiskers) was staying in our house for this night, as he was to be my father's best man on the morrow. He sat up with my father to enjoy "a quiet cigar" before retiring to bed. I entered their room to say "good night."

My father was standing on the hearth-rug, knocking off the ash of his cigar as I went in.

I paused for a moment, and looked at him wistfully.

His attitude before the fire-place reminded me of our first meeting in Aunt Clym's drawing-room. The idea seemed to cross me that I would, as it were, give him the last chance of changing his mind, and making it up with me again, once and for all. I felt that we had quarrelled, without a word having been uttered on either side. A gulf had been opened between us, and by whom, or how, was it to be filled up? I put down my candle hesitatingly.

"I didn't know you were going to be married," I said,

timidly, and with the old choking feeling coming up
again in my throat.

As I spoke I did not dare look at him, but at my
candlestick.

"Didn't you?" he replied, in an off-hand, careless
manner. "I thought I told you in my letter."

"No, Papa, you didn't."

"Ah! I thought I did."

Then, turning to his friend, he observed, alluding to me.
"It won't make any difference to him, will it? He's provided for."

"Oh, of course," returned the gentleman with the
whiskers, in an easy assenting manner, "it won't make
any difference to him."

I smiled. I could master myself for no more. I felt
that this off-hand answer only implied that my father's
marriage would make no difference to the gentleman with
the whiskers, that was all. It did not convince me.

"Good-night, Mr. Telderton; good-night, Papa."

"Good-night, Cecil."

Sadly I left them, and went to my own room.

"It would make no difference to him," they had said.
They were talking of money. I knew that, when they
used the phrase "provided for."

I was not thinking of money; I was thinking of affection. Everything about me in my room that night seemed
cold and cheerless. I had never before realized the
loneliness of my position. Could I have had then my
dear old friend, Nurse Davis, at whose knees I could
have bowed my head, and poured forth all my sorrow,
I should at least have felt the consolation of kindly
sympathy. Not the thought of Nurse Davis of yesterday
by the riverside came to me now, but the memory of
the honest, kindly face, when years ago she taught
me to fold my hands and "Pray God bless papa," then
far away in India; and, as this softening influence crept
over me, I stole, with a quickly beating heart, from
my room to my father's, where my mother's portrait
hung.

Seized with an uncontrollable impulse, I mounted a

chair, detached it from the wall, and, embracing it with both arms, returned with it to my own room.

Then I laid it gently on the bed, and falling down on my knees, I threw out my arms, and bowed my head over the picture till my lips touched hers. With the first kiss, the fountain was unsealed, and the passionate tears, flowing uncontrolled, relieved the parching fever of my grief.

"My darling mother! my darling mother!" I cried.

Then, becoming calmer, I prayed against my wicked thoughts of hatred and anger; I prayed that I might like (I could not say love) the woman who was to be my stepmother. I could scarcely utter the hard word; and then, once again, I used the first prayer Nurse Davis had taught me, and used it with all my heart and soul.

"God bless papa this night—and always."

Then I laid the picture gently by my side, feeling as though my mother had only me to love her now, and so, kissing it once more, I fell asleep.

CHAPTER XXVII.

MISS CAVANDER married my father the day after the dinner-party, to an account of which important ceremony the previous chapter was devoted, and, on the decease of my grandmother, the Dowager, which happened six months after my father's second marriage, Lady John Colvin obtained her social step, and became Lady Colvin.

My first instincts had been only too true. My step-mother began her rule by being excessively polite to me, and, as it seemed to the uninitiated, going out of her way to make me comfortable and happy. If she discouraged the visits of my young companions at our house, it was done so gently as to afford me no opportunity for an open rupture without my putting myself, in the eyes of my relatives, and of course and specially of my father, utterly in the wrong.

She was glacial. She had less sense of humour than any woman I have ever met; and, apart from her school-girlish education, and her proficiency at the piano, she had very scanty acquaintance with any subject in the literature or art of either the past or the present. I have before said she was an influence in the house. Exactly. I felt she was there, somewhere, probably watching me in a cat-like manner; and I knew that whatever I did which might not be precisely in accordance with her notions, would be immediately discovered, and would be certainly followed by some sort of punishment. Then I was deprived of the society of Holyshadian friends. My amusements were to be gradually curtailed, if not absolutely stopped. Formerly I had done as I liked at home; now I was to be made aware that my selfishness must be made to yield to her selfishness.

The servants curried favour with her and neglected me. Restrictions were being placed upon me for the first time in my life, just at the very moment when they were being removed from the companions of my own age. Had I not been brought up "to be a man," and forced prematurely into, as it were, the perfect freedom of bachelorhood—for, as I have shown, nothing short of this had I enjoyed as a boy—I should not have found the restraint put upon my actions by the presence of a stepmother so unbearable. But my wings were to be clipped when my companion fledgelings were preparing for flight.

I left Holyshade after an affecting interview with Dr. Courtley, who presented me with a handsomely bound copy of *Hallam's Constitutional History* in two volumes, and with great tact and delicacy, acquired by long practice, pretended to occupy himself with something out of doors which he could only see from the recess of the windows of his study, while I deposited on his drawing-room, or dining-room table, an envelope containing ten, or fifteen pounds, in notes.

Good heavens! ten or fifteen pounds—for what? Why should I have had to give my father's fifteen pounds to Dr Courtley? For flogging me? Well, he had only had that pleasure twice, and that would have been dearly bought, including the birch itself—to which, such was the tradition, any swished Holyshadian had a right after his swishing—at fifteen pounds. The charge for a "swishing," including the birch to be given to the Swishee, was, I have always understood, five shillings. It was, I believe, regularly charged in the bill, but the apple-twigs were not bestowed on the boy after the punishment. They should have been made into the sem-semblance of a laurel wreath. I suppose the birches were among the perquisites of Dr. Courtley's servant. In the course of My Time I regret much wasted money, whether mine by earning or by inheritance, but I have never got over that leaving gift of fifteen pounds to Dr. Courtley, and the other ten to my tutor. Why should they have been fee'd on my going away? Had not they been already well paid, both of them? What was that fee for? Had they either of them any power to detain me if I had not given them this money, or was it to console them for the loss of so delightful a companion as myself? They lost many equally delightful companions about that time, and must have been overwhelmed by such substantial consolations. Some idea lurked in my mind that Dr. Courtley would give it me back, or offer to share it with me, or at all events appear very grateful for so handsome a present. Not a bit of it. He lisped out—

"I with you ev'wy prothpewity in your future caweer. Good bye."

That was all I got for fifteen pounds. A good wish in a stereotyped formula. Perhaps, when I had retired, he quickly opened the envelope to see if the inclosed fee was in notes or a cheque.

I paid something more to old Phidler, Dr. Courtley's shuffling pantaloon of a servant, to carve my name on one of the panels of Upper School, as a memorial of My Time at Holyshade. Most Holyshadians left their mark in this way.

With a university career before me, it became necessary to examine my position. This I had to do for myself, and shape my own course.

At that renowned seat of learning, Holyshade College, Learning, as far as I was concerned, had sat remarkably still. Her ladyship seemed to have been asleep. She has, I imagine, bestirred herself since then. What gifts was I bringing away with me of her bestowing?

Well, I could make Latin verses *à la mode de Gradus ad Parnassum*, and had a respectable acquaintance with Virgil, Ovid, Horace, Homer, and their talented assistants —I mean their translators. I was well up, as are all

Holyshadians, in quantities: the Holyshadian maxim with regard to verse-making having been, in my time, "Quantity, not quality."

In Greek I had never felt any interest, and the beauties of the Greek drama had never been pointed out to me. I knew enough of the language to pass an examination in the Anabasis, if the examination did not venture upon details. I had the usual Holyshadian knowledge of "Derivations," and in construing was not likely to take δε by itself and translate it badly as "but." And what else? Nothing, except that I could play a first-rate game of Fives, was fond of "football at the wall," could row, swim, and play billiards. As to moral and religious training, I have already stated how much we had of that, and just so much I carried away; the amount being rather less than what I had brought with me. Of the value of either time or money I knew nothing, except that both could be spent pleasantly, and the more one had of both, the greater the enjoyment of existence. With English literature I was better acquainted than most boys of my age, in consequence of the bias given to my taste by my early friendship for Austin Comberwood. He started me with Scott's novels, and after that, I read everything and anything within my reach.

But when I heard from Austin that a candidate for undergraduateship at Bulford must undergo a preliminary examination, and that this was far from easy, my valour oozed away, and I decided for the sister university of Cowbridge, where I was given to understand the studies were eminently mathematical, which had the attraction for me of being an entirely new branch of learning.

There was, too, another inducement, and that was the prospect of an easy life at a private tutor's, away from the home now ruled over by Lady Colvin. My father gave me my choice, and I chose Cowbridge University, taking care to point out to him, at the same time, that I was, as yet, neither old enough nor learned enough in mathematics, to be entered on the books of Tudor College. My father consulted Cavander on this subject, as he now did on everything, and the result was that a private tutor was found for me, far away in the country, who was to take me under his care for a year or so, in order, to state it plainly, that I might make up for some of the time lost at Holyshade.

The Cavanders, brother and sister, governed my father's house both in and out of the City, and I was not aware, until later, that by this time Colvin and Cavander was the name of the firm.

The marriage did not seem to have brought my parent unalloyed happiness. He gave more parties, I believe; and Lady Colvin worked to restore him to that position in society which he ought long ago to have held. The Colvin title was like a horse's trappings, hung up in a damp room and allowed to rust for want of use; Lady Colvin had at once taken it down, and had commenced polishing bit and bridle, for Sir John was to be put through his paces and made to move in his proper circle. So far she was right, and in this respect my father had been undoubtedly wrong.

" Wrong ! " exclaimed my aunt Clym; " yes, and my brother has not gone the best way to set himself right. He never could take good advice "—by this she meant her own—" but was too fond of trusting anyone who'd only flatter him enough."

My aunt seemed to feel a kind of pleasure now in making these remarks in my presence. As to the Cavander family, she was inveterate against them.

" If ever there was a man I thoroughly distrusted," said my Aunt Clym, " Cavander is that man. His sister is not so clever as he is—that's the only difference between 'em. I pity that unfortunate piece of putty, his wife ; but as to him, I wouldn't believe him on his oath, not if he took it on the Bible."

Uncle Van fidgetted, and looked at my Uncle Herbert, to see what he would say.

" I don't think that form of swearing would offer any obstacle to him, if he thought it worth his while to take an oath," observed Uncle Herbert, languidly. He considered Cavander a sharp fellow, but Uncle Herbert's formula being " Speak of a man as you find him," he had always taken very good care to find every man so that he could be well spoken of.

Everybody was, or might be, useful to Herbert Pritchard. He did not envy his neighbour's carriage, horses, yachts, and so forth, but looked upon these luxuries as kept for his, Uncle Herbert's, use.

"If," he said, "you can't afford to keep these things yourself, take care to make yourself agreeable to those who do keep them. If you can't belong to all the best London clubs, the next best thing is to have friends in every one of them."

Cavander had been useful to him in a small way in the City, and Uncle Herbert had been assisted by him to the few odd pounds that are to be picked up by City *flâneurs*, who keep their eyes and ears open and are ready to take good advice on the spur of the moment.

Uncle Van was not fond of Cavander, but, being of a fishy nature, he was incapable of strong emotion, and had found, by experience, that it was generally safer, and more conducive to domestic comfort, to follow his wife's lead, in likes and dislikes.

Aunt Clym did not care how freely she spoke out her mind before me. I had told her how I could not get on with my stepmother, and in spite of what Aunt Clym had said to me on the eve of the marriage, she had not since then ever counselled me to try. The Van Clyms gradually left off visiting at our house, and a coldness sprang up between my father and his sister, which ended in the suspension of all friendly interchanges. I used, of course, to go and see my cousins, for the Clym family now sided with me, and considered me as decidedly and most unwarrantably injured in my rights.

"You'll see what will happen," said Mrs. Clym, oracularly, to her husband: "one of these days there'll be an exposure, and the wicked will cease to prosper."

Uncle Van intimated pleasantly to me that he hoped he, personally, should not lose by the cessation of the wicked's prosperity."

Your uncle makes jokes on those things," said my aunt, austerely, "but—"

"I do not make jox, my dear," protested Uncle Van. It was true, he did not.

My aunt went on, addressing him—

"You trust your money where you think it safe. You will see. I am glad for the children's sakes, that mine cannot be touched. I would not put it in Mr. Cavander's power to speculate—for speculate he does, and would lead you into it, too—not if he was twenty times the respectable man he appears to be, and five hundred times over again my brother's partner."

Uncle Van looked at me with a frightened air. I had accompanied him into the City the day before, and had heard him giving Cavander a commission.

"You shoot not mention what I too in the City," he said to me afterwards.

"I havn't said a word about it to Aunt," I told him; but I think he had lost faith in me. Fortunately, on this occasion he did take his wife's advice, and as the breach between the two families widened, so Uncle Van visited the office only at rare intervals, and his transactions with Cavander became less and less frequent, until they ceased altogether.

I was welcomed, too, by Aunt Clym, because I brought news to her about Mrs. Cavander, who often came to our house, and whom I generally discovered in tears.

She would speak to anyone and everyone of her sorrows.

"You know," she would say, after walking with me from our house to Mrs. Clym's, and talking to me all the way on her one subject and in invariably the same style, "James is very clever, and I can never expect to be as clever as he is. He is very handsome, too, and I feel that I am not equal to other women whom he meets in society. I know he doesn't wish me to go about with him."

"I should like to hear Mr. Van Clym saying such a thing as that to me," said my aunt, bristling up. "But you really ought to insist upon Mr. Cavander not going without you."

"I can't insist," returned the feeble woman; "how can I?"

Aunt Clym gave herself a shake, as though she would

have liked to perform a similar operation, only with greater violence, on Mrs. Cavander, just to shake her into action.

Here I interposed. I had heard Mrs. Cavander's Jeremiads, and they had by this time no interest for me, and obtained no sort of sympathy from her sister-in-law, now my stepmother, who evidently considered her a fool who was treated according to her deserts. The object of my visit was simply to say good-bye to the Clyms, as I was off to Ringhurst Whiteboys on a short stay, previous to my going to my private tutor's, where it had been arranged I was to make up for that portion of My Time which I had lost at Holyshade, and to prepare myself for the university.

"Miss Comberwood is considered very clever," Mrs. Cavander suddenly commenced.

"Yes, I believe so," I said, feeling that I was beginning to blush.

I was at the blushing age. It is a time when we do not care to sail under false colours, when, at the word of command, we display our flag, and acknowledge under what queen we are serving. At this season the face of a boy is like the graduated thermometer, with a heart for a bulb, and blood for mercury; you can mark off love, sin, shame, mirth, anger, on his face as certainly as you can the mean between zero and the highest temperature on a Fahrenheit scale.

I had corresponded with Alice while at Holyshade, and no one knew of it, at least so I thought, except her brother Austin. The disparity of our ages was, I suppose, in my opinion more than equalized by the superiority of the male over the female. Of course I could not have formulated this, but I fancy some such feeling underlies all these juvenile affairs of the heart. It is always Thumbling and the Princess. In after-life, if a Thumbling marries a Glumdalca, it is ten to one that the latter is his most obedient slave, and perhaps tyrannical Thomas Thumb whops her unmercifully. However, we did not go into this question then, and it has no place here without travelling out of the record of this history.

" Miss Comberwood has stayed with you often, hasn't she ? " asked Aunt Clym.

" Yes," sighed Mrs. Cavander. It was a heavy, dull, stupid sigh.

" She is very clever, and James likes talking with her," continued Mrs. Cavander, with a whimper in her voice expressive of utter helplessness. " They talk of things that I really do not understand, though I try very hard to."

" Your stepmother," said my aunt, turning to me, " told me Miss Comberwood was going to be married. Have you heard ? "

" I think I have," I answered.

I remembered Holyshade and Sir Frederick Sladen. I was indignant with him on the Verneys' account, for I had not forgotten the picnic, and Nurse Davis's speech on that occasion.

I did not wish, however, to prolong my interview with the two ladies, nor did they offer any opposition to my withdrawing, as they evidently had still got a good deal to say to one another which my Aunt would rather I should not hear, though as to Mrs. Cavander, she, poor babbling soul, would not have been offended had the butler, footman, and all the domestics been summoned as an audience of her woes.

Austin Comberwood had by this time returned to England. He had sent me a long letter, concluding with the invitation to Ringhurst Whiteboys, of which I was now about to avail myself. His brother Dick was at Woolwich, reading for the Army. Alice was at home. No obstacle was placed in my way by Lady Colvin, who was probably as pleased at my departure as I was myself. Her objection to the presence of my schoolboy friends at our house, I should now say at *her* house, was a polite method of hinting that my room was preferable to my company ; and as I was now placed under such restraints as made my former free-and-easy enjoyment of life in town impossible, I was only too glad to seize every opportunity of absenting myself, as much as I could, from the place which I could no longer regard as my home.

My father, too, seemed to shirk me as much as, at Holyshade, we had shirked masters when out of bounds. As yet my stepmother had not interfered with my father's financial arrangements in my regard, which had always been of a most openhanded character, and I felt that now he was paying me for being quiet and keeping out of the way.

Of business, of economy, of the value of a shilling, except in stamps for letters, I still knew nothing. Of such matters I had been studiously kept as ignorant as were the Egyptian neophytes of the sacred mysteries of Isis.

Other youths of my age could not, so they told me, run to this or that expense, because their allowance would not permit it; and this I was unable to understand. When Austin Comberwood informed me that his father had given him two hundred and fifty pounds a year for his university career, out of which he was to pay everything, and not to bring home a single bill, I considered Austin a very lucky fellow, and nothing would thenceforth satisfy me but a similar allowance. The distinction between Austin's and my view of this sum was, that *he* rightly considered it as intended for necessaries in the first place, and luxuries if possible, whereas I placed luxuries before necessaries, which I could have allowed to take care of themselves, like the pounds in the old proverb; and where Austin, with a bag of sovereigns, would have carefully calculated the cost of every day in the year, I should have played the game of life with sovereigns for counters, and spent them all in one day, or one hour, under the firm conviction that there were not only more, but plenty more, in the bank whence these were issued, and which would refuse my father nothing.

That I should have adopted this view was scarcely my fault, though it was, as events proved, undoubtedly my misfortune. From the first, even from Nurse Davis, I had always been led to believe my destiny to be cast among the richest, and the Colvin City mine inexhaustible. When my Aunt Clym expressed her annoyance with me for consorting with the Verneys, when afterwards she had reasoned with her brother on his

R

abdication of the family dignity, and of his choosing his
companions from a society beneath that in which he was
born to move, she never failed to allude to the resources
at his command, with which she used to say he might do
so much good, and if he like, repurchase the old Colvin
estates, and make a name in Parliament.   But my father
preferred the City for himself, and entertained such ideas
of his son's future as Aunt Clym would have had him act
upon for his own.   Strangely enough, he saw how fitting
this career was for another Colvin Baronet, but declined
the honour for himself.   He was to be the last of the line
in business, and I was to be the first of the modern race
on whom the State was to shower its rewards.   I was
certainly not qualifying for Chancellor of the Exchequer,
and of any profession I had no notion except what I had
derived from Austin when he had sometimes spoken of
being a clergyman.   I had seen a good deal of clergymen
as masters at Holyshade, and they were as other men,
their title to our reverence being, not in their ecclesiastical, but in their scholastic dignity.   I looked forward
to the day when, as an undergraduate I should be entitled
to wear a college cap and gown, in which costume, it
seemed to me, I should be as good a clergyman as any
one of them.

At Holyshade, as I have before remarked, I had seen
something of the Army, and barrack-life had no attraction
for me, as it appeared, save for the uniform, so uncommonly like Holyshade life at "my Tutor's" over again,
with just a thought more liberty for smoking.

Nearing the critical age of seventeen I had no sort of
bias.   I had begun, partly in consequence of the change
at home, to be restless and fond of wandering.   The course
of my education had gone far towards "making a man of
me;" that is, such a man as my father had contemplated,
and as I have before described in this record; but the
introduction of a stepmother had suddenly braced me up
to look out into the world, and act for myself.   In this
discontented frame of mind I went down to Ringhurst,
which after the chill of our household was like walking
out of a dank cave into the warm sunlight.

A change had come over Alice. Her brother had noticed it on his return. Her enthusiasm for ornate services, and her fondness for discussing any ecclesiastical or theological subject that might come up in the course of conversation, seemed to belong to a phase of her existence gradually passing away. Now she was inclined to question, where a very few years since she had been eager to teach.

"I think," said Austin to me, as we sat together one autumn evening in the fir plantation opposite the house, "this sudden love affair, if it is a love affair, has unsettled her. Perhaps one gets unsettled as one grows older."

Such a grave subject, treated, too, so gravely, was new to me, except in such novels and romances as had provided me with whatever knowledge I then had of life. But with Austin, and only with him, was I ever content to listen and speak seriously. I was, unconsciously, from time to time, yielding myself to his influence, an influence always for good, as my retrospect proves.

"Alice will be Lady Sladen," I said, giving him, as it were, a text for his discourse.

It was a lazy evening after a hot day, and I was in the humour for being talked to.

"Yes," he replied, thoughtfully, "and my mother and my father, too, are immensely pleased. Dick tells me that it was quite sudden, and he speaks of Sladen as a 'poor sort of fellow.' But Dick is hot-tempered, and I think would be inclined to resent anyone's taking Alice away from us. You know it all happened while I was away, so that I have scarcely had time to make his acquaintance."

"I don't think much of him," I said; and, in a confidential mood, I contributed my quota of scandal, saying, however, as little as possible, on my own account, about the Verneys.

Austin heard me to the end, and then remarked that at all events "no harm had come of it," meaning the affair between Sladen and Lottie, and this, as far as my information went, and I was not old enough to draw inferences, was a fair conclusion.

We then fell to comparing notes, how had Austin been occupied while I had been idling at Holyshade? and so forth. Now, with other youths, whether so much my seniors as to be almost young men, like Austin, or of my own age, my conversation would have flowed freely.

I should have talked about amusements at Holyshade, or during the holidays; I should have given my experience of life about town, of the joys and delights of a fast style; I should have boasted of my acquaintance by sight (and sometimes I romanced a good deal on this subject) with the celebrities of the day, whether famous or notorious, and would have given the rein to that sort of light and airy discourse which was, at that time, in vogue among us "Old Holyshadians." For at this distinction I had arrived, though not, as yet, at the enviable one of being dubbed a "Worthy." However, were I an "Unworthy" it would have been no more than were seven hundred out of the eight hundred scholars. The two most wicked cities this world has ever known, however, would have been saved for the sake of one godly resident: therefore, if my estimate be correct, Holyshade, after all, was in a comparatively hopeful state.

On such topics as those to which I have above alluded, I was as silent, in Austin's company, as I would have been in that of his mother or sister.

I liked, indeed, to exhibit myself to him as a lad of some mettle and anything but slow, yet I could not bear the idea of his supposing me to be a mere trifler.

In my correspondence with him, during his absence, I had been at pains to present him with the better side of my character, and though I really enjoyed writing to him, yet I experienced a certain relief when I had finished the letter, and had resumed my own natural self.

I always "felt good," as I expressed it to myself, when with Austin, and, even between sixteen and seventeen, it was through him that I occasionally opened my eyes to a brighter light than that to which I had, till then, been accustomed. But there were to be many progressive temptations by which I was to be tried, before I could

live in the pure atmosphere of the planet where Austin
Comberwood dwelt.

So it chanced that I had little to say, but much to hear.
For my friend had travelled in France, Germany, and
Italy, and had allowed few things worthy of note to
escape his observation.

"And now you finish by going up to Bulford," I said,
"and then you'll be a clergyman."

"I do not know," was his reply, which surprised me,
as I had never known him waver in a course when he
himself had fixed the goal.

"Austin says he doesn't think he'll be a clergyman,"
I said to Alice, who had now joined us.

"We have talked it over together," said Austin, looking
up affectionately at his sister, "though we do not talk
over so many things as we used to; but I suppose that's
because my Alice is to have another confidant——"

"Never mind that now," Alice interrupted him, as if
annoyed by even this passing allusion to her marriage.
"We don't know what may happen between now and—
that time."

I had never before heard her speak with even the
slightest degree of petulance to her favourite brother.

For the moment her tone shocked me, and I could have
resented it for Austin's sake, but for his resuming quietly—

"No; nor do I care about anticipating our separation.
Papa talks of settling in London, and Mamma considers
it absolutely necessary. Dick will go abroad, probably,
with his regiment, and I shall be in my cap and gown at
the university. My father seems to wish that I should
go to the Bar, where his interest, he says, would be of the
greatest use to me. I do not care about it much myself;
but, on the other hand, I begin to think of a clergyman's
profession as involving a very great responsibility."

"I am sure Austin is right," observed Alice. "He
would never of course be such a clergyman as is Mr.
Tabberer, our rector, who looks upon Sunday as his professional day, and is a country squire and market gardener
for the rest of the week. Why he is more interested in
his fruits and flowers than in all his poor at Ringhurst

taken together. I've visited among them, and I know it. And Austin could never be like Mr. Kershaw, at Hyde Mallow, who only took the curacy because there was good hunting and shooting in the neighbourhood, and who visits the sick cottagers with a small pack of fox-terriers at his heels. Then there's Mr. Greeve, of Wylborne, who dresses as if he were always ready for an evening party, and who drives miles to go to a dance. No, I would rather see Austin a barrister than a clergyman of that sort."

Here it suddenly occurred to me that the masters at Holyshade were clergymen, and I expressed a hope that Austin would never resemble any one of these ecclesiastics, from the unwieldy Provost, who used to puff and blow over the first part of the Communion Service, and the Vice-Provost, who piped out the Commandments in a shrill perky tone, or his reverence the Bursar, who began his sentences in the pulpit with a bellow and ended in a whisper, down to my old tutor, Mr. Raab, who used to take an occasional duty for a friend three miles from Holyshade, when it was his wont to be accompanied by a few of his pupils, to whom he gave leave out of school chapel in order that they might have the treat of a pleasant walk across the meadows by the river-side on a fine summer morning, and form a portion of the scanty congregation assembled in the little parish church of Stockfield to hear him preach.

I owned I did not know what kind of clergyman I should have liked Austin to be, but my ideas on all such subjects were of the vaguest description.

I knew my catechism, because I couldn't help that, and I had been confirmed at Holyshade by the Right Rev. Father in God Bishop of Sawder, for which I had been prepared by Miss Raab, my tutor's sister, who presented me with a packet of tracts, which, with pictures, afforded us scapegraces considerable amusement; and it was on this solemn occasion that I took the opportunity of refreshing my memory of the earlier-acquired catechism.

"And then," said Austin, "you should see our clergymen abroad. I really don't know where they come from. Mr.

Venn, who was with me at first, knew some of them, and I'm sure I never wished to meet any of them again : except one at Nice, who was very fond of music, and who went with me to all the grand services in the churches there."

"But they were Catholic churches, weren't they?" I asked. Had he told me they were Mahometan Mosques or Pagan Temples, I should have accepted his account of it.

"Yes," he replied, "and of course our dreary place for Anglican Church worship wasn't to be compared for a moment with one of these splendid churches. I should have preferred my own service to any of theirs, I think, could I have had our own old church of Whiteboys, with even Alice's old enemy, the rector, to conduct it. But the carelessness, the irreverence I witnessed Sunday after Sunday——"

"In Roman Catholic churches?" asked Alice.

"No, in our English place of worship; it was simply revolting. As for the sermons, they were generally stupid. All the English went as a matter of nationality, and out of compassion for the clergyman, who, I believe, had only a small allowance to live on, in addition to his congregation's subscriptions. There was a fairly respectable specimen where we were staying. I was not impressed, personally, by him, when on meeting him, subsequently, at a *table-d'hôte* I heard him inform my tutor that he didn't make a very good thing of it."

"Was he married?" asked Alice.

"Yes," answered Austin, "and there were three daughters whom the poor man had to take to all the parties and dances throughout the season, in the hope of their making good matches, and so relieving him of a portion of his burden. I once came across a good-natured Bulford man, a married English clergyman, who tried to affect the dress of the native Catholic priests. He was very angry because our German landlady would not understand his pretensions, and when he attempted to explain to her that he was a priest, she shook her head, smiled, addressed him as *Herr Pasteur*, and asked after his wife and five grown-up daughters, who had the reputation of being the greatest flirts in the place."

Alice sighed. "It is difficult, most difficult, to believe in such men being divinely set apart for their office," she said.

"It is," returned Austin, gravely; and, as I was saying to you yesterday, Alice dear, what proof shall I ever have or those about me, that I should be so set apart? And if the clergy are not divinely commissioned, in what are they in the least superior to other ordinary men, who know just as much about religion, and sometimes more, than those who set themselves up to be their teachers?"

He was talking far above the capacity of my youthful intelligence, yet I have no doubt but that his words were seeds dropped on a likely soil. As tares spring up among the wheat, so, on the other hand, sweet wild strawberries grow in the rank grass by the side of a stagnant pond. Whence the seed came, when it took root, none can tell, but innocent children discover the bright red berries with shouts of delight, as Heaven's angels, who have sown as silently, but more carefully, than their fallen brethren, may point exultingly to the good fruit, dwarfed indeed, but flourishing, in the midst of nettles and noisome weeds.

Subsequent events brought this conversation vividly to my mind, and though I was wearied with the subject, which was then almost unintelligible to me, I well remember Alice's manner, as being, in its restlessness, so different from her former impassioned self. Two years before she would have attacked Austin for what she would have deemed his profanity, and would have professed herself unable to understand how he could, for a moment, admit one doubt as to the sacred character of the priesthood of her ideal Church of England.

Since then she had fallen under another influence, but it angered her to have it said, even by her dear brother, that her hold upon the standard, under which she had enlisted, had been relaxed by a force to which she had gradually been compelled to yield. This flag was no longer her pride and her encouragement; it embarrassed her movements. She made some show of still grasping her colours, but it was evident to those who understood her at that time, that she was often on the point of flinging them down on the march, and abandoning them for ever.

"It would be better," she said, "for you to be a barrister than to be teaching either what you did not believe, or did not understand."

"My dear Alice," Austin began in a tone of remonstrance, but his sister took him up quickly, and with more of her old impetuosity than I had hitherto noticed.

"I too have seen something of clergymen," she said. "Besides Mr. Tabberer and Mr. Kershaw, look at Andrew." She alluded to her brother-in-law, Mr. McCracken. "Why, old Mr. Tabberer said he admired floral decorations, and did not mind—fancy! did not mind—having a cross on the altar, only he objected to my using the word altar, not because, he said, there really was any harm in it, but because it might engender superstition. I asked him, for you know I had been reading a good deal about it,"—Alice considered herself something of a theologian—"what particular grace was conferred by the Bishop's laying on of hands at his ordination——"

"And what could he say?" asked Austin.

"Say! He had nothing to say, except that the subject was too far above me, that there were certain formal words which every candidate for orders had to read, and that on the whole he considered his ordination as a solemn ceremony; and just as the consecration of a church might be the setting apart a building, so the ordination would be the setting apart a person for a special purpose. Mr. Amphthill, his curate, who was here for a short time, gave me a very different view of the matter; *he* said he was a successor of the Apostles, and that old Mr. Tabberer was also."

"Without being aware of it," said Austin, smiling.

"That is what Mr. Cavander said—" she stopped suddenly, as though she would have recalled these words had she been able.

"I know you talked all over this with him," Austin observed, and then, as if unwilling to pursue this part of the subject any further, he reverted to her mention of Mr. McCracken, and inquired, " What did Andrew say ?"

"He told me that Mr. Tabberer was too much of a Tory, and was of the old-fashioned Church and State type, which hated dissent, where, after all, there was real hearty spiritual life. He expressed his opinion that Mr. Amphthill was a Jesuit."

At this point I *was* interested. I had read about Jesuits in romances, and my notion of them was grotesque. I had never seen one, and from the flavour I had got of them in fiction, I could have described such a creature with about as much accuracy, as a man, blind from his birth, might be expected to describe a crab, only from having tasted the delicacy with pepper and vinegar. The word Jesuit conveyed to my mind inquisitions, tortures, prisoners in disguise, and a number of creeping, crawling things, half fiend, half human, with, perhaps, tails. What a Jesuit was in reality, I honestly had not the smallest idea, so powerful had been the national English traditions influencing my mind through the channels of Romances founded on so-called History. It is thus that ignorant prejudices are fostered, and how few of us in after-life have the time, or the will, to sift the rubbish of the dustbin of History on the chance of discovering the diamond of Truth.

" *Was* he a Jesuit ?" I asked innocently.

Alice paid no attention to my question, for she was in earnest now.

"I told Andrew that Mr. Amphthill hoped to see confession restored in the Church of England; whereat he was horrified. I pointed out to Andrew that both he and Mr. Amphthill had to use the awfully solemn form of absolution in the Visitation of the Sick to be pronounced by an English clergyman over a dying person who had confessed. Andrew replied, that there was a great deal in the Prayer-book that wanted altering, that this particular instance was merely a form meant for the solace of a certain' sort of weak mind—like mine I suppose he meant—that the use of it was optional, and that it had been allowed to remain in order to conciliate Catholics at the Reformation, and that no one with a grain of sense believed in the existence of such a power; and that, speaking for himself, if he pretended to possess it, he would be no minister of the Church of England. Yet," she continued meditatively, more as if communing with herself than addressing us, "were there such a mission of forgiveness, could one indeed be sure of——"

She paused, and, bending her head, plucked the grass fitfully. Austin leaned over her, and put his arm round her neck.

"We think together," he said; "and I have three years of study before me. I wish I could be a clergyman; we have both of us always wished that. Don't you remember how gravely we had settled our future; neither of us to marry, but you to keep house for me at the parsonage or the rectory ?"

"Yes."

"All that, so far, is changed now. You are going to be married, and I have not yet made up my mind as to what I shall be when I leave the university. Come, dear, there's the supper bell, and we've quite tired out poor Cecil."

I call to mind now how that night, sitting alone in my room at Ringhurst, I reflected on this conversation, and was puzzled by it. A change seemed to be coming over me, and over those whom I loved best. So much I perceived distinctly, but I was too young to trace results to causes, and too much engrossed with my own domestic affairs to bestow more than a passing thought on those of others, however near or dear to me they might be.

That Austin was contemplating an alteration in the plan of his life, that his sister was going to be married (an event which was being looked forward to by Mrs. Cavander with unconcealed satisfaction), that I detested Sir Frederick Sladen on sufficient grounds, and that somehow in the midst of all this a comparison between Alice and Julie would thrust itself upon me to the disadvantage of the former,—all these subjects of interest presented themselves to my mind as in the jumble of a dream, to be ultimately absorbed into my own personal and present grievance, namely, my father's recent marriage.

My Holyshadian habit of keeping an irregular sort of diary was at this time a source of great relief to me. This diary, kept from time to time in various old-fashioned account books with clasps, served me as a confidential friend, into whose ear I would pour my griefs, my complaints, and such observations on my friends' words and deeds as I could not have made to anyone likely to repeat them. On looking over a drawer full of these sketchy records, I have been surprised to find how briskly my memory has been refreshed as to details, concerning My Time, which have been necessary to my evidence when appearing as a "witness to character," that character being my own.

I quitted Ringhurst Whiteboys a few days after. Alice had gone on a visit to some friends (she was always going away on visits now, Austin said). And only stopping in London to call at the office in the City, where, according to my father's directions, I was provided with ample funds for my journey and my residence at my private tutor's, I set out for Hillborough House, Collington, Devonshire, where I was to pass the interval between Holyshade and the University.

CHAPTER XXVIII.

A FRESH SCENE—A PUPIL—PRIVATE HISTORY—THE DRIVE—
NEW IDEAS—DOMESTIC ECONOMY OF HILLBOROUGH—MR.
BLUMSTEAD APPEARS—FURTHER DESCRIPTION—HIS REPU-
TATION.

HILLBOROUGH House, near Collington, Devonshire, was
the strangest possible residence for a country parson like
my tutor, the Rev. John Henry Blumstead.

A curly-headed pupil in a pony-carriage was waiting to
receive me at Collington Station. His name was Ashton,
and he was about eighteen. He wore a pea-jacket, boating trousers, and a tarpaulined straw hat, whence I
inferred that he had lately come off the river. It appeared, however, that this nautical taste of his was the
consequence, not of his having come off a river, for there
was not one for miles round, but of his having been to
sea, which profession he had quitted in disgust, and had
come to Mr Blumstead's to prepare himself for Bulford.
This, and much more as to the amusements of Hillborough
House, Ashton told me as we went along; and before we
had reached my tutor's abode I was pretty well master
of my companion's family history, and was prepared
for the best or the worst, as it might come, at Hillborough.

It was a lovely autumn evening, and every fresh ascent
(we were perpetually dipping down and coming up again
in a way that reminded me of bathing), opened before us
an ever-varying aspect of the undulating fields and

meadows, terminating in distant hills of such a bright blue as I had never till now noticed out of a landscape-painting. The rocks about us, for it was a very rough way, were of a rich brown, not unlike the colour of a wedding-cake, and the herbage of a deep ultramarine formed a strongly marked foreground to the picture, making the distance all the brighter and lighter by the contrast. The swiftly passing clouds drew, as it were, cloth after cloth from off the face of the fields, suggesting to my Holyshadian mind the brown holland covering being rapidly removed from a series of well-kept billiard-tables.

The view was entirely new to me, who had never before seen a hill country. We bumped over a rutty road, past many hovels and a few well-kept cottages, which, I was informed, represented a portion of Hill-borough parish. Ringhurst Whiteboys was a town compared with this. The country folks, too, spoke a dialect which was almost unintelligible to my ears. My companion seemed to be well up in the _patois_, and amused himself, and me, considerably by addressing the rustics in their own native tongue, and then translating the conversation for my benefit.

Altogether I was charmed with the novelty.

"You'll keep a horse or a pony and a trap here, of course," said Ashton.

This was a novel idea to me, but it was one that coincided with my own notions of luxury and self-inportance. However, never having mentioned the subject to my father, I thought it as well to enquire what necessity existed for such an outlay at Hillborough. Ashton explained :—

"You see," he said, "you'll want to go about to picnics and parties, and old Blumstead doesn't keep a trap himself, and so it depends upon us whether the ladies go or not They're very jolly, and we take them. You can't hire anything here, not even a donkey, as there's no town, bar Collington, for miles."

"And who are the ladies ?" I asked, naturally enough.

"There's Mrs. Fowler, she's Blummy's sister; she's a

widow, and he's a widower," Ashton answered. "Then there's the eldest Miss Blumstead, rather starchy, but pretty; Mrs. Fowler looks after her," added my knowing young friend, giving me a side glance, and the horse an encouraging flick, which caused him to go ahead with a jerk that nearly landed me on his back over the dashboard. "The two other girls, I mean her sisters, are away just now, staying with my aunt, who always has some companions with her, whom she takes a fancy to for some time. You must know my aunt. Very jolly, and got a beautiful yacht."

So he finished, reverting, illogically, to his first theme, "You must have an animal and a trap."

This was a suggestion upon which I determined to act as soon as possible.

It had long been an ambition of mine to possess a horse and vehicle of some sort, having envied the old Holyshadians in barracks their neat turn-outs, and now that the opportunity presented itself, I would not let a week pass without furnishing myself with what Ashton had clearly demonstrated to be an absolute necessity. As to the cost, that never troubled me for a moment. I protested that nothing but a dog-cart and a fast trotter would suit *me*, and from that moment, Ashton, who regretted his own inability to afford so expensive an equipage, was my admiring friend and sworn ally. Now for the first time I began to appreciate the advantage which a youth, who has been at Holyshade, possesses over one who has not; and as this gradually broke upon me, and we drove up to the front door, I felt more as if I had come to teach than to receive instruction.

I have already said that Hillborough House was a strange residence for a simple country parson, and I think its description will bear me out in this remark.

It was a very large house, of the Italian style, looking as though some eccentric person had brought a London club-house down here, and had set it on the top of a hill, for the benefit of the pure country air.

It was perfectly square, and painted a bright glaring white, unrelieved by any colour, whether from a venetian blind or a geranium. A colonnade, the roof of which was supported by plain columns like those in a child's box of wooden bricks, went all round it, and formed a useful promenade in wet weather.

On the plan of a Pompeian house, the rooms were in the corridors that inclosed the central hall, the height of which was that of the house itself. This hall, which was lighted by windows in a dome above, contained the grand staircase, while the servants' staircase was concealed, and within the walls on one side of the quadrangle.

On the whole it had so classic an air about it, that had the Rev. John Henry Blumstead issued from the front door and appeared in the colonnade in a toga, with a garland round his head, and sandals on his feet, I should not have been very much surprised.

The house had been built by a nobleman, who had given it up after trying it for a short time, and had then conferred it upon its present occupant, to whom he had given the small living of Hillborough.

Mr. Blumstead, who was a Bulford man, with a scholarly reputation, had soon found it necessary to follow his sister's advice, and take pupils. There was plenty of room for them, and they were more profitable than pigs or poultry. There was, too, no difficulty in obtaining them, as, thanks to the reputation for scholarship above mentioned, many of his most aristocratic friends, whom he had years before assiduously cultivated at the university, were only too glad to avail themselves of his services for their sons who were to follow in their own footsteps. Not that they remembered Mr. Blumstead's having in any way distinguished himself while at College; he had only come out as a B.A. without honours, and had subsequently taken his M.A., which step, as everyone is aware, requires only the payment of certain fees into the university chest, and something more for the good of the college of which you may happen to be a member. Yet he had been credited by everyone with the possession of high mathematical attainments, which, in his day, were, they explained to one another, of small value except at Cowbridge, to which university it was clearly his misfortune, and not his fault, that he did not belong.

Ashton informed me that he believed, from what he had heard from his father, that Mr. Blumstead owed his name for classical scholarship to the fact that he had successfully coached Lord Cricklewood through his degree, after that unlucky young nobleman had twice failed in the most gallant attempts. Lord Cricklewood, now Earl of Willesden, had never forgotten this feat of tutorship, and when Mr. Blumstead wrote to him announcing his intention of regularly taking pupils, he recommended him to all his friends as a man of such erudition, and so skilful in imparting his knowledge to others, as to be unrivalled by any living professor. The Earl quoted himself as an instance of Mr. Blumstead's skill, saying, "'Gad, sir, he got *me* through!" which was a lifelong wonder to himself, and rendered his lordship a splendid advertisement for his former coach.

This highly recommended preceptor of youth had a pear-shaped head, big at the cranium, and diminishing towards the chin. His neck, encircled by a loose white tie, was as it were the stalk of the pear. He was bald, and grey hair rose up on each side from the temples to the back, like the sea froth about a polished boulder.

Allowing for Lord Cricklewood's degree as a fluke in the annals of private tuition, just as an outsider from an unknown stable may falsify all prognostications about a Derby favourite, and immortalize his trainer,—I say putting this aside as a chance hit, to what had Mr. Blumstead owed whatever success in life he had achieved ? I answer, unhesitatingly, he owed it to his broad massive forehead, and his nose of the genuine Roman type. In the most flourishing era of Paganism he would have been Blumstedius, the chief augur, and had he met his most intimate friend in the whole College of Augurs, he (Blumstedius) would not for one second have tolerated a smile or a wink, but would have valued himself and the secret of his own incapacity too highly, to admit the truth even in confidence and unofficially, to the man who had best reason to know that the chief augur was only a solemn idiot.

s

The Rev. Mr. Blumstead's face, like that of the milk-maid in the song, had been his fortune. No one—so fathers who were acting upon my Lord Cricklewood's recommendation reasoned—no one with such a brow as Blumstead's could be a fool. And indeed it would have been difficult to convict him of folly out of his own mouth, for in society he had seldom opened it but to agree, or to utter in a sonorous tone, and with a calm air of peaceful superiority, platitudes which sounded at the time like the words of true wisdom. He manufactured sermons in his library, where he had indeed a formidable array of theological works. He belonged to no religious party in the Church. His "views" were, so to speak, held for him by his sister, and his daughters, who followed their aunt's teaching. Were all Anglican clergymen like Mr. Blumstead, the English Church would be at peace: but, it would be a corpse.

Next to being rich, it is best to have the reputation for wealth, and next to being clever, it is best to be given credit for talent. To give credit is a phrase implying no pressure for immediate payment. Mr. Blumstead presented his creditors with his forehead for their security. This, backed by that brilliant living example already quoted, namely, the Earl of Willesden, was quite sufficient. The Earl did business with Sir John's house in the City, and had there mentioned Mr. Blumstead.

He had his faults, like other great men. He was of a choleric disposition. A stupid, passionate man will go at a stone wall like a mad bull. Fortunately for him, his sister held the reins with a tight hand, and did with him what she pleased.

He had his accomplishments, too, for he was passionately fond of the science of music; and associating this with the idea of keeping up his reputation for high mathematics, he would pass his hours of recreation in attempting logarithms on the German flute.

Everybody liked Blumstead: his pupils would have done anything for him, and he certainly possessed the knack of imparting knowledge, of "coaching" in the best possible manner, and in innoculating the student with a desire to know more and learn more thoroughly. I write with loving respect of dear old Blumstead, though his weaknesses amuse me even now.

The flute and the bugle were his instruments, and I had reason to sincerely wish they had not been.

Mrs. Fowler permitted their use, as I discovered, for a certain wise purpose. The flute had been fashioned according to his own order and design, years and years ago, and had twice as many holes as any ordinary one. This, he thought, gave him more chance of producing such correct and exact notes as, he would explain, must lie, even though expressed in logarithms, between b and c, or between e and f, which had no semitone between them. His pupils were unable to plumb the depth of these mysteries, but of one they were all quite sure, that if the flute had twice as many holes as any other, it made, at all events, twice as much noise.

Mr. Blumstead's innocent ambition was to perfect the flute, but the difficulty increased with the size and number of the holes. Everyone in Hillborough House, except perhaps Mrs. Fowler, sincerely hoped that this object might be speedily accomplished. When the flute should be perfected, it was probable that he would then be satisfied, and experimentalize no more.

I have hinted that Mrs. Fowler had a sufficient reason for encouraging the performance. She continued to do so because when she had first come to reside with him after his bereavement, her brother discovered that he had 'temper.' She hit upon the flute as an expedient, and a look from her was enough; so that when he felt he was no longer master of himself (the most trivial thing would make him boil over, like the "shallow pot" in the old proverb, which is "soon hot"), he would, from sheer force of habit, walk sharply out of the room, and the next instant we were sure to hear the shrieks of the flute, through the holes of which he blew off his steam in the study.

The key-bugle he blew regularly every morning. It was used instead of a bell, or a gong, to rouse the sleepers. He only knew a few cavalry calls on it, and I often wished he had learnt a tune.

Mrs. Fowler was sharp, clever, and a thorough woman of the world.

Ashton and myself became fast friends, though his was a friendship of a very different type from Austin's. I soon found that the Hillborough party was never omitted from any of the country festivities, of which, at all times of the year there was more than enough to prevent one ever complaining of the dulness of a provincial life.

I now set to work with a will to prepare myself for Cowbridge. I rejoiced in a new kind of life which was free from the irksome restraint of Lady Colvin's presence, and, having within a very short time suited myself not only with a dog-cart, bright harness, a high-stepping bay, and a small boy out of the village, dressed in a tiger's livery, I felt that I had completely set up for myself *en garçon*, and, at the end of six weeks at Hillborough, I imagined myself at least four years older than I had been on my arrival.

For me the present time was more than a mere change of scene; it was, as it were, a new drama, with new interests, new action, and an entire novelty in the *dramatis personæ*.

For a while I could forget the Cavanders, and even became negligent in my correspondence with Austin Comberwood. My Time at Hillborough, which was the *entr'acte* between Holyshade and Cowbridge, would not have demanded any especial notice from me here, but for one event which I must hasten to record.

CHAPTER XXIX.

ASHTON and myself were Mr. Blumstead's only pupils, and he was therefore able to bestow on us his individual attention.

Now, for the first time, I conceived a liking for study, for our tutor was sufficiently well versed in his subjects to be able to arouse the curiosity of any pupil of an inquiring turn. He showed us difficulties in mathematics, and left us to solve them. He seldom answered a question in classics, but observed that *his* way was invariably to refer to authorities. These authorities were dictionaries, grammars, and lexicons, on accessible shelves, and Mr. Blumstead himself must have acquired a vast amount of erudition, and considerably strengthened the muscles of his calves by climbing his library ladder, in the course of his teaching *me*.

What I learnt then, I learnt thoroughly; and I pay this tribute to Blumstead's memory, that he acted as master of the ceremonies in introducing me to the "authorities" above mentioned, whose acquaintance I might, perhaps, have never made, but for his intervention.

My time at Blumstead's was not thrown away After two harmless upsets, and consequent expenses—for there is no exception to the rule of paying for experience—I learnt to drive, and my showy dog-cart, with a tiger behind, quite threw into the shade my companion Ashton's low four-wheeled chaise, and little rough-and-ready pony.

Among the numerous picnics to which we were invited, there was one alone which, as bearing in any way on my future, I must not omit from these confidential records. It was given by Mr. and Mrs. Burdon, relations of Ashton's, who had taken a house near Dawlish for the summer.

Mr. and Mrs. Burdon were the most popular couple I have ever met. They were known everywhere as Mr. and Mrs. Robert Burdon, to distinguish them from the Toms and Dicks of their family; and as Mr. Burdon had from his earliest schooldays been known familiarly as Bob, so Mrs. Robert, who was as warm-hearted, lively, and "jolly," as her husband, had been, very soon after her marriage, christened Mrs. Bob, and ever afterwards, by her own wish, so addressed by her intimates.

It was a great privilege for a youngster to be a friend of Mrs. Bob's It was a recommendation to their own circle, and it was a *passe-partout* outside.

The Bob Burdons were very rich and spent their money well and wisely. Their house, wherever it was, and they were always changing it, preferring to have no fixed residence, was invariably open to all comers, and their hearty "Come and see us" really meant that the giver of the invitation would be honestly disappointed if it were not accepted. They had travelled much, and reckoned a number of foreigners among their acquaintances, who on coming to England were sure of a hospitable welcome from Mr. and Mrs. Bob. They had no children, but several pets, which travelled with them, and Mrs. Bob was invariably accompanied by some young lady, frequently by two, whom she had chosen for such distinguishing social qualities as would be of assistance to her in her informal and chatty receptions, and would supply the place of a grown-up daughter, when in the absence of excitement Mrs. Bob might happen to be thrown on her own domestic resources.

Their yacht was in reality their home, for this was kept in trim all the year round, and, as they always took a furnished house or apartments, when on shore, it was no trouble to them, at any moment, to order their things to be packed up, to embark on board the *Stella*, and start for Norway and Sweden, or the Mediterranean, as their caprice might suggest.

When I first met this happy couple, they had been married about fifteen years, and I do not suppose there had ever been one minute in the course of their lives when they had repented their union.

Mrs. Bob informed me that she already knew one of my relations very well indeed; that, indeed, he was one of their most intimate friends, and never missed a season's yachting with them.

After this I scarcely required to be told that this relative was Uncle Herbert.

The "Bobs" were just the people he would love. The honest fellow would have said to them with fervour, "Your home shall be my home; your table my table; your yacht my yacht; and where thou goest I also will go, at your expense."

So it was not long ere he appeared in all his glory of summer costume, at Corfield, which was the name of Mr. and Mrs. Bob's temporary residence, and was the life and soul of the picnic parties, and of the house generally.

It was he who handed his host's best cigars about to friends, who commanded the servants, who suggested plans for the day's amusement, and a stranger arriving at Corfield would have concluded that Uncle Herbert was the generous and hospitable entertainer, and the "Bobs" his old friends, staying with him for some time.

Between my own willingness to make a confidante of Mrs. Bob, and my uncle's readiness to impart his information on the subject, the Colvin family history had been long known in detail to the Burdons, who sincerely condoled with me on the change which had lately taken place in Sir John's household.

The Burdon party at this time consisted of Mr. and Mrs. Tom, Miss Fanny Blumstead, who was my tutor's second daughter, a pretty, fair-haired, blue-eyed, fresh-coloured, lively girl, and Mrs. Tom's resident *protégée,* Miss Clara Wenslow.

One evening, in Ashton's absence, Uncle Herbert drove with me to the station, on our return from a fishing excursion, off Dawlish.

"Cecil," said Uncle Herbert, abruptly.

I was all attention. He so seldom spoke with an air of conviction, that a smack of real earnestness in his tone put me immediately on the *qui vive.*

"You're a young fellow yet," said Uncle Herbert, "quite a boy, and therefore it's just as well to warn you against making a fool of yourself. I know the world, and I know young men in it, and am perfectly aware that, as a rule, with scarcely an exception, advice is utterly thrown away."

"Not on me," I ventured to reply.

"Ah," he returned, dubiously, "we shall see. What I'm going to observe is this. You're very easily taken in. Every impulsive chap at your time of life is—by—" he paused for a second, as if considering.

"By whom?" I asked.

"By himself," answered Uncle Herbert, decidedly. "I mean by his own vanity and love of admiration. A girl expresses herself your admirer, and immediately you become hers; a girl shows a preference for you, and you fall head over ears in love with her."

I felt myself blushing, and did not feel inclined to ask at whom his allusion pointed.

"I am putting you on your guard," he went on; "there is no such mistake in life as marrying too early. I don't say that you are going to make an ass of yourself just yet, before you are even of age; but I foresee that unless you have some one at your elbow to guide you, you'll lose yourself, and be precious sorry for it afterwards."

"My dear uncle, I have no sort of intention," I began.

"Precisely. That's just it. You don't intend to fall in love when you set out in the morning, but before lunch-time you've done it. You don't intend to go one step farther than a flirtation, but half-an-hour after you've commenced, you find you've passed the limits, and are caught. There's no way out of it; the only thing is to take my advice, and don't go in for it. If my sister had lived, and you had had a mother at home to look after you in this respect, I should not have been advising you. But you ask Mrs. Bob. I'll get her to have a chat with you, for the best companion and guide a young man can have on entering the world is a clever middle-aged married woman, who knows the ins and outs of society. Her influence will do more for him than any lectures either from father or uncles."

Herbert Pritchard was right, but of course I could not at that time be expected to agree with him on such a nice point.

I simply protested that I had no idea of anything like a serious attachment, and for that matter, speaking honestly, I did not then know the meaning of the phrase. How can the words " serious attachment" mean anything to a lad of seventeen or eighteen, however precocious he may be ?

And yet it seems to me, reviewing the past, that young men now-a-days *do* understand the phrase, and more, know how to guard themselves against yielding to any such absurd sentiments. The other day I was lecturing, a young friend in much the same style as Uncle Herbert had lectured me—no matter how many years ago— enough that it has been here recorded—and what does he get up and say ? Why this :—

"My dear Ganache,"—he did not use this word, but it was *subauditum*, and underlay the speech—"I am not such a fool as I look. I can't afford to do any more than flirt; the merest innocent flirtation. *Je ne suis pas un parti, moi, vous comprenez—*" this is another modern affectation; we in our time did not interlard our discourse with French, but then I am bound to add that that elegant and charming language was only taught as an "extra" at Holyshade—"and so mamma runs after me for her daughters. I'm more like the *maître de ballet*, or one of his merry men—I'm hired out to dance. That's my profession at present, dancing.

In return they give me suppers and dinners, and as, fortunately, I happen to sing, they add invitations to their country houses. I am not ornamental, perhaps, but I am useful, and I fill a gap. No, *mon vieux,* if I marry, I must marry money. One and one make two, and that is quite enough without going further into arithmetic. No, love is a luxury, and marriage isn't a necessity."

Now these were not the Colvin sentiments at any time in the history of our family. Impulse: *dum vivo, ago,* was the Colvin motto, and *ago* is better than *spero.*

With all my knowledge of London life, I knew at this time very little of society. That must be put to my account. Romances and novels had been my chief pabulum; and the theatres and such-like places of amusement my recreation. Sir John had never gone into society, and society had stopped short of our door. Such friends as by father gathered round him I have already described. What I wish to convey is that I was now making my *entrée* into society without such a guide as (and here Herbert Pritchard was undoubtedly right) my mother would have been.

And had I fallen in love with Miss Clara Wenslow, Mrs. Bob's *protégée?* This was what Uncle Herbert's lecture pointed at.

Fair-haired, petite, older than myself—of course—and decidedly accomplished. She wrote poetry, she sang, I thought, *then,* deliciously: she adored Tennyson, quoted Shelley, and kept an album full of scraps. I have to thank her for my introduction to a taste for poetry. A taste, not much, but enough for scraps.

Miss Clara amused Mrs. Bob vastly, and so, I suppose, did I.

As for her nephew, Frank Ashton, he was having a desperate flirtation with Miss Fanny Blumstead, and Mrs. Bob had an eye for both of us. We should not kick over the traces and bolt as long as she held the reins, and she did hold them, and knew how to manage the team perfectly.

I think this was at the time somewhat irksome to

her companion, Clara Wenslow, who would have had me down on my knees before I knew where I was, and would have sent me off to her parents (her father was a retired naval officer living in the north of England) by the next train. But Mrs. Bob knew all the moves, and I was not to be the only young man in attendance.

Besides, Uncle Herbert, too, was not blind, and so, thank goodness, I was prevented from making an utter idiot of myself before I had arrived at the use of my reasoning faculties.

Legally an infant, I suppose my promise to pay on a hymeneal bond would have been worthless. But then there would have been the Colvin honour.

Talking over our mode of life with Ashton one evening, he observed,

"If a fellow must have a profession, it would be very jolly to settle down as a country parson with a nice wife."

"Yes, we see a good deal of them, don't we?" I returned. "They seem very happy."

"And it doesn't cost much," remarked Ashton, to whom money was an object.

"I don't think I shall be anything," I replied, with an assumption of indifference as to all monetary questions. "My father wants me to take to the Bar, and be a Chancellor or something. I mean after Cowbridge, of course. I've got to take my degree first."

"Well, on my word," said Ashton, returning to the subject, "I think if I were to go and take a degree I'd come back here, find a nice country girl for a wife—a clergyman's daughter's the best"—he was thinking of the younger Miss Blumstead—"and settle down with a vicarage or a curacy, or whatever it is."

"It does seem comfortable enough; and for my part I like country life immensely."

I uttered this with enthusiasm, Hillborough having been my first experience of living out of London.

In after-life I have returned to most of these first impressions, and therefore I conclude the Colvin impulsiveness to be but a froth which must be blown off before we come to the true liquor. Of course we discussed the ladies, our likes and dislikes. We disliked youths of our own age who came in the way, and we liked those who did not interfere with us.

"I've an invitation for you," said Herbert Pritchard one morning, "and most likely when you return to Hillborough you'll find yours waiting for you in due form."

"From home ?"

"No. Try again."

"From Uncle Van, or," I added vaguely, with some idea of Mr. Verney and Julie flitting across my mind, "from the Baa-lambs."

"Ah, I forgot you knew all about the Lambs," said Uncle Herbert, laughing, "but it's nothing to do with either Van or them. You're not half sharp. I thought even you Holyshade fellows were quicker than that. It's an invitation to a wedding. Now then, whose ?—No, Cecil, not your father's again—no, not quite so quick as that."

Oddly and stupidly enough that notion had occurred to me, of course to be dismissed as a joke, if so serious a subject ever admits of such treatment.

"Alice Comberwood," he began——

"To Sir Frederick Sladen, I know!" I cried, finishing his sentence for him. "I know him."

I did of course, and entertained for him, solely on the Verney's account, a dislike which was of a very mild character compared with my feeling towards Mr. Cavander.

The news did not delight me.

"We'll go together," said Uncle Herbert, "we shall be back here before the end of the week."

My invitation had arrived in my absence, and we were to leave the next day. Austin sent me a short note, but said hardly anything of the important event. Alice wrote herself. It was some time since I had had a letter from her. She wrote to me as an old friend. When, as friends, we are all young together, we are all old friends. She had been, as the reader will recollect, among my first loves, when I was a mere private schoolboy. It had never occurred to me that she was so much my senior, and though

I could smile at the fact when she was going to be married to Sladen, yet I failed to see that history was repeating itself in my new attachment to Miss Clara Wenslow. Not that I would compare the two girls for one instant: nor did I at that time.

But as I sat conning the two letters and meditating on the marriage, my thoughts reverted to Cavander and to all that I had heard and seen of him and Alice. I felt certain that to his influence alone Alice owed the change that both her brother and myself had so recently noticed in her.

She had commenced a dangerous game; that of converting an older and cleverer person than herself, a person, too, whom we knew she both feared and admired. And why did he, of all men, pretend to sit at her feet? Was it that thus commencing, he could rise to his knees and so gain her ear for the serpent's whisper? Time and opportunity and inclination were not wanting, for Alice had lived an idle life, the more idle because her employment was of her own choosing, and her whole day had been composed of leisure hours. The work she had set herself was in the village and the Church. The latter she had discontinued, whereat the family were astonished, and her Evangelical brother-in-law highly pleased. When she came gradually to absenting herself from all Church services, the Rev. Andrew McCracken talked this over with his wife, who, however, represented it to him as a phase in her sister's character, and so cheered him.

But Austin, who knew her better, soon arrived at her real reason, and respected her honesty, though he was puzzled by the problems which she placed before him (second-hand, indeed, and *he* saw clearly enough whence they emanated), but of which none the less could he find the solution.

Yet Austin was a plodder. I have previously described how brother and sister would treat a book. So they dealt with difficulties. Alice would have cleared them at a bound, had she been able. She could not do this, nor could she break or hew her way through them. She was stopped, and must take up new open ground, which was

No Man's Land, or rather No Deity's Land, and there she would wander.

Austin, with these obstacles brought before him sooner than they would otherwise have occurred to him in his career, supposing they occurred at all, set himself to work, not to scale or climb, and so surmount the wall, but to make a breach in it and then to utterly destroy it.

The above is a summary of our conversation at Ringhurst on the first evening of my arrival, the day before the marriage. I think its key-note had been struck by my report of the domestic happiness of parsonage life about Collington, and by my repeating Ashton's views on the subject to Austin, who was now at Bulford, and had just obtained one of the best scholarships of his college. This first step seemed to give a bias to his line in life, and the alteration in Alice's sentiments had, he owned to me, led him to look upon his future course as a matter for the gravest consideration.

The next day was one of bustle and excitement among the ladies. We were got out of the way, anywhere. Of Alice I saw nothing till dinner-time.

Then I thought she was livelier than I had ever seen her. Sir Frederick seemed to be a very happy man, and old Mr. Comberwood could not repress his evident exultation at the possession of a real Baronet for his son-in-law. Lady Sladen was condescending and gracious. Having been a tradesman's daughter herself, it was natural she should look with coldness on such a retrograde step as the union of her son, the Baronet, with the daughter of a solicitor.

Had she been permitted to be present behind the scenes, as I was by the merest chance, on the night before the wedding, she might have successfully interfered to prevent the tying of the knot.

CHAPTER XXX.

HOLYSHADIAN HABITS—A REMAINDER—AT RINGHURST AGAIN
—UNDER RESTRAINT—SELFISHNESS—FANCIED NECESSITY—
THE CIGAR—DIFFICULTIES—A LOVELY NIGHT—I AM PLACED
IN AN AWKWARD POSITION—I OVERHEAR—I BECOME THE
MASTER OF A SECRET—MY DIARY—A DREAM—AWAKENING
—AN ENTRY—THE WEDDING—PUZZLEMENTS—I AM IN-
FORMED OF MY FATHER'S ILL-HEALTH—AFTER THE WED-
DING—THOUGHTS—SOMETHING ABOUT UNCLE HERBERT—
THE BLANK PAGE—THE UNFINISHED SENTENCE.

I HAD brought with me from Holyshade several habits
more or less expensive. Not that I then considered them
in that light; on the contrary. I really was unacquainted
with the word expense; but the habits were none the less
deserving of the epithet on that account.

Among these habits I do, undoubtedly, include smoking. Not as the luxury of after years when friends and
loves having failed us, the pipe is sought as the sure confidant and sympathiser.

To the smoker it is the pipe, not time, that is the
consoler.

But the grave and philosophic pipe is not for the jaunty
season of youth. This latter is best fitted with the cigar,
which carried as easily between the lips as the protesta-
tions of a flirt, is for public display and not for private
comfort. Frivolity is associated with the notion of cigars;
gravity with that of the pipe. Of course I speak of the

pipe that gives constant employment to the hands as well as to the mouth; and what I praise, is the lawful use, and not the abuse which has often caused the pipe to share with wine the reproach of being the enemy that man has put into his mouth to steal away his brains.

At Holyshade, of course, smoking was a necessary complement of "fastness," and we imitated our elders. Many of us suffered martyrdom in the cause, and experienced strange sensations. We smoked, not because we liked it, but because we liked to smoke.

At Hillborough I was my own master, and cultivated the habit to such an extent, that, to visit Ringhurst, where no smoking was allowed, except in the greenhouse, where it was supposed to hurt nobody, and benefit the plants, was to me, now, a deprivation of no ordinary character. I ought to add here, that, in all frankness (for which I trust this record is remarkable) I must omit the words "of an ordinary character," as implying that I *was* accustomed to some deprivations; this would convey to the reader an idea of my life, at this time, scarcely in accordance with facts. I knew nothing of deprivations. I could only see around me everybody living for themselves, and it had never occurred to me that I or anyone should live for anybody else. I indeed was of opinion that my father ought to have considered my happiness before his own, when the idea of a second Lady Colvin had first entered his head, but as he had not done so, his example was only another confirmation of my view of the general selfishness of life.

The "independent spirit," which it was the boast of Holyshade training to cultivate in its *alumni,* comes very easily to mean, simply, selfishness.

Had it not been for the special occasion of Alice's wedding, and that my dear Austin was there, I fancy that Ringhurst Whiteboys would not have been honoured with my presence, because of the general restriction placed on tobacco by Mrs. Comberwood, who rather looked upon it as something questionable if not absolutely wicked; and by Mr. Comberwood, who disliked it, not only on account of the feeling of nausea which it usually caused him, but because it was in his mind generally associated with what he styled "young puppyism."

I could not understand why he could tolerate a cigar in Sir Frederick's, or Cavander's, or my Uncle Herbert's mouth, and sneer at it as "puppyism" in mine.

However, my pipe, I mean my cigar, was to be put out on this occasion, and I felt myself therefore under a restraint perfectly new to me.

On retiring for the night (everybody wanted to go to bed more or less early, and neither Austin nor his brother were inclined to stop up and "talk"), I moodily opened my *valise* and took out my diary, so negligently kept about this time, as to resemble a partly finished house, with the parlours and second story taken, and no one in the drawing room or attics; and, with my diary, out came my cigar-case.

There was the temptation.

My little room was without a fire-place; indeed, it was only an out-of-the-way store-closet, temporarily used for sleeping accommodation, and there was no exit for the tell-tale smoke that way.

The window was, evidently, not a bad notion, *faute de mieux*, but then I was sure that the smoke would obstinately persist in entering my apartment, and I firmly believed that the unaccustomed perfume would have roused the household.

The longer I eyed my cigars, the greater the obstacles to their enjoyment, the stronger grew my desire to achieve the feat of smoking on the forbidden ground.

It was a fine warm night; other windows besides mine might be open, and the smell of the tobacco would be everywhere.

I looked out on to the garden. Immediately below me, not three feet from the window sill, was a sort of landing-place, about six feet square, with a leaden gutter running round it. Nothing could have been easier than to have stepped out, placed a chair for myself, shut my window, and smoked comfortably.

I stepped out. The other windows were all closed. Lights out and everybody asleep, or, at all events in bed.

T

Not a sound. Now, as the merest chance would have it. a careless gardener, contrary, of course, to reiterated orders of the strictest character, had left a ladder against the side of this projection. He had, probably, been interrupted in nailing up some trellis, which I noticed to be in a somewhat dilapidated condition, and, without a thought, had left his ladder where it now stood.

My mind was made up. I locked my door, put out my candle, took my cigars, cautiously shut my window after me, and descended the ladder.

I landed on the dewy lawn, and was congratulating myself on not having forgotten the fuzees (smokers are generally dependent upon accident for their lights), when it occurred to me that one of the seats now under the verandah would make my position more comfortable.

Ringhurst was (I have before described) Elizabethan, and as angular as the plan of a fortification by Vauban. The verandah had been carried well-nigh all round the house, and had been ingeniously contrived to fit into the several triangles of the building.

Thus Mr. Comberwood's study was situated in a recess, at, so to speak, the apex of the triangle, at one extreme corner of whose base I had just descended. As I turned into the verandah to carry into execution my idea about the chair, I saw the window of Mr. Comberwood's study suddenly opened, and the window thrown up.

The little light that there was within came from the green-shaded candles which only lit a small circle around them on a table covered with books and papers. At the window stood Mr. Comberwood himself, with his necktie off, and, in an easy dressing gown, was evidently refreshing his head after some work of reading and writing.

I thought I would wait quietly, for it would not be long before he would close the window and withdraw.

He could not see me, as I was blotted into the shade of a corner, but I felt certain that he would have heard the striking of a light, and would have scented the forbidden weed after the first puff.

The night air seemed to have the desired effect, for he passed his hand over his forehead, as if smoothing away the wrinkle of some recent trouble, and half turning towards the chair whence he had, I suppose, just risen, he said, in a low voice, but perfectly audible to me where I stood—

"There, that's enough. You are not a child, and yet you really seem to wish me to think you one, by your extraordinary behaviour."

Whom was he addressing ? It was evidently the finish of a conversation, and the opening of the window had served as a relief perhaps to its intensity, and as a signal to the person with whom he had been engaged, that it was now time to make an end of it.

Such was my impression from his whole manner. Whatever it was I ought not to hear it; still there was, I felt sure, not much more to be heard, and every instant I fully expected to see him close the window; and then, when the light should have disappeared, I would indulge in my cigar.

He quitted the window, and, as well as I could see, re-seated himself at his table.

Somebody was standing by him, I fancied, but as his chair was on the same side as my hiding-place, I could only catch a glimpse of him now by stretching forward, and this I fancied might lead to discovery.

I dared not move, and began to hope that I might not be able to hear.

But neither dared I, in my own behalf, stop my ears; so, trusting to the speedy termination of the conference whatever it might be, I remained where I was, and against my will, I was forced to listen.

"Must it be to-morrow ? Oh, papa, it cannot be too late even now."

It was Alice speaking, in a tone so earnest, so imploring, that even had I been able to stir from the spot without risking detection, I should have felt myself spell-bound by the force of my own suddenly awakened interest.

Mr. Comberwood replied. He was evidently vexed, and spoke in his most abrupt manner.

"Nonsense, Alice ; this is a whim, a fancy—a fancy. You are nervous, you know, and—and—over excited."

" No," she answered, almost despairingly.   " I have struggled with myself, and against myself till now.   And now—" she paused, and presently added, in a voice that died away, as though hope too had died in the heart that gave utterance to the words, " I dread to-morrow."

I think she must have been kneeling by his chair, and that at this moment Mr. Comberwood rose and paced the room for a few seconds.   Then he spoke, this time severely.

" Alice, this is folly, sentimental folly.   You have been encouraged too much in this sort of thing—always spoilt —from a child—so that you never knew your own mind."

He waited, as if expecting some interruption on her part; none came, however, and he continued, with less severity, but with increasing firmness.

" This match was deferred once on your account.   Your mother yielded to your wishes, so did we all.   The Sladens were satisfied, and Sir Frederick behaved uncommonly well—very well.   You must understand, Alice, that you cannot play fast and loose with a serious engagement, as you can with sentiments and opinions, taking up one view one day, and another the next."

A heavy sigh was the only comment upon this part of her father's speech.   He seemed to take it as corroborative evidence of the truth of his statement, and in some sort as an expression of repentance for the past.

He resumed—

" You do not sufficiently consider others.   You owe a duty to your parents, a duty which seems to be omitted in some of the new religious notions you've adopted from time to time."

" No, indeed, father," she broke in with, but wearily. " It is for mamma's sake and for yours, more than for mine, that I speak now."

" I'm glad to hear you say that, at all events," returned Mr. Comberwood, catching at an admission which he saw he could turn to his own account, " as, if you are sincere in your desire to please us, we have only to intimate what our wishes in this matter really are, in order to insure your compliance."

" But, father," said Alice, speaking slowly, as though she were picking her way along a path beset by difficulties at every step, " if you knew—if I tell you—that this marriage cannot bring me happiness—if I own that I was wrong in giving my consent——"

Mr. Comberwood dashed his fist down on the table, and broke out angrily—

"*If* you told me that *now*, I should tell you that it's all of a piece with your character, that you don't know what you're talking about, that we cannot be made fools of in the eyes of everyone ; and that—that if you didn't want to marry him you should not have accepted, and that having accepted, you cannot go from your word. It's too late, too late. Get up, and don't let me hear any more of such trash."

When next Alice spoke, her voice trembled through her effort to be calm.

" You will not forget this night, father ; you will remember that at the last moment I implored you to defer this marriage,"—I heard Mr. Comberwood's movement of impatience—" but do not be afraid for mamma's and your sake, and for the sake of those whose good opinion you seem to consider of greater importance than my happiness—hear me out, father ; it is of no use to be angry and impatient with me now. I will do what you consider to be my duty in this wretched matter."

There was by this time a third person on the scene. It was Mrs. Comberwood. I gathered her observation rather from Alice's reply than from what I heard her say.

" If Alice would but give us a reason——"

" There is no reason, mother, that I can give you."

" Of course not—she has no reason," said Mr. Comberwood, brusquely, as though his patience had reached its limits. " She is unreasonable—always was, always has been."

" It will do no good to speak like that," said his wife, reprovingly.

" Nothing will do any good now," was the irritable reply ; " I've done with it—I wash my hands of it. To-morrow she'll be married, and years hence she'll be very glad we didn't listen to her fanciful whimsies." Then he added, with a return of his old hearty manner, " *There !* we'll all be looking like chief mourners to-morrow if we don't get to bed. Come, Alice, kiss me. God bless you. Now, wife! wife!" And therewith followed the closing of the windows, the extinction of the candles, and then the door was closed softly, and that scene in the drama of Alice's life was over.

I did not smoke my cigar.

I stole back to my room by the way I had come, and sat down before my diary which I had left on the table.

At this distance of time, I have a clear recollection of the immediate effect produced on me by the conversation I had just heard.

It occurred to me at once, to write down, not the conversation itself, but my remarks on it; and as I set myself to this task the whole scene reproduced itself to my mind, so vividly, as to give the impression of its being rather a continuation of what I had partially witnessed in the study than its mental representation. My imagination coming to my aid, added dramatic action to the incident, which, clear at first, gradually became merged harmoniously into other past events, the line of demarcation being gradually softened by the moist brush with which Sleep, the artist of dreams, blends subject with subject, until we are no longer able to distinguish cloud and sky from mountain and sea.

Bending over my diary, I fell asleep.

In an hour's time I awoke to find myself shivering, and the candle guttering in the socket.

Nothing was real, then, except the cold at my knees, and in my feet.

In a few minutes, I was in bed and asleep.

The next morning commenced with a tremendous bustle and excitement.

I thought I was still at Hillborough, and expected every minute to hear the bugle-call with which Mr. Blumstead was wont to summon the sleepers.

A servant came for my clothes, and then I awoke thoroughly to a consciousness of the business of the day.

Alice's wedding.

Then recurred to me the dream of the past night. Was it a dream, or had I indeed heard her imploring that the ceremony of this day might be deferred?

I decided, in bed, upon its having been a dream.

On rising I saw my diary open on the table.

I had written, evidently with some hesitation, as there were several erasures, some sentences under a date, and the time of night. The first few sentences betrayed remembrance of the style of the latest novel I had been reading, and were descriptive, but the last, where I had been interrupted and taken by force into dreamland, stood thus:—"*She begged she might not be married to-morrow, and told her father that if he sought her happiness——*"

Here the entry ceased.

I questioned with myself whether I should tell Austin or not, but when I came to stow away the diary in my bag (for I was to leave in the afternoon), I packed up with it the memory of what it contained, and as no one of the family appeared to have time for standing still and conversing, but all, on the contrary, were hurrying to and fro the whole of the morning, I was soon employed as one of the general crowd, ready to cheer the bride and bridegroom, officially, and without any further question as to private and personal opinion, than is expected of a professional mourner at a funeral, or a chorus-singer in the grand opera.

Alice looked rather pale and anxious, that is, to my eyes. Everybody said she was looking "charming." Sir Frederick was resplendent, and nervous; Lady Sladen grand and condescending; Mrs. Comberwood fussy and tearful. Dick Comberwood wore the air of a member of the family who was permitting what he was powerless to prevent. However, even he was occasionally radiant, as conscious of having passed a first-rate examination, and in view of the novelty of Indian life. Of Dick I have not said much hitherto. He was of a roving disposition and hot-tempered. For home he had never cared, that is, as a place where to remain and be at rest.

It remained to be seen whether what both Austin and myself would have called the monotony of soldier's life, would satisfy his "craving" for liberty. I have intimated how deeply attached Dick was to his sister, and he showed it in his own peculiar manner.

"Well, Ally dear," he said to his sister, "it'll be a long time before I go in for this sort of thing. What a fuss! When I marry, which I don't suppose I ever shall, I shall run away with somebody—an Indian perhaps —and live on shooting and spoil generally. I say," he continued, "I'll send you lots of things when I am in India; and mind you write. Oh!" he cried, "why I shall have to send to you by a new address. How odd it will seem! Lady Frederick Sladen! Dear Ally!" and he kissed her affectionately. She returned his kiss and was smiling, when he in his careless light way, whispered something in her ear which made her break from him almost indignantly.

"My darling Ally," he went on in a low voice, "I really didn't mean—you know I wouldn't——Don't," he urged repentantly, "don't let us quarrel on this subject now, of all times."

He held out his hand.

She took it, sighed, and the calm of her old manner returned, as she replied—

"No Dick dear; we won't have a single word now. Perhaps you have been right: perhaps I have been wrong."

She paused. What she would have been led on in another second and under a fresh impulse to say, I can only guess; but for my part I felt inclined at that moment to ask her for an explanation of the conversation in the study on the previous night, with some sort of a very vague knight-errant idea in my mind, that if she were to be rescued now, Dick and I would do it.

But her mother called her away at this instant, and time pressed.

Dick was sorry he had put her out, he said to me. "I asked her," he went on confidentially, for he knew how much of his altercation with Alice I had witnessed, and how I was quite on his side on the subject; "I asked her about Cavander."

" Why ?"

" He's not here."

" No ?" I wasn't certain.

"I hate the fellow," said Dick gratuitously; adding, immediately, "I suppose I ought to beg your pardon, as he's your father's partner, but I know *you* don't like him."

"I like him better than I did," I returned; but I don't think I had any good reason for saying so, except that he was not intruding himself at Alice's marriage.

"Ah, do you ?" said Dick, as if he rather doubted my statement: then he went on, "Well, I'm precious glad he isn't here now; and I don't suppose, now Alice is gone, they'll have much of his company at Ringhurst. I'm sorry for the reason he can't come, though; only, I ought to have thought of that before. How *is* your father ?"

"How is he ?" I replied, being rather startled by the question; "he is well, I—I—I believe."

It suddenly occurred to me that I had not heard from him for some time. Uncle Herbert had not spoken of him to me, except occasionally; but then, I knew that Uncle Herbert was always about somewhere, and would not have even seen my father so lately as I had.

"Mr. Cavander," Dick explained, said he could not come, as he was detained in the city by the absence of his partner (your father, I mean), who was at home, and ill."

It was the first I had heard of it. My stepmother never wrote to me, and my father had never been a regular correspondent.

However, I was returning to Hillborough *vid* London, and would take Langoran House, Kensington, on my road.

Now followed the religious service in church, where, whatever might have been experienced by the others, Mr. Comberwood enjoyed himself (as he always did in church), amazingly. He was parson, clerk, bride, and bridegroom, one after the other, and came out with question, and answer, and a running accompaniment to the prayers, sometimes in advance, having turned over a page hastily, sometimes lagging behind, having turned two pages back and again got wrong, remaining perfectly happy in his error, too, until set right by Mrs. McCracken, whose husband was assisting Mr. Tabberer at the communion rails, when he said "Hey? um—ah!" and after shoving his spectacles up, and looked under them to see if everything was going on correctly, he set himself at the prayer-book again with a will, and gave away the bride with a good, strong, stout voice, that recalled nothing of those irritable answers to his daughter in the study, still less of Alice's last piteous request.

The skeleton was under lock and key in the study cupboard at Ringhurst, and all were a maying in festive costume, and pledging themselves, or attesting the pledges of those who would have risked perjury before the Judge of Heaven and Earth rather than make an *esclandre*, or incur the displeasure of that little circle which they called the world. Who reads aright the old saying, that "marriages are made in heaven"? How many will face Heaven's Registrar with a clear conscience?

Great Jove, the old heathen said, laughs at lovers' perjuries. But not even the lightest French writer has made *Le Bon Dieu* (which is in such writers' mouths the lowest form of Divine amiability, the creation of a modern Voltairianized Christianity) approve conjugal infidelity, though often adjured to pity it, to avert any unhappy consequences, and finally to unite the lovers in a Paradise where there are no husbands. Such a Garden, deprived of its Adams, would be all Eves and Serpents.

Well——

Alice Comberwood became Lady Frederick Sladen. The happy pair did all that the journal of fashionable intelligence recorded of them. There were certain little touches in that paragraph which I am sure were furnished by Uncle Herbert Pritchard, who had his own reasons for blowing a trumpet on this occasion.

He (Uncle Herbert) had made *the* speech of the day.

No eulogies, he had said, either of the bride, or the bride-groom, or of their parents, could be too much for their deserts. He wished them every sort of happiness most cordially, most sincerely, most heartily. Of his sincerity, no one who knew Uncle Herbert could have entertained the slightest doubt. To him, the marriage was the esta-blishing of one more "house of call," where, as he ex-pressed it himself, he "could hang his hat up in the hall, find his knife and fork on the table, and a shakedown somewhere about." He was starting Sir Frederick and his wife in a house of entertainment, licensed to be open, at all hours, to Herbert Pritchard.

I always admired Uncle Herbert, and, indeed, was really fond of him. He went out of his way to give me some good advice, and treated me as a companion, and not merely as a nephew, which coming from a man so greatly in demand, was most flattering. His advice never offended, and the confidences concerning his own *vie intime*, which it suited his purpose occasionally to entrust to some, temporarily, very particular friend, were of so harmless a character, as to be pointless should they ever be turned as weapons against himself. He acted upon the maxim of treating a friend as one who in time might become an enemy, and thus no one had a word to say against him, but, on the contrary, very much in his favour. He had the great talent of attaching himself to a person, or to a family, without being considered a bore, and knew the exact moment to leave even the most hospitable mansion, so that his departure should be re-gretted. Could he have chosen his own time for quitting the world, I am sure he would have arranged it in such an artistic manner, socially speaking, as to have left behind him a large circle of friends and acquaintances on whose lips there would have been nothing but the most laudatory epitaphs, and the strongest expressions of sorrow, at his having been taken from them so early. In Society's calendar, Herbert Pritchard would have been canonized.

And so the party broke up.

Austin to the university. Dick to Woolwich, thence

speedily to India.   Mr. Comberwood's first son-in-law
and his wife, the McCrackens, had kindly consented to
remain at Ringhurst and cheer the lonely couple.

What would Mr. and Mrs. Comberwood have to talk
about now Alice was gone, and their pet scheme accomplished ?   For it *had* been their pet scheme; there could
be no doubt of that.

I fancy that each would have been anxious to throw
the responsibility of this match on the other's shoulders.

I never continued that sentence in the boyish diary I
was then keeping.   It is by me now, and save for those
two lines, that page remains a blank.

CHAPTER XXXI.

A VISIT—DISAPPOINTMENT—INTERVIEW WITH MY LADY COLVIN
—SIR JOHN—A GRAVE CHARGE—SURPRISES—A NIGHT IN
TOWN—I AM RESTORED TO A SCENE OF MY CHILDHOOD.

UNCLE Herbert accompanied me to town, where, at this
time of year, he could not show himself in public, except
arrayed in a countryfied suit, when, if he met a friend,
he would at once explain that he (Uncle Herbert) was
only "passing through." He said he should dine at his
club, and go on by the night train to Devonshire, as he
had promised Mr. and Mrs. Bob to meet them at Dawlish
as early as possible next day.

On arriving in London, I proceeded at once to make a
dutiful call at Langoran House.

"Sir John was at home, yes, Mr. Cecil, and had not
been very well for the last few weeks. Of course he will
see you sir, at once."

The servant's "of course he will see you sir, at once,"
caused my heart to beat violently. I was very deeply
attached to my father, and the thought of our becoming
gradually estranged was a bitter one for me. As on my
father's return to England, when I was a mite of a child,
I longed to embrace him, so the same yearning seized me
now. That he should be ill, and I not to be called to his
side—that he should be suffering, and perhaps suffering
the more because of the apparent indifference of his only
son, was to me almost insupportable. I loved him more
than any such wife as the present Lady Colvin can could

have loved him; for I represented in myself my dear mother's love for her husband, and my own for my father. As I stood there in the hall I pictured to myself our meeting—the grasp of the hand, the words "Father," "Cecil, my dear boy," and the moment of silence when words are insufficient, and heart speaks to heart, and the eyes are moist from the deep springs of the most holy love.

The servant returned less buoyantly than he had left me. He had been disappointed, I saw *that.* He brought back with him the chill of the atmosphere he had just quitted.

"My lady will see you, sir, in the drawing-room."

I ascended to the drawing-room.

Lady Colvin evidently considered herself as the recognized medium of communication between father and son. She was waiting in the centre of the room, frigid and polite, somewhat altered in appearance, and not, it seemed to me, for the better.

I found it impossible to be at my ease in her presence. It was necessary to talk the ordinary nothings of society in order to restrain myself from giving utterance to my feelings.

I resented her interference, and it was with the greatest difficulty I could refrain from inquiring by what right she placed herself between me and my father.

My manner, in spite of all my attempts at vapid conversation, betrayed my distraction, and from time to time I could not avoid regarding the door, where I expected my father would present himself. In the presence of my stepmother I was as anxiously longing for the sound of my father's approach, as could have been the most ardent lover compelled to chat with the duenna, when he is bending to catch his mistress' footstep on the threshold.

Lady Colvin and myself sat and conversed, if this could be called conversation.

As we sat there I became more and more certain that the duel *à la morte* between us must come before long. Not at this interview; for though the buttons were off the foils, yet we were only saluting one another with the extremest courtesy and politeness.

Still I felt equally certain that she might have gained me over to her side, had she been so inclined. I have since asked myself how would this have advantaged her? She needed no ally, at least no such ally as I should have been.

"You had a very gay wedding I suppose yesterday?" she commenced, after I had inquired after my father's health, and received for answer that he was considerably better, and would come down to the drawing-room (she explained this as the granting of a favour to which she had opposed no obstacle) to see me.

"Yes. It was lively; that is, about as lively as most weddings are, I suppose."

"This was dangerous ground. I had only been to one wedding, and she could not forget at whose I had had the extreme pleasure of assisting.

"She shirked it, remarking, "Yes, so much crying generally, really a wedding is in most cases a miserable affair. Your young friend—young Master, I should say, Mister Comberwood——"

"Austin," I suggested, politely.

She knew the name as well as I did myself. It was one of those petty gnat-bites that will ruffle an equable temperament on the very calmest summer evening.

"Ah yes, Austin—he has gone to College, has he not?"

"Yes, to Bulford."

"Let me see, you go to Cowbridge in October next?"

"Yes. I return to Hillborough to-morrow."

"Then you are stoping in town to-night?"

"Yes, but" I hastened to explain, "I have left some of my things at the station, as, my father being unwell, I thought I would not put you out by coming here."

I could not say I had left all my things at the station, the fact being that only having one portmanteau I had brought it with me, never for one moment supposing that I should be denied a bed at home.

When I clearly saw that my present proceeding was looked upon as utterly informal, I withdrew from my position, and requested her, as it were, to give me credit for at least not being wanting in consideration.

"Of course, Cecil"—I could scarcely bear to hear my name from her lips, it seemed like a sneer—"you could always have a bed here, if you only let us know just a day or two before. But you see, your father being unwell, and one thing and another, just now makes it rather inconvenient, or else——"

"Pray don't bother yourself on my account. I assure you I intended to stay at a hotel."

"Oh, well," she returned, assuming the air of a person making a concession. "Oh, well, if you've already taken your room, why as its only for one night, it will be useless to disturb the arrangement. Will you dine here? We are very quiet, perhaps too dull for you. Only your father and myself."

I hesitated. Had my father asked me, I should have accepted at once.

She rose from the sofa, and went towards the door.

"If you decide to dine here," she said, "please say so now, because of course anybody coming in suddenly makes a difference, and I must give some orders.

This was enough for me.

"No thank you," I replied. "I was only considering whether I could have put off a friend who is engaged to dine with me at Broad's to-night."

"Do you stay at Broad's?" she inquired, with an air of surprise.

"Yes. It's very convenient. Lots of Holyshade men go there."

"It's very expensive, is it not?"

"No, I don't think so," I answered in an off-hand manner.

How could I have known whether Broad's, of Bond Street, was expensive or not? I had been there frequently with Holyshadians, but I had never asked a price, but had paid whatever had been charged ungrudgingly, or had left it "till next time," and then settled my small account in a lump.

The amiable proprietor beamed upon any one of our Holyshadian set who honoured him with such custom as we brought him. Colvin was a good name in the City.

"I will see if your father is ready," said Lady Colvin, "because I dare say you'll be glad to get away to your hotel."

So she went out, and left me to press my lips, clench my fists, and rage by myself.

Here was my welcome.

Impelled by affection for my father, I had come home. Could I have seen him at once, my warmth would have been reciprocated.

So I paced the room, grinding my teeth.

"Confound it!" I growled to myself, "I came to see *him*, not *her*. She'll go and complain of my upsetting her plans, how I prefer a hotel to coming here, and—and—" To have dashed my hand through a window, and have caused myself some physical pain, would have relieved me.

The door opened, and my father entered.

He was aged, and altered for the worse. His manner was irritable and nervous. He shook hands with me with a forced geniality, which, I think, was in reality more chilling than my stepmother's frigidity, and then he averted his eyes as though unwilling to face me boldly. Immediately after this greeting, he made some remark about the temperature of the room, which led to a discussion between them as to the advisability of fires in the drawing-room at this early season of the year, and as to what the doctor had recommended, and various other household matters, which in no way concerned me, but which appeared to be so many small ways of deferring his conversation with me as long as possible. At last my stepmother, who had brought him so far, placed him in position, as it were, by saying—

"Cecil won't stop to dine here."

"Ah," observed my father. "Well, he can't expect, of course,"—turning to me—"you can't expect, you know, that we can keep open house for anybody who comes in at hap-hazard. Why didn't you write and tell us you were coming? We should have been prepared for you then. But no!" he continued, impatient of any sign of interruption on my part, and in an injured tone, "of

U

course not, you don't consider me, you don't consider your—your mamma." This came out awkwardly, and Lady Colvin appeared to have the satisfied air of a governess listening to the result of her careful instruction, and interested in the success of her pupil. "You don't consider me, or any one, only yourself. You come up to town suddenly, *we* don't hear anything of it, you dash away to a hotel, then you dash down here, and you expect to find a room ready, and dinner, and everything, just merely for yourself. You really should be more considerate."

I was astonished, and sensibly pained by this sudden attack. My father had tried to work himself up into a passion, and had partially succeeded.

I noticed his look towards my stepmother when he had come to an end, as if inquiring whether so far he had not remembered his lesson to perfection.

"My dear father," I said, being determined to say something in my own justification, "I heard only yesterday you were ill, and I came at once to see you."

Lady Colvin said nothing.

My father spoke, impatiently—

"*Heard* I was ill. You might have inquired before. You never write, except it is for money. But I can't go on like this. I can't go on spending everything on you, and you making no sort of return. When you go up to Cowbridge you shall have a fixed sum, and not a penny more."

Lady Colvin took out her basket, and pretended to be occupied in some work, as though we were discussing matters wherein she could not possibly feel any sort of interest.

"I shall be very glad to have a regular allowance," I replied; "and I should be glad," I added, on the impulse of the moment, "to live more at home than I have lately."

"What's the good of your saying that?" asked my father, for whom the line set down seemed to have been that of quarrelling with everything I could possibly say. "What's the good of telling me that? You want your friends here, and to give parties. You've got a dog-cart and a groom, I hear, now——" He threw this in quite inconsequently.

"Yes, I have; in Devonshire it is really necessary."

"Oh, of course," he returned sarcastically, "you'd find a reason for it: you can always do that. At your age I wasn't driving about the country in a dog-cart and a tiger behind. I had to work in the counting-house and learn the value of every sixpence, which you seem to think nothing of spending. But it's always been the same. And if you think to come and stop here, and keep the servants up night after night and upset the house, why you're very much mistaken, and I won't have it."

This was the most extraordinary turn that any well-intentioned filial visit could have taken. The guns were banging about my ears, I was confused by all these shots at once, and fell back on my former explanation in order to be in time.

"I was told yesterday that you had been unwell; I immediately came up to see you. I'm very sorry if I've done anything to offend you, but really——"

"Done anything to offend me!" My father interrupted me with an ironical imitation of my apologetic tone. "What have you done to please me? that's the question. But there, I don't want to talk of it now. I've been ill, and I'm not strong. Only understand, that when you go up to Cowbridge I shall fix your allowance, and not a penny shall you spend beyond it."

With this ultimatum he reclined in his arm-chair, apparently rather exhausted.

Lady Colvin broke the silence.

"What time do you dine?" she asked me, quite pleasantly.

"Half-past six," I replied, looking at my watch, and inventing my dinner-hour because I found it was now just half-past five.

"Where?" asked my father.

Now remembering what Lady Colvin had said about Broad's, I foresaw the storm which in my father's present temper would follow upon my announcement of that place of entertainment as the one I had fixed on. But there was no help out of it.   The truth being that I might dine there or might not.

"At Broad's."

"The most expensive place in London.   Upon my soul the way you go on, at your age, is perfectly absurd. Dinner, Opera, Theatre—ah! there'll be a stop to it all, one day."

After this ebullition he once more leant back in his chair, carefully averting his eyes from mine, in the peculiar manner I had already noticed.

For a second a rejoinder arose to my lips; I was on the point of asking him to whom I owed my initiation into what he was now stigmatizing as "the way I was going on, at my age;" but I felt that it would be undutiful and ungenerous.   Besides, I was sure that it was not his heart speaking, but that he was only repeating what he had learnt by rote.

Determined to appease him if possible, I said, as I rose to depart:—

"I don't think my evening is going to be an expensive one.   I am dining with a friend at Broad's.   I am his guest; he isn't mine.

There was no answer to this pleasantry.

"Good-bye," I said to Lady Colvin.

"She touched hands, and rang the bell.   I could have thanked her for this latter action, as it helped to abbreviate the leave-taking.

"Good-bye," I said to my father, trying to revive in my tone all the affectionate warmth which had been chilled by his reception.   "I am so glad to see you so much better than I expected; I hope when I return from Hillborough on my way to Cowbridge, you'll be perfectly recovered."

"I hope so," he returned, drily, "Good-bye."

I went to the door.

"Mind," he said suddenly, as if there were just a parting shot he wanted to give me for his own satisfaction; "when you are coming up again, let your mamma know a few days beforehand, and then we shall be able to put you up."

"Thank you. I won't forget. Good-bye."

I resolved as I went down stairs that it should be a long time before I again entered Langoran House.

A servant went out, at his peril I believe, to procure me a cab, into which I put my portmanteau and drove off to Broad's.

What was the meaning of all this at home?

There was a starveling air about the place. It was a house, and no longer a home.

Why was there so much fuss made about preparations to receive me?

"They don't want me there," I said to myself, sadly; 'at least *she* doesn't want me there."

Then this reiterated charge about my expensive habits; and the fixed allowance. As to the latter, I desired nothing better; as to the former, I did not understand it. I was doing what I had been trained to do. That was all. If the tutor does not teach arithmetic, it is evidently unfair to blame his pupil for not being acquainted with the rule of three. Again, if the tutor not only does not teach it, but has always carefully avoided any reference, however indirect, to such a subject, it is palpably unjust to be violently angry with the pupil on account of his ignorance of the multiplication-table. I recognised the truth that I had, by force of circumstances, begun life very early, and that between seventeen and eighteen I was beyond my *æquales* of Holyshade in many respects, and was on an equality with any young Guardsman of twenty-two who had passed four or five seasons in London.

In attributing this sudden change in my father's manner, to the dislike entertained for me by my step-mother, I was only partially right. The real sore lay far below the surface, and I had yet to probe its depth.

Langoran House was large enough to have accommodated myself and half a dozen unexpected visitors, if my Lady Colvin had been hospitably minded. However, there was no doubt about the fact that I had been politely shown out, and so I descended at Broad's and took a room.

As within the next three years I was frequently at

Broad's, I may point out that it was at this time an expense thrust upon me, and not of my own seeking. Hotel life was a novelty to me. Colvins find novelty charming; I like the easy style amazingly. But then look at the frigid reception I had just left. To be refused admittance at home was heartbreaking; but to find that every comfort could be had for the asking, almost for the wishing, in such a gloriously lighted, warm, cheerful, gay place as Broad's, why it was the revelation of such a new and pleasant life as to a mercurial temperament, was a death-blow to domesticity.

Here, at Broad's, I had no one to consider, save myself. As to expense, my father had talked of it, and had said he would "allowance" me. Well, 'twas the very thing I desired. Broad's was a land of plenty, and meeting with two or three old Holyshadians, I soon forgot my step-mother, and thought, indeed, of nothing else that evening except making the best of an unexpected night in town.

"A night in town," at that period, meant a good deal more, I expect, than it does now-a-days. I fancy, "from information I have received," that, in these degenerate days young men take their pleasures with something more of refinement than did the "good fellows" of a generation or two ago. We considered ourselves an improvement on the ancestral model, and door-knocker wrenching, street-fighting, and suchlike rowdyism, was not in our line. Look at Tom and Jerry, and see in what those noble spirits delighted. There was a remnant of the taste yet remaining among a few of the old Holy-shadians who had lately "joined," and who, as pupils of some professor of the art of self-defence, were anxious to practise upon any amateur whom they could induce to pick a quarrel with them. Vauxhall was generally chosen as the battle ground. There were chances of a pugilistic encounter at that place of entertainment, not to be obtained elsewhere. The exhilarating supper in the alcoves, the band playing dance music, the lights, the crowd composed of well-nigh every grade of society; and the best opportunity was invariably afforded by the gay and gallant young shopkeeper who had taken the young person, with whom he was a-keeping company, to make her courtesy to the chivalric Mr. Simpson, to say "Oh" at the fireworks, to take an *al fresco* supper, and to join hands in the mazy dance. Their gyrations would not probably be of the steadiest, and if the youthful "swell" had been smiled upon by Mr. Counterjumper's coy partner, the former considered everything fair in love and war, and would by some act of gallantry not altogether unwarranted by the occasion, so excite the jealousy of the latter that blows soon followed words, and a genuine *fracas* ensued. If the swell succeeded in punching the snob's head, the former was pleased and satisfied; he condoned by a handsome gratuity on the spot, so as to mend a crack with gold, reported himself at Tom Mawley's head-quarters next day and continued his practice with the gloves, thirsting for further gore. If, on the other hand, the swell received more than he gave, then it cost him something in fees to policemen, more in the suffering consequent on defeat; and it entailed upon him heavier work than ever at Tom Mawley's. The professors of the "noble art" had a good time of it even in those days.

Quitting Vauxhall, there were numerous places open, brilliant as stars in the firmament of a night's dissipation. Falling stars, that have disappeared into space long since.

It is evident, that, in those good old times, or bad old times, for what had preceded them were worse old times by ever so much, there was no lack of amusement when you had once commenced; and the ball could be kept rolling from one place to another, from any time after seven o'clock in the evening to the same hour next morning, when jaded, pale-faced votaries of "pleasure," in their tumbled and seedy-looking black, might be seen purchasing early bouquets in Covent Garden, for the express purpose of inventing some reason for spending the last sovereign left in their pockets; when they had not any reason, they pulled out their sovereigns and tossed for them on the flagstones.

Had this ever been my amusement, my father's reproaches would have been well merited. Although, as I have said, considerably ahead of myself at my own age, I never had had any liking for the lower forms of reckless dissipation, nor had I any inclination towards gambling in any shape. I was prodigal from ignorance; and this ignorance was bliss, of a certain sort, at the time.

I must pay that tribute to Holyshadian teaching; it had kept some of us in ignorance. And therefore I can count on a few years of my life passed in the successful pursuit of pleasure, which were enjoyable because they brought no remorse; thoroughly enjoyable to one who was conscious of the gratification, and, to a certain extent, irresponsible. The law would have considered me an infant, and my father, who would have had me become a man at twelve, had lectured me, at eighteen, as though I were still a child.

We did not moralize thus on the evening in question: far from it. There was little Lord Pilchard, on his way to his country seat, and there was Parry, my accomplice in the swan-murder, both at Broad's, and both equally determined upon making a night of it; which phrase I soon discovered, was in their mouths, equivalent to making a morning of it; as their efforts seemed to be directed towards the highly laudable object of seeing the lark well up and on his way to heaven's gate before they sought their hardly earned repose.

When that wicked little nobleman, Lord Pilchard, proposed Vauxhall, Parry acquiesced at one; and I, who had been there twice before (when I had been taken by my father with a party of city bachelor friends), replied that, of course, nothing would suit me better.

Everyone at Broad's knew little Lord Pilchard, and he was treated with as much deference as though he had possessed the wisdom of all our hereditary legislators in his youthful cranium.

None the clearer in our intellects for the wine we had taken, we arrived at the Gardens. It was, to my thinking, very full, but my better informed companions considered it as empty as it ought to be at that unfashionable season.

A concert was going on when we arrived, and we stood

at the outskirts of the throng, in front of the brilliant pavilion.

Somehow or other we were separated from one another, and in trying to recover my companions I came up against a gentleman who was carrying a shawl over his arm.

" I beg your pardon, sir," said a full, rich voice, which sounded very familiar to my ear.

I looked him full in the face, and collected myself for an effort of memory.

" Mr. Verney."

" Mr. Cecil Colvin," he returned, shaking my hand heartily, " I am indeed pleased to see you. A gay scene this, reminding one of the oriental descriptions in the Thousand and One Lamps, I mean Nights. You are really so much grown, so filled out " (here he filled himself out, as an illustration of his meaning), so much, in fact, the man, that, had it not been for your recognition of me, I do believe that, excellent as is my memory for faces and names—I think I remember everyone of any celebrity in the many circuits I have been engaged on during my professional career—I should have failed, I fancy, to associate you in my mind with the youth whom so lately I saw in the appropriate costume of boyhood."

Of course I asked after the family.

" All well, I thank you, and prospering. I shall be in management before another year is over, and I intend to show the theatrical public something that will restore the palmy days of the drama, and elevate the stage in the eyes of the people. My eldest daughter, Beatrice, has written a play, which,—though of course you will think me prejudiced,—yet I assure you she has no more severe critic than her own father—is as good a thing as I have read, or seen, for many a long day. She is married, and married well. Her husband has money, and is anxious that she should continue in her profession."

" I thought," I said, " that Miss Beatrice was to have been a singer."

" She studied under the distinguished Monsieur Némorin, but after a short residence in Paris, whether she went to perfect her accent—she speaks French like a native—she was advised not to risk her strength on the Operatic stage, and, indeed, she has since developed so decided a talent, I may say, genius, for there is the divine afflatus there, sir"— I hadn't a notion what he meant, any more than he had, I believe, but I said " Certainly "; and he went on—"the divine afflatus, without which there can be no dramatic instinct, no real dramatic life."

" Is she here ? " I asked.

" Oh dear no ; she is at her own home, studying. My daughters Lottie and Julie are here. They have taken a short engagement in the off season to sing a duet and one song—Lottie has a fine contralto—for a limited number of nights. They are then going down to breathe the pure air of heaven with their aunt, near Liverpool."

" Mrs. Davis ? "

" Yes. I will remember you to her. She will be delighted. My son Charles Edmund is also here. He is able to get away some nights. He is rising in his line ; humble but honest : and to be honest, as this world goes, is to be as one man picked out of ten thousand. He's got a good appointment at his station, is a favourite with the Company, been complimented by the directors, and—— excuse me one minute; I am beckoned by Mr. Johnson, the manager here. I shall see you again."

He bowed, taking off his hat with much politeness. Then replaced it on his head, looking round upon the un-initiated as though to say, "*That* is the way that one gentleman should salute another," and so he strutted away.

I remained apart from the crowd, and at the back of the orchestra, wondering whether I should be able to see Julie, when a small door opened, and, as if in answer to my wish, she came out.

Lottie was following. They were not a little surprised at meeting me, and after a few minutes' conversation, Lottie slipped off to join her father, whom she said she perceived talking to the afore-mentioned manager.

Julie and I were left alone together.

With a freedom of speech, but not of tongue, the cause of which I am afraid she divined without any explanation on my part, I confided to her my grievances, to which she listened attentively. She appeared to pity me, and yet to be giving me good advice, which, strange to say, seemed to me at that moment totally uncalled for.

I managed to change the conversation and to ask about herself. She was never afraid, she said, of telling me anything, but she would wait for another time. I could not understand her reticence.

Under her influence, however, I became calmer, and as we strolled on together away from the crowd—we were to return and meet her father and brother on the spot where we had been standing and where they would wait for her—once more I experienced that *attrait* towards her, which had its commencement in the purest and best time of my life.

Through the wine the truth came out. I was on the road to—what Uncle Herbert had called when advising me about Miss Wenslow—"making a fool of myself." Would that my folly had never been worse than then. What nonsense I talked in that dark walk! And yet, through it all, how clearly do I remember her soft steady voice replying—

"You have not seen as much as I have. You cannot know whether you really love me or not. You may think so at this moment. No, please. We must turn back. Father and Lottie will be waiting."

Therewith I became sulky; I could not understand her, or myself. A gentleman whom I had not before noticed was following us, and eyeing Julie in what seemed to me to be a peculiarly offensive manner. She grasped my arm closer, and was for hurrying me on. But no, I was bent on showing her I was no longer a mere boy. I returned the man's impertinent gaze defiantly, whereat he seemed immensely amused, and stepping up addressed himself to Julie, who now fairly trembled on my arm, and this tremor of helplessness made me the more determined to prove myself her champion.

"I think," said the gentleman, or whatever he was, with easy familiarity, "we have met before."

Julie urged me onward, but I was for standing to my

guns and presenting a bold front. I don't know what I intended to say or to do, but seeing him offer his arm, or rather push it rudely against Julie, I wheeled right round and confronted him, asking "how he dared insult——"

I did not get any further in my heroics. In another second I was staggered by a tremendous buffet, which came with sledge-hammer-like force on my right ear, and, losing my balance, I stumbled over a row of oil-lamps which decorated the border of the basin of Neptune's fountain.

My recovery was instantaneous, as a strong hand pulled me out by the legs, and on being landed in the midst of a crowd, I was pleased (as far as I could be in the circumstances), to find myself among friends, for I was sitting at Mr. Verney's feet, while the cause of my immersion was lying prostrate on the ground, where he had been sent by a well-directed blow from young Charles Edmund, whom professional railway duties had gifted with an herculean muscle. Fortunately, the Verneys being well known, we had no difficulty in making our way to a temporary retreat in the manager's room, where I was soon dried, and put right again, with the exception of my hat, which had filled, and disappeared somewhere under Neptune's three fish-tailed horses.

Julie informed her party of my heroic conduct, omitting all mention of how it had been solely through my fault that she had been placed in such an unpleasant situation. After this, the thanks of the company were given to me, and Mr. Verney insisted upon my accompanying them home to supper. We all went in one cab; and once more the merest accident had brought me into the old pleasant society of Frampton Court, though not to the Court itself; the Verneys having removed, according to their improved circumstances, to more airy and fashionable quarters in one of the streets in the neighbourhood of Russell Square.

It was past one when I took my leave of this merry party, and Julie saw me to the door.

"Julie," I stopped to say, as she was letting me out, "I really mean't what I told you to-night."

She smiled, gave me her hand, and by an irresistible impulse I drew her towards me and kissed her on the forehead. She looked up suddenly——

"Julie!" cried Mrs. Verney from upstairs. She was as sniffling and fidgetty as ever, and her hair not one whit tidier than it had been when I had first seen her.

"Mother's calling," said Julie, nodding to me. "Good night."

The door closed. I walked slowly on. I haven't the smallest idea what I was thinking about. Not about my father; not about my stepmother; not about any grievances; certainly not about Hillborough, or Miss Clara Wenslow.

What was I thinking about?

That kiss on her forehead.

I did not feel inclined to go in search of my dinner companions, though from knowing their London haunts, I should not have had much difficulty in finding them. So after losing myself in the neighbourhood of the Verneys' residence, I hailed a cab, and was soon reposing at Broad's Hotel. The last thing that occurred to me was the strangeness of events that had driven me from home, once more to be welcomed by my old friends of Frampton Court. After all, the World's a very small circle.

CHAPTER XXXII.

THE MORNING AFTER—AT THE HOTEL—CONFUSING RECOLLEC-
TIONS—GENERALLY SHOWING WHAT I WAS DOING WITH MY
TIME—A BOX OF DOLLS—COLVIN AFFECTIONS—ATTEMPT—
FAILURE—ANOTHER DUTY CALL—MRS. CAVANDER—FRESH
REVELATIONS—THE NEW COUSINS—A LECTURE POSTPONED
—I NEARLY MISS A TRAIN—REFLECTIONS ON COLVIN
PECULIARITIES—RETURN TO HILLBOROUGH—A YACHTING
LUNCHEON—MR. AND MRS. BOB'S FAREWELL—TACTICS—A
LETTER FROM HOME—I AM A MILLIONAIRE—AND MEET WITH
A SUDDEN AND UNEXPECTED REVERSE.

THE next morning I was considerably puzzled to find
myself neither at Hillborough, nor in Neptune's pond, nor
at Frampton Court, having been in all these places at
once during the night in my confused dreams.

The apparition of the Boots soon cleared up my doubts.
I was at Broad's, and it was much later than I could have
wished, seeing that my previous good intention had been
to leave for Hillborough by an early train.

There was not another (Collington was our station) for
four hours; that is, I mean one that went at anything
like a decent speed; and so, having got so far into my
day, I determined to make the best use of it I could in
town.

My head was not as clear and fresh as that of a youth
nearly eighteen should have been. I had Vauxhall on
the brain; and as I gradually extricated myself from the
labyrinth of dreams, I began to wonder about what I had

said to Julie, and not only to wonder at what I had said
or what I had done, but to be astonished at myself for
this strange conduct.

When the Boots reappeared I inquired after Lord
Pilchard.

" His lordship won't be hup for a hour-or-more yet,
p'raps not then : his servant 'as orders to 'ave everything
ready for the two ten train."

" And Mr. Parry ? "

" Come in very late, night porter said, sir ; 'ad his bath,
sir, and breakfast and was off, sir, a hour-or-more agone.
Shall I order breakfast for you, sir ? "

It was a new sensation—this hotel life. I was my
own master ; and this I should not have been at Langoran House under the present *régime*. Once as the
Dauphin Colvin, I had been a little monarch of all I surveyed in my father's house. But the true Prince had
been exiled by the queen stepmother, and was to seek a
new home, new friends, fresh acquaintances.

I fell in with this novelty very easily ; it fitted me as
though made on purpose for me, or I for it.

So I ordered a sumptuous breakfast, and rose to lounge
over my toilette with as *blasé* an air as though I had
been jaded by the gaieties of several May seasons, and
was tired of London life.

From time to time during the morning, the image of
Julie presented itself to my mind. Then followed other
images of Alice Comberwood and Lady Sladen, Miss
Blumstead and her sister, and then of Clara Wenslow,
and one after the other I replaced these dolls in my play
box in order that I might once more take up the one that
I seemed to myself to prize the most—the one that appeared not inanimate as did the others, but gifted with a
voice that *could* tenderly reply " Cecil " when I murmured to myself " Julie."

I have described myself as having supper with Mr.
Verney at his new lodgings near Russell Square : this
description is given with such accuracy as was compatible with the exciting events of the previous night.

In the daytime, after breakfast, I tried to find Mr.

Verney's house, but failed. One street was just like
another, the houses were all of the same family—especially about the windows, which may be termed the eyes,
and the doors, which one may set down as the mouths.
The complexions, too, were within a shade the same.
The costumes differed; here and there flowers made one
of them a trifle gayer than its brothers and sisters, and
curtains, hangings, and blinds made all the difference
between coquettishness and sobriety.

Feeling that I was wasting my time—a feeling not
common to me, as may have been perceived, at this period
of my life—I determined upon returning to my first
resolution of improving the occasion by a duty call, that
is, by paying a flying visit to my Aunt Clym.

Annette, my eldest cousin, whom I had not met for a
long time, greeted me. She was just twenty, had grown
almost out of knowledge, and was as pretty, though
dollish, a blonde as you'd wish to see. She put her finger
to her lips mysteriously, and beckoned me into the
dining-room.

"What's the matter, Annette?"

She closed the door.

"Mamma's got some one here whom she wants to get
rid of, and if she saw you she'd step in and chatter all the
morning."

"Who? My aunt?"

"No, no," returned Annette, laughing, "Mrs. Cavander."

"With a history of grievances," I inquired.

"Yes. Mamma says that she's afraid she's not quite
right in her mind, and that she's been driven distracted
by ill-treatment."

"*His?*" I asked.

Annette nodded.

Hush!" she added, listening at the door; "I think
she's coming downstairs now. Mamma is never at home
to her now, but unfortunately she came early, caught
papa on the doorstep, and so frightened him, that he rang
the bell and the servant let her in."

"Uncle Van's in the city?"

"Yes, as he always is. Arty's in business now, Uncle

John "—she meant my father—" offered to take him
into his office, but mamma flatly declined to receive
any favour from Mr. Cavander, or, indeed, to have anything to do with a place of which he might have the
direction."

"And he has?"

"Yes, so papa and mamma say; Mr. Cavander is
everything, and that Uncle John is scarcely ever seen
there at all."

At this moment there was a considerable amount of
sobbing, and rustling, and tearful associations in the
passage, and presently the door banged, and I caught
sight of Mrs. Cavander passing before the house.

"Is that Mrs. Cavander?" I exclaimed. "I don't think
I should have known her again."

"No, indeed," replied my Aunt Clym, curtly, and
drawing in her breath. She paused for a minute, as
though considering whether it would be well to say much
on the subject before me. She glanced at Annette
suspiciously, and Annette met her frankly.

"I have told Cecil all about Mrs. Cavander."

"Not more than I should have known very soon, in all
probability, or that I might have guessed for myself," I
said, wishing to exculpate my pretty cousin.

It pleased me to find I had so pretty a cousin.

"Where's Nellie?" asked my aunt.

"Upstairs. Shall I tell her Cecil's here?"

"Yes."

When we were alone Aunt Clym asked me if I had
been home.

I recounted my visit and told my grievance.

She was indignant on my behalf. She, too, had called
at Langoran House.

"I hadn't," she said, "been there for some time, but I
heard, from your uncle, of John's illness, and so I went.
I saw *her*, not him, and I can tell you I cut the interview
very short. A large sum of money and the house have
been settled on her. I know that much. Her brother,
Mr. Cavander, arranged it all, and *he* is the master in the
city and *she* is the master at Langoran House. There's

x

evil to come of this, and John is kept like a prisoner; upon my word it's like the man in the iron mask."

This was to her, evidently, so horrible a simile, that she stood aghast at the awful image she had conjured up.

I told her how irritable my father had been with me, and how for the first time he had talked about my expensive habits.

"I don't blame him for that," said Aunt Clym; "only he ought to have begun it some time ago when you went to Holyshade. But you've been neglected."

Here she shook her head and shut her eyes, as though mourning over my unenlightened state. "However, it's as well you should be careful now. There's nothing that Cavander won't do. Why, as to that poor woman, I mean his wife, who was here just now—" My aunt having gone so far, ran on—"He has neglected her, though it was she who brought him out of the mire at first; he has positively ill-treated her; his sister shut the door in her face; her own friends are powerless to help her, because, I must confess it, she is still so absurdly fond—it is idiotically, not absurdly, I ought to say—so idiotically fond of that bad man, that she will hear of no interference, and would rather be his slave, and I do believe clean his boots than remain unnoticed by him. And—" here she looked round to see if her daughters were returning—" I am very—very much afraid that by her foolish conduct she will soon give him the opportunity he has been eagerly seeking for some time past."

I knew so little of life that I failed to understand her.

"Annette," I said, "told me that you thought Mrs. Cavander rather out of her mind."

My aunt shook her head sorrowfully.

"It will come to that. She has taken the first step on the road. From what I hear, Mr. Cavander is pitied by his friends. Don't speak of it any more before your cousins. It will be time enough for them when they have reached my age to know of the existence of such sin and misery, even within our own family."

Still I did not fully comprehend her meaning. I was honoured by her confidence, and she, too, had not treated me as a boy. At this time, in appearance and manner I was several years my own senior. This was an involuntary deception. As long as I was silent I might be mistaken for the lion; but from my bray it might be inferred that I was a younger donkey than I really was.

On this occasion I had the tact of silence, and was credited with the possession of considerable discretion.

Annette now returned with little Nellie. I had two pretty cousins, and it was very easy to please them with a full, true, and particular account of the wedding at which I had so lately been assisting.

My aunt, too, was interested, and asked many questions about Alice Comberwood, whom she had met sometimes in town. My aunt mentioned how she had been introduced to Alice at my father's, and again we drifted into the Cavander channel, for Miss Alice had been at different times Mrs. Cavander's guest.

My Aunt expressed her opinion strongly as to Alice.

"Had she been one of my girls," she said, "I would not put up with all this High Church nonsense. She never was to be satisfied unless she was drawing someone into an argument about Church matters. I set her down once, for she really seemed to despise her elders, and to consider us as little better than heathens."

My cousins smiled, covertly. I took up my hat, for we were approaching dangerous ground, and I had known my aunt, on the slightest provocation, produce a book of Evangelical sermons, select a passage which proved something or other incontestably, to her own mind, without carrying conviction to that of any other person, and then following up this attack with a charge of heavy divines, backed by a perfect cannonade of texts.

My watch, stationed like a sentinel at the outposts, saved me! I was not to be surprised on this occasion.

The train was to leave at such and such a time (which as to exactitude I more or less invented *sur le champ*) and my studies required my attendance at Hillborough.

This led to a discussion of my prospects.

The mention of Cowbridge University pleased my

aunt prodigiously. There, she had been told, I should
indeed hear sound doctrine, and perhaps that portion
of my early education, which had been taken so inju-
diciously out of her hands—here she alluded with sorrow
to the companionship of Nurse Davis and the Verneys—
and since then so little attended to, would now be
cultivated, and the small amount of good seed which
she had been able to sow would, she hoped, bring forth
abundantly.

Once more she had mounted her hobby, and once
more I was saved by little cousin Nellie, who pointed
to the clock on the mantle-piece.

I took my leave of them with many friendly and
cousinly wishes for our next meeting, for, with a genuine
Colvin impulse, I had conceived such a sudden and
violent liking for both fair cousins that it required time
so to improve the acquaintance as to enable me to
determine to which of the two I should devote myself.
Had it not been for Aunt Clym I might have missed
my train to Hillborough that day.

A Colvin nature is capricious. It had been hitherto
exemplified in such members of the family, including
myself, as have figured in these records.

But in these later days I have a theory founded
on experience. It is as to caprice in affairs of the heart.
I affirm that no man, or woman, loves twice in a lifetime.
I do not use the word "Love" lightly, but in the
fullest sense that can be given to human, as distinguished
from Divine love.

And the theory is that, as a man or a woman loves
truly and really but once in a lifetime, so his or her
likings and caprices are stronger, or weaker, in proportion to the resemblance which their varying objects
bear to that First Object of love. A manner in one,
a feature in another, a tone in another, and so on, may
recall the first love, and so far satisfy for the moment.

This may seem, perhaps is, an apology for caprice
in the art of love, but I do not think so. The subject
must, however, be remitted to a separate treatise. At
present how the theory practically bears on this history

will be seen, should the reader honour me by remembering it during the subsequent portion of this record.

Varium et mutabile Colvin.

I had carefully abstained from mentioning anything about my amusements in London the night before, though I daresay had I remained much longer with Annette and Nellie I should have gratified them with a vivid picture of Vauxhall and of my own prowess, in order to impress upon them that I was no longer "little Cecil," but a young man about town of an age to take care of himself, and to offer his protection to others.

However, Aunt Clym had prevented this, and when I left her house I rather suspect I had added two new dolls to my box of playthings, and their names were Annette and Nellie.

I don't think they lasted me much farther than Bath. Between Somersetshire and Devon the entourage reminded me that I had left—I was going to say my heart, but of course it couldn't have been that—but a representative of my heart somewhere in the neighbourhood with Clara Wenslow.

For it seems to me that my heart about this time was a county divided into several ridings and boroughs, and able to return many members, and that the elections were perpetually going on, and the whole county consequently in a hubbub.

I personally possessed great influence, and could give the casting vote everywhere in this heart-county. Yet so many and varied were the interests involved, and so conflicting the claims, that I hesitated to proceed to a definite choice in any one instance.

It might have been then evident to a looker-on, like, for instance, Mrs. Bob or Uncle Herbert, that one of these days, and at no great distance, I should be forced to proclaim myself an autocrat, sweep away the petty divisions, consolidate the interests, and rule over a united kingdom.

Ashton was waiting for me at Collington, having just come in from Exeter. The "Bobs" were to give their last party on board their yacht next day, and all the Hillborough House party, including my tutor, were invited.

My dog-cart and Ashton's pony-trap were in requisition, and early next morning we set out to catch the train for Dawlish. We had a long day before us, and the weather was lovely.

Uncle Herbert was on board, and everyone was in high spirits. There was breeze enough for sailing, and there were no qualms to interfere with appetite. At luncheon the conversation happened to turn on the recent marriage of Miss Comberwood, which one of the ladies had read in the morning paper. I gave my account of it, and Mrs. Bob said she had heard it was quite a love at first sight affair.

"I don't believe in love at first sight," said Uncle Herbert.

Clara Wenslow was separated from me by Ashton, and I was seated next to Mrs. Bob. I looked up at Clara. She smiled slightly, and the next minute evinced the greatest interest in the conversation.

"You're a heathen and don't believe in anything except dinner," growled Mr. Bob.

He generally growled, and very seldom troubled himself to look at the person he was addressing. He preferred catching somebody else's eye to watch the effect of his speech on a third party.

"Ah !" said Mrs. Bob, "you wait till you're married before you venture an opinion."

"Perhaps Mr. Pritchard will find that rather too long," quietly observed Mrs. Fowler.

"I don't see why I'm to wait until I'm married in order to give my opinion on love at first sight," urged Uncle Herbert.

"There are a great many things you don't see yet," growled Mr. Bob, winking at Ashton.

"I don't see the sherry," said Herbert.

"And yet it's under your nose," was Mr. Bob's triumphant repartee.

"Well, anyhow," said my uncle presently, "it was a deuced good match for her. And if it was only a *mariage de convenance*—I don't say it was mind——"

"Well! if it were ?" asked Mrs. Bob.

"If it were?" returned Herbert. "Well, if it were, I wish there were more of them. Young people are too young to choose for themselves: their elders know what's best for them, and if there's a reasonable attachment, without violent passion, that's quite enough. Indeed, on reflection," added Uncle Herbert, watching the ignition of his fuzee, "I'm not at all certain if love oughtn't to come after marriage and not before."

"Oh, Mr. Pritchard?" exclaimed Miss Clara, as if shocked at these loose sounding sentiments; "do you *indeed really* think all you say? Oh, Mrs. Bob he doesn't, does he?"

"I don't know, I'm sure," replied Mrs. Bob, always good-humoured, but a trifle curt in her answer when addressed gushingly. Italics in a girls' conversation annoyed her. "You've heard him say he doesn't believe in love."

"Excuse me," said Uncle Herbert, placidly, "I distinctly mentioned 'at first sight.'"

"I loved Bob at first sight, didn't I?" inquired Mrs. Bob of her spouse.

"You told me so," was the response.

"And you told me so too," rejoined Mrs. Bob.

"Of course I did," returned her husband, "and I rather think I added 'long before I saw you.'"

"Ugh!"

And Mrs. Bob threatened him with a roll.

"Of course," said Uncle Herbert, who seemed to have some object in dwelling on this theme so long; "of course there are brilliant exceptions. But look at what are called love matches, made in haste, repented of at leisure. No, thank you," continued Uncle Herbert, knowingly; "no love for me, if you please, if it is to lead to so much social misery as I see around me——"

"Not at this moment," put in Mrs. Bob.

"Exceptions, of course, as present company; but if I were allowed to lecture a college of young men on Social Science—and there ought to be such a Professor—I should say, unless you've got some clever people to arrange a marriage for you, remain a bachelor till you're thirty; don't believe in love, it's all a snare and a delusion."

Mrs. Fowler would not listen to such sentiments any longer.

"My dear Mr. Pritchard." she said, and her tone compelled our attention, "because some instruments play it out of tune, is that a sufficient reason for finding fault with the original melody?"

"Bravo!" shouted Mr. Bob, and drank Mrs. Fowler's "health and sentiment," as he phrased it, on the spot.

Uncle Herbert evidently felt himself tackled. He would not risk a pitched battle, for fear of losing everything. He saw by my nodding at Mrs. Fowler how soon I should enlist under her banner, and being once her soldier, he would be obliged to give me up as a recruit of his own.

"Mrs. Fowler," he said politely, "I am not a musician."

"Therefore," she retorted quickly, "you are no judge of the original melody."

"I have never heard it," he replied. "You must not expect a man without an ear to give you a correct account of a tune."

"No, decidedly not, any more than I expect anyone colour-blind to deny the existence of colour merely for the reason that he himself is deficient in his perception of it. Let him acknowledge his own deficiency."

"I would willingly have done so up to this moment," said Uncle Herbert demurely.

"And why not now?" added Mrs. Bob, thinking she was coming as an ally to Mrs. Fowler's help.

"Because since Mrs. Fowler has taken me in hand, I begin to feel that I am capable of recognizing and appreciating the original melody."

He had turned aside his adversary's point, and, amid the merriment that followed his last polite speech, Mr. Bob, who, to do him justice, never lost an opportunity of conviviality, insisted upon drinking Uncle Herbert's health, then Mrs. Fowler's again, then that of both combatants united; and then—Mr. Bob had the sherry taken away from him, whereupon he simply said, "Quite right," and lit a pipe.

This afternoon when I was not with Mrs. Bob, who seemed to be perpetually requiring my assistance, or else wishing to speak with me about the present state of affairs at home, I was captured by Mr. Blumstead, or Mrs. Fowler, or I was told off to assist one of the Misses Blumstead, the other generally being with Ashton, while Clara Wenslow appeared to me to be entirely engrossed by my Uncle Herbert.

I was unable to say more than half-a-dozen sentences to her, apparently unimportant. She gave me her father's address. Might I write? I could do as I liked—but——. Here again I was hastily summoned, but before I quitted her she had answered "Yes."

Mrs. Bob begged me to send to her whenever I felt inclined for a sea-trip, or to enjoy myself in the country on shore. Uncle Herbert, she told me, would be able to give me their whereabouts always. She spoke most generously, and shook my hand with a warm, honest grasp.

"I don't have many *friends*," she said to me emphatically, "but I'll count you as one. And perhaps at some time or other he won't be sorry for it, eh Bob?"

Her husband, who was standing at her elbow looking out to sea through a telescope, not to examine anything in particular, but from mere force of a habit common to all yachting men, dropped his glass and turned to me.

"She's A 1, lad. The missus always means what she says." And he tucked his wife's arm under his own, and gave it a squeeze.

When I repeated to Herbert Mrs. Bob's farewell, he was immensely delighted.

"You see," he said, "I can introduce you to some good people." He forgot that it was Ashton who had brought me in among them. "I can take you everywhere; and you'll find, if you only stick to what I tell you, you'll have as jolly a life before you as any youngster can have. When are you off for Cowbridge?"

"In a few weeks."

"All right. When you're settled I'll come and see you there. Don't bother about the governor at home. That'll all come straight. Good-bye, Cecil, and look here—mind you always confide in me in a difficulty; it'll save you heaps of trouble."

I promised I would. I intended to do so. I rather wished I had told him about Clara having given me her address; but, as yet, I didn't see I was in any difficulty requiring Uncle Herbert's advice. If he hadn't sailed away that evening, or if I had been going to remain on board, I should have given him full particulars of the Verneys, of my night in town (which I had only partially recounted), and I should have there and then established him as *pro tem.* my guide, philosopher, and friend.

But I did not sail with them. Clara was leaving to spend a few days with some friends near Collington, whose address she gave me, but which, owing to one of the many interruptions above mentioned, I was unable to write down, and so it slipped my memory. Ashton, who was going to stay longer than myself at Hillborough House, had obtained leave of absence, and was starting with the Bobs for a short cruise.

There were a few details to be settled before quitting my private tutors for the University, to which event I was now looking forward with expectations of the greatest possible pleasure.

Whether these were to be realised it will be now my part to show.

I had to a certain extent made up for lost Holyshadian time by a fair amount of application, at Hillborough, to such studies as had recommended themselves to my taste. Mr. Blumstead was a capital tutor.

He never objected to my having a holiday, as he used to take that opportunity of cramming himself for my next day's task.

Whenever I asked him for the explanation of a word, he used to tell me to "look it out." I did; found the correct meaning, and *then* he, at the same time having found it in a much larger dictionary full of references and quotations, would explain it to me with an assumption of erudition that took me in at first, but ever afterwards amused me immensely.

It would be more in accordance with facts to say, that instead of my sitting at Blumstead's feet as a disciple, he and I read together—he as senior, I as junior pupil, our masters being Messrs. Lexicon, Dictionary, and the Keys to algebraic problems.

He had one advantage over me, and he kept it.

He possessed his own MS. copy of algebraic problems with their solutions.

I had had a very pleasant life at Hillborough, and when I drove away with my tiger behind, I was really sorry that my time there for the present had come to an end.

On the morning of my departure I received a letter from my father (an acknowledgment of two I had written to him hoping to hear better accounts of his health) informing me that he had instructed Mr. Cavander to pay the sum of three hundred pounds sterling regularly to my account per annum at a Cowbridge banker's, adding that this, he was informed, was a very handsome allowance, and further telling me that it would be no use my calling at Langoran House, as "I and your mamma are on the point of starting for the Continent for the benefit of my health."

Three hundred a year! I felt myself a millionaire. I gave such a flourish to my whip as I drove away from Hillborough House, and rattled to the station, at such a pace, that poor little Jemmy had to hold on by the back as though his life depended on it.

And it did, almost.

The last corner settled it.

The horse, sharing my excitement, dashed round a right-angled corner, the boy spun out and went head-foremost into a duck-puddle on the opposite side, the shafts went right round, I saw nothing except a medley of horse and trap all in one, I heard a smashing and cracking, and the next instant I lay insensible on the road hard by the Collington turnpike.

CHAPTER XXXIII.

I AWOKE to consciousness in a bedroom of an old country inn, which the enterprising landlord, not to be behind his time, had recently christened "The Railway Arms."

The accident had happened near the station, and a couple of labouring men, who, like many other labouring men up and down the country, were gaining their livelihood for the day by loafing about and doing nothing in particular, looking upon me as blown into their arms by the proverbial breeze which does not bring bad fortune to everyone, had carried me into the house, where I had been laid out in state by the obliging host. My wrist was very painful, and my arm much swollen.

The bandages, which Jemmy was fomenting from time to time, were so neatly wound about the injured limb, that I could not help remarking it, and praising either, as

I thought, Jemmy's skill, or that of the attendants at the inn.

"The doctor did that, sir," said Jemmy.

"What doctor?" I asked.

"None as b'longs here, sir; he comed from a walking about the country, and missed thic—I mean I he missed this train."

For Jemmy had learnt civilized English since he had been in my service. When he had first entered it he used to say "thic" for this, "thar" for there, "plai" for play. When we subsequently parted company, I was afraid lest he should return to the family hovel and rub off all his polish, much as a Fiji islander, after being caught and taught to dress and speak like Mr. Smith of Fleet Street, and credited with Smith's ideas, being once more turned loose among his compatriots, is soon fetched out of his finery, and in less than a week is the whole Fiji again, none the better, but perhaps a few thoughts the worse for his brief glimpse of another and, let us hope by comparison, a better world than where he had been accustomed to dwell.

However, I have the satisfaction of knowing that Jemmy Boots—as Ashton used to call him, in allusion to his tops—got another situation very soon, and enlisted in the "Bob" family, Mrs. Bob taking him on my representation.

"Is he a London doctor?" I asked.

Jemmy did not know, but was of opinion that he was a precious sharp 'un, whoever he was.

"Lor, sir!" said Jemmy, "he had me out o' the duck-pond in no time, and I was put in a hot bath and steamed in the kitchen, and then he gave me some gruel with brandy in it."

Quite a holiday for Jemmy.

It was uncommonly fortunate for me that there happened to be a doctor on the spot who had missed his train.

I then wondered who might be suffering by the doctor's mischance and my good luck. Perhaps he was on the road to a patient.

" No," Jemmy explained, " he was walking about, doing nothing, and not at all like a regular doctor."

I understand Jemmy's meaning, and certainly was rather anxious to know to whom I was obliged for this present timely attention.

" He went out," said Jemmy, on whom I think the cordials had slightly taken effect, "and saw Tommy shot, sir." Here Jemmy broke down. Tommy was the horse, and a pet with everyone. This was a blow to some of my hopes. Considering the formidable lecture to which I had been so lately exposed at home, I dared not re-start myself *en voiture* on my first appearance at Cowbridge.

" The trap ? "

" Smashed to haddoms ! " was Jemmy's concise reply.

" The harness ? " I asked.

" Had to be cut to get Tommy out, sir. You never see such a thing, sir. I was by, in my clothes, wet through —they're quite spoiled now—till I was taken off by doctor's orders."

" What are you wearing now ? "

" Billy Coombes's Sunday things. He's the son o' Mr. Coombes as keeps this here."

" And you're all right now, Jemmy ? "

" Yes, sir, thankye kindly, sir. I'm as right as ninepence now, sir."

While Jemmy went at the fomentations once more, there presented themselves to my mind two subjects for meditation:

First, the unexpected presence of a doctor; secondly, the phrase " Right as ninepence."

I had often noticed in newspaper reports of accidents how a medical man is so often, and so providentially, on the spot. Also I had noticed that the reporter was most careful to mention the doctor's name and address, so that in some instances his fortune may have taken its rise from the accident of that day.

It was not likely, indeed, that in my particular case the doctor's happening upon me should lead him on to fame and fortune. Yet who could tell ? Had I been a great nobleman, or a prince, then I could have understood the exact value to *him* of an accident to *me*. But an un-fledged undergraduate (and hardly that yet), on his way to *Alma Mater*, putting out his wrist, how on earth could this benefit the doctor, who, perhaps, by missing a train, had lost a practice? We should see.

Then the boy's being as "Right as ninepence."

Now, were it not that I have other considerations of greater importance in view, I would take this opportunity of discussing the exact and precise meaning of this pro-verbial similitude—I mean about the rightness of nine-pence. I must reserve my remarks on this subject, though I own 'tis a great temptation, seeing it so close to me at this moment, and knowing that the time once allowed to slip can never be recalled—I say it *is* a great temptation to me to lay aside, temporarily, this narrative, to give myself a few minutes' rest, really necessary after the peril of the dogcart, and while lying on the bed in the Railway Arms, to dreamily think out the oppositeness of the similarity existing between the sum of ninepence, current coin of the realm, and the possession of perfect health.

At some period of history the amount indicated by ninepence must have stood for the commercial prosperity of the individual. But how came this about?

Well, the Roman penny——

I might perhaps, in a drowsy state, have got as far as this in my communing with myself on this subject, when I was aroused by Jemmy informing me that the doctor was now coming up to see me.

Having heard that his being there at all was the merest accident—the consequence of his missing a train—I was anxious to see my assistant-preserver, who, Jemmy had moreover informed me, had seemed to recognise me when he "fust comed up."

I had not long to wait in suspense. The door opened. Dressed in a dark tweed suit, a foreign-looking man, with close-cropped reddish beard and moustache, stood before me. I knew him again directly, in spite of his growth of hair, in spite of his bronzed complexion, I knew him again directly by his lack of eyebrows, by his trowel-shaped nose, and that peculiar mouth which the moustache could not conceal.

I knew him directly ; but remembrance of faces, coupled with inability to recall names, is a Colvinistic peculiarity.

"Mr. Cecil Colvin," said the doctor, with something of a foreign accent.

"Mr. Venn, isn't it ? " I exclaimed as the name seemed to be flipped on to my tongue and off again. I felt it must be used at once or lost. A Colvin impulse. A scheming nature would have kept the discovery quiet, and worked the mystery out to its own advantage.

"Yes," said Mr. Venn, "you are right. I was afraid I was so altered you would have forgotten me."

"But, I say," I went on frankly, though, I admit, after a minute's hesitation, "you're not a doctor."

Now this doubt was not, the reader who has followed this record with anything like care, will own, altogether unreasonable. I had first known him as an usher. I had then seen him in such circumstances as caused me to feel considerably perplexed as to what he might really be; and, finally, at the recommendation of Mr. Cavander, he had travelled as Austin's private tutor, and, from what I gathered, had subsequently obtained an appointment abroad, as in some official way connected with one of our small consulates, or as migrating chaplain, travelling for the spiritual benefit of church-going Anglicans in foreign parts, which would of course result in certain pecuniary advantages to himself.

"Yes, I am," he smilingly answered,—that is as much as Mr. Venn ever could smile—with the most perfect equanimity ; "and it's rather lucky for you that I am, or you would have had a great deal more trouble with your wrist than you have now. So. It's better already ; but a sprain is often worse in its effects than a positive simple fracture. Once properly set, the latter is all right, but the effects of a sprain you'll feel for years. You may not, it's true, but ten to one you will. With an impromptu sling you will be able to travel on as comfortably as possible to London."

"I am going farther than that," I replied, quite thrown off the scent of my own inquiry about himself.

"Are you ?   Where ? "

"Cowbridge."

"Cowbridge !" he exclaimed; "why we shall be travelling together."

"You're not at college," I said, in a tone which, I am afraid, implied that my respect for a university of which Mr. Venn could be a member would be rather diminished.

"No," he answered; "I'm too old for that now.   My student's days ended years ago at Heidelberg."

"You were at college in Germany ?"

"Yes, that's where I got my medical degree and diploma.   Ah! there you see practice, and the system is far superior to anything here."

"Is it really ! " I said indifferently, though at the same time admiring the bandage.

"Yes," he went on, "you're in my hands now, and I'll have you on your legs again in no time.   What college are you at ?"

"I haven't matriculated yet."

"I thought not, or I must have seen you at Cowbridge. Why, I know everybody there, and can introduce you to some capital fellows."

Mr Venn's heartiness did not become him.   His geniality was forced; and forced geniality scorches, but fails to warm.

I was bound to bear with him now, and gratitude evicted prejudice.

"I am going up to Tudor College," I informed him.

"Will you live in or out of college ?" he asked.

Bless him !   I didn't know.   He had lighted upon a thorough fledgling.   I was—I could not help myself—in his hands.

This last sentence is literally true : morally and physically I was for a while helpless.   However, I was well enough to set off by the next train for town, where the Doctor advised we should break our journey.

So also, by his advice, we broke it at Broad's.   That evening he kindly went out and purchased a sling for my

Y

arm; he ordered my dinner, an excellent one, with such dainty little specialities of Italian, French, and German cookery as caused the waiters to wonder, the *chef* to be respectful, and brought out of his private office the impassible Mr. Broad himself, who listened, smiled, made mental notes, approved with a nod, and retired.

After dinner I do not remember that any prejudices remained.

With the wider view of life that Mr. Venn put before me, even my thorough-going dislike of Cavander would have soon melted away.

But, strange to say, though my old friend, with a new face, was full of conversation, quite different from the reserved usher I remembered at Old Carter's; yet though, to my surprise, I found myself on common ground with him as regarded Cavander, he became suddenly guarded and reticent on any subject connected, however remotely, with this latter gentleman; and it is no wonder that even my unsuspicious nature, at my most unsuspecting age, should have suddenly been aroused, seeing that during the time we had been together I had mentally recalled the three mysterious occasions when I had seen more than Mr. Venn had ever imagined.

We stayed another day in London, so that, as the Doctor said, I might go up sound as a bell.

The great advantage of being in London seemed to consist in the fact that I could obtain an unlimited supply of ice, which Mr. Venn used very freely.

The great disadvantage (which I did *not* observe at the time) was, that I was running up a considerable bill at Broad's, and that I was really retarding my cure with one hand while helping it onwards with the other.

The second night we became more confidential. The Doctor amused me with anecdotes of Cowbridge, which I soon decided must be the most delightful place in the world.

"When I left your young friend Austin," said Mr. Venn," I did, as you were rightly informed, avail myself of the fact of my having in early life taken orders in the Church of England, and as, fortunately, I had the necessary certificates with me, I was able to be of some use to a few travellers here and there. But I had studied, years ago, another profession, and that was medicine. The idea seized me, and, being free to do what I liked, I resumed my place in the college in Germany where I had previously been, and obtained my diploma. I grew this moustache after one of our students' duels, in which I got a severe cut on the upper lip. As there was no opening for me in the Church, and as I had some little money left me about this time, on condition, oddly enough, that of my changing my name to Falkner "——he broke off at this point, seeing my surprised look.

"Then," I exclaimed, "you're not Mr. Venn any longer."

"No, I'm Dr. Falkner. I keep the Venn as a Christian name, and sign myself Dr. V. Falkner. My diploma is for Falkner, not for Venn."

"Oh! then the money was left you while you were studying?"

"Just so," replied Dr. Venn Falkner; "and as Dr. Falkner I practise at Cowbridge. I am getting on very well, but the regular college ignoramuses of medical men, with their old exploded methods, are, of course, dead against me."

This, I said, I thought very hard on Dr. Falkner. I slipt into calling him Falkner as easily as though I had known him by this name all my life. Indeed, it became so easy that I began to think of my Mr. Venn of the past as a being totally distinct from the sharp-eyed, foreign-looking medical man seated at table with me in a private room at Broad's tossing off champagne and telling story after story of his adventures at home and abroad.

Unable any longer to resist the impulse, I blurted out one of my questions point blank :—

"Do you remember walking in Kensington Gardens with that woman you knew, who afterwards died at the hospital, and meeting Mr. Cavander?"

The *ci-devant* Mr. Venn looked at me in a manner that at once ·recalled to my mind the afternoon when he had shut the back door of Old Carter's on me, after warning me (in effect) about minding my own business without interesting myself in his.

This searching look was evidently intended to prove the depth of my consciousness at that precise moment. The difficulty that had arisen in his mind probably was whether I had only repeated hearsay, or had interrogated him from my own knowledge of the fact.

He parried the thrust, and returned,

"What on earth put that into your head?"

In a champagney manner I thought I should triumphantly render all evasion on his part impossible by bearing witness to my own evidence, and so I unhesitatingly replied,

"What put it into my head? Nothing. I saw you."

To my surprise, Mr. Venn seemed suddenly to be shaken by a fit of silent, but uncontrollable laughter. Stopping himself by an effort, he requested me to repeat what I had just told him, and. if possible, to give my narrative in detail. We had some more wine, and I recounted the incident, as already given in this record.

Its recital seemed to amuse him vastly, and when I had finished he took the trouble to point out to me how remarkable were the coincidences which associated him in my mind with the unfortunate woman at whose disease we had both been present.

"Had you seen this woman anywhere, and with a person dressed as I used to be in those days—that is, in nothing which could in any way distinguish me from a hundred and ninety-nine other seedy ushers in and about London, you would very naturally have said to yourself, boylike, 'Why that's Mr. Venn!' I don't say you would do so now that you are a man and know what's going on in the world."

I said, certainly I should not do so now, and thought my former preceptor a very intelligent person.

"Besides," he continued, as if rummaging his memory, "though it's difficult at this distance of time to say where one was and what exactly one was doing—this is excellent champagne and can do you no harm; on the contrary,— yet I dare say you may remember that for those holidays

I had gone to Switzerland, and—dear me, how vividly all these minutiæ return to one!—and you pointed out to Bifford, Puggy Bifford, on the map, where Switzerland was, and he was very angry, and then he and his brother fought it out between them."

Yes, as Mr. Venn had observed, these minutiæ did return to my mind most vividly, and I certainly *did* recollect the incidents to which he referred, therefrom concluding, for I had had quite enough of the subject, and too much of the wine, that I must have been mistaken, as Mr. Venn, who must himself best know where he himself was at any particular time, was doubtless in Switzerland on the memorable day when I could have sworn to him in Kensington Gardens.

The matter was allowed to drop, and I did not take it up again. Once or twice it occurred to me to question him as to the half-witted creature who had frightened me at Old Carter's, but somehow or other I never did mention it to him from that time forth.

Under the able guidance of Dr. Falkner I went up to Cowbridge.

What my preconceived notions of a University were it would be difficult to describe.

I thought it would be Holyshade over again, only that we should all wear caps and gowns.

When I first saw Cowbridge I could not realize the fact of my being in a University town.

Nor was this very wonderful, as on quitting the railway station—a squalid affair, by the way, for such a place—Dr. Falkner (whom henceforth I shall style by his new name of Dr. Falkner, for by this only was he known at Cowbridge) took me to his apartments in Meadow Terrace, the shortest route to which place lay through a number of narrow back-passage-like streets, where frowsy mothers stood or sat on their doorsteps, and gutter children threatened our fly as it rolled on towards its destination. Slouching men stood at tavern doors; and, in short, anything more unacademical, or more like a provincial edition of the Seven Dials, I could not have imagined.

All my enthusiasm vanished. But that I was a man, and all but a Cowbridgian, I could have wept for sheer disappointment.

"Where," I asked, "is the University?"

For I had some idea that the University was one large building, just as Holyshade was one large college, and that this grand and imposing pile would occupy the centre of a splendid square, itself in the centre of an ancient and magnificent town.

"The colleges," said Dr. Falkner, "lie in the other direction;" indicating the opposite to that in which we were going. "We," he continued, "are now nearer Badwell, and my rooms are just on the outskirts. It is not," he added, reassuringly, "ten minutes' walk from my place to the Tudor Gate, only this fellow's come a round-about way."

The drive, indeed, was not a long one, but my vexation had rendered every minute's delay more tiresome than it would otherwise have been.

We descended at Dr. Falkner's in Meadow Terrace. It was a neat little house, one of a row of ordinary lodging-houses (of a very second-class order, I thought, on seeing them for the first time, though after a day or two I soon came to regard them as good as any others in the great University town of Cowbridge) facing some meadows that ran down to the river Cowe.

Having deposited my luggage in the passage, and discharged the fly, I proceeded with Dr. Falkner to make my first inspection of the University.

At the sister University of Bulford the colleges thrust themselves upon you and overpower you. At Cowbridge you have to hunt them out for yourself. In some instances you go down a narrow passage between two high walls, come to an old archway, push open a door (timidly in all probability), and startle yourself with the exclamation—

"Why, bless me, here's a college!"

Then, again, it often happens that one college, like one false step, leads to another. You cross a bridge, or go through a gate, or come out of a small archway into a narrow street, only to pass through a similar archway on to the opposite side, and then you are in another college.

The colleges of learned St. Bolt's and respectable Little Tudor were literally crowded out by the houses, which, as it were, just gave Tudor street—more a street-let than a street—room to run between the two steep banks.

When Dr. Burleigh, the master of Tudor, was Vice-Chancellor, Tudor Street was just big enough for this majestic personage to pass from the senate house to his college, with his silver poker and other implements borne before him, as if he were going out to spend the winter with a friend who had asked him to come and bring his own fire-irons.

So scattered are the colleges at Cowbridge that I can quite imagine a studious young man at St. Saviour's (which you will pass on your road to the station, and, perhaps, take for a Contagious Disease Hospital in an outlying district), who should confine his exercise to within the boundaries of his own college, remaining at the University without seeing any colleges, except St. Henry's, which he could hardly fail to notice on account of its proximity to the senate house, where my imaginary student would perforce (unless ill and examined in his own chamber at St. Saviour's) visit first for his "little go," and secondly for his degree.

Dr. Falkner asked me on whose side I was, and I remembered that I had been told off to Mr Smyler's side.

To call on the Rev. Dumley Smyler was my first duty.

He lived in one of the towers of Tudor College, and shared the rooms over the gateway north with the clock and the founder's statue. At least, this was my impression. My subsequent visits to my tutor's chamber were angelical in their infrequency, but diabolical in the manner of my apparition, as I only showed myself when, like Mephistopheles, or any other familiar, I was forced to appear by the summoner's possession of some potent spell.

I took good care on this my first visit to make him perfectly acquainted with my serious dogcart accident.

By Dr. Falkner's advice I kept on my sling, and trusted to Mr. Smyler's compassion for a mitigation of the severity of my matriculation.

There was no necessity for the employment of so much art. Matriculation time came and passed, and so did I. It was a farce from beginning to end. What its object was I do not know. It proved that at eighteen I had got up certain subjects which had been fixed by collegiate authority long beforehand. However, it satisfied them—that is, it pleased them, and it did me no particular harm, except that it gave me a low, and, at the same time, an incorrect notion of all University examinations.

Mr. Smyler, my tutor, was very glad to see me. He did not recognize my name, and called me by that of somebody else. This difficulty overcome, he asked after my father, with whom he was totally unacquainted, I know, and of whose health, he was, he said, sorry to hear so poor an account. I, thoughtfully (in view of this matriculation, which I then dreaded as an unknown terror), added my father's illness to my accident, in order to affect Mr. Smyler to greater pity for the lonely undergraduate, who, by coming "on his side" had, as it were, appealed to his patronal protection against cruel examiners.

"Was I going to live in college? Because, if so, he was afraid that there would be some difficulty about rooms, unless——"

Here I relieved his mind. I was going to live out of college.

"Then," said he, rising, "in that case I won't detain you, as you will want to install yourself as soon as possible."

We wished each other "Good day," with much courtesy, and, on descending, I found the Doctor waiting for me at the foot of the stairs, talking to a tall, good-looking young fellow in a pea-jacket, with a knobby stick peeping out of his pocket, and his hat very much on one side.

"Nice fellow Smyler seems," I observed.

"Yes, pretty well, as Dons go," answered my worthy monitor. "I wouldn't recommend you to be too gushing with him at first. Let me introduce you to my friend,

Mr. Rowdie." The lengthy young man smiled, and saluted me in a gentlemanly and courteous manner, that strangely contrasted with his slangy appearance.

"Rowdie will put you up to a good deal as to being on too friendly terms with tutors, eh?" observed Doctor Falkner.

Mr. Rowdie shook his light locks in a knowing manner.

"If you go to lectures," said Mr. Rowdie, with a wink at me, expressive of the most overwhelming knowingness on his part, "when you first come, you're done for: and you'll always have to go to lectures; they'll expect it of you; and if they don't see your familiar face, they'll send to know why you don't honour them, and then you'll get into a heap of trouble."

I was really much interested. Till then I had heard that, though a University was undoubtedly a most pleasant place for a young man fond of amusing himself, yet that there were drawbacks to his giving himself up entirely to enjoyment, in the shape of studies, necessitated by the existence of tutors, lecturers, examinations, and examiners.

"Now," said Mr. Rowdie, confidentially, "I was put up to it when I first came, and I'll put *you* up to it, as it is a wrinkle. You be *ægrotat* as soon as you conveniently can; the doctor here will manage it, and if he won't, I'll give you a prescription which will do all you want with the regular practitioners——"

"I don't quite understand."

"Well, I mean, you get on the sick list—be excused lectures and chapels. Then get an *exeat*."

"A what?"

"An '*exeat*,'" explained the Doctor, "means a permission from your tutor, and the Dean, to stay away as long as you like. With an *absit* you can only be away one day and a night."

"Yes," said Rowdie; "then come up late, but in time to keep your turn in Hall. You keep it by eating four dinners a week for half a term, and by then they'll have forgotten all about you. I," he continued, bringing himself forward as evidence, "seldom patronize lectures, but I've had to do chapels lately. Good-bye; see you again."

It occurred to the Doctor that if the rooms under where the Honourable Malcolm Rowdie "kept" (which is the Cowbridgian for "lodged") were vacant, I could not do better that take them.

Thither, therefore, we shaped our course.

During our walk I came across several Holyshadians, either freshmen like myself, or undergraduates of some standing.

I longed to don a cap and gown, and could not conceive how any undergraduate could allow his academicals to run to such utter rack and ruin, as I saw they did; or how so tattered and battered a costume could be permitted by the University authorities.

I saw and wondered at the proctors and their bull-dogs, and learnt all about the academical system, which compels a respectable clergyman to become, for one year, a sort of police-sergeant, with a couple of constables in plain clothes at his heels, whose duties in the town and at night are far more irksome, and, in some cases, more repugnant to a man of refined taste, than those of an ordinary policeman, and, of course, quite out of keeping with their position as educated gentlemen.

As to the mode of the hiring of apartments, the Doctor knew all about this, and on our road recommended to my notice two or three places where, he explained to me, I could do pretty much as I liked, this being evidently the chief object of my coming to Cowbridge.

The rooms under Mr. Rowdie's were fortunately vacant. And, being strongly urged thereto by Dr. Falkner, I took them without further hesitation.

Then came the furnishing. Most other youths had been duly instructed before coming up to college, or were accompanied by someone who could regulate their expenses, and assist them with his experience. As I had not the slightest idea of the value of any one article, from a hand-shovel to a pair of window-curtains, and as I did not make any inquiries as to prices, and as the generous and high-minded tradesmen of Cowbridge—one and all—professed themselves utterly incapable of any such meanness as sending in a bill, or accepting ready money,

making me feel quite ashamed, indeed, of even ordering
anything at all of them, it will not astonish any lady, who
may do me the honour of reading this simple record, to
learn that in one afternoon I had, without being aware of
it, expended something uncommonly near the amount of
my one year's allowance ; and for it I could show a fair
quantity of various wines, cigar boxes, easy-chairs, sofas,
prints, and such decorations for my rooms as seemed to
me to be, after all, only absolutely necessary.

Once installed, I began my University life with such a
genuine appreciation of its pleasures, and such a hearty
capacity for enjoyment, as few, even of my own age,
possessed, and which, alas! was not to be of very long
duration, I say "alas!" And *eheu ! fugaces annos,*
rises to my lips, as it has to those of so many others since
that old heathen *bon vivant* first struck the chord of
middle-aged sympathy.

But I am not about to linger unnecessarily over these
scenes of *ma première jeunesse,* like a disembodied spirit
recently set free, which is, according to certain theories,
said to hover about the spots on earth it once loved so
well, and from which it has departed with regret.

My Time at Cowbridge was for the most part a thoughtless, careless, happy, idle, selfish time spent in a Paradise
without resident Eves, and where one went peaceably to
sleep within the shadow of the ancient Tree of Knowledge.   There stood the Tree ; the industrious climbed it
and plucked its fruits, the lazy remained beneath, and,
instead of plucking, were themselves plucked.   Some
thrived on the windfalls.   Those who were neither studious nor idle, or whose taste lay in a direction different
from that in which the University insisted upon her sons
taking their way if they would profit by the rewards and
prizes in her gift, took such fruit as lay within their
reach, and finally wrote B.A. or B.C.L. after their names,
and with this valuable addition entered the world of
work outside the borders of the University.

One morning, during my third term, as I was lounging
over breakfast, two letters were brought to me by our
worthy landlady, Mrs. Freshly (excellent, motherly,

respectable, old lady you were, and sorely tried by Mr. Freshly, whose reputation as a trowser-cutter was only excelled by his fame as a bruiser), one from Langoran House, and the other from Austin.

The latter had more interest for me, so after debating with myself to which I should give the preference in order of opening, I finally decided for Austin's.

"DEAR CECIL,—It is a long time since you heard from me. Once more I have been abroad, and not abroad only, but half over England since we last met. I have no good news to tell, and sooner or later you will hear of what has happened, from some friend or other, and I can tell you no more than they can, for in spite of every effort to unravel the mystery, we are—and, I am deeply grieved to think that for a long time we shall be—without any safe clue to guide us in this unhappy affair. I cannot now write at length to you, as I am bound by a promise to my father to pursue what will prove, as I have already expressed my fear, an ineffectual search before communicating with my brother in India, from whose impulsive and hot character we are led to apprehend some violence."

Up to this point the letter that Lord Monteagle received was a plain and simple statement compared with this of Austin's, whose correspondence had invariably been remarkable for its perspicacity, its thoughtful method, and its cheerful tone.

The thought that now occurred to me in reading seemed to have struck him in writing, as, after a dash with the pen, implying a break in the sequence of his ideas, he went on to say—

"*I stop to look over what I have written.* Were I to destroy it, perhaps I should not now write at all. But I find that I have not told you—it seemed to me that everyone knew it, and that you at all events would have learnt it ere this should have reached you—hear it then from me—Alice has left her home. There are two letters of hers : one to her husband, one to my mother, enclosing a message for me. It is now more than a month since she disappeared, and as yet we have been unable to trace her movements. Sir Frederick Sladen has made no extraordinary effort to discover her; and his mother has written to express a wish that further intercourse between our families may at once cease, intimating that, as at present advised, her son will take the necessary steps to free himself from the tie by which, against her (his mother's) advice, he had bound himself. The message enclosed to me is a sad one. Poor Alice! once so religious, so devoted to all that was good, seems to have become a soul without faith in God, or trust in man. Two years since I noticed, sadly, but not without hope, the change that was gradually coming over her. Alas, my experience then was only a boy's—was only that of a young and loving brother, who had grown up to pet and spoil his sister. True, that we conversed earnestly on grave subjects, and that while she leapt to conclusions, my slower mind was contented to wait until I could prove by a logical method whether her conclusions were correct. She looked up to me, I know, for guidance and instruction; it was she who determined me on carrying out my own bent towards the Church, but from the moment I began to study the questions which such an exalted profession seemed to entail upon me, I was unable to direct her, for I myself had already begun to lose myself in doubt. Then when I could no longer conscientiously answer her difficulties, when, indeed, my replies only confirmed her in her growing scepticism, then she no longer sought my guidance, but that of some other, who had been, for his own vile purposes, slowly but surely poisoning the pure well of her mind, and the impulse that would before have driven her almost to fanaticism for an ideal cause, good and holy in itself, now urged her on a downward career where it is impossible to retrace her steps. Such, my dear Cecil, my dear friend, is *my* view. Who is to blame for all this? as yet I dare not say, nor would I venture now to hint my suspicions. You know my deep affection for our Alice, and this shock seems to have aged me more in a short time than I could have imagined of any, even the most bitter, grief. You will scarcely know me again.

On my return, I have made up my mind to finish my course here as quickly as I can; indeed, if my father does not object, I shall leave Bulford without taking a degree (I can come up and do that at any future time), and shall proceed to St. Bede's, the Diocesan Theological College, where, in perfect retirement, I am informed, I can devote my whole time to the special studies for which it was instituted. A friend, a clergyman, has offered to give me an opportunity of seeing what practical village work is whenever I liked to go and spend a part of my vacation with him in North Wales. A letter to my college will find me at present; but you shall hear from me again shortly, when I hope against hope to have some better tidings to give you than are contained in this letter from your

" Most sincere friend,
" AUSTIN."

With this letter in my hand, I sat in my chair for half an hour or more meditating vaguely. Now, I vividly recalled the conversations to which I had listened in the past, and as Alice's life, as I had known it, gradually unfolded itself before me, I, too, began to wonder of what use had been all those pious sentiments and practices of hers against *the* one temptation when it came.

The day on which I received the letter from Austin I felt was one to be recorded carefully in my diary; the very diary that contained the other unfinished entry, of which, alas! this must form the continuation,—And the end?

I have said before, that I did not intend to dwell upon the details of life at Tudor College, Cowbridge, except as they might crop up incidentally, and be involved in my own personal narrative. And this is why I have already skipped over my two first terms as being, in regard to my present object in view, void of particular interest. Dr. Falkner continued to be popular; I increased my circle of acquaintances; we all did pretty much what we liked, doing it also pretty well when we liked; and, as Uncle Herbert observed, who had been on a visit to me for three weeks (having nowhere else just then to go, and University life being a novelty to him), "You have a remarkably pleasant time of it; but when do you work?"

The answer to this I had yet to supply for myself. Uncle Herbert was delighted at having a new place where, as his phrase was, "he could hang up his hat;" for he was one of those companionable beings who cannot get on without someone on whom to lean, to which someone the leaner may, indeed, be far from useless. This was Uncle Herbert exactly. Alone, he was as helpless as a detached cart-wheel lying by the roadside; and I am of opinion that nature can present us no stronger instance of utter hopeless helplessness than that melancholy spectacle of a solitary cart-wheel.

"So," said my Uncle, on this double-letter morning, entering the room quickly, contrary to his usual habit, "I see you've some correspondence from home." It was lying on the table while I was making a careful memorandum in my diary.

"Yes. I haven't opened it yet."

"No?" exclaimed Uncle Herbert. He walked to the window and fidgetted.

"I've been to the Chatham," he said presently, mentioning a club to which I had obtained for him the *entrée*, so long as he might be my guest at the University.

"Ah!" I said, continuing my diary.

"And seen the papers," he continued.

"Anything in them?" I asked, for the sake of civility.

"Yes," returned my Uncle. "I don't often read the *Births, Deaths, and Marriages,*, but it's a most extraordinary thing, that whenever I do I always find somebody mentioned whom I know."

"Odd."

It had struck me, at first, that he might have fallen upon this news about Lady Frederick Sladen, but evidently he was not leading up to that now.

"Open your letter," he said.

"It's my father's hand," I remarked; then, on observing it more closely, I detected a marked difference between his writing and that on this envelope.

" Yes.   That's Cavander's," said Uncle Herbert; "I suppose, from long partnership, he and your father write so much alike I can hardly tell the distinction : their clerks write like them, too.   Dangerous faculty, imitation. What does he say ? "

" He writes, he says, for my father, who is not very strong just now.   It is to apprize me that—good heavens !——"

And I broke off abruptly, for I could scarcely believe my eyes.

" I thought you'd be astonished," said Uncle Herbert, gloomily.

" You knew it, then ? "

" I bought a paper."

He produced one from his pocket, and while I continued staring stupidly at the same intelligence conveyed in Cavander's letter, he read aloud—

On the 9th instant, at Langoran House, Kensington, Lady Colvin, wife of Sir John Colvin, Bart., of a son.

CHAPTER XXXIV.

LETTER—REPLY—WHERE TO GO NEXT—ADVICE—UNCLE HER-
BERT DEPARTS—DANGEROUS CORRESPONDENCE—I KEEP A
SECRET—MORE OF COWBRIDGE—CLUBS—SCIENCES—ARTS—
THEATRICALS—MARMY DENNE—DR. FALKNER IN A RE-
SPONSIBLE POSITION—LANGORAN AGAIN—BROAD'S—CALL
ON THE VAN CLYMS—OF MRS. CAVANDER—ABOUT VERNEY
—I BECOME MORE AND MORE UNSETTLED—I START NORTH-
WARDS—I MEET THE BIFFORDS—I LOSE MY ROAD—I COME
UPON CLARA AND HER GRANDFATHER—WELCOME—A DAMPER
—MRS. WENSLOW—VISITORS EXPECTED—DANGERS—THE
FOUNTAIN—THE GOLD FISHES—I AM CARRIED OFF—A NEW
FAVOURITE—I JOIN AUSTIN AND MAKE A DISCOVERY.

I COULD not honestly write my congratulations. Like
the Amen in Macbeth's throat, the words would not
come out.

"You must send something civil," said Uncle Herbert,
who now very rarely called at Langoran House.

This I achieved, after having torn up several sheets
of paper, and having, as it were, written all round the
subject in order to avoid calling Lady Colvin either
"mother" or "mamma," and at the same time so mentioning her as not to pain my father.

In reply to this, I received a letter intimating that
if my vacation were commencing soon, it would be
as well to defer my coming home until the house should
be a little more in order; as the advent of so illustrious
a visitor as The New Baby had, it would be understood,

z

thrown the establishment rather out of gear, temporarily, of course; but for a few weeks or so it would not be, I was given to understand, convenient to receive so gay and independent a young bachelor as myself as an inmate.

"Broad's?" I said to Uncle Herbert.

He shook his head.

"Don't overdo it, Cecil. You're inclined to go fast without knowing it, and the sooner you pull up the better. You don't gamble, thank goodness; and a little harmless loo, such as I've seen here among the best set, won't hurt you, or them. But not a step beyond. And as I'm going away, and while we are on the subject, let me warn you against"—he hesitated, then continued —"You won't take it ill if I mention a man here who seems to be more a friend of yours than he is of any-body's——"

"Rowdie?" I asked, feeling pretty sure that my Uncle did *not* mean him.

"No, no, not Rowdie. He's fast and noisy, but he comes of a good stock, and, *au fond*, he's a gentleman. Besides, when *he* has seen more of the world, he will tone down. No, I mean Dr. Falkner. I know the man somehow," said my Uncle, meditatively; "and I've seen him somewhere, and however I know him, or wherever I've seen him, I'm certain of one thing, and that is that I would not trust that man with sixpence. Besides, he has no more right to be mixing with gentlemen; and specially with such open-hearted, open-handed boys as you all are here"—Uncle Herbert owned to having been treated *en prince* —"than has one of those cads who sell toy terriers and fancy French Lulu dogs in your streets."

"I know some fellows speak against him; and Rowdie was blackballed for the Minerva"—this was the aristo-cratic Club at Cowbridge—"in consequence of his keeping up his acquaintance with him. But Rowdie says he won't give up a friend for a parcel of snobs, and I think he's right."

"You do *not* think he is right, Cecil," returned my Uncle. "You really admire Rowdie for what you call his pluck in sticking by his friend. And so should I if Dr. Falkner *were* a friend, but he's not; he's only an acquaintance, and a disreputable acquaintance too. He lives on you young fellows. Recollect he's twenty years older than any of you here."

"Well, well; I'm not going to lend him any money."

"I hope not. Though, by the way, if you did, I'm not sure if it wouldn't be the best way to get rid of him. He's a bad 'un, mind that; and before long he'll turn out to be all I've said, and more."

Privately, I was entirely of my Uncle's opinion. Publicly, I acted with Rowdie; and we, with a few others equally careless, were Falkner's supporters, though not, perhaps, altogether his admirers.

In truth I had forgotten him as Mr. Venn; but this conversation with Uncle Herbert recalled to my mind all that I had previously known of this mysterious personage; and I determined to take Rowdie into my confidence, as to the Doctor's antecedents, on the first opportunity.

It being the commencement of the London season, Uncle Herbert regretted that he should have to leave me in order to fulfil an engagement with some friends in town, in whose house he had the usual peg for his hat. He begged me earnestly not to omit calling on Mr. and Mrs. Bob, at their London house, and to provide myself with visiting cards.

Once only, just as I was seeing him off at the station, did Uncle Herbert allude to Clara Wenslow. He pretended to rally me on this subject. But I confess to not having felt exactly at ease at being reminded of this episode in my time at Hillborough.

She had written to me, once, on some pretext about some pictures of Cowbridge which I had promised her, but from the tone of her letter it was evidently intended to bring to my mind the sentiments which I had professed to entertain for her at our last interview, and it startled me to find that I had gone further than I had thought, or that she, at all events, had understood me to be more in earnest than I had really been.

This letter I had answered by a promise to bring

the drawings myself during the vacation, when I hoped to renew our, to *me*, (I said) most delightful acquaintance.

In the present unsettled state of affairs at home, I thought I could not do better than revisit that part of the country where I had found so many friends, and had spent such a pleasant time.

One letter more arrived from her thanking me for my answer, and informing me that in all probability she would, in July and August, be staying at her grandfather's at Vale House, near Windermere, where she was sure her relatives would be only too delighted to make my acquaintance.

As Uncle Herbert had left before the arrival of this second epistle from Clara, I had no opportunity of informing him as to my progress in that quarter, and as I had not considered it necessary to say anything about the two previous letters when he had started the subject at the last moment at the railway station, Uncle Herbert went away satisfied that I was a wiser young man than he had given me credit for being, and pleased with himself for having given me such timely advice when we were last together in Devonshire.

I felt some compunction in having kept a secret of this nature from so kind and valuable a friend as was Uncle Herbert, but I consoled myself with the consideration, that, after all, it might, and probably would, come to nothing, and in the meantime it was no use bothering him about what was of so little consequence.

Term time came to an end with no further news from Austin, who had sent no reply to my answer to his letter. I concluded, therefore, that he was still travelling, and I now set myself, being absolutely my own master, to map out some sort of a plan for a vacation tour.

One most important incident occurred before the end of this term.

Cowbridge, as every Cowbridgian reader knows, is a University of clubs.

Man is a gregarious animal, but the University man is perhaps the most fully developed species of the genus.

Whiggism and Toryism, of the most ancient kind, are

represented by dining clubs, where youthful politicians emulate the example of their political ancestors by attempting to swallow, each one "to his own cheek," two or three bottles of such port wine as is easier imagined than described, in drinking loyal and patriotic toasts, after which they hoped to be able to speak; for had they not heard of such feats performed by the greatest orators of old, and had they not some vague ideas about Mr. Fox, Mr. Pitt, and Mr. Sheridan having achieved their successes in consequence, rather than in spite of, their magnificent potations? There were modern instances, but they were contented with those of a time when debates were fiery, when the old English gentleman could lick any seven Frenchmen, when the duello had not gone entirely out of fashion, and men had not yet learned the habit of putting water in their wine.

Cowbridge had its rowing clubs innumerable, its public school clubs, its general sociable clubs, its dining clubs, its debating clubs, its reading and writing rooms (also called a club), its aristocratic club, its sporting clubs, its swimming club, its cricket clubs, and I dare say many others of which I have never heard; for there were religious societies, chiefly professing Evangelicalism, which, while shrinking from the name, were practically clubs, with settled objects, meetings, and subscriptions. There was also a High Church club, a feeble and priggish affair, whose supporters were chiefly remarkable as being of an effeminate and dilettante character. Of course the members did not style themselves a Club, nor would they adopt the Exeter-"hall-mark," and form themselves into a "Society," but they got hold of the mediæval word "Guild;" and this pleased them immensely.

But, certes, in my time, religious fervour was not the distinguishing characteristic of this University, as some years before, during the marvellous period of Catholic revivalism, had been the case with its sister Bulford.

Neither did the arts flourish at Cowbridge. Sciences had it almost entirely to themselves, though some of the most useful were not taught at all; and others coming under the same category were, so to speak, taught in holes and corners, to which access was difficult. Special instruction was kept a secret from the many, and as in no case was it prominently brought before the eyes of the ordinary careless undergraduate, who, like Gallio, only with far better excuse than had that eminent statesman, "cared for none of these things," so even those who would work, and wanted to work, had to hunt up their own professors, whose lectures were interesting to the specialist, but were useless for a degree, whether in classics or mathematics.

Music had its votaries, and was honoured by the University in its chief scientific exponent. There was also a musical society which gave concerts in the Town Hall, and was patronized by deans and dons, by masters of colleges and their wives, and by the first-class townsfolk, with their wives and daughters, and by all that devoted band of ladies unattached, who, somehow or another, seem to hang about the township of a University, like October flies on a warm plate.

The Drama had been hitherto unrepresented at Cowbridge. Amateur theatricals had not be seen for years since "somebody," who had become quite a legendary person, had started a University Theatre, which had been very soon closed by order of the Proctors.

It was destined for Marmy Denne in our time to start the idea. He was of my standing, and remarkable at the University for belonging to no particular set, though welcomed as a genial companion by all. He was a sharp, quick, odd, little man, with a round mobile face and rough hair, which, with a good voice, several songs, and a facility as a pianist, were his stock-in-trade for the amusement of his *convives.* He was one of the very few men who, uninvited, could drop in at a party and be welcomed. Rowdie and myself inclined towards him on account of his strong theatrical tastes, which, in my view, were ever associated with the earliest, and perhaps the happiest, portion of my life. The Hon. Malcolm, my co-lodger, liked Denne immensely, because of his eccentricity; for Rowdie took up with anyone who was outside the ordinary circle of University acquaintance, and it amused him to have in his room as heterogeneous a collection as he could get together, including a professor of the noble art of self-defence, another professor of the quarter-staff, a conjurer, a fiddler, Marmy Denne giving illustrations of popular actors to Dr. Falkner, who was smoking a pipe in a corner, while the action of the scene was accompanied on the piano, capitally played by a young undergraduate, who, having received the greater part of his education in Paris, was thoroughly acquainted with all the most sparkling and the latest airs popular in that gay capital.

Boxing, single-stick, fencing, fiddling, playing on the piano, singing, eating, drinking, talking, and games of cards, were, more often than not, all going on simultaneously in Rowdie's two rooms. The noise was rather too much for me, and Rowdie himself was gradually becoming too much for every respectable Tudor man. Thank goodness, he discovered one day that his soul could be no longer fettered by our restricted premises. He gave notice to quit, and changed his lodgings.

By this separation it came about that we met less frequently than heretofore, and my eccentric friend left the University long before my time there came to an end. Having said this much of him, I may add that he has since entered the ministry of the Church of England, and has come out as a first-rate preacher—a man in the front ranks of the Evangelicals; distinguished, however, from his brethren, by the liberality of his sentiments. Further, he is incumbent of a popular church, in a fashionable district, and, if he had but been a schoolmaster, there would be hardly any room to doubt that, sooner or later, he must be fitted into a Bishopric. In any case, he is the respected father of a family; he is the "Honourable and Reverend," is on the high road to preferment, and, as the celebrated epitaph has it, "of such is the kingdom of heaven."

Marmy Denne had surrounded himself with undergraduates. Theatrically inclined, he had started a club, which came to be, both for its members within and their friends without, one of the most popular institutions

founded by University men for intellectual and harmless
recreation. It would take too long to dwell upon the
history of this club, which, in its way, is as interesting,
and far more amusing, than that of its ancient and
honourable brother, the Junction Debating Society. The
annals of the latter have often been referred to by com-
pilers of statesmen's lives; the annals of the former have
yet to be written. To this temptation, now, I will not
yield. My only object in mentioning its existence in this
place is, to tell just so much connected with this institution as affects my own private and personal narrative.

Mr. Venn—I mean Dr. Falkner—was admitted to this
club as an honorary member, though his entrance at all
was strongly opposed at first. Rowdie, Denne, and myself
backed him, and our energy won the day. Nor was
this all. Uncle Herbert's mistrust of Mr. Venn-Falkner
chiefly arose from his having seen what an influence he
had obtained over some men in this particular club. Mr.
Venn's stories of Germany, German theatres, of London
literary society, tickled us all immensely; and though
Uncle Herbert, in whose presence Venn would not expose
himself to the chance of a cross-examination, insisted that
the man could never have been in any such good society
as he represented, yet Rowdie and Denne and many
others made a clique to support their protégé, and when
one after the other of the members declined the treasurer-
ship of the club, Rowdie actually went so far as to
nominate my old usher as a fit and proper person for
the office. This raised a storm; but we were all going
away for our vacation: Venn-Falkner would be on the
spot, able to look after our rooms and our interests
generally; and as none of us were, after all, inclined to
treat the affair as a serious matter of business, except
one Irish member, who observed, " We ought to be
mighty careful in our dealings with money matters,"
and who, having been secretary for one term, had run
our ship into the very quicksands of debt; reasoning also
that not to accede to Rowdie's proposition would be
to imply a distrust of him and his friend, we finally
handed over our cash-box to the honorary member,

who was accredited with full powers, in the absence of the committee.

This was the last event of this term time, and then we separated.

At Langoran House I called.

Plemdale, the butler, was gravely pleased to see me, but the cheery welcome of old times was wanting.

"How is my father?" I asked.

"Sir John is not so well as we could wish," answered Plemdale. "Lady Colvin is doing well; and," added Plemdale, with a meaning smile, "so is the little baby."

"Not at home?" I asked, with as great a show of carelessness as I could affect.

"No, Mr. Cecil. At Dover. We don't expect 'em back for some weeks now."

It was absurd to ask whether I could stop at Langoran House,—in my own home. Plemdale had no orders on the subject; the room wasn't ready. There were, of course, plenty of rooms, and there was no difficulty; only, the servants were on board wages, and in fact, Plemdale repeated, in a tone that implied his own personal dissatisfaction with the present state of affairs, "I haven't had no orders on the subject, Mister Cecil."

I professed the most complete indifference, and took my luggage to Broad's.

"Horrid expensive!" said little Lord Pilchard, who was always in the coffee-room, looking out of window. Little Pilchard was enormously rich. The Earl of Dawlish, his father, having been a saving man, had also had the good fortune to marry an heiress of a noble Scotch family, daughter of the M'Kerrel of M'Kerrel. These facts I did not then know. Lord Pilchard was still, to me, only "little Pilchy" of Holyshade, with as much pocket-money as I had; that is, with as good a supply of counters to play for amusement as was in my possession.

"It is horrid expensive?" I returned, with the most utter *insouciance.* "Is it? Ah! I haven't seen the bill."

Nor had Lord Pilchard.

I made a duty call on the Van Clyms, and saw my

uncle for a few minutes. The girls and my Aunt were out shopping.

"Kee, kee, kee!" Chuckled my worthy Uncle Van, jingling keys and small change in his pockets. "Your Aunt won't vizit at Langoran. Your couzans never go tere. Nor I. No, not to te countink-ouze in te city. Tat Cavanter he manishes everything now. Ton't like te looks of it. Zomething's wrong; kee, kee, kee!" And he shook his head, chuckled, snuffled, and laughed, as if he'd been describing a most humorous state of affairs.

"And Mrs. Cavander?" I asked.

"Ah!" replied Uncle Clym, drawing a long breath, and opening his eyes so wide that I really began to think he would never be able to shut them again; "ah! you 'ave not hert?" He meant "heard."

"No, uncle."

"Not from Erbert?"

"No."

"Ah!" he repeated, as if my answers had unsettled him in his former purpose of recounting to me some tragic history which would be better kept secret.

"What is it?" I asked.

"Vell," he replied, slowly, but always with something of a smile on his countenance, though speaking in the most serious tone, "I'll tell you. She vas left-at-ome too mosh, an' ven tey are left-a-tome too mosh, vat vill dey do to amuse temselves? I ton't blame her. She vent mat."

"Mad!" I exclaimed, startled by the suddenness of the intelligence.

"Tey *say* so," said Uncle Van. "It was necessary"— the "rr"s seemed to stick in his throat—"to put her under rrrestraint zumvere. She is gone."

"What! locked up?" I inquired energetically. In truth, I had only come across such things in romances, and could not realize them as fact so close to home.

"Yes. It is no bizniss of mine;" and here Uncle Van broke into a nervous laugh. "She is not my vife."

No, it was no business of his, or of anybody's, except Cavander's. The further conversation was interrupted by Mr. Pipkison, who looked in, having heard from a. friend that Uncle Clym had not been seen at Lloyds' that day. He wanted to know if Van was too indisposed to join the Baa-lambs' dinner next day.

"An old friend of yours was with us at our last gathering," said Pipkison to me. "Mr. Verney. He was in high feather. Someone with money has trusted him—a novelty in that line, I believe, and Mr. Verney is to have a theatre in town, and, on the first opportunity, is to produce a piece which a long time since has been written by his eldest daughter."

"I know it," I said; "at least I think I remember having heard it years ago. Mr. Verney has always had that piece coming out. I suppose his daughter will play in it."

"I don't imagine so; one may. But I gather from the old boy himself that his eldest daughter, the authoress, has made a splendid marriage—something millionairish, and baffling description. I think it's her husband who takes the theatre; that another is just going to be married, and a third—he's got three, hasn't he?—ah, I thought so; and a third has had an offer, and is going to quit the stage altogether."

"An offer!—marriage?" I asked.

I felt he must be speaking of Julie, and, though the last thing in my thoughts would have been to marry Julie, or anybody else at that time, yet I did not like the idea of her belonging to anybody else. Julie had always been to me, though separated by position, as a sister—a sister of my own age—a confidante. That strong feeling came back to me on that idiotic night at Vauxhall. Then immediately after that it had occurred to me that I was her lover. And then I had thought of Alice, who had been to me as an elder sister, and lately of Clara Wenslow, whom, but for this information of Pipkison's, I should, without further consideration, have gone to visit at the Lakes.

Pipkison replied to my question as to the nature of the offer, that he supposed it to mean marriage, but had not inquired.

My time was my own to do what I would with it. Where was Mr. Verney? Pipkison didn't know. He had left town and given up his lodgings.

I remember his having mentioned "Heaven's own air" at Liverpool, and called to mind the fact that Nurse Davis was living somewhere near them.

This was all in my way to the Lakes. My tour was to comprise the north generally, with Liverpool to begin with, or Clara Wenslow first at Windermere, and Liverpool to finish.

There never was such a haphazard time as this vacation. No sooner had I decided upon taking Liverpool last than little Lord Pilchard, to whom I confided my plans, said he knew of a yacht at Liverpool which could be hired, that Rowdie had promised to join him. Would I make a third?

Certainly. My only knowledge of yachting was connected with the Bobs; but it seemed to me to be a pleasant way of spending part of a vacation, and so I settled with Pilchard, and we named a date of meeting.

So I took the Lakes first, and met the Bifford Brothers on a walking tour, perpetually quarrelling as to their route, and as to which should carry the umbrella. We put up at the same hotel, and had some pleasant evenings.

As to discovering Miss Wenslow's house, which was the ostensible object of my visit, my real one being to amuse myself with novelties, that appeared to me to be a consummation devoutly to be wished for, but unattainable. Nobody knew it.

I have often noticed this in the country, that the nearer you get to the place of which you are in search, the less the resident peasantry can tell you about it.

The Biffords were walking on to Ullswater from Patterdale, and I determined to join them up to a certain point, when I would return.

This plan I carried out, but on coming back I managed to diverge from the path in order to take shelter from that not remarkably uncommon event in the Lake district, a storm; and fancying that I was making straight for Patterdale, I found, after an hour's walk, that I had completely missed the road.

I did not see a soul to speak to, no sheep even, which would have indicated a shepherd at some distance at all events, and not the slightest sign of a habitation of any description.

"Thank goodness," I thought, "I am in a valley:" for I had heard and read such mysterious stories of wanderers perishing in the hills, that I had come to look upon losing your way in the Lake district as something akin to the commencement of a German legend. I had followed the course of a small stream, and had now entered a thick plantation, which seemed to me unenclosed, and showed no marks of cultivation or preservation. I pushed on for some time, and at length, to my surprise, came out upon a wild and picturesque looking tarn, such as I had met with up in the hills.

I now discerned two figures, of a man and a woman seated in a boat, at the end of the tarn farthest from me. Towards them I made. In a few minutes I found myself in the presence of Clara and her grandfather, old Mr. Wenslow.

Mr. Wenslow was the limpest man I have ever met. He was feeble, to such an extent of feebleness, that it seemed as if he had never had the slightest, faintest shadow of a will of his own. He had a watery smile, and humid mild eyes; he was flabby about the gills, and flabby about the nose, which seemed to have been wrung till it was loose, or injured by too much blowing. In fact, it being pear-shaped, richly tinged, and full towards what ought to have been the point, I say that, without offence, this feature could be fairly described as a full-blown nose.

Clara was charmed, she said, to see me, and blushed—at least I think she blushed. If she did, she did not appear confused. Whereas, in the presence of old Wenslow, my courage seemed to have oozed out, and I felt as though I had been caught trespassing.

"Very glad to see you, sir," said the little flabby old

gentleman, landing, and holding out to me his flapping hand.

Fishing from a little boat on this tarn was Mr. Wenslow's favourite occupation, and so anyone from his appearance would have thought.

"Have you had good sport to-day, sir ?" said I.

"So, so," he replied, feebly; "there's not much sport here. I'm afraid you'll find it very dull."

He seemed to think I was going to live on the tarn, or in it.

Clara reminded him that they would be delighted to see me at dinner.

"Oh, yes," said the weak old man, smiling at the prospect of such an excitement; "we shall, indeed. Mrs. Wenslow will be delighted to see you at dinner. We've only ourselves, and I don't know how we shall amuse you. I'm afraid you will find it rather dull."

He repeated this hopelessly, with a despairing glance round the tarn, from which it almost appeared as though he was expecting from it some corroboration as to his statement about the dullness which was to be my portion.

"Dull ?" I returned, politely; "I am sure this is the last place to be dull in."

I meant it; not satirically, but as a truth at that moment, and as a compliment.

"You are right," he replied, shaking his nose (I knew that he shook his head, but one lost sight of the cause in the effect) sadly; "it *is* the last place to be dull in. I shall never be in another. No, no."

Here he fell into a sort of brown study, from which Clara aroused him by jogging his elbow.

"It's getting late, grandpapa," she said, "and mamma said you weren't on any account to stop out after there was any chance of damp."

"Ah, yes," he said, rousing himself. Then, once more extending his hand to me, "Welcome to Greygill Holm. If you are not a fisherman, I—I,"—he looked at the time for a suggestion, but finding that none came, he dropped my hand, and added, slowly, and almost despairingly, "I'm afraid you will find it very dull."

Clara seemed somewhat annoyed, I thought, at this exhibition of second childishness.

We had some little distance to walk before reaching the house, which was one of those quaint, sleepy old mansions seldom to be met with now-a-days in England, and bearing a strong family resemblance to those old châteaux of Normandy and Brittany. The house was not a large one, but it had a deliciously cool courtyard, where we found Mrs. Wenslow, Clara's mother (a widow lady), in a Bath-chair, drawn by a shy-looking, shock-headed boy, talking to her gardener.

Mrs. Wenslow was a sharp-eyed, fashionably and well-dressed elderly matron, with quick, brisk brown eyes, sharply-cut features, excellent teeth, which were generally very much *en évidence*, and thin lips; but her figure inclined becomingly towards *embonpoint*.

She was motherly in her style of reception, and removed all difficulties as to my dress—for I was in tourist's costume—with so ladylike and pleasant a bearing as at once put me at my ease. Her tendencies, she explained, were rheumatic, and this would account to me for her being wheeled about in a Bath-chair.

Their pony-chaise would take me back to Patterdale, and though they were unable to offer me a bed, owing to some friends being hourly expected, and their accommodation being limited, yet if I would only make their home mine while I remained, "we shall be," said Mrs. Wenslow, "only *too* delighted."

Grandpapa joined in this, but was still of opinion that I should find it very dull. This being his firm conviction, no one seemed to care to disagree with him about it.

Mother and daughter were remarkably attentive to the old man, and Clara seemed to me to be gifted with a most affectionate disposition.

Our conversation naturally turned upon the "Bobs."

Mrs. Wenslow upon this exclaimed, "Why, dear me, of course I forgot to mention it. We are expecting them. They promised to be here this morning, but I know how uncertain they are; and really, at this distance from a civilized town, it is impossible to count on anything like punctuality. But they have been so kind to Clara, that of course, when I heard they were likely to be in this neighbourhood, I could not think of their passing us without a visit."

" I've heard," said Clara, while we were discussing the Bobs, " that Mrs. Bob was, at one time of her life, a concert singer."

"My dear!" protested her mother, "you should be really more careful. Mrs. Burdon is most highly connected, and so is her husband. Let me see—his father was one of the Southdownshires; I forget whether she is their cousin, or nearer than that. I don't mean," she continued, turning to me, as though to set herself right with a member of the aristocracy on a certain point, when she had unwittingly fallen into a slight error, "I don't mean the Southdownshires of Cropland; that of course was the elder branch, with which the barony goes, though they *do* say, as *you* know well enough, of course, that the present Lord Woolcombe is *not* really a member of the family at all."

She raised her eyebrows, and nodded her head at me ominously thrice.

"Indeed!" I said, being of course much interested.

"Well, of course," she went on, with a little refreshing sniff, " it's nothing to me; I don't— " with a sharp laugh —" I don't belong to the aristocracy. But if I did, I *think* I should feel a little sore if I were the real heir, and saw another put into possession by present agreement of the family. For my part, I don't know how such things are done."

Nor did I. Nor did Clara. As for grandpapa, he followed the discourse at a distance; and only once, on the removal of the soup, he was heard to murmur, "I'm afraid you'll find it a little dull;" but on the appearance of the fish he cheered up again. When we had quite changed the subject—I cannot, though, veraciously say that the subject was ever quite changed, for, so long as Mrs. Wenslow led the conversation, it continued to be about lords and ladies, the crests of various noble families, their public and private scandals, their sayings and doings

—in fact, we only played variations on the original theme, which was the aristocracy; however, half-an-hour after we had dropped the Southdownshires, grandpapa broke in on a conversation about the Davie Toffies, of Toffshire, Wales, descended, as everyone knows, from that most famous Saxon Earl, Harold Hardbake; "the Hardbakes having gradually altered their spelling to Hardebayke, and married with the Harmond Rockworths, of Rock-craggie, Toothshire," explained Mrs. Wenslow. It was into this interesting conversation the old man broke, with— "I remember young Charles Chopp at the University. He was somehow connected with the Southdownshires;" and, having favoured us with this contribution, he subsided for another half-hour.

Whenever he thus joined in the conversation, we three looked straight at him, smiled, and then went on with our own subject again—that is, Mrs. Wenslow went on with *her* own subject again.

The Bobs sent a letter to say they could not stay, and, indeed, should only be able to take advantage of Mrs. Wenslow's kind invitation, *en passant*, as they were coming from the north, were going down to Morecambe Bay, and so to Liverpool, where their yacht was waiting to take them to the Isle of Man.

"They were at Liverpool some little time ago," observed Mrs. Wenslow.

"Yes," said Clara, in a tone which showed she was not best pleased with Mrs. Burdon's present proceedings, "they stopped some time there. They never asked me, and they don't ask me to accompany them now. Mrs. Bob's very fickle, I believe. I daresay she has picked up some one whom she likes better than me."

Here she shot a glance across at me, as who would say, "Do you think there *can* be any one to be liked better than yours truly, Clara Wenslow?"

For the moment I did not.

But oh! it was a dangerous place for a young couple to be left alone in, with a sharp general of a mother and a doddling old grandfather to act as sheep-dog, as a toothless, barkless, harmless guardian.

2 A

To stand by that old fountain in the courtyard was enough to suggest a proposal to the most bashful; for the basin being shallow, and of a peculiar curve, the drops trickled over regularly from above, and played little marriage-bell tunes on the water below.

The gold-fish eyed you suspiciously out of the corner of their eyes, as they halted meditatively in the sunlight for a second, then darted off at angles as if to fetch a friend, but only to reappear at the same point—all alone, as before—and repeat the evolution over and over again, as though it were some part of a game.

Then the fish, seeing a couple standing by the brink of their domain, would come up to the top, open their mouths, as if saying, "Oh, I didn't know you were there! I beg pardon! Oh!" going off again as quickly as might be consistent with good-breeding. There are certain creatures in whose presence love-making is easy. Fish belong to this class. Singing birds are a trifle too noisy, and the presence of a tame bullfinch, with two-thirds of a tune in its puffy little throat, is simply intolerable.

That fountain had much to answer for. But in the midst of this, a whirlwind came and carried me away. The whirlwind was a party consisting of the Bobs and my Uncle Herbert.

"Come with us for a cruise! that'll do you good," said hearty Mrs. Bob; and Uncle Herbert not only cautioned me against refusing, but insisted upon my accepting so hospitable an offer, as he pointed out I could not refuse without positive rudeness.

I was carried off; but those three weeks at the Lakes had been fraught with danger to my peace of mind for some time to come.

There was, I ascertained, a good reason for Mrs. Bob not having invited Clara Wenslow to join them; what it was, Uncle Herbert intimated, I should know later.

"Had she got another favourite?" I asked, being indignant on Clara's account.

"It's nothing to you if she has, Cecil," replied Uncle Herbert. "You can't do better than stick to Mrs. Bob, and listen to my advice, mind that."

I was not, however, destined for the cruise with them, for, as it suddenly occurred to me, I was bound to Lord Pilchard, who with Rowdie descended at the Turtle Hotel, Liverpool, two days after our arrival.

I had promised to keep up a correspondence with Clara, and I began well, that is all I can say.

I pass over the absurd yachting expedition of us three, who know nothing whatever about the matter; and after a month of it we returned to our starting point, Rowdie left us, and Lord Pilchard took me to his place near Shrewsbury. We had it all to ourselves, and idled our time away well into August, when his little lordship was off to Scotland; and I, left to my own resources, was only too glad to receive a letter from Austin, who was now at a small place called Clyn Strytton, North Wales, where he was staying with my old tutor, Mr. Blumstead, who had taken charge of this parish by way of a holiday employment for himself, and in order to enable its then clergyman—an old college friend—to get away for his vacation. Austin had arranged to spend a month at Clyn Strytton, for change and repose, and to see something of the work which a country curate with a scattered parish has to perform. When his friend wrote to Austin to say that he regretted being compelled to accept the only chance presented to him of a holiday, and mentioned Mr. Blumstead as his *locum tenens pro tem.*, Austin, associating my name with this latter, proposed to keep the engagement as it originally stood, and then wrote to me.

Clyn Strytton was almost out of the reach of English civilization. The people spoke only Welsh, and the church had for years been almost deserted, save by the minister and his family.

It was a quaint old place, the date of whose erection was lost in antiquity.

Mr. Blumstead seemed to suit it exactly. His congregation consisted of ourselves and two or three Welsh peasants, who might happen to be in the neighbourhood by accident and looked in out of curiosity. They had their meeting-house at some distance off, and their out-of-door preachments in their own native tongue.

It was a holiday for my old tutor, who amused himself in the mountains waking the echoes, as he used to wake us at Hillborough, with his cornet, and giving himself what my friend Rowdie called, when I subsequently described it to him, "a regular good blow-out on the heights."

Austin and myself had much to converse about, but alas! much on which to be silent.

His search had been fruitless. Nothing had been heard of or from Alice since Austin's last letter to me.

His mother, he said, was ill, but not at present so seriously as to suggest the probability of danger. He was, however, in daily expectation of a letter from his elder sister, Mrs. McCracken, with whom Mrs. Comberwood was staying.

His next duty was to write to his brother Dick in India, and the consequences of this he feared.

He had determined, at the end of the year, upon carrying out his plan of entering St. Bede's College. He prayed daily, he said, without affectation and in most perfect humility, for the safety of his sister, that she might be reclaimed, and that she might be led to him in her repentance, so that she should be repelled by no Pharisaical severity. "I do not speak," he said, "of the disgrace she has brought on our family, on our name. I esteem these as a matter of comparatively light importance. But, knowing how *she* will come to look back on all this, I dread her being driven to despair."

It was our amusement on a Saturday night to put the old church in order; and Mrs. Fowler, who had accompanied her brother-in-law, was glad to have something of the sort to do.

The ladies, in fact, were perpetually cleaning and brushing it up, as if a glossy appearance would induce the scattered flock to try the pasture provided for them by a maternal establishment, which they looked upon with about as much cordiality as I regarded my stepmother. This English Church was a strange mother forsooth, that could speak intelligibly neither to their hearts nor ears.

There was a worn-out old safe in a corner which belied

its name immediately we attempted the lock. Here we found some musty books and a register, carelessly kept, of years gone by.   Different hands were visible at various times, and we smiled at some of the odd names occurring here and there among the births, deaths, and marriages.

I was standing alone in the vestry lazily inspecting this book, when my own surname caught my eye.

There was no doubt of it, and the entry was that of a marriage; it was one of the few where the date and names were clear.

And the names that preceded the clergyman's signature (who wrote himself Daniel Gere) were—

John Colvin: Sarah Wingrove.

The remainder of the page had been torn across.

CHAPTER XXXV.

THESE names on the register. What was their history?
what there purport for me? Neither "John Colvin" nor
"Sarah Wingrove" were absolutely uncommon. But had
not the latter haunted my life? Had it ever been allowed
to drop out of my memory's grasp? Never, entirely.

I turned it over and over in my mind, and could make
nothing of it. I consulted Austin, and he would have
been for dismissing the subject as a matter of the merest
coincidence, but for my mentioning the story of Mr. Venn
at Old Carter's, and the death of the strange woman
whom I had seen with Venn and Cavander in Kensington
Gardens. I arrived at a determination.

"I will ask my father point blank," I said.

Austin shook his head over this proposition.

"Of what use," he inquired, "will such a course be to
you?"

I could not exactly say, but it struck me it would lead
to some catastrophe, which would include, at all events,
an explanation, whether satisfactory or unsatisfactory I
could not pretend to conjecture.

"No," returned Austin, "I do not think I would
mention it until you and your father should be once

more upon such terms of intimacy as would warrant an allusion to what may be either a painful incident in the family history—for it does not follow that the John here mentioned was your father—or an accidental concurrence of the names, which, as it happens, are of peculiar interest to yourself personally."

"I might tell Uncle Herbert," I suggested.

"You would be wrong to do so. Evidently, if it concerns your father at all, Sir John is the first person to be informed of your discovery, and that, not by a third person, even though he should be so near a relation as Mr. Herbert Pritchard, but by the discoverer himself."

"Then I must wait for an opportunity; for as long as my father is so guarded by my stepmother, and so entirely under the Cavander control as he now is, I shall have as much chance of seeing him alone, as anyone had of an interview with the Man in the Iron Mask."

This was the result of our consultation. I made a copy of the entry, and placed it in my diary. Gradually it ceased to trouble me, and by the time of my return to Cowbridge, I had well nigh forgotten its existence.

Had I acted upon the impulse of the moment, and gone at once to my father, register-entry in hand, I should have learnt what might, or might not have been its importance; but once having let myself stand to cool, I soon found plenty of other subjects of more immediate and special interest, whereon to expend my energy.

On the third day of term, Marmy Denne entered my room.

"Here's a go!" he exclaimed, throwing himself into an armchair, and looking as blank as the empty grate at which he was standing.

"What is it, Marmy?"

"Why, Thingammy—I mean Dr. Falkner's bolted."

"Bolted!" I exclaimed.

At this season of early youth, I could not imagine any one in real life "bolting." I knew something of bailiffs, and writs and warrants, in novels and plays, but of their existence, save as expedients for the use of romancists and dramatists, and therefore as creations of the brain, I could at that time form no idea. Such words as time, money, trouble, sorrow, had for me rather less meaning than the strange characters on the Assyrian stones.

"Bolted!" I repeated. "What on earth has he bolted for?"

"Debt; so they say here," answered Marmy. "I've been talking to old Sam Lincoln and his wife"—he alluded to the proprietors of a well-known confectioner's, the back room of whose shop was laid out like a small restaurant's, where those who either could not, or would not dine, or, at all events, had not dined, in Hall, were wont to take a simple well-cooked late dinner—"and they said he was a regular bad lot, and obliged to cut and run. He'd done all the tradesmen here, and in a heap of other places too, old Sam says."

"How does he know?"

"Lor!" replied Marmy, "he knows everything that goes on here."

Old Sam Lincoln was certainly a trustworthy authority.

"And," continued Marmy, "I met Jack Freshly"—he was my landlord, and as good a gossip as any in Cowbridge—"who told me that the police had been after him, and he wasn't away a minute too soon. I didn't quite make out whether it was police or bailiffs, but, anyhow, the Doctor bolted, and I rather think Master Jack has helped him to mizzle."

Marmy had a free-and-easy way with him, but was less slangy than Rowdie, who now came in with his usual big knobbly-stick, projecting out of his very short P-jacket. Why the Honourable Malcolm Rowdie adopted this costume it was impossible to say. His best reason was because he chose to do so, and having chosen, he was not going to alter his style for anybody. I rather fancy that, if Professor Manley (of the P.R.) had hinted that his patron's costume was not quite the thing, it might have had some effect upon Rowdie. However, we took him as he was, and for what he was; and those who really knew him, honestly liked him. He began with a laugh; he always began with a laugh, which, in writing, it is impossible to describe exactly; the nearest approach I can make to conveying any idea of the effect of this laugh is to say that, like an orator's cough, it was generally prefatial; and, like a semicolon, it hitched up the conversation, in such a manner that for some one else to have spoken, under the impression that Rowdie had finished, would have been resented by the latter as a rude interruption.

"Oho!" laughed Rowdie, "Here's a pretty blessed boil over!"

"You've heard?" asked Marmy.

"Rayther so!" answered Rowdie, who preferred any slang to the pronunciation and terms of ordinary respectable society. In fact he had become worse than ever.

"I know," continued Rowdie, "what you coves will say. You'll say that I got him into our lot, and that I forced the card on the club."

A sudden light broke upon me.

"Why," I exclaimed, "we have entrusted him with the club funds!"

"Of course," rejoined Rowdie; "we were such a clever lot o' fellows, we were. But it's my fault, and so pr'aps, if you'll just send out to the Committee to come to my rooms, I'll offer to pay the little lot, and put myself right that way."

"No, no," protested Marmy, "you shan't do that. I voted for him too."

So had I, as Rowdie's friend.

The Committee however did meet, and the result was to place the whole matter in a solicitor's hands.

This, I think, was my first introduction to anything resembling important business. We made "a whip round" for the sum required, and the funds of the club soon looked as fresh as ever.

The third week after this I received a note which had been lying at the post-office under cover of initials, with direction on the outer envelope to the effect that if the letter were not called for within five days, the Postmaster was to break the seal and deliver it to where the letter was addressed. This was evidently a plan to render the post-mark useless. It was from Mr. Venn, alias Dr. Falkner.

In it he owned his guilt, and pleaded his necessities. He begged me not to proceed to extremities, as he had a wife and family dependent upon him, of whom I had never till that moment heard, and I was inclined to think that they had been invented for the occasion.

He wrote further:—

"If you will deal with me mercifully in this matter, and God knows I have troubles enough to weigh me down (from which may you always be spared), I say, if you will deal mercifully, and get your friends, who have been such good friends to me that I curse the moment of fearful pressure when I yielded to this dire temptation—and get your friends to deal kindly with me also (for I do swear I will work my fingers to the bone in order to repay them what,—had I had but the courage to ask as a loan, they would have granted), I will *put you in possession of some information which will most certainly be of the greatest importance* to you hereafter, and a clue to the nature of which you will find in one conversation (if you can call it to mind) at Broad's, when we were both on our way to Cowbridge,—after your accident in the dogcart. Let me implore you to attend to this, and, believe me, I am not using vain words. I can be of the utmost use to you; and one day you will, if you refuse me this request, deeply regret not having acceded to it. It is in *your* power to help me; it is in your power, even by the advance of a small sum and getting your friends to consider these funds (which I had intended merely to use and return with interest; I assure you upon my oath, this is true) as a loan, to reinstate me in my position, or at least to start me in another, where I shall recommence practice and honestly pay my debts. A line addressed to John Hunter, 16, Rue des Carmes, Boulogne, will ultimately find me, but I cannot say how long it will be ere it arrives at its destination. I am in deep distress. But *the information that it is in my power to give you would make my liberty well worth your purchase-money.* It may so happen that circumstances *will prevent my ever returning to England;* if so, the secret will be safe with me, wherever I am, till you send to buy it. Let me know your decision, and believe me faithfully yours, V. Falkner."

This letter I showed only to Rowdie.

Rowdie was of opinion at once that it was "a dodge."

"The Doctor's a sly old fox," said Rowdie; "and all he wants is some more tin. He thinks you're a sort of soft-hearted cove, who'll be just before he's generous, with a lot of ready cash to spare, and nothing to do with it; and he imagines that you'll get the other fellows—he don't write to *me*, by the way," he suddenly interpolated, in a rather injured tone; then he went on—"He thinks you'll soft-sawder the others, that they'll say 'all serene,' and have the old boy back. But," said Rowdie, laying a finger significantly against his nose, "I would'nt have him back; no, siree, not on no account! though, at the same time, I wouldn't be hard on the poor beggar."

I was inclined to take this view of it myself.

Rowdie was right. Venn had appealed to my soft-heartedness, which was, at that time, another name for my green-hornedness. For, see, I had never detected any thorough hypocrite; I had never, to my knowledge, met with such a creature as a swindler; and my youthful profession of faith was, "All men are truthful."

The supposition that Venn should have a wife and family, whose existence he had not, for reasons of his own, mentioned to me, or to any of us, seemed, on second thought, not at all improbable; and the more consideration I bestowed upon Venn's letter, the more thoroughly convinced did I become of his honesty and virtue, which had bent, not broken, beneath some temporary pressure.

This theory of mine was, it is needless to say, laughed out of court; and the result was to leave matters *in statu quo,* that is, we, as a Committee of a Club, were to proceed against Dr. Falkner on the criminal charge. Rowdie explained the case fully to me, and advised me to give the Doctor, so to speak, law, in a sporting sense, by not furnishing the solicitor with the address I had in my possession.

"After all," said Rowdie, "it'll be enough if he doesn't come back here. That'll be a good punishment for him; for he won't live so well anywhere else; and as we should never get our tinnums back, what's the good of transporting the ruffian?"

"But what do you think of his offer of valuable information to me, eh?" I asked Rowdie when we were talking over the affair alone.

"Bosh!" returned Rowdie, laughing; "all bosh. You recollect the story of the Irishman going to the jeweller's, and asking what would be given for a lump of gold the size of an ostrich egg. The jeweller dined him, liquored him, and tried to get over him in every possible way. Pat ate the dinner (he hadn't had one for a long time), and made himself thoroughly at home until a late hour, when he was leaving without ever having said a word about the prize supposed to be in his possession.

"'What about the crock of gold as big as an ostrich egg?' inquired the jeweller, nervously.

"'The gold as big as an ostrich egg?' says Pat, who seemed to have forgotten about it. Then, as if suddenly remembering, he replied, 'Ah sure I was only axing wat would you be inclined to give for a lump of gold the size of an ostrich egg, *supposing I should be after finding such a thing.*' I fancy that's about the size of the Doctor's valuable information."

"Then, perhaps, I had better not answer the letter?" I asked, hesitatingly.

"Perhaps!" rejoined Rowdie, laughing at the utter absurdity of such an idea. "Of course not."

So the letter remained unanswered. Probably it went into the waste-paper basket, thence into the grate, and there was an end of it.

The remainder of My Time at Cowbridge, though far from uneventful, is of no importance to this record, except inasmuch as I gained no more experience of life than I had up to my entering at Tudor. My vacations I spent in visits, often to the Bobs, once to the Wenslows, when they had a house near London, and Clara Wenslow I frequently met at Mrs. Bob's.

My Uncle Herbert kept ward and watch over me, and was, while I was in his sight, ever on the alert to prevent me from plunging headlong into a deep matrimonial abyss. Still, for all this, and separated for a length of time together, I somehow felt myself gradually bound more and more towards Clara Wenslow.

We corresponded, clandestinely on my part, which was dishonest: openly on her part, which was perfectly fair: at least so it seemed to me.

Of Alice Comberwood no intelligence had been received by any of her family.

Dick learnt such news as there was to be learnt of her while he was in India, and having obtained leave of absence, himself attempted to discover her retreat.

His suspicions fell on one man, but he found himself utterly helpless in bringing the crime home to him. Had not Austin, had not I, had not the Clyms' suspicions all been directed towards one quarter? Towards whom? Towards a man who Mr. Comberwood professed to consider as one of his best friends, to whom he was bound in business, and who had already been the cause of such an increase to his wealth, by recommending judicious speculation, as had far exceeded the hitherto careful lawyer's old-fashioned notions.

True that Mrs. Comberwood regarded these dealings with anxiety; but in business her husband was out of her control, and, heart-broken by her child's desertion, she lacked all her former spirit and energy.

They were, neither of them, the same as of yore; their geniality had vanished; they were irritable, and shared their grief in separate burdens, which they bore apart, neither speaking to the other of the load, nor offering to lighten it. Mr. Comberwood was living for money, and showed no pleasure in anything else. Austin's object in life had no interest for his father. His mother was still affectionate with him, as was he with her, and through her he seemed to hope to touch his father's heart, which, strange to say, had been hardened by the same blow that had broken his mother's.

The home of the Comberwoods had ceased to exist.

Thus, though from totally different causes, Austin and myself were placed in a similar position.

. Sir Frederick was a careless man, and not a wise one. He shrank from making the scandal public property. He accepted his situation, saying that he had tried married life, and had no wish to return to it. He never spoke of his wife, and henceforth lived as a bachelor. In a short time his name was amongst the foremost at races, steeple-chases, where he rode himself, and at all meetings of a sporting character. Dick Comberwood called on Sir Frederick, and, from what Austin hinted, I gathered that the baronet had not come with flying colours out of *that* interview.

My visits at Langoran House were of the most formal character. When in London I stopped at Broad's and enjoyed myself. Rowdie and Marmy Denne were my constant companions, and serving as a link between their tastes, I was pulled first to this side, then to that, taken here, taken there, until I had seen as much of London life as would have sufficed for me for many a year to come. Rowdie was hand-and-glove with all the sporting-men, publicans, with little rat-killing dogs, retired prizefighters, prizefighters not retired, while Marmy's tastes lay in the direction of theatres and theatrical clubs. His name was "up," he informed me, with great delight, for the Roscius Club, "where you meet everybody, all the actors, artists, and literary men," and he had already managed, through myself, who had introduced him to Mr. Pipkison, to be elected an honorary member of the Baa Lambs. He was looking forward to quitting Cowbridge and residing in town, with the greatest possible anticipation of pleasure. On the several occasions of my dining at the Lambs' hospitable table Mr. Verney was absent. It was reported of him that he was engaged in beating up recruits in the provinces for his great Metropolitan undertaking. His eldest daughter had married "money," and Mr. Verney was to open a theatre on his own account, or rather with the account of his son-in-law, whose wife, playing under her maiden name, was to be the leading actress, the bright particular star of the new company.

Once, and once only, in my last long vacation, before my degree term, when I was passing a few weeks with the Bobs at Southsea (which, as a station, Mr. Bob preferred to "the Island"), I came across Mr. Verney and Julie. He had been recruiting, and Julie had been playing. To my surprise, Mr. Verney approached Mrs. Bob with his politest bow, taking off his hat with such a flourish, as, had there been a breeze, would have sent it into the sea.

Mrs. Bob had seen Julie at some provincial theatre, and had taken a great fancy to her.

I was delighted at hearing this; but Clara Wenslow was with us at the time of our meeting, and I had no opportunity of speaking alone with Julie.

This annoyed me considerably; and, somehow, from that moment I began to consider myself more firmly bound than ever to Clara (as I see by my diary), and at the same time to look upon the attachment which had sprung up between us, and which I felt was strong on her part, as an irksome tie. And whenever I named Clara, I thought of Julie.

"You're enjoying yourself here, Mr. Verney?" observed good-natured Mrs. Bob, who, I found, took great delight in drawing out her new acquaintance.

"My dear madam," replied Mr. Verney, turning so as to face the sea for his audience (we were on the promenade) and speaking more *at* Mrs. Bob on his right, than *to* her; "My dear madam, this is life; this is the pure air of heaven, and the revivification, the recuperation of the vital forces. The system," he continued, settling his hat slightly on one side with both hands, "requires it; and when Nature, who is of your own sex, madam, commands,—what remains for us poor mortals, being men, but to obey? 'When lovely women,' etc.," said Mr. Verney, stopping abruptly in his quotation, with a short laugh which showed either that he had forgotten the rest of it, or had suddenly become alive to its inapplicability to the present circumstances. However, he threw into his look just so much expression as would eke out the blank which he had made in his address, and before any of us could put in a word, he had waved his right hand as a sort of preliminary danger signal to give notice that his express train of thought was coming along the line, and all others must get out of the way for fear of accidents, and thus recommenced :—" Yes, my dear madam, I like Southsea, for a while: the air is bracing, the sky is open and clear; the offing is full of life with its ships, its yachts, and its steamers; on the greensward, a trifle too dusty, perhaps, and sunburnt—but you must be sunburnt by the sea-side—I say on the greensward from morning to night you can witness evolutions of troops to the beat of drum, and the sound of the stirring fife. Beauty is here more beautiful, being radiant with health; and to sit in the coffee-room of your hotel at breakfast, nice white table-cloth, a plateful of fresh-coloured prawns, a crisp French roll, a delicate pat of butter, and a homely pot of tea, with your morning's newspaper at your side, and a whiff of the briny stealing in through the open window, this appears to me to be the acme of earthly happiness, if not absolutely an anticipation of future bliss."

" You describe it feelingly," observed Mrs. Bob.

"Madam," returned Mr. Verney, "my heart expands like the petals of the tropical convolvulus (a beautiful flower, but little cultivated in this climate) beneath the rays of the morning sun. And, after breakfast, being here for a holiday, I stick my cigar in my larboard gill— you, as a yachtswoman, if I may so say, will appreciate the expression—and I walk out on to the pier, where the sea-gulls perch, one on each shoulder, like a pair of epaulettes, and some genuine old salt in charge of the guns, or the tackle, or employed as the man at the 'look-out,' spins yarns to me as long as my arm by the quarter-of-an-hour, in return for a timely pipeful of tobacco which causes me no loss, and renders him for ever grateful."

"You haven't yet finished your engagement here," said Mrs. Bob, addressing Julie."

" To-morrow is my last night," answered Julie,' in her quiet voice. "I have not forgotten your kind note,

Mrs. Burdon, and I think you gave me till to-morrow to answer it."

"Yes, or till you get to town, and can consult your father and mother together."

"My daughter *has* consulted me already," said Mr. Verney; "and it only remains to hear what Mrs. Verney has to say; because, my dear madam, though at first sight——"

"I don't think we'll discuss it now," interrupted Mrs. Burdon, somewhat hastily; "it will be time enough if I hear within the next two months. I suppose you are going up to London the day after to-morrow?"

"My poverty and not my will consents," said Mr. Verney. "I mean that the business which now engages my attention must be done by me personally on the spot, though indeed I grieve to leave this romantic and healthful situation, not to mention the most comfortable hotel, which I can recommend to any one in search of quiet home comforts, where I have a small room, cosy as carpet slippers, snug as the winter nest of a dormouse," here he pointed his description as though he were arranging a scene on his own stage, "with a practicable window, left, looking out on to the sea, fireplace for ventilation, right centre, and door in flat: I go out and come in as I like. In the morning I stroll into the town, visit the fruiterer's, buy my green fig, the juice of which (for you must carefully cast aside the skin and the small residuum of hard stalk) cools the system generally, while the ozoic properties of the atmosphere so brace up the larynx, that a strong-voiced man can reach E flat in alt, or whatever the high pitch may be, I forget now, with comparative ease and certainty, and without distressing his physique. I have no hesitation in saying that all things considered, a few days at such a sea-side resort as this, spent in the manner I have described, must represent the summum bonum—I may almost say the *summerum bonum*—of terrestrial felicity."

Mr Verney's speech ought to have been taken down in shorthand by an employé of the hotel he was patronizing: it would have served the proprietors admirably for an advertisement. Mr. Verney, it has since occurred to me, was himself quite an advertisement to them, and they certainly could have afforded (though I am not aware they adopted this plan) to let him stop there gratis. I believe had they done so they would have been the gainers by it to a considerable extent.

I record this occasion of our meeting, as it was not for some time afterwards that I had the opportunity of speaking with Julie.

"What was Mrs. Bob talking about to Mr. Verney?" I asked Uncle Herbert afterwards.

Uncle Herbert didn't know exactly.

"Doesn't Old Verney go out and get up private theatricals, and your little friend, his pretty daughter, Miss Julie, doesn't she go out, too, and act?" suggested Uncle Herbert in the form of a question.

"Ah, of course. I remember;" and the performances at Ringhurst Whiteboys flashed across me.

How I call to mind Alice entering the hall, and her look of contempt for the young professional, who had played a page in an opera. Alice would not then have thought her worthy to have assisted her in holding a garland of flowers for the decoration of Ringhurst chancel. And now—where was Alice, with all her religious training and her æstheticism? Alas! I knew not, nor did any one of those who loved her most, know more than this, that, by her own confession, she had fallen, fallen for ever from her high estate here—and for the rest it was a blank. But Julie, the little Miss Publican, scarce daring to raise her eyes to Heaven while my Lady Pharisee swept proudly by, how had *she* stood her trial—that trial which to my knowledge had come so early and with such strong inducement, such powerful temptation? Whence had she those principles which resisted the evil as soon as it was whispered in her ear, which made her strong not only to save herself, but to save her whom she loved so truly, her own sister? What education had she beyond the lowest Sunday and day school teaching, when from her earliest years she had been earning her own livelihood on the boards of the Theatre?

Our meeting had given birth to such thoughts as the above, which I have since found recorded in my diary. Sometimes I fancy that in my last vacation before my degree term at Cowbridge, this day when I met Julie at Southsea was the turning-point of my life. Henceforth I was to take a more serious view of my future career; but I could only come unto the light very, very, very gradually; and I was moving onwards, unconscious of my progress as is a ship of its own motion.

CHAPTER XXXVI.

DEGREE TIME—COACHING—THE GOAL AT LAST—THE FETTERED
BIRD—DIFFICULTIES—A NEW PAVEMENT—ADDITION—PRO-
FESSION—A CHANGE—NEW LIGHTS—A SUMMONS—AT HOME
—AN INTERVIEW—SENTENCE—CLOSED FOR EVER—HOME-
LESS—A FAINT—I ARRIVE AT MY OLD STARTING POINT.

THE time at length came when a Bachelor's degree was
to crown the tower of my academical career.

The "good old coaching days" were revived, and teams
of men who, till their last term, had scarcely (save for
their little-go) opened a book, were now harnessed, made
to step well together, rendered accustomed to the main
road, and were finally trotted through the examination
papers at an easy pace—arriving at their journey's end
without exhibiting the slightest signs of distress. We, of
this set, proposed to go in for a pass; honours were out
of the question, and a pass we most of us obtained. The
moment of reading out the list in the Senate House was
an anxious one for many, and the successful undergraduate did not often stop to hear any other name after
he was certain of his own being on the list.

The coaches, too, were nervous, and, outside the Senate
House, awaited the return of their men. Congratulations
were flying about in all directions, and the plucked ones
were trying to dissimulate their chagrin as best they
could. Some of the latter at once sought their coaches,
and pointed out to them the exact spot on the papers

where they knew they had come to grief. A few protested their inability to understand why they had failed, and some energetic spirits called on the examiners individually in order to ascertain in what subject they had fallen short of the minimum.

Here two or three men were to be seen old in intellectual feebleness, who had been plucked for the fourth time and were contented with the result, looking forward to the time when their degree would have, by University law, to be conferred upon them, gratis, as qualified "ten-year men."

This ordeal over, nothing now remains for me but to go through the solemn ceremony of receiving my degree at the hands of the Vice-Chancellor, before whom the undergraduate kneels, and places his hands, clasped in an attitude of prayer, between the palms of the Vice-Chancellor, who whispers in his ear something in Latin, and gives him his blessing—*in nomine Patris et Filii et Spiritûs Sancti. Amen.* Then the newly-created Bachelor rises, proudly, as though he had been knighted on the field of battle, with the insignia of his degree over his shoulders, a white tie about his neck, and the strings of his baccalaureate gown fluttering in the draughts of the Senate House.

How the blushing youth is welcomed by his father, who, from the crowd around, grasps him by the hand; by his mother, who well-nigh sheds tears of joy over the first distinction won by her gallant son, whom she then and there considers as far greater than anyone else in the University, the Vice-Chancellor himself not excepted. Then, the fond sisters, who will cling to his arms all day, and never be tired of being lionized. Ah! happy hours! happy men! wistfully eyed by me, who indeed took my degree, though not at the appointed time, but later on, quietly, and without any excitement; only to retire afterwards to my rooms, throw my new robes on one chair, seat myself in another, and wonder if that day there was any one much more unhappy than myself.

At this point my life of carelessness, of unconscious prodigality was to end, for once and for ever.

I had lived, never wisely, always too well.

Tradesmen had trusted me, that is, they had fastened a line round my leg which they had from time to time lengthened out so that I could hop about in apparent freedom, forgetful of the tie that bound me to them. They never would let me pay them. My father's city reputation had, doubtless, suggested this line of conduct to them; and perhaps the decline of that reputation, or some vague rumours from Cornhill, had decided them to come upon me suddenly, and press for a settlement, when it was impossible to refuse without sacrificing my degree.

There was nothing for it but to collect all my bills and present them at home. I shall never forget the feeling of utter hopeless dismay that came over me on arriving at the sum total.

In for a penny in for a pound; and it now occurred to me to send for Broad's bill for the last three years.

In fact I collected them round, with all the straightforward determination of setting my house in order, or, rather, of having it set in order for me; and further, I resolved to sacrifice two-thirds of my allowance for the next any number of years in order to make up for my past folly.

I began laying down a splendid pavement of good intentions, and wrote a penitential letter to my father announcing my plan for the future if he would only free me in the present.

To this I received an answer from Mr. Cavander, to the effect that my father was very unwell, and unable to attend to business matters, but that my affairs should be at once placed under consideration.

I should have mentioned before this that Lady Colvin had been blessed with a second child within two years of the appearance of her firstborn. This had as before furnished me with an additional reason for not visiting Langoran House, where I found myself quite *de trop.*

In a state of great suspense I remained at college, having nothing to do except to commence the practice of economy. Other men of my own standing were studying for their "Voluntary Examination" for the Church, and attending the lectures of some Theological Professor.

It suddenly occurred to me that my choice must now be made of a definite line in life.

My intimate college friends had gone down, and the few whom I knew remaining "up" were engaged as I have said above.

Those belonging to the former category had already been keeping their terms at one of the Inns of Court, and were commencing legal studies, or had set themselves to whatever serious occupation might be required of them as scions of old county families, or as successors to their father's business.

It seemed to me at this time that I was isolated; left, as it were, high and dry, by the tide of pleasure receding on all sides.

The last day of a happy, pleasant University career is the end of the first volume of life. The merry company breaks up and departs this way and that, some never to meet again this side the grave. New faces appear, new customs and manners come into vogue which the solitary man left behind by his companions pretends to despise because he is unable to associate himself with them. University life is of so short a duration, that Time marches at the double, and in a few weeks a new generation has arisen, not one that "does not know Joseph," but that does know him, and considers him a fogey.

For lack of ought better to do, and because my thoughts seemed, as I have already indicated, to have taken a more serious turn, I considered that my time could not be better employed than in attending the Divinity lectures. Certainly they dealt with a subject which had not often attracted my attention, and on which I had seldom heard any one speak except Austin, and with him Alice in the old Ringhurst days.

I was really a sort of prisoner for debt at the University, and for the first time I began to awake to the fact that money was an object, and that, except a small sum of which I was at present possessed, I had not, unless my father were well disposed towards me—and this I could not expect—much of a prospect for some time to come. I had no reason to suppose that all would not end as well as it had begun; but my father's continued silence was ominous.

So about this time I took to attending these Divinity lectures, and by way of parallel reading, I commenced studying Paley's Evidences, which I had only crammed up for little-go years before, and the History of the Reformation.

This new course of reading so highly delighted me, and I put myself at it with so much zest and vigour, that had I only been brought up to turning my Colvin impulsiveness in the direction of classics and mathematics, I would have engaged to have been well placed in the Tripos, or high up among the Wranglers.

English literature, from the time when Austin had started me with Scott's novels, had always possessed the greatest, indeed the only, charm for me at once as a study, and as a recreation. Holyshade training had introduced Homer to me as a wandering old heathen who had written hundreds and hundreds of lines which we boys had to try and learn by heart, or to write out as pœnas. Who, thus taught, could love Homer? There have been brilliant exceptions; but I am speaking of the rule. And in proof, what is the cry now-a-days? Why, that Greek is of no use, save to divines, and that modern education should be only utilitarian. An examination question of the future may be, " Who was Homer? " and the answer will probably be rendered, " Sir, he was an author who wrote in a language called Greek, which is now happily and deservedly obsolete."

At length came a summons from my father. He wished to see me. I was to come up to town immediately—there was nothing more.

It was a dull, leaden morning in March when I presented myself at Langoran House.

Our old servant, Plemdale, opened the door respectfully, but sadly, and ushered me into the dining-room. He was as unlike himself as possible.

I stood there, and gazed around. I knew it all so well, yet I was a stranger, or, at best, an unwelcome guest in my own home.

I wondered what my father would say; how he would receive me: if I should, at least, see him alone—this was my great desire—and be able to say more for myself to prove that my own affection for him had never diminished, but had rather been increased and strengthened by our separation, which had dated from the night I had sat next my Aunt Clym, at that table, in that very dining-room, where I was now standing, and learnt from her the secret which he had feared to tell me.

I was ready to own myself a prodigal, but I also fully expected him to perform his part of the prodigal's father. I had erred in ignorance, and, though I did not intend to utter one word of reproach, which would have been unbefitting our relative positions and the occasion, yet I vaguely expected him to own that he himself had not been entirely free from blame.

Finally my bent was turned towards the Church, and this, too, it seemed to me, would show my inclination for reform. I would tell him how I had begun to study, and how seriously I was meditating on the choice of a profession. I would tell him how I was now awaking to responsibility; and then it suddenly occurred to me, would it not be a favourable opportunity to consult him about Clara Wenslow, and to ask him what step I ought to take in the matter? In short, he should be at once and immediately my confidant, should be to me the father I had always pictured to myself—my best guide, my best friend, my constant companion—and for his sake I would accommodate myself to the circumstances of his family life, and remain at peace with my step-mother. Such was the ideal I was drawing for myself of the lamb reclining by the side of the lioness, when Plemdale opened the door, and requested me to follow him into the study.

This room I have mentioned before, small and gloomy. The day was dark, the blinds were drawn, and shaded candles partially illumined the apartment. There was a small fire in the grate; on the table were two ledgerlike-looking books, and a collection of my letters, which I at once recognized. My father was in an easy-chair placed between the fireplace and the table.

As I entered, Mr. Cavander was leaning with his elbow on the mantelpiece and his cheek on his hand, evidently in deep thought, while the rustle of a dress on the stairs behind me caused me to turn, and I became aware of Lady Colvin having only that instant quitted the study.

I was glad of this. But her brother was there, and all my old antagonistic feeling, intensified by recent events, rose up against him, and from that minute I thought less of conciliating my father than of ousting *him* from his usurped position.

I was advancing to shake my father's hand, when Cavander at once stopped me.

"We will not," he said harshly, "put you on false ground at the outset. Your father, who is too ill and weak to speak much to you himself, has deputed me to deliver his decision in this painful matter."

I looked towards my father, who merely inclined his head towards the fireplace. He seemed weak and feeble, and his hair was fast becoming grey.

Unprepared for such a scene as this, I hesitated. Then I spoke, anticipating Mr. Cavander.

"I have come, by my father's wish, to see him, and him alone."

Mr. Cavander nodded to my father, as much as to imply, "There! I told you so! I thought he'd begin in this way! Just his obstinacy."

I continued.

"I have come to own myself very sorry for my expenses, for my extravagance. I assure you," I said, addressing my father, "I had not the smallest idea of their extent. I feel that I have wasted my time, but I have already begun to try and repair the past, and for the future——"

"The future will speak for itself, as the past does now," said Cavander, interrupting me, and facing round so as to fix me with his eyes.

I confronted him fearlessly.

"Had you shown yourself," he went on, "a credit to your name—had you even proved yourself anxious to be a companion to your father, a dutiful son, one to whom he could entrust his business when he had earned his repose—then what I have to say now would have been left unsaid. There was an old agreement between Sir John and myself on this matter, an agreement by which, in justice to others, neither your father nor myself can any longer be bound. Had your conduct been all that could have been desired, our task would have been rendered more painful and more difficult; but your own acts of extravagance, your own course of life which you have chosen for yourself, and which have separated you so entirely from all family ties, have given us an opportunity of which, as I have just said, in mere justice to others, your father feels bound to avail himself. I believe I have not said one word too much?" he added, addressing Sir John, who had been nervously interlacing his fingers, and looking at the fire.

"No, no, not a word," my father replied, with more decision of manner than I had expected from him. It occurred to me afterwards that he had been given his rôle, and had played it out from previous instruction. "He has been very ungrateful for all I've done for him. Most ungrateful."

"I have not been ungrateful," I returned, scarcely knowing how to defend myself against so general a charge, " unless extravagance, which I own, and am sorry for——"

But Cavander cut me short.

"Your extravagance is only part and parcel of the return you've made for all Sir John's kindness. When have you ever done anything to please him ? When have you ever put yourself out of the way to do what he has wished ? How have you spent your time up till now ? And might not every penny expended upon your education have been just as well thrown into the gutter? You profess to be sorry now : it is time you were. You will be put to the proof. Up to this time you have been most generously dealt with by an indulgent father, and have been treated as though you had claims upon him which it will now be my duty to tell you you have never possessed."

"A son has some claim on his father, at all events up to a certain age," I said, earnestly wishing to make them understand how eager I was for an opportunity of retrieving the past.

"A legitimate son," answered Mr. Cavander slowly, and emphasizing every word, "has a legitimate claim. An illegitimate son has but a natural claim."

"I do not understand?"

"I think you do," returned Cavander, calmly, "for you have been to Clyn Strytton, and have seen the register in the church."

My breath came with difficulty, and my throat was suddenly dry and parched. My father's face was averted from me, as he leant back in his chair.

"You saw the date," Mr. Cavander went on.

He need not have said one word more. I knew it all now.

"Under the impression that Sarah Wingrove, Mrs. Colvin, during the lifetime of your grandfather, had died in Australia, Sir John married into the Pritchard family. You were, fortunately, present at the death of this very Sarah Wingrove, the real Lady Colvin, at St. Winifrid's Hospital. Your father has been legally married only twice, once to Sarah Wingrove, and to my sister. You can now understand the precise nature of your claim on Sir John."

I was stupified. I had no answer. I was dazed. I could make no appeal.

"I had kept this as a family secret with which from the first I had been intrusted, till, in justice to others, to the children of the present Lady Colvin, your father considered that you should no longer be kept in ignorance of your real position. You know what that position is now. Apart from what it is by the illegitimacy of your birth, you would have, had you indeed been Sir John's heir, estranged yourself from him by your heartless and ungrateful conduct. Sir John wishes me to inform you that your debts will be discharged, that he will make you a certain small allowance which will enable you to start in the world, where it is to be hoped your education will prove of some service to you; and when you shall have made a name for yourself—for remember you do not bear that of Colvin now save by your father's permission—then you may return to this house, but—*not till then !*"

I stood silent. Should I leave the room, and the house at once ? Should I appeal to my father ? What should I do ?

Strange as it may seem to the reader of this, who would have expected a " scene," I, for my part, never felt less inclined to make one than at this moment.

A knock-down blow stuns for the time, and the victim cannot do much when prostrate and senseless. Such a blow had I received; and I could neither do anything nor say one word. I *had* seen the register; how Mr. Cavander had learnt the fact I did not care to inquire. I had been present at Sarah Wingrove's death. To announce my illegitimacy now, after so many years of silence, appeared to me to be cruel, yet I could not but admit his plea of justice to the others, and I had already testified against myself by owning my sorrow for my past, and my honest determination for good in the future.

I was no hand at duplicity; I was incapable of suspecting a plot. I could not imagine that my father would have allowed Mr. Cavander to speak for him, and to warn me from the door, had he not believed himself and his adviser actuated by only the strictest sense of the requirements of truth and justice.

Presently, however, my father broke the silence—

" I must think of others now ; I have thought too much of you, without any return. You have always been disobedient and ungrateful."

Again I had nothing to say. I could not ask for special instances of my disobedience and ingratitude. All I could find to say, and that, with the greatest difficulty, was—

" I have never intended to be either disobedient or ungrateful."

" Never intended," repeated my father irritably; " but you *have* been. It isn't what you intended : it's what you've done."

He had been primed up to this point; he had learnt his lesson; and anything I could have said would, I saw, have been useless.

The enemy was in the possession of the capital; nothing was left for me but flight.

" You need not stay any longer. One of our clerks will settle these bills at Cowbridge, and you will receive a hundred pounds a year in quarterly payments. You can go."

At that instant the name of Alice Comberwood flashed across me. An uncontrollable impulse forced from me the question—

" Mr. Cavander, where is Alice Comberwood ? "

For one second the shot staggered him. I saw and noticed it. But, ere I had time to take advantage of the effect I had produced, he had perfectly recovered his composure, and replied,

" Do you mean Lady Frederick Sladen ? You will find Sir Frederick's address in the Court Guide."

So saying, he rang the bell, as an intimation that the interview was at an end.

My father's face was turned away from me, as I said, huskily, and tremblingly,

"Good-bye."

I heard him reply, shortly—

" Good-bye."

Then I passed out into the hall, closing the study door. What it had cost my father to dismiss me thus, I could imagine. Thank Heaven, I entertained no angry feeling against him, either at that moment, or at any other time since. I pitied him more than I pitied myself; I forgave him as I could not forgive myself, for I began to magnify my carelessness and selfishness into unexampled crimes.

I should have fairly broken down, so miserable was I, had not my pride come to the rescue, on seeing Plemdale, who, waiting at the hall door, eyed me curiously.

It was, perhaps, could I have seen myself in a glass, but a lame attempt at carrying it off, jauntily, with a smile, but I managed its counterfeit to the best of my ability.

" My father does not seem well," I said, to Plemdale, as

though my visit had been one of the most ordinary duty.

"No, Mr. Cecil," replied Plemdale, "Sir John is far from well. And he hardly moves out at all now, sir."

The thought that occurred to me then was, does Plemdale know all about it, and if so, what does he think of *me?* And, strange to say, it seemed more important to me at that moment to have Plemdale's good opinion than anything else in the world. I can understand the impulse which causes the prisoner to take the gaoler, or the police-man who captures him, into his confidence, and I can realize his anxiety to secure at least one person who will listen to his own explanation of what appears to others his inexcusable crime.

On the other hand, I wished to ignore Plemdale alto-gether. True, he was an old servant; but what had he to do with my affairs.

Thus, at the door we both hesitated; he, as though expecting me to speak, and I as uncertain whether to speak or not.

The hesitation passed, and, turning on my heel, I said—

"Good-bye, Plemdale."

"Good-bye, sir," he returned.

Then the door was closed against me for ever.

It had begun to drizzle as I walked along, trying to fix myself to some immediate and definite line of action.

The familiar streets, the well-known thoroughfares, seemed now all different. It appeared as though I were seeing them in some contradictory dream, where I both recognized and was unable to recognize objects at one and the same time.

The names over the shops struck me, especially one "Dumper" over a baker's, and I had a sort of vague idea that now or never the man Dumper was the man to help me. But I gave up Dumper, and wandered on in a state of indecision, until I had left Dumper's a long way behind. Then I was attracted by a name which seemed to have got itself out of the alphabet in a regular tangle of letters; it was "Migligen." Migligen was a dealer in old china and second-hand umbrellas, and at Migligen's private door, on the knocker, was a large card, stating that the

upper part of Migligen's was to be let out in apartments
to single gentlemen.

This caused me to halt, and to remind myself that after
that term, when my lodgings at Cowbridge would have
to be given up, I should be houseless and homeless.

Besides, except to pack up and remove my movables, I
had no object in returning to the University.

There were no friends there of whom I could make
confidants. So I hurried on, debating within myself on
my next step. And, in another second, I had decided on
seeking Austin Comberwood, wherever he might be.

I could talk it all over with him before seeing Uncle
Herbert. Yes, this is what I would do, and at once—at
once.

This active decision seemed to startle me as much as
my bringing my stick sharply down on the pavement
startled a small child, who had just crossed the road with
a small can of milk.

All of a sudden I began to shiver, then the next
moment to be flushed with a heat which left me colder
than before. In five minutes I felt very ill, and all I
could think of at the moment was, that to see Austin
then and there was an absolute necessity.

I felt faint, and lifted my hat to cool my forehead.
Then there arose in my ears a sound like the rushing of
water, and I became unconscious.

    *   *   *   *   *

That the world is but a small place after all has been
remarked before now, but never was there occasion for
me to be so strongly impressed by the fact as when on
awaking I found myself in a small but most comfortable
room : a kettle singing on the hob, medicines on a table
near the bed, a stout elderly matron dozing in an arm-
chair, while, bending over some work, was Julie.

My exclamation of surprise aroused them both. The
other was nurse Davis.

CHAPTER XXXVII.

AND where was I?

" Why, my dear," said Nurse Davis, " you've come back
to the point where you first began life.   This is my apartment over Gander's dairy, where you were born. Polly
Gander's married, and the name's Verney, for Polly Gander married Charles Edmund, who's quite a gentleman
now, and doing very well indeed, being head something
at the railway ; and so as I took always a great fancy to
this place, they made a home of it for me when I come to
town, to stay and see the gaieties of London."

And so here I was, beginning life again, and from the
same starting-point.

Charles Edmund, a tall handsome young man, with
very little of the awkward lad about him now, had
worked hard and had been steadily promoted. He was,
for his station in life, already more than comfortably off,
and buxom Polly Gander, who was exactly his own age,
had come in for something at her mother's decease.

Charles Edmund was now occupied with some mechanical invention which, adapted to railway requirements, would, Nurse Davis told me, make his fortune, and perhaps do more than that.

"Why," said Nurse Davis, "he may have a title afore he dies. Who knows? More unlikely things than that have happened before now."

This set me a-thinking. Should I confide in them or not. Should I tell them how it had come about, that it was far more probable that Charles Edmund should win a new title, than that I should gain, what, till now, I had been brought up to look upon as my right.

Nurse Davis had sent to Langoran House, intimating that I was ill, and giving the address. But no answer had been received.

Julie was the tenderest of nurses, and when they would allow me to talk, I gradually fell into confidences.

On the fourth morning of my being there, Julie told me that Mrs. Burdon begged to be remembered to me, and this puzzled me. Then Julie said that that very morning she had heard from Mrs. Burdon, but that as I had my secrets from her (Julie), she would have her's from me.

And so it oozed out, and I told them all.

Then Nurse Davis said, quietly, but firmly:—

"That Cavander's a liar, and, please God I live, I'll prove him one. But, name or no name, legitimate or not legitimate, you're the son of your dear mother, whom I loved as though she'd been my own daughter, and you as my child too, left to my care by her; and whatever you are, or may be, you'll never want for a home, as long as I've one to offer you."

"Thanks, dear nurse. And Julie?" I said, turning to her.

She put her hand in mine.

"We were brought up together, and in spite of our different positions I have always thought of you as a brother. Besides," she added, cheerfully, "*now* your friends are mine. For I've retired from the stage, and am a lady at large."

" What do you mean ?"

" Why," she answered merrily, " I'm a sort of adopted child. Would you have any objection to my being the daughter of Mrs. Burdon?"

It appeared that Mrs. Bob had taken a great fancy to Little Julie, and, tired of a change of faces in her young lady companions, who had all turned out more or less flirty or flighty, Mrs. Bob, after carefully studying Julie's character during a two-month's stay (when Julie had conceived a strong attachment for her), had made Julie such an offer, that even her own family would not stand in the way of her accepting it, and Julie, whose physique was unequal to the exigencies of the stage as a profession, willingly consented to Mrs. Burdon's proposition.

She was now "on leave," and permitted to remain with her aunt during the early portion of my convalescence.

As to my own affairs, it was arranged that for a time nothing should be done or said until I had consulted my friend Austin, from whom I had lately received a letter addressed to me at Cowbridge, and brought thence to Gander's by Charles Edmund, who had kindly undertaken the removal of my goods and chattels, and the disposition of such furniture as would bring in a trifle, and for which I had, of course, no present use.

There was, too, something in my mind, at this very unsettled time, about being a clergyman. This came out of the quasi-serious turn I had taken during my last term, and the line of study I had resorted to after my degree. Austin's example (he was at St. Bede's Theological College, near Bulford) had some weight with me; and there was still one remaining difficulty which I dared not mention to any one except to Austin; this was how I stood with regard to Clara Wenslow.

In fact, this last consideration was perhaps of all others what troubled me most. I felt myself bound to tell *her* the truth; and then supposing she said, " What matters a name; pursue your profession," at the Church or Bar, " and I will marry you "—for it had reached this climax in my own imagination—what was I to do ?

Uncle Herbert had warned me against this entanglement, but entangled I was, and indeed, in the very batch of letters which contained the one already mentioned from Austin, was one from Clara, pressing me to tell my family of our attachment, as she had already informed her mother and grandfather, and that they said it ought not any longer to be concealed from Sir John.

Here it was evident I could not take either Nurse Davis, or Julie, into my confidence. Thus it came about that I ultimately carried out my first intention of consulting Austin.

"Dear Cecil," he wrote in reply to me, "your letter shows me you are in great trouble. Come to me. I have obtained leave from the Principal here to receive you as my guest at the College, and a spare room is at your service. It is a very quiet studious life, suiting me exactly, and if, as you hint, you too are thinking of what is, wrongly, called 'going into the Church,' then you could not do better than take advantage of a course of study at St. Bede's. But in whatever way I can be of use to you, you have only to name it, and I put myself at your disposition to the best of my power. But first come up here, and tell me your trouble. Expecting to see you within the next two days, I am, your always devoted friend, AUSTIN COMBERWOOD."

This determined my movements.

Julie returned to Mrs. Burdon, and Nurse Davis remained in town, both under promise of secrecy as to my affairs, until I should give them permission to speak.

Nurse Davis hinted, more than once, that she was sure she could be of use in this matter, or, if not, that her brother-in-law could, though she wouldn't have him brought into it, till he was absolutely wanted. At present, unfortunately, my faithful old nurse was only a witness to the death of Sarah Wingrove in the hospital, and she had, she said, reason to remember a name like that long before, "though," she added mysteriously, but disappointingly, "that wouldn't prove much, not even if it was the same."

As she was not inclined to explain this oracular utterance, I contented myself with agreeing with her, that when we *did* take steps, they should be decisive ones. Then I set off for St. Bede's Theological College, near Bulford.

So from Gander's Dairy I sallied forth with a firm determination to fight my own way onwards in the world. And, as I journeyed down to Bulford, I looked back upon my time, considering what I had done with it up till then, and resolved that henceforth, come what might, nameless or with a name, wronged or righted, I would use my best endeavours to make up for the time lost in the days of my ignorance.

I now debated with myself as to the propriety of travelling first, or second, class. I considered the difference of price, and went second.

I think this was the first occasion of my practising economy.

Henceforth, farewell to Broad's, and to all my old expensive habits. Whether Cavander's story was true or not—and, in spite of Nurse Davis's mysterious hint, its truth was forced upon me by my father's sanction—I, pecuniarily, should be in no better position. I thanked Heaven for my health and for the true friends I possessed; and at the end of my journey Austin was on the platform, ready to grasp me warmly by the hand.

We deferred our confidential talk till the evening, when we should be alone in the room; and so, neither of his sorrows, nor of mine, did we say one word, as we drove along towards St. Bede's.

He described the College and its object to me. It was founded by the Bishop of Bulford, for the benefit of those who, not having been at a university, wished for a thorough theological training before ordination; and also for those who, having taken their degree, required something more satisfactory than the University Divinity lectures, as the preparation for a life so different from what they had hitherto led.

"This place," said Austin, "makes, you see, a break between the university life of an undergraduate, and the profession of the ministry of the Church. For myself, I don't understand how a man, ordinarily speaking, who has been either merely enjoying himself at the University, or reading only classics, or mathematics, is qualified to pass at once into the Diaconate, and then into the Priesthood of the Church."

I noticed his use of the word Priest. Except in the few Divinity lectures I had attended, I had never heard this term applied to the clergy of the English Church. I had always thought (but I admit my ignorance of such matters then) that Priest meant a Catholic Priest.

My ideas were to be considerably enlarged on all theological subjects during my brief stay at St. Bede's.

A Gothic college, with its grounds and chapel, far away from the gentle hum of even the neighbouring University-town of Bulford, was the very picture of an ecclesiastical seminary, and the place, above all others, to which one in need of rest and quiet meditation would wish to retire. The building seemed to repose in a sort of monastic atmosphere. It only wanted antiquity to perfect its charms, for, despite its close imitation of the architectural style of the old Catholic days, St. Bede's was but a modern invention of the last quarter of a century, I mean at the time I first knew it.

It was erected to show of what the English Church was capable, when her teaching, in all its fulness, could be thoroughly and boldy proclaimed. The object of its energetic founder was to prove to hesitating Churchmen, that it was not Rome alone that had a system of training her clergy. Moreover, it was intended to exhibit within the collegiate walls a ritual which, though, distinctly Anglican, should be as impressive, solemn, and as attractive to certain minds, as that of the Church of Rome. It was furthermore intended to declare, in the teaching and practice of St. Bede's, that it was not the Roman Church only that held the full sacramental doctrine, but that the English branch of the Catholic Church possessed all this, and more, wherever it could bear fruit uninjured by the presence of sectarian plants. The atmosphere of Bulford was supposed to be peculiarly congenial to her healthy existence.

This theory had attracted the thoughtful Austin, who, with a natural bias towards the ministry, had determined not to enter it blindfolded, but, at any sacrifice, to follow the truth, wherever its light should lead him.

As far as my own affairs were concerned, Austin's advice was, that the best thing I could do would be to draw out the case on paper, and place it in the hands of a solicitor.

"Why not your father?" I suggested.

To this he replied, after some hesitation, that there were objections to such a course. However, on this we would decide in a few days; but the first thing I was bound to do was to write to Miss Wenslow and her mother, stating plainly and fully my altered prospects, and releasing her from any engagement she might suppose herself to have contracted in my regard.

As no answer to this was likely to arrive for at least three or four days, if not more, on account of her frequent change of residence, I was at liberty to enjoy my time of convalescence at the College, and, if I liked, to fall in with its style of living, and its course of studies.

"I must introduce you to our Principal," said Austin, "as a matter of courtesy."

Dr. Poddeley lived with his wife and family, in a house standing in St. Bede's grounds, but apart from the College.

We found him in his study. He was a short, round, bald-headed man, in an archdeacon's dress, looking as though he only wanted one touch more to make him into a bishop.

He rose politely on our being announced, and received us most cordially.

He had not, I found out from our conversation, always been a clergyman, but had commenced life as a doctor, and had tried his fortune in youth in the Colonies.

"However,"—said Dr. Poddeley, smiling and stretching himself before his fire—"the Colonies did not agree with me, and it being a case of 'Physician, heal thyself,' I was forced to return to England. Like our friend here," alluding to Austin, "I felt a powerful *attrait* towards the Church, and took a similar course to that which he is now pursuing. No man should undertake such a step without a due sense of his responsibility."

Here the Principal yawned, and a nurse entering to make some inquiry respecting one of the children, we rose to depart.

CHAPTER XXXVIII.

THERE are breathing points in the journey through life, when we can consider and reconsider.

Thus at St. Bede's I halted to take counsel with myself and with my best friend, Austin Comberwood.

After carefully penning a letter to Clara Wenslow, wherein it was difficult not to express the secret wish (which I had not even dared reveal to Austin), that she should reject me, and leave me free, my final decision was to do nothing hastily, to obey no first impulse until I had well weighed and deliberated upon the consequences, to disengage my thoughts as far as possible from my immediate difficulties, and occupy my time with profitable study.

A new world could not have presented more novelty to me than did the life at St. Bede's Theological College.

My bent had been latterly in the direction of the Church, and Austin's example seemed to me a beacon light in my unsettled state.

"I am puzzled here," said Austin, speaking in frank confidence to me. "I own I am puzzled. Yet what perplexes *me* seems to others to be as clear as daylight. I must believe everything, or nothing. I am speaking for myself alone, and I am forced to do so, for I find that I am alone in my opinion. The other men here seem to belong already to the High Church party, either as a matter of æstheticism, or as the more gentlemanly side, or as coming of Tory families, or as being proud of enlisting under the banner of such as Andrewes, Laud, Ken, Bull, Sherlock, Wilson, the Non-Jurors, and, finally, John Henry Newman."

It was almost all new to me. I was contented to listen. So apt a disciple could pick up, from such a master, more in one evening's discourse, than ordinary students could learn from a dry and learned lecturer in a course of six weeks.

Besides, though comparatively ignorant of such matters, I seemed, to my astonishment, to grasp his meaning intuitively, to master at once the first principles, and, in some instances, to jump boldly from premiss to the conclusion, which he indeed foresaw, but whereat he refused to arrive, except by logical sequence.

"There are," he said, "some shallow pates here who are dazzled by great names, and overwhelmed by their auctoritas—I mean, by the weight of character of a single leader."

He conversed with me as though I were his equal, as though he remembered only our room at Old Carter's, and his hundred and one nights of Sir Walter Scott.

"I am dissatisfied with what are called the Anglo-Catholic school of Divines, or rather they satisfy me as far as they go; but, like Paley's evidences for Christianity itself, they do not go far enough. They are fettered, as partisans of a system, in which the accident of birth has placed them. One and all are constantly shaping their theories to fit these facts. You have seen, in these few days, enough of our Principal to know that he is simply a comfortable Church of England clergyman, of what is called 'high,' but not extreme opinions, and he has been placed here by the Bishop——"

"The Bishop of Bulford ?" I asked.

"By the Bishop of Bulford," he went on, "who, knowing exactly how to trim his ship, has placed worthy Dr. Poddeley at the head of affairs here, to act as something more than a counterweight to our Vice-Principal, for whom the Bishop shows a marked regard, and of whom he is rather afraid. It was better to place such a man as Mr. Glyde, our Vice-Principal, in a responsible post, with plenty of congenial occupation, and the prospect of certain preferment, than to allow him to nurse his doubts, and feed his disaffection in the solitude of some country parsonage. In such a position Mr. Glyde would be a disciple, *here* he is a teacher; and no one knows better than the Bishop that the leader of a school of thought is the last person to be converted."

"Converted?"

"Yes; I use it in a general sense. Privates may desert to the enemy, and their defection is a matter of small importance; but with the Colonel it is another matter—you may be sure *he* would rather die than yield; and, putting the question of heroism entirely aside, were a captain of a vessel asked whether he would not prefer going down, with his sinking ship, to being saved with a remnant, he would undoubtedly choose certain death, rather than risk the barest chance of dishonour."

"Do you mean, then, that most leaders of thought are dishonest?"

Austin sighed.

"I am afraid," he said, "that, at all events, they are in great danger of becoming mere special pleaders. They seem to me to lose their sense of, if one may so call it, fair-play, and if they deceive others, it is only the consequence of their having first of all deceived themselves. To *myself*, I am conscious of an honest purpose, at least so it appears to *me*, and as yet I have no ground for supposing I am mistaken; on the contrary, as I have no theory to support, and am very far from being a Master in Israel, I only profess myself a disciple, an inquirer after Truth in Religion, and only so far a sceptic, that I will deliver over my intellect captive to no *man*, to no teacher who is unable to convince my reason of the existence of a supernatural claim to my obedience."

This remark struck me forcibly at the time, for I was ready to follow Austin as my guide.

"But, my dear Austin," I said, "a person uninstructed in such matters—in any matter, in fact—and as far as religious opinion is concerned, I may fairly instance myself and my own bringing up—must he not learn from a teacher ?"

"True. A child is under instruction, and grows up with the bias, specially in religion, of his education. But there comes a time when he is bound to use his own reason, and in such matters he must act for himself, for he is *in foro conscientiæ*, and is responsible to no human being. I cannot understand sectarianism in Christianity, in the face of such a dictum as 'Call no *man* your master.' What do all these terms Irvingite, Puseyite, Wesleyan, and so forth, mean, if not that those who choose so to style themselves have called that man their master, whose opinions they profess, and on whose authority they rely ?"

"And Protestant and Papist ?" I suggested.

"No; Protestant is the generic term under which come the hundred specific variations. It merely signifies the existence of a multitude of sects whose only common bond is a protestation against Popery. A Papist signifies a follower of the Pope, it is true; but the Pope, as I apprehend their theory, has no followers in the same sense that Wesley, or Irving, or Pusey has. The Pope's private opinion is entitled to just so much weight on a theological point as the *obiter dicta* of a Lord Chancellor on a point of law. When the Pope does speak, officially, his utterances are not his, but are taken to be the Divine explanation of some particular portion of a Divinely-given revelation. Granting the Catholic premiss, the system is perfectly logical, the reasoning consistent throughout. For Protestantism, as a whole, it is Hamlet without Hamlet. It is not a system in any way. Its basis is the assertion of the right of Free Inquiry; and though it asserts such a right, it not only does not impose it on individuals as a duty, but even persecutes those who make full and free use of their liberty This is a matter for every man's conscience. I find myself placed as a member of the English Church, an institution which the majority agree in calling decidedly Protestant, while a small minority among its members call it Catholic, or rather Anglo-Catholic. Now, before I take office in such a community, it seems to me necessary to inquire what it really is. The school calling itself Anglo-Catholic—of whose views our Vice-Principal is an exponent—seems to me to have something to say for itself well worthy the attention of an inquirer. It claims for the English Church an authority equal to that which the Roman Church claims for itself. Of course it cannot pretend to more than Rome. All I am concerned to ascertain now is, can it substantiate these claims? if not, then I must look elsewhere for that Divine authority which alone can compel my allegiance. Should I fail to find it, should I be forced to the conclusion that no revelation has ever been given to man, and that on this side of the grave the soul's ignorance is its happiness, and the greatest scepticism its highest form of worshipping the Unknown Creator, then so, honestly, will I be prepared to live out my time here, doing my share of the world's work, whatever it may be."

Here Austin paused. Then, folding his hands, he walked slowly along the gravel path in front of the College, his head bent down, his eyes on the ground, absorbed in thought.

At this instant the Vice-Principal, Mr. D'Oyley Glyde, came from the College door towards us. Sallow complexioned, his black hair cropped short, and closely shaven face, in his long cassock, and white band round his throat, in imitation of—what I subsequently ascertained to be— a Roman collar, Mr. D'Oyley Glyde was, to my mind, at that time, the very picture of a wily Italian priest.

I could understand his being, should the opportunity arise, accused of Popish plots, mentioned with suspicion as being a Romanist in disguise, a Jesuit in the English Church, and as being the object of any other absurd charge brought by the extreme party of one school against the extreme party of another co-existing under the same liberal establishment.

The Vice-Principal struck me as a man who was hold-

ing himself in, who was constantly struggling to achieve
a victory, to restrain a hasty temper, and to repress giving expression to an almost overpowering sense of the
ludicrous.   This gave him an air of artificiality which at
once inspired me with distrust.

His bright sparkling eyes were the lamps to his words.

By their light those who cared might read his meaning.
He liked Austin because Austin thoroughly appreciated
him ; but at the same time he must have envied his pupil
that entire liberty which he himself was gradually giving
up.   He admired Dr. Trimmer, Bishop of Bulford, but
deplored the necessity of the times which forced Dr.
Trimmer to blow hot and cold as occasion required;
though Mr. Glyde consoled himself that even in these
tactics "the dear Bishop" (as the Vice-Principal invariably called him) was eminently apostolic, for was he not
perpetually being, or trying to be, "all things to all
men ?"

"The dear Bishop," said Mr. Glyde to us, his eyes
showing us, in spite of himself, exactly what he thought
of his idolised prelate, "is coming here to-morrow.   He
will preach in the parish church.   After the sermon there
will be a celebration."

I had only lately learnt the meaning of this term.   At
Cowbridge we were aware of their being certain Communion Sundays in the year, but we none of us knew
much about it.   Tudor College Chapel had only been a
school for irreverence and negligence.   I well remember
that one part of the Chapel nearest the Communion rails
was known as "Iniquity Corner."   I had also known
young men, devoutly inclined, who, having been present
at one Communion Service in the College Chapel, had
shrunk with horror from ever attending another during
their term of residence.   Till now the clergyman to
whose duty this portion of the service had fallen I had
always heard spoken of as the one "who read the Communion Service."   At St. Bede's I found he was called
"the celebrant."

One of the students, a delicate-looking young man,
came up to Mr. Glyde.

"You want to speak to me?" asked the Vice-Principal, smiling encouragingly.

The student, whose name was Vincent, and who had been my senior by some years at Tudor College, replied "Yes, Vice-Principal."

"Well," said Mr. Glyde, softly, with his head inclined on one side, and intensifying his usually insinuating smile; "what is the difficulty?"

"This is the difficulty," answered Vincent, who was evidently much troubled: "the Bishop has said that none of us are to stay in church unless we communicate. Now, what with the confirmation and the sermon and the full choral service, the celebration won't be till past one. I don't think I can fast till then; and if I go to early communion, at seven, in our chapel, I shall have to walk out when the Bishop celebrates at one o'clock, and I can't do this. I've been talking it over with several of the others, and we all agree that to leave the church at that moment, would be entirely contrary to our principles; while to break our fast, before communicating, would be against the practice of the Primitive Church."

The Vice-Principal's smile had gradually disappeared, and his eyes sought the ground for a few seconds; then resuming his habitually caressing manner, he placed his left hand affectionately on Vincent's shoulder, and eyed him, inquiringly, while replying to the question implied in his statement.

"My dear Vincent, you come to me to ask me for advice. What shall you do? Well, I own it is a painful case. Our dear Bishop is peculiar on some points, and I regret his decision in this instance; a decision, however, to which we, who are immediately under his authority, must bow. The ordinance of fasting before communicating is, probably, of apostolic origin, but, like all other matters of mere discipline, it admits of modification, and, within certain limits, of relaxation."

"Then to break one's fast is permissible in order to avoid so great a scandal as the fact of so many students going out of church, at such a time, would be in the eyes of all the people?"

The Vice-Principal smiled and patted Vincent on the shoulder.

"Quite so," answered Mr. Glyde, "quite so. You can be present at the Principal's celebration in chapel in the morning, and can defer communicating till after matins."

"What will *you* do, Vice-Principal?" asked Vincent, boldly coming to the point.

Austin was carefully watching Mr. Glyde's countenance.

"For myself," replied the Vice, in his softest and sweetest manner, "I shall merely take a cup of tea, and a small piece of bread. Nothing more."

"Then one *may* do that?" asked Vincent, evidently somewhat astonished.

"Oh surely, surely," responded Mr. Glyde, smiling. "In doctrine, we must be firm and stedfast; in matters, which are purely of discipline, we are not bound by a hard and-fast line."

"But," observed Austin, quietly, "where discipline is a logical and necessary consequence of a fundamental doctrine, surely relaxation is in the highest degree dangerous to the doctrine itself."

"Quite so, quite so," replied Mr. Glyde, his manner becoming more and more insinuating; "but I have already qualified the relaxation by putting it 'within certain limits.' In this special instance we are bound by our obedience to the Bishop's wish, and by our charity for our weaker brethren."

Austin slightly shrugged his shoulders, a movement which I saw did not escape Mr. Glyde's observation, though he addressed himself, markedly, to Vincent, who gradually became reassured by the Vice-Principal's tone of conviction.

"You recollect those cases, my dear Vincent," Mr. Glyde went on, "in the Primitive Church, to which I alluded in our last Greek Testament Lecture, when, during a severe persecution, the communicants, of both sexes, were allowed to take away the consecrated bread to their houses, so that, though unable to unite in the assembling of themselves together, they might not be deprived of their spiritual food. These were very important exceptions to the general rule, and only permitted under the unprecedented pressure."

"Then," remarked Austin, "these people communicated in one kind only, and, therefore, according to the Church of England, their communion would have been such a mutilation of a sacrament as she charges the Church of Rome with. And a mutilation of a sacrament is a sacrilege. Therefore, these holy martyrs and confessors, suffering for their religion, were, according to Anglican teaching, as I understand it, guilty of sacrilegious communion."

"My dear Comberwood, may I ask where the Church has spoken, as you say she has, on this grave matter?"

Vincent took upon himself to reply.

"I have something of the sort down in my notes of the Principal's Article Lecture yesterday."

Mr. Glyde sighed, and smiled.

"You must have misapprehended the Principal's meaning. It is true that in the heat of argument some of our older controversialists have brought the charge of mutilation against our erring sister, founded upon a misconception of the Catholic doctrine in its entirety; but this line has been given up by moderns, who are also inclined to take a more just and a wider view of the sense of the Thirtieth Article than has been hitherto adopted. When the Church, in that Article, uses the word 'ought,' it is, evidently, a very different thing from the positive *command* which would have been forced upon us by the use of the imperative '*must.*' By the way, my dear Vincent, you were asking me the other morning what the Roman theologian Perrone said on the question of Anglican ' orders.' If you will come into my study I will show you his own words. He appeared to be in favour of their validity."

So saying, the Vice-Principal took Vincent's arm, and walked him into the college.

"Now," said Austin, " you will notice the result of this. Vincent will return flattered by the Vice-Principal's interest in him personally, and full of the statement that Perrone, the great Roman theologian, is entirely in favour

2 D

of the validity of Anglican orders. His assertion will
not lose by repetition, he will innoculate his inquiring
friends with the same motion, and, if unchecked by some
counter-statement, coming from at least equal authority,
he will gradually come to believe that Anglicans have all
that a Divine system can possibly possess, and are only
separated from the other parts of the same whole by
ministerial differences of opinion."

"And the authority they have gone to consult?"

"Perrone, an excellent one, true, but the note to which
the Vice-Principal alludes will not bear the gloss the
latter puts on it. Vincent will glance at it hastily, will
accept Mr. Glyde's reading of it, will feel himself highly
complimented in being considered at all by so eminent a
scholar as our Vice-Principal, and, by thus unconsciously
shifting his responsibility, he will have taken one step
more towards making himself a mere theological partisan,
instead of an honest inquirer after truth."

"But you do not think that Mr. Glyde is purposely
deceiving or misleading Vincent?"

"No, I do not think he is. But he is trying different
remedies on different minds. What will not suffice to
convince Mr. Glyde himself may satisfy the doubts, and
remove the difficulties, not only of Vincent, but of many
others. This will re-act on Mr. Glyde himself, until he
will, so to speak, arrive at believing in himself on the testimony of others. He is weakest when defending his
own position, and strongest when attacking anti-chris-
tian philosophy, or professed infidelity. But, as it seems
to me at present, for members of the English Church
scarcely three hundred years old, to style themselves
'Catholics,' in order to identify themselves with the
members of the ancient Roman Church, is as though
some modern cockney Smith or Brown, lately titled on
account of his money, were to claim blood-relationship
with the Howards."

Such conversation as this occupied us during our walks,
for we had tacitly decided upon not referring to my immediate difficulties until I should receive a reply to my
letter.

After a week the expected answer arrived. It was from Mrs. Wenslow.

She refused to allow Clara to write herself; she upbraided me for trifling with her daughter's affections, and, with scant courtesy, wished it to be clearly understood that any engagement I might have looked upon as existing between her daughter and myself was now at an end. She had made inquiries, she candidly added, which entirely corroborated my own statement, and had received additional information, not at all favourable to my moral character. Her informant had, clearly, been Mr. Cavander himself.

Clara Wenslow *did* write, but it was only to reiterate her mother's sentiments, and to weep for herself, "as a blighted flower struck by the withering blast."

Here ended the Clara Wenslow chapter, and thereupon I was sincerely congratulated by Austin Comberwood. Uncle Herbert had not been far wrong in his estimate of this young lady's character, and I do not wonder at thorough Mrs. Burdon having given her up.

"Now that that obstacle is out of the road," said Austin, "your next best step will be to put the whole matter into the hands of a good solicitor. He will employ means to discover where the fraud is, if any exists, and of this, taking into consideration Mr. Cavander's long reticence, and the circumstances under which he at length breaks silence, there can scarcely be a doubt, and thus you will be able not only to right your own position, but you will release your father from a burden of which, you may depend upon it, he would most gladly be rid. I will write to a friend in town, and inquire, without stating names, who would be the best man to employ in such a case."

Austin at once wrote to his friend, and we were to receive his answer the following night.

There was a late post which arrived at about eight o'clock, and, while we were walking up and down discussing probabilities, Dr. Poddeley, happening to pass us on his way towards his residence, courteously invited us both within.

We could not refuse, and were soon seated in Dr. Poddeley's drawing-room, drinking tea poured out by Mrs. Poddeley.

The conversation, as a matter of course, began with the weather, and questions concerning the children's health, and so forth; then Mrs. Poddeley, who had lately been fitting up a magnificent medicine chest, under the professional assistance of her husband—once Doctor of Medicine, now Doctor of Divinity—discoursed learnedly on the complaints of the villagers, and extolled the office of the English parson's wife, whose duty, she observed, was to know something of doctoring.

"But, Mrs. Poddeley," said Austin, "it is not every lady who has the good fortune to have the advantage of such excellent instruction."

"I had a natural taste for it, I think; I fancy I was always fond of medicines," said Mrs. Poddeley.

"Not of taking them, my dear," observed Dr. Poddeley, adding, with a ponderous sort of playfulness, "unless you took them to other people."

And so we fell to talking about doctoring generally, and his experience in particular, and why he gave it up, and as to where and when he practised.

"I took it into my head," said Dr. Poddeley, making two acute angles of his elbows on the arm-chair by bringing his hands together, in a sort of prayerful attitude, on a level with his chin, while he slowly moved his right leg crossed easily over his left knee, and looked occasionally towards us, but mostly towards the fire; "I took it into my head, in commencing professional life, to try Australia. Everyone told me I should make my fortune there, or rather, that there was some chance of doing so *there* and none whatever *here.* I went, and tried. *Veni, vidi,* but I can't add *vici.* On the contrary. Melbourne itself was then only a rising place—a city of the future; and while the city would be growing the Doctor would be starving. I wasn't the only one doomed to disappointment; however, it was not to be my vocation in life, and I am grateful for the use which so much knowledge of life as I was then able to pick up has been to me."

"It is a rare thing for the same man to be at once physician of souls and bodies," remarked Austin.

"Now-a-days it is so; but formerly monasteries were excellent dispensaries, and Brother So-and-so was chemist, druggist, herbalist, and doctor. The Jesuits, too, at a later date, were proficients in the healing art, and their missioners were in many instances bound to make themselves acquainted with the science of medicine. We have the 'Jesuits' bark' handed down to us now. Many a time," continued Dr. Poddeley, reflectively, "would the combination of the two offices have been singularly serviceable to me. I remember—indeed I shall never forget it—being called to the bedside of a dying woman, connected, as I understood, with a company of strolling players, who had come out for the same reasons that had induced most of us to leave England. The poor woman was sensible, but powerless to express her meaning by words or signs. She had lived, I could see, a careless, dissipated life, and at the supreme moment it was the clergyman who was wanted more than the physician. She lay dying in the house of her married sister, who, with her husband, was away from home at the time. Only two of her theatrical companions were with her—a good, sensible young woman who nursed her tenderly, and a pompous person, whose distraction, under any other circumstances, would have been really most diverting. He it was who had fetched me, and on my arrival I administered restoratives, and despatched him for a clergyman. I whispered to the poor woman, now rapidly sinking, such consolatory words as I could think of; a light of sudden intelligence beamed in her eyes, and she stretched her hands with unexpected energy towards the door. It opened, and our messenger had returned with a Catholic priest. He was a foreigner. I shall never forget that moment. By instinct I yielded my place to him, and as he knelt by her pillow he placed in her hands a small crucifix which he gently moved towards her lips. Then, being unable to speak English, he said, clearly and distinctly, the '*Confiteor*' of the Romish Church, which the poor woman evidently recognized as familiar to her, and, we could tell

by her eyes, that she followed it sentence by sentence.
Then the priest pronounced the absolution in Latin, and
as for the last time she bowed her head as if doing grateful homage to the well-known words, a calm, contented
smile lighted up her pallid face, and, as the priest made
the sign of the cross over her the stertorous breathing
was suddenly checked, and with a long-drawn sigh of
weariness of the world, she passed away to her eternal
rest. Then we knelt and prayed. The sudden slamming
of the door caused us all to raise our heads, and to our
astonishment—and for a second, to my horror—there,
dressed in tawdry finery, stood before us the living image
of the dead woman."

"Who was it?" we asked.

"Her twin sister, so like in face to the one lying dead
before us, that at first we could scarcely credit the evidence
of our senses. The awful lesson of that evening was lost
on that unhappy woman, who, however, had been, I was
informed, more sinned against than sinning. Her husband
had married her for such money as she had possessed, and
had recently deserted her."

"Did you ever see her again?" I asked.

"Once only, on registering the death. The priest, too,
had left; indeed, his presence there at all was almost
miraculous, as he was a French missioner who was sailing
for England the very next morning. The dead woman
had been but a lax Catholic, I was given to understand
by her theatrical friends, and in fact had not practised
her religion for years. The following week I myself
quitted Melbourne, but I date from that evening the first,
as it were, setting of my resolution to forsake the calling
of a physician for that of a clergyman."

There was a pause of a minute or so, and then Austin
broke the silence.

"I almost wonder, Dr. Poddeley, that your experience
on that evening did not lead you towards becoming a
Catholic priest."

"It did at first," replied Dr. Poddeley, with a satisfied
air, "as I confess I was so taken with the idea of the
system which rendered a French priest to be useful to

the poor wretched, dying Englishwoman, without understanding the language. But that system, fascinating as it is, will not, you will find out when you have studied it as I have, bear investigation. The Church of England has a great future before her, not for this country alone, but for the world at large."

"Then, these actors, her friends, knew she was a Catholic?" I asked.

"Yes, as I have said, they had some vague ideas on the subject, and Verney——"

"Verney!" I exclaimed.

"Yes, that was his name; he thought the clergyman of one creed just as good as another in such an emergency, and was not aware until afterwards what a real service he had rendered the unhappy woman."

What Nurse Davis had hinted at now impelled me to the next question. Could it be possible that I was indeed on the very track of which I was in search?

"Can you, Dr. Poddeley," I asked, trembling with excitement, "remember the other names?"

"Aye, well enough; the woman who died was Sarah Wingrove, her sister's name was Susan, but at this moment I cannot exactly recall the married name of the latter."

I started from my chair so energetically that Mrs Poddeley screamed.

"You may thank Heaven for this," said Austin; "it comes most opportunely."

Then he told my story to Dr. Poddeley, who forthwith begged me to make what use I chose of the information.

CHAPTER XXXIX.

PROGRESS—LAST OF ST. BEDE'S—THE DEAR BISHOP—SKETCH—
FAREWELL—MY OWN BUSINESS—INTERVIEW WITH SOLICITOR
—HOPEFUL—FRIENDS OLD AND NEW—MR. VERNEY AGAIN—
MY AUNT SUSAN—HELP—A PROFESSION—WORK AT LAST—A
CITY PANIC—COLVIN AND CAVANDER—FAILURE—FLIGHT—
SIR JOHN'S LAST ILLNESS.

AUSTIN soon put my affairs in train. One Saturday
afternoon he placed in my hands the name and address
of a certain solicitor's firm, in whose peculiar province
lay the work necessary for forwarding such a case as
mine. To Ladbrook, Lewson, and Son, therefore, I at
once wrote, making an appointment for the following
Monday.

One day more remained to me at St. Bede's, which,
indeed, I was loth to quit. Still, if there were one lesson
more than another which I had been taught by the
recent shock, it was that of shaking off sloth, and rousing
myself to fight for my own existence in the struggle
of life.

Fortunately the weapons were to hand. I had a
doughty squire in Austin, and, in Julie, a fair lady to
bestow the wreath; but the squire does not fight the
knight's battle, nor do the brave who "deserve" the
fair invariably win her. The prize is to the victor.

Therefore, much as I would have liked to have stayed
within the precincts of St. Bede's, to have continued
theological studies, to have argued and reasoned with

Austin on his doubts and difficulties, and, above all, to have gathered from the religious instruction given in the College such a realization of existence as would set before me the highest motives even in the most ordinary occupations of duty, I was unable to do so now. Yet I had seen enough to know that the teaching at St. Bede's was tainted throughout with partisanship. This was a necessity of its position as a theological seminary for men of certain opinions in the Church of England—men who were by birth and education Protestant, but, by taste, Catholic.

·Fettered by the Articles, whose sense he would explain away until they were reduced to nonsense; fettered by his collegiate superior's caution and timidity; fettered by his "dear Bishop's" want of boldness and candour; fettered by his own disinclination to break with his party, his College, or his Bishop—the Vice-Principal, Mr. Glyde, must have had a trying time at St. Bede's.

The "dear Bishop," Dr. Trimmer, was an optimist. He acted and spoke as though he considered himself the best man for the place, and doubtless looked upon his appointment as, so to speak, a triumph in the dispensations of Providence, in regard to the Church of England. His Lordship occasionally regretted his being insular, and not œcumenical. He would have liked to have shaken hands all round the Christian world, without yielding a point in his own belief or practice to Pope, Emperor, or President of a Conference. But, on the other hand, he would have had them acknowledge him the Right Rev. Thomas Trimmer, D.D., to be a real and true Bishop, as real and as true as the Pope himself, about the validity of whose orders it would be manifestly suicidal to entertain a doubt.

The Bishop had a full-flavoured story for wavering young men as to how he (the Bishop) had been recognised in his episcopal capacity by an eminent Prelate of the Gallican Church; but the story, being subsequently tested, only showed that the latter eminent Prelate having made the acquaintance of Dr. Trimmer, and finding him called Bishop and "my Lord," had naturally,

and courteously, so styled him, but without having in
any way expressed his opinion as to the reality of his
existence as a veritable Bishop of the Catholic Church,
on which matter it may be supposed the French Bishop
was charitably and politely silent.　But the superficial
story was good enough for Dr. Trimmer's purpose and
such weak-minded candidates for orders as were contented to take him at his own valuation.

The Bishop was an "all-round" man, physically and
morally.　Anglicanism was associated in his ideas with
angularity, and he wished the sharp points to be worn
down by intercourse with outsiders.

He was, according to his scriptural authority for so
being, "constant in season and out of season."　I do not
know how *he* read this text in *all* its bearings, but
his Lordship on a cob was certainly an institution in
Rotten Row for the two most fashionable months in
the London year; and his nag's hoofs splashed up more
mud, or threw up more dust, than that of any rider,
clerical or lay, in that assembly.　Of course it was
necessary he should be in town, for his seat on horseback
by way of exercise was only a corollary of his seat in
the Upper House.

The "dear Bishop" visited St. Bede's on the last
Sunday of my stay.　Dr. Trimmer looked the after-
dinner Bishop to the life.　His sermons were admirable,
but his speeches on festive occasions were better.　He
invariably "improved the occasion," and never forgot
the Bishop, while playing the charming guest.　He set
young men at their ease immediately with a cordial
shake of the hand.

It could not have been more cordial had his Lordship
known the person for many years.　As a matter of
fact, an old friend, perhaps, would have received the
same sort of shake from his Lordship.　It was his way
of greeting: it was a hearty way: it was a taking way,
specially with young men, when the grasp of affection
was given by a Bishop.　And by such a Bishop too!

The Right Reverend Dr. Trimmer scandalised some
of the more fervent spirits at St. Bede's by his method

of performing the Communion Service. He would stand
in the old-fashioned Protestant way at the north side
of the table, with the Principal of St. Bede's at the south.

The exact position of "the celebrant" was a little
uncertain at St. Bede's. The Vice-Principal, in the
College chapel, would stand with his back to the small
congregation of students, and would contrive to make
the service resemble as much as possible what I have
since ascertained to be a "Low Mass." The Principal,
who, for the sake of his influential subordinate, did
not like to adhere too closely to the old, and on his
own account did not care about yielding in all points
to the new style, adopted a half-and-half fashion, which
was neither one thing nor the other, but a shuffling
via media. He stood at the corner of the table, so
that he presented his back to a part of the congregation
on his left, and his profile to the other part on his right.
Had it been possible for the three—Bishop, Principal,
and Vice—to have officiated at the same time, in the
same capacity, there would have been room enough for
the trio, arranged thus, each according to his views.
The Bishop at the north end, sideways to the congregation, as of old. The Principal with the corner of the
table fitting into his lowest waistcoat button, representing
in himself the translational state; and the Vice-Principal
in front with his back to the congregation. The last
would have said the service *sotto voce*, the second in
a moderate tone, and the first would have given it out *ore
rotundo*, with immense unction, with a special enjoyment
of the commandments and the offertory sentences.

It seemed as if a new proverb had been invented
specially for St. Bede's, founded, in sound at all events,
upon the old one which declares "possession" to be
"nine points of the law;" here the pupils were to read
it thus—"position is nine points of the Gospel."

St. Bedesmen, with no ideas of their own, must have
quitted the College with very confused notions on most
subjects in which they had come there to be specially
instructed. A want of certainty was felt throughout the
place. Little could be taught with authority. One

eminent divine contradicted another on essentials. Austin Comberwood sighed and smiled over his summing-up of the teaching at St. Bede's, as he bade me farewell for the present, and wished me success in the prosecution of my inquiries.

Mr. Lewson, junior partner in Ladbrook, Lewson, and Son, heard my statement, made his notes, took down such names in my recital as might be of service to him, and promised to use all diligence in order to bring about a favourable result.

The difficulties were not insuperable, but they were certainly difficulties of a sufficiently grave nature to make him cautious of expressing himself in too sanguine terms as to my future.

The case lay in a nutshell.

My father had married in Wales. This was not disputed on either side. I had seen the register.

Had my father re-married, his first wife being still alive?

Who was the woman called Sarah Wingrove, at whose death I had been present at St. Winifrid's Hospital?

"Who," asked Mr. Lewson, "on that occasion gave the information as to her name?"

This for the first time brought into the subject the mention of Mr. Venn, *alias* Dr. Venn Falkner.

Premising that much of what I had to say might appear to Mr. Lewson foreign to the inquiry, I gave, as briefly as possible, all my knowledge concerning Mr. Venn, not omitting the episodes of the mysterious woman, his questioning me as a boy, his interest in my mother's family name, and many other matters which had evidently deeply impressed me at the time, and which only required an extra exertion of the memory to reproduce.

"Venn," observed Mr. Lewson, thoughtfully, "seems to have been an active agent in this affair. And he knew Mr. Cavander." He considered awhile, and then he asked me—

"Was Dr. Venn Falkner ever proceeded against for that fraud upon your club funds at the University?"

No, I did not think he had been.

" Um ! " said Mr. Lewson, meditatively. Then he brightened up.

" I think to a certain extent our way is pretty clear. I shall put the case in trustworthy hands, and all that can be ascertained about these parties shall be in our hands in a few weeks, it may be in a few days."

I thanked him heartily.

" The difficulty I have hitherto experienced in similar cases," continued Mr. Lewson, " in consequence of the laxity of official system years ago in our colonies, would surprise any one accustomed to the regularity of our home proceedings. Things are different *now*, it is true ; but it is not, unfortunately, with the present we have to deal. Why, it was only recently I had to apply, for a burial certificate, to a department of the United States, and the trouble it was to procure it, for the books had been changed, or lost, or mutilated, or had been taken away by a retiring official and not demanded by his successor, or at all events something or other prevented our getting at the document in question for so long a time that the case seemed on the point of breaking down altogether, when an accident crowned our efforts with success. May it be so in this instance !"

Thus chatting Mr. Lewson inspired me with hope. He went on—

" I do not say in a short time, but without any un-reasonable delay, we shall be able, I have little doubt, to establish her identity beyond question."

He read over to me his list of witnesses, which included the names of Dr. Poddeley, Mr. and Mrs. Verney, and that of the clergyman who had celebrated the marriage in Wales, Nurse Davis, and Mr. Venn, *alias* Dr. Venn Falkner.

It became a question with me now—for really I seemed alone in the world—whether I should go for a lodging to Uncle Van's, Mrs. Gander's at the Dairy, or rely upon Uncle Herbert.

The last-mentioned, however, generally being occupied in " hanging up his hat " in somebody else's house, had seldom even a *pied à terre* in London.

As for Mrs. Gander's—well Polly and her husband would have been glad enough to see me; but Nurse Davis was no longer there, and Julie had of course returned to her friend Mrs. Burdon.

The Burdon's! Yes, to them I would go. Uncle Herbert had advised me to call upon them merely as a matter of civility, but now there was a stronger reason for my paying them a visit.

I should see Julie. This I knew to be the secret influence at work, but I studiously ignored its existence; reminding myself that Mrs. Burdon took a deep interest in my welfare, and sympathised with me in my present trouble.

Besides, Julie could assist me here, for I had promised to send her father's address to Messrs. Ladbrook and Co.

Mrs. Bob was at home, and Julie was with her as her companion. Uncle Herbert was not staying with them in town. He only used their house or yacht in the country. In London he resided at the Pantheon Club Chambers, where Mrs. Bob was of opinion it would be more convenient for me to stay than at her house, though she would be delighted to offer me hospitality, supposing Uncle Herbert unable to put me up.

I forwarded Mr. Verney's address to my solicitor. Had I been consulting the newspapers lately, I should have discovered that Mr. Verney had appeared in London as a manager, and was about to produce *the* celebrated play written by his eldest daughter, Beatrice Sarah, entitled *The Wife's Vengeance*.

Beatrice Sarah had married a Mr. Farley, a pleasant, amiable man, in his prime, of a liberal disposition, and with plenty of money with which to be liberal. The drama was a hobby of his. In fact, it was with Mr. Farley's capital that my esteemed friend Mr. Verney had opened his theatre. At this time the glossiness of Mr. Verney's hat, the brilliancy of his overcoat, with a flower in the button-hole, and the brightness of his gloves and boots, were things to be seen and remembered hereafter.

He was the picture of a successful theatrical manager, *before* he had ever admitted the public to his theatre.

He gave a dinner to the Burlington Lambs, at which, you may be sure, Pipkison was to be present as Vice, with a happy speech in honour of the occasion and genuinely hearty good wishes for his host's future. When Pipkison turns up this record, slight as my mention is of him at this time, yet on no other mere acquaintance does my memory dwell with so much pleasure. The even tenor of his life's way must have been envied by many, while he was never envious of any one, no matter to what heights of good fortune his friend might attain, perhaps at Pipkison's expense or over Pipkison's shoulders, who might have even bowed to give him, as it were, a back, and so lost by politeness. But pleasant as is the recollection, I have no time now to dwell on Pipkison. He has reappeared at this point in connection with this invitation to the Burlington Lambs' dinner and Mr. Verney.

Mrs. Verney, with whom Mr. Lewson and myself had an interview, certainly did not do much to keep up the outward managerial dignity of her husband. But what she did do within the four walls of that theatre saved, in the future, Mr. Verney many hundreds, and prevented him from what he called "launching out," which apparently meant spending money in every conceivable way without any advantage accruing from the outlay. He was inclined to dismiss small bills, or mean-looking items, with a wave of the hand. His Treasurer would see to this; his Manager to that; his Secretary to something else; his Under-manager to so and so; his Wardrobe-keeper "to those sort of things," and so forth; and Mr. Verney within a very short time would have been surrounded by such a swarm of flies as would have sucked up all the honey, had it not been for hardworking Mrs. Verney, who was here, there, and everywhere, sweeping out, diving in, cutting up dresses, cutting down expenses, seeing that no cats were on the establishment that didn't catch mice; and, in short, being the real life and soul of the business.

Her memory was perfect of the circumstances of Sarah Wingrove's death. She corroborated Dr. Poddeley; as did Mr. Verney, who, finding himself of importance and likely to become a witness in an important trial, at once gave us, as it were, a sort of rehearsal of himself in the witness-box, occasionally varying the entertainment to suppose the questions put by the judge, the counsel, and the jury, who were all finally to compliment him on the admirable manner in which he had given his evidence.

"And on the whole," he summed up, "it would be a remarkably good advertisement for the theatre." With this view he quite looked forward to a trial. Mr. Lewson rather damped his ardour by hinting at the improbability of this case ever coming into court, whereupon he ceased to take so much interest in it as he hitherto had, until it suddenly occurred to him that there were certain incidents in my story which would make a good plot for a drama, with a great part for himself and daughter. From this moment he devoted himself to my cause with all his heart and soul.

Uncle Herbert was in new quarters. He had undertaken to act as warming-pan in a house which his brother-in-law, Philip Waring, who had married my dear Aunt Susan, to whom I had always been most sincerely attached, had recently taken. Thus it came about that Uncle Herbert was able to let me occupy his chambers until my relatives should arrive. On their taking up their residence in town, they at once, and most warmly, espoused my cause. Aunt Susan, who, I had always heard, nearly resembled my mother, was for most violent measures against Cavander.

It was in vain she attempted to see her brother-in-law. My father was too ill: and it was reported that he scarcely ever left his room, and we also heard that Lady Colvin was unremitting in her attentions to him.

Mr. Lewson pointed out to our family party, now split up into two factions—the Van Clyms on one side, and the Warings and Herbert Pritchard on the other—that there must be a certain amount of delay consequent upon the obtaining possession of the Australian registration. That this being once in our hands, coupled with such evidence as we were already able to produce, our case would be so complete as to render any attempt at litigation utterly absurd.

"In the meantime," said Aunt Susan, "Cecil must get to work. We won't," she added, looking at Uncle Herbert, "have another idler in the family."

"Certainly not," assented Uncle Herbert, stretching himself on a fauteuil.

"Therefore Philip agrees with me that Cecil had better become a barrister. We'll arrange it all; only you" (this to me) "must promise to work."

"There's no good to be done without work," observed my Uncle Waring, decisively. "Herbert and myself will be your sponsors, and you shall enter at Lincoln's Inn or the Temple next week. There you'll keep your terms; you won't have so many to keep as a non-university man, and you'll read with an old college friend of mine; who's a great man now. I'll put you in his chambers, and the rest remains with yourself."

I was only too delighted at such a prospect.

What a letter I wrote to Austin! My Colvin impulse stood me in good stead for a start, and for many a month there was not a more persevering pupil in Mr. Birkett's chambers than your humble servant. Nay, I endeavoured to draw Austin towards the law, but he had, so he wrote, elected his course, though his letter on this important subject did not contain positive information.

Mr. Lewson was right. It was a very long time before we could get anything like satisfactory information from Australia.

In the meanwhile events came about in the city which affected the fortunes of many families. From Uncle Herbert we had frequently heard how Mr. Cavander had been engaged in such gigantic operations, which were not only out of the regular legitimate business of the firm, but were of too speculative a nature for any but a most solidly-founded business concern, and dangerous for even that. Had they all been successful, Mr. Cavander, it is true, would have been *fêted* as the Emperor of Finance, would have lent money to crowned heads, to royal families, would have purchased constituencies, bought lands and a title, and have been spoken of with admiration by all.   But, unfortunately, they were not successful. The whole chain stretching across a channel was solid, the hooks firm, but the staple at one end, which appeared to be the strongest possible, yielded to pressure, suddenly parted company with the cliff, and came down heavily, bringing the chain and the other staple with it in its fall.   Its weight carried it to the bottom of the river, and every link in that chain representing small and large firms, steady or speculative houses of business, agencies, bill discounters, shareholders, capitalists, and hopeful investors, disappeared at once and for ever.   Divers might, perhaps, some time hence, bring it in parts up again to the surface, but for the present the breaking of that staple was the total disappearance of all the links.

Circling wider and wider round the place where it had fallen, spread the effects of the panic.

With several other houses, "Colvin and Cavander" was ruined.

Ruined utterly.   Other firms could face—nay could court—inquiry, but this one could not.   And an inquiry was held, but Cavander, long ere this, had fled.   He had expected such a crash, had anticipated it as a part of his speculation to be calculated among other chances, and was prepared not to face it, but to fly from it; and he had fled.

But more important results followed, so damaging to the reputation of Colvin and Cavander, that never again could that firm rear its head in the city.   Within a few days a warrant had been issued for the arrest of James Cavander.

Langoran House was a desolation.   Lady Colvin, to whom a considerable property had been secured, was still the nurse at my father's bedside.   My aunts, both Mrs. Van Clym and Susan Waring, insisted on being admitted.

Lady Colvin permitted them to have their way, and I took the first opportunity now afforded me of re-entering Langoran House—my home.

Ah! as I stood in the hall, and paused to think what might have been, and what was—of what I might have been, and what I had not been : of my time thrown away, frittered away as to some of the best of the earliest years, I blamed only myself—and yet, at that moment, I seemed to vow that, should I ever be the father of children, and left with one, or more, alone, as my father had been left with me, my companionship and example should, from my son's earliest years, make me his guide and his friend. What might interest my boy, should interest me ; what I could teach, he should learn. Religion, inculcating love, should be the basis of education.

Thus meditating, I ascended to my father's door.

Already, before the events above recorded, his memory had become seriously impaired.

Of the great ruin he knew nothing.

Lady Colvin was most assiduous in her attentions. For once there was a truce between us, and we watched and nursed together.

One thing deeply grieved me. It was that I had never had the opportunity of speaking to my father on the subject of religion.

It was too late now.

Mrs. Clym came several times, and read chapters from the Bible, and "occasional prayers" to him. But as far as we could ascertain, he could neither follow her reading, nor comprehend her meaning, He was aware of her presence, and appeared rather annoyed at it. That was all. The clergyman of the parish, too, having been thereto urged by Mrs. Van Clym, paid my poor father an official visit. The worthy, well-meaning man was unable to do anything. My father smiled at him and feebly held out his hand under the evident impression that his visitor was a doctor, who had come to feel his pulse. But had the poor invalid been in the possession of his faculties, of what avail would a clergyman have been? Words of consolation? Well, other unofficial Christians could have said as much and said them better.

No, I thought of Austin's reasoning, and of what I

had heard at St. Bede's: and I called to mind the death-scene of Sarah Wingrove, as described by Dr. Poddeley.

One day, it was the tenth of my regular attendance at Langoran House, a ray of intelligence shone in his eyes. He had slept well, and seemed to have gathered strength from his repose. It was a lovely morning when he awoke, and made a movement with his hands, by which I understood him to express a wish to be raised up on his pillows.

Lady Colvin was still sleeping.

The nurse assisted me, and we placed him in a more comfortable position.

The sun streamed in through the blinds, and the light fell on the foot of the bed. The nurse was for drawing the curtain, but her intention seemed to be anticipated by my father, who whispered in my ear, "No, no," and a minute afterwards he murmured, "Light, light." I directed the nurse to pull up the blind, and to lower it immediately, if it should be found too strong. This seemed to please him, as on seeing the clear sunlight, he smiled, and gently pressed my hand. Then he sighed deeply.

For a few seconds he was restless, turning his head, and moving his hands as if in search of something. Then, what was the greatest grief to me, he tried to whisper in my ear a connected speech. Thrice he failed in his attempt.

There was something that troubled him, and of which he would have disburdened himself. But it was not to be. After the third effort he himself appeared to be aware that what was now unsaid must so remain unto the end. Once again he whispered faintly. One word, "air." The nurse opened the windows, and from below arose the hum of the streets, the careless song and cry, and the rumbling of vehicles.

Then, as he seemed to wish for more support, I passed my arm behind him, and so lifted him that he lay more on my shoulder than on his pillow.

I saw now it was but a question of minutes, perhaps seconds.

The nurse went noiselessly for Lady Colvin.

We were alone.

Unrestrained, from my heart, and with all my heart, I prayed aloud, fervently. The prayer of prayers alone rose to my lips, and I then realized something of its wealth of meaning, of its applicability to every circumstance of life, of the divine force of its petitions; and, inspired by its words, a fire of faith, hope, and love seemed to glow in my heart.

"Thy will be done."

My father's lips moved, and he turned his head towards me. "Forgive us our trespasses, as we forgive them that trespass against us."

I felt, once again, the gentle pressure of his hand; our souls were together in communion, pleading before God, and we understood each other at last.

Then he drew a long, deep, cavernous breath, his hold on me relaxed, and he lay back against my arm, on his pillow. Dead.

CHAPTER XL.

TITLED OR UNTITLED ?—WORK—MAKING UP FOR LOST TIME—
LADY COLVIN—DR. VENN FALKNER REAPPEARS—USEFUL—
A REVELATION—DIFFICULTIES DISAPPEAR—SETTLED—JULIE
—AUSTIN ONCE MORE—BROTHER AND SISTER—MEMENTO OF
A FIRST MEETING AT RINGHURST—END OF THE RECORD OF
THE MEMBER OF THE COLVIN FAMILY.

AFTER my father's decease a considerable time elapsed
before my case progressed another stage.

As Mr. Lewson had predicted, there were many
Australian difficulties arising out of carelessness, change
of officials, accidents to the books, and so forth, until
at length we began to imagine the registry of death
as a piece of evidence unobtainable.

In the meanwhile I was employing myself in chambers
and working as I had never worked before.

I had an object in view. I began to understand the
value of Time, of money, and, under the tuition of my
best and kindest friends, my Aunt Susan and her husband,
Mrs. Bob, and Uncle Herbert (who, if he would not
take his own advice and act upon it, was prepared to
give it on all occasions, and it was well worth having)
I acquired a knowledge of the responsibilities of life,
and learned to appreciate the worth of labour.

At my father's death, in consequence of the failure
of Colvin and Cavander, I was left without a shilling.
Lady Colvin was comparatively well off. She made me
no offer of assistance, nor could I have accepted any
at her hands.

The fact of my inheritance of the title was now in dispute: and my friends hastened to make good my claim. For my part, I saw nothing in the empty honour, and would willingly have relinquished it. In justice, however, of course I had no option but to substantiate my legitimacy.

About this time Mr. Lewson sent for me in haste. He had been concerned for a man named Vere, who had been recently tried for forgery and found guilty. Whereupon, at the close of the case, a detective had volunteered some further statements concerning the prisoner, against whom, it appeared, there had been a warrant issued years ago, when bearing the name of Geare, or Geere. And being a clergyman of the Church of England, he had committed a forgery on Owen Brothers, merchants, of Shrewsbury. The evidence further went on to show that, in consequence of some delay in the proceedings, when the capture was to have been effected, it was discovered that Mr. Geare had disappeared.

From that day to this he had not been heard of, but a woman to whom he had promised marriage in England, and with whose little property he had decamped, had come forward to swear to the identity of the prisoner, now calling himself Vere, with the man whom she had known as Geere or Geare.

This man, on being now convicted and sentenced, had confided to Mr. Lewson his confession, and had requested to be allowed to see me.

Vere, *alias* Geare, was Mr. Venn—Dr. Venn Falkner.

What he had to tell me was very important.

He had, as he had formerly informed me, been a clergyman in Wales. He had married Mr. Colvin to one Sarah Wingrove, one of a strolling company of players.

Sarah Wingrove encouraged the attentions of only two out of many admirers. One was a Mr. James Cavander, and the other Mr. John Colvin. These two young gentlemen were apparently great friends, the former being some years older than the latter.

"That Cavander never intended marriage was," Venn said, "quite certain. He was too ambitious and clever for that. That he was as deeply in love with Sarah Wingrove—that is, as far as such a man can be in love with any woman—is equally certain. He was thwarted in his scheme by the simplicity and impulsiveness of his young companion, who, ignorant of a seducer's arts and of the consequences of the false step he was about to take, married the strolling actress. Their union was kept a profound secret. I think in all this Cavander had his own designs. I know I had mine. It was Cavander who helped me out of the country when the forged draft on Owen Brothers was discovered; and for some time I was in frequent communication with him."

Venn's confession now went on to relate, circumstantially, how in Australia he had come across Susan Wingrove, twin sister of Sarah, and, foreseeing that, at some future time, the relationship might be of considerable service to him, he married her. She had a little money of her own: but as might be expected, their union was not a happy one. Both sisters, Sarah and Susan, seemed to have lived a dissipated, idle life, and in throwing off the exercise of their religion (they had been brought up by Catholic parents, who had, unfortunately, died while the girls were still children) they had rapidly deteriorated, and had gradually developed that craving for excitement which tries to satisfy itself with stimulants.

This fatal disease soon led to a separation between Mr. Colvin and Sarah, who went out to Australia, where she joined her sister (during the protracted absence of Venn himself from his own home), in whose house she died. There were present at her death the two Verneys and Dr. Poddeley. Her sister Susan attested the entry of the correct name in the registry, and before Mr. Venn returned, she had herself written to Mr. Cavander, of Owen Brothers, Shrewsbury, to inform him of the death of Mrs. Colvin, or as by that time she would have been Lady John Colvin, though of this both Venn and his wife were ignorant.

This information Mr. Cavander must have imparted to Sir John, who placed implicit faith in his confidential friend, and within a few years Sir John married Miss Pritchard.

Mr. Venn returned after a while to England, leaving his wife to her fate in Australia. Her intemperate habits rendered her unfit for his purposes, whether as a tool or a confederate. Having had a good education, Mr. Venn obtained his situation at Old Carter's by certain means, in the use of which he was by this time an adept. Here he came across me, and was naturally interested in my family affairs.

The appearance of his wife, who had contrived to follow him and discover him in England, suggested a new fraud, and one in which he could protect himself by involving another, who had once befriended him, and on whose cherished hate for the man who had been his successful rival, Venn felt sure he could count.

He was right. Cavander's whole course had been taken with one fixed aim—there could apparently be no other, so every transaction that has since come to light seems to show—and that was, my father's ruin. He hated him with a vindictive, fiendish hate. And he hated *me;* I felt it instinctively the moment I first saw him in the office, when I was a boy. His one object was his own and his family's aggrandisement; he would secure his sister's rights; he would see me displaced; he would make himself the firm, and then leave his senior partner to get on, as best he could, without him.

Venn acknowledged that on the occasion when I had seen himself and wife with Mr. Cavander in Kensington Gardens, they were arranging how the fraud was to be accomplished. Susan's likeness to her sister was the stock in hand. Unfortunately, she herself could not be trusted with their secret.

They hit upon this scheme. Sir John, who had never recovered the shock of hearing of his wife being alive; and who was totally ignorant of the existence of a twin sister, was carefully reminded by Cavander of the outrageous habits of Sarah Wingrove, of her fatal propensity for drink, and how indulgence changes the expression, and makes awful ravages in the most lovely features.

Premising this, Cavander offered to show Sir John

the very Sarah Wingrove whom he had married in
Wales, and who was now the one legitimate Lady
John Colvin.

My father saw her: the unhappy woman had been
carefully plied with drink, and Venn himself was on
the spot to testify to the identity of this woman with
the one to whom he had married Sir John years ago.

Changed slightly, and for the worse, Sir John saw
and recognized, as he thought, the woman to whom
he had been once so passionately attached.

From that day he was a broken man. From that
day Cavander did as he pleased in my father's house,
and in the office.

Sir John could scarcely bear me in his sight. Now,
the past was explained.

The accident which brought about the death of Susan
at St. Winifrid's in the presence of my father, freed
him, and bound Venn to the lie. He lived abroad on
Cavander's bounty for some time, but at length this
failed, and then he returned to England with a false
German diploma, and practised on the gullibility of
Cowbridge undergraduates.

When, on decamping with the club funds, he had
offered me information which would be of the greatest
possible service to me, he had done so in good faith;
and the confession which, through Mr. Lewson, he had
placed in my hands, was but the amplification of what
he would have given me long before had I been willing
to accept it.

The Verneys remembered all the case perfectly, for
Sarah Wingrove turned out to be the very girl of whom
Mrs. Verney had been so jealous on that northern circuit
of which she would have spoken more frequently, but
that her husband had assured her that the allusion
pained him considerably. They too were witnesses to
the extraordinary resemblance between the two sisters;
and they could swear that it was Susan who entered
the room and stood by her dead sister Sarah's bed.

Cavander's admission could not be obtained. We did
not, however, require it. For the man himself, I believe

he is past the justice of human law. He lived and grew rich in California, and was one morning found on his face before his own door. He had probably been murdered with a sling shot, as there was one wound found behind the ear.

His wife had died, so my Aunt Clym informed me, in an asylum, knowing nothing of her husband's crimes. His sister, Lady Colvin, had no desire to contest my claims. Satisfied with the evidence, she soon retired from the field, and we saw her no more.

And so progressed My Time, and in my diary I was able day by day to note down satisfactory results. Our name had to be made once more, not on 'Change, but at the bar.

I shrank from no work. I was determined to deserve the kindness of those who, whatever my fortune or misfortune might have been, would never have deserted me.

I worked, as it were, to repay them the interest in their outlay.

My Time past had been, save for the latter part, Time lost. The remainder of the life of Cecil Colvin must be making up for lost time.

I had lived entirely for myself—now for others. And need I say for whom it is the happiness of my life to work? who is my comfort in sorrow, my adviser in difficulties, my sympathiser in every variation of joy or grief? who, but Julie, my little Julie, my wife!

We were by the sea-side, Julie and I. Our choice of a watering-place out of the season, for it was the week before Easter, was guided by certain judicious reasons. Both of us preferred the quiet drowsiness of the sea-beach to the excitement and gaiety of a lounger's promenade. This alone would have been enough to have prevented our spending even a week at Brompton-by-the-Sea. But our arrival was in answer to a letter from Austin Comberwood, received long since, who, congratulating me on my marriage, and on the successful issue out of my difficulties, informed me that he had become a Catholic, and having determined on trying his vocation for the priesthood, he was now studying as a novice in a Religious House, belonging to the Mission at Lullingham, where, should our journeyings take us so far, he hoped to see us.

Thus it came about that, on the evening of Good Friday, Julie and I were sitting in the little church, watching the people, as they knelt in meditation before the representation of the sepulchre, after quitting the confessionals on each side of the building. There was a considerable Catholic element in the population of Lullingham, and the two priests (for it was only a depôt from a larger house in Liverpool) found their time fully occupied. It was a touching sight in that dim light to note penitent after penitent bending low in prayer, and presently quitting the church with a brighter mien and a firmer tread as conscious of a burden removed.

So we sat and watched, and thought, and in our minds went back to those early days when as children we were taken to the little Catholic chapel in some out-of-the-way corner of London, where I had wandered about the aisle, and curiously examined the congregation.

We supposed ourselves the last in the church, for the one remaining priest, who had been detained longer than his companion, after carefully peering forth into the gloom, evidently came to the conclusion that his services were no longer required, and, having hung up his surplice and stole within the confessional, he withdrew by a side door which led into the house.

We arose too, wondering at our own delay, when from the small door just mentioned came Austin, who, in obedience to his superior's orders, now acting as sacristan, had to see the church securely closed for the night, attend to the lamps, and everything duly and reverently bestowed in its own proper place.

We were just rising to bid him "good night," and ask him a few questions about the coming Easter ceremonies, when we were startled by a deeply-drawn heart-breaking sigh, issuing apparently from the darkest corner of the church close by the sepulchre.

There, hitherto unperceived by us, perhaps by any, and certainly by the priest as he passed, a woman, or rather, a dark shadowy form of a woman, crouched kneeling, with her head buried in her hands in an agony of grief.

Austin whispered to me, "Father Charles must have left without seeing her. Perhaps she was afraid to approach the confessional."

He approached the stricken figure, and asked, gently, "Have you been to confession?"

She shook her head, almost passionately; then seemed to abase herself lower and lower as though to shrink even from her kind questioner.

"Do you wish to go to confession now?" continued Austin, kindly. "If so, I will tell one of the fathers at once."

An inexplicable sympathy, and no mere curiosity, held us spectators of this scene.

Slowly and painfully the kneeling figure answered—
"I am not of your faith."

The tone reached me. I recognized it, not clearly at once, but gradually.

It had struck to Austin's heart, as it had to mine. For a few seconds he was silent.

"There is hope for all and there is salvation for all," he said.

"Yes, if I could but believe!" she cried, as, with a sudden impulse of despair, she stretched out her arms towards the large crucifix on the wall.

This action discovered her face, on which the lamp of the sepulchre cast its pale steady light.

Austin uttered a sharp cry, and her name passed his lips, as she turned towards him and showed the face, care-worn and sadly altered, but still handsome, and, above all, still the features of Lady Frederick Sladen, once Alice Comberwood.

Walking home, I repeated to my wife so much of poor Alice's story as I knew, and told her of my suspicious with regard to Cavander.

"I remember her," said Julie thoughtfully, as we walked home. "When I went to Ringhurst with my father——"

Julie stopped herself. I knew what was passing in her mind.

I never saw Alice again. Some time after Austin confided to me her story. She had from a girl had the deepest admiration for Cavander. He had fascinated her, and, clever man as he undoubtedly was, his vanity was so flattered by the worship of this girl, that flattering her in turn by the condescension of his great talents, he used his utmost art to desolate the fair land which, in its approach to womanhood, was putting forth signs of so great promise. It was a devil's design to rob heaven of a soul.

Cavander would gladly have seen her married to Sir Frederick. It was he who had urged it on old Mr. Comberwood. Alice struggled against the match to the last, but, for her father's sake (as I had learnt outside the window at Ringhurst) consented. Then she fled, and trusted to Cavander. Within a year her trust in him had gone for ever; and she was left alone in the world, wishing she could believe in nothing, and so die. But, in the merciful providence of heaven, this was not to be. She was to be brought back, to a true home, to be welcomed by the brother who had never ceased to mourn and pray for her, to be taught by him whom she had left at the threshold of Faith, and who was now to take her by the hand, and show her where, in this world, she could be comforted with the assurance of pardon. Devoted to the care of the poorest outcasts of society Alice thenceforth lived; and in this charitable service she died, resigned to Heaven's will, happy in suffering what Justice might demand, humbly trusting in the Divine Mercy that she might be saved, "yet so as by fire."

She was buried at Lullingham. In the early morning we sought her grave. The fresh-cut turf was wet with dew as though with the tears of angels.

On her grave is only this; beneath a cross cut in the stone are the initials A. C., then the date. Then these words:

"*I am not worthy. Pray for me.*"

And the prayer followed:

"*May she rest in peace. Amen.*"

And here the story of "My Time" ends.

THE END.